WAR OF THE LONG LAKE

TREK TO THE MOUNTAIN FORTRESS

JOHANN SORENSON

iUniverse, Inc.
New York   Bloomington

War of the Long Lake

iUniverse books may be ordered through booksellers or by contacting:

iUniverse
1663 Liberty Drive
Bloomington, IN 47403
www.iuniverse.com
1-800-Authors (1-800-288-4677)

ISBN: 978-1-4502-6372-6 (sc)
ISBN: 978-1-4502-6373-3 (dj)
ISBN: 978-1-4502-6374-0 (ebook)

Printed in the United States of America

iUniverse rev. date: 11/23/2010

For my mother, Gloria, my wife, Judy, and my daughter, Suzanne. Thank you for all your support.

PART ONE

THE BEGINNING

S KYE PUT HER PEN to the paper.

Chapter One.

The End.

"That's a stupid way to start your hist. You can't start at the end." Her charge's voice ground on Skye's nerves.

She kept her focus on the page in front of her. "It is my history, and I'll start it the way I like." She resumed writing.

My older brother, Richard, was born on September 11, 2001. My father said the world changed that day. I can't truly say if it changed, as I don't really know what the world was like before that, because I was not there, as this happened years before I was born. But my father said it changed, and I have found most of the things he told me to be true.

I've heard the stories and seen some videos of the time before, but the vid players are mostly broken now, and we only bring out the one that works on special occasions.

Eagle looked over her shoulder, read the lines, and then spoke again. "That's boring. Nobody cares who was born or when, or what vids you got to watch. But at least you got to watch them before the players all wore out."

Skye suppressed her irritation and looked at Eagle and thought about his knowledge of the world. He was four years younger than her eighteen. The fall of the world was just talk to him, ancient history. For him life had always been lived here, in Stehekin, at the end of Lake Chelan, which over time they had come to refer to as the Long Lake. The fjord-like lake stretched fifty-five miles along the base of the towering Cascade Mountains that protected the village from intruders on three sides. Eagle did not have a memory of a walk down a big city street, had never taken a car ride on a freeway, and had never even seen an airplane.

He did not know what it meant when the buildings fell and the people burned. He did not know the agony that followed years later when the bio-weapons were unleashed. She had been schooled in the 9/11 disaster by those who knew of it firsthand. She had been there on the desperate journey from Seattle when her father fought off looters and bandits who tried to rob and kill his family. These were only old stories to Eagle, not something he had lived.

Skye's mother, Sharon, had told her now that she was of age she must write her version of the history so it would not be lost to the next generations. She wondered if there would be next generations.

Eagle stood as if to leave and asked, "Do you think our fathers will ever come back?"

Skye always hated this question. It cut her to think about it. She had only been six when the men of the village left for the war. All she knew was that they had not been seen since. She answered Eagle the way she always did. "I think that when they can, they will."

"After almost twelve years, do you still think that is true?" He looked at her with clear brown eyes that were more intense than usual.

She turned away from his gaze. "I have to make myself believe it. I just have to."

"Do you remember your father?"

Skye closed her eyes and visualized the tall blond man with the big smile who used to pick her up and carry her on his back and then sometimes twirl her in circles until she was dizzy and laughing so hard it hurt. She remembered crawling into bed between him and her mother and being in the safest place in the world. She caught a deep breath.

"Yes, I remember him. When I was very young he seemed a happy man, though I don't think he much liked this place."

"Do you remember my father?" He asked the question, not looking at her but staring out the window toward the forest.

She answered, "Yes, he had a kind smile and was always nice to me."

Eagle moved to the door. "I don't remember him. I don't know if he was ever nice to me or not. Seems like they left us."

Skye clenched her teeth and breathed, "They went to war for us."

She looked at Eagle, who made an impudent face and sauntered away. He acted as if he cared not what she thought, and she understood why the record needed to be made.

Skye took a breath and let the air out soft and slow. She brushed a wisp of blonde hair from her eyes and gripped the pen. It felt good in her hand, and she was pleased she could still write. It had been months since she had put pen to paper. The fact that her protégée had wandered off made it just a tad easier to write. She was a little tempted to follow him.

She glanced out the window and watched as he trotted up the trail into the forest. She guessed he was now almost five and a half feet tall, still shorter than she. His bare arms, darkened by the sun, moved in rhythm. He carried a bow with an arrow ready to be loaded in his left hand. His long brown hair fell just to his lean shoulders and danced over the fading dragon on his blue sweatshirt as he disappeared from sight.

No doubt he was going to practice with the bow, his favorite weapon, or spend the morning working with Top, the only adult male left in the village and the chief instructor of all things defensive. She worried about that because Eagle was now nearly as good as she was at close combat, and she wanted to keep her edge. She resolved that she would have to work harder to make up for missing out.

They had so few free days, it seemed a waste to spend much of it in the house writing. But she could feel the story wanting to come out.

At first she had not known where to start, there was so much to tell. Then she closed her eyes and thought of her earliest memories. She thought of the time when her father had taken her and her mother in the car to visit her grandfather.

Thirteen years after the towers fell, I was six years old. We went to visit my grandfather, taking a ferry that glided across the water, and we laughed in excitement when we spotted a pod of orca whales splashing in the wake of the boat. I did not know then, but I know now that the world was on the verge of the worst war ever. The war that changed civilization forever. The time we call the end.

Her thoughts stayed on that day, and she recalled that Grandfather lived on a beautiful green island with pebble beaches that went on for miles and were washed by crisp blue water. She pictured her little brother, David, as he squealed in delight as the wake from a passing freighter made cold waves crash on the rocks and dash over his feet and ankles.

She thought of digging clams that day and the way Grandfather smiled, except when he watched the news on the TV. Even though she did not understand all that was happening, and though the adults tried not to show it, she knew something dreadful was on their minds.

Then her thoughts turned black and her insides drew tight as she remembered the dark times, the time of destruction and panic. She remembered seeing her neighbors' bodies stacked in the streets and the time she had cowered in her father's truck while they made their escape to the safe haven they had helped build in Stehekin. As mobs chased them, her mother fired shot after shot out the window. Skye's eyes had stung as the truck's cab filled with acrid smoke and hot, spent shell casings. Then she recalled the high-pitched scream David made when the bullet ripped through his chest.

Skye sat up and choked back a sob. She put the pen down and went to the sink and pumped up cold water from the well. She splashed it on her face and looked at the pen and paper on the table. She knew then that she had to record her history from the end, to what she prayed was a beginning.

"Pirates! Pirates at the landing!"

Skye leapt to her feet with the pen in her hand and wanted not to believe what she heard. It was unmistakably Eagle's voice, and even a prankster like him would never turn the village to alarm by crying out a falsehood. This could only mean the lookout had failed and that raiders from the lake might penetrate the shore gates. That would be a disaster.

Skye bolted from the table and reflexively grabbed her closest weapons, a longbow and knife-belt, and ran out the door. The bow was not her first choice of weapons for a fight; she used it mainly for hunting because it was quiet and accurate; however, it was close at hand and would have to do. She strapped on the belt that held the combat-sharp eight-inch KaBar knife over her shorts. She wished she was wearing something more substantial than her Winnie the Pooh Bear tee shirt.

Skye broke into a run and searched the tree line for Eagle. He called again as the other women of the village turned out armed with rifles, bows, knives, and clubs.

Eagle pleaded, "Hurry, they've almost reached the gate! Only your mother and Captain Lynn are there to hold them off."

Skye sprinted past the older women, some dressed in day skirts and tops to match the hot weather, some in work clothes as they were coming in from the vineyards. Eagle came to her side and matched her speed. The sound of gunshots cracked from the landing. Skye didn't break stride but her insides made a knot in her belly. Eagle glanced at her and said, "This is new. I don't remember them having guns for a long time. What do we do?"

Skye wanted to make it sound simple. "We go down there and we kill them."

Eagle grunted, "Good. I thought you were going to have us make nice and try to capture them and then send them home with a stern warning not to come back."

Skye and Eagle reached the defensive stone wall ahead of the others. It was five feet high on the village side, but there was a ten-foot drop on the other. It had commanding fields of fire into the dock and landing area of the village. It made a great U that covered half a mile around the head of the lake and butted against steep cliffs on either end. In the center was great wooden gate that was the only passageway to get from the water to the village.

Skye took a position behind the wall to observe the landing and docks. She gasped at the sight. Three large cruisers flying crimson flags were pulling up to the village docks. She guessed the boats were thirty feet long and their decks overflowed with mostly men and a few scrawny women; she estimated there were over twenty. They were all armed with guns of various sizes and were dressed in all manner of clothes that, even from this distance, almost seventy yards away, looked dirty and scruffy.

"Eagle, look how many there are. Not including the kids, at most we are only two hundred strong, and today almost everyone is up the mountain in the vineyards."

She could hear the concern in Eagle's voice. "And the people here are mainly old women."

Skye tried to encourage him. "They are experienced fighters; they've held this place since you were born."

"I think we'll need more than experience to beat these guys."

The sound of shots below caught her attention, and she saw her mother and Captain Lynn of the village defenders, kneeling behind a pallet of lumber and shooting at the pirate boats. Her mother's long gray hair draped back over her strong shoulders. Their shots had deadly effect, but their weapons were not automatic, and the pirates immediately returned a huge, though uncoordinated, barrage at the women, forcing them to keep mostly behind the cover of the lumber they hid behind.

Skye recoiled at the sight. Her mother was almost certainly

trapped. She had never seen so many pirates. Stories of kidnapping and enslavement flashed through her mind, causing her to take an involuntary gasp of air. The first two boats touched the dock, and the invaders swarmed off the vessels and started running to the shore, shouting with bone-chilling screams and shrieks and firing their guns in the general direction of the wall.

Skye loaded an arrow into her bow and fired at the lead pirate on the dock. The shot was true and the arrow hit him square in the chest; she loaded another as more of the village defenders arrived at the wall and started shooting rifles and arrows at the marauders below.

Damn, why the hell didn't I bring a rifle? Had no idea there would be so many. She fired again and another pirate fell with an arrow in his thigh. The air filled with the smell of gunpowder and the continued war cries of combatants on each side. More women, many panting and out of breath, joined the defense, taking position behind the wall and adding their firepower to the effort.

The sheer number of pirates was overwhelming. Those who fell were pushed off the dock or stepped over by those behind. The leaders made it to shore and started to rush the gate. Skye immediately saw they were going to cut off her mother and the captain. Worse, if they made the gate, they would penetrate the defense.

A great *VHOOM* sounded from the last of the pirate boats. A moment later, an explosion went off behind the wall fifty feet from her and blew two of the defenders off their feet, where they lay bleeding on the ground. Skye shouted to Eagle, "They've got mortar!"

Another *VHOOM* sounded and the projectile landed even closer to her this time; three defenders fell, and she was sure they were dead. Some of the women started to retreat and then Lieutenant Delta, a tall, black-and-gray-haired, ebony-skinned woman who was considered by most to be one of the best fighters in village, shouted, "Stand fast, we have to keep them outside the gate!" A new explosion ripped through the air, and Skye saw Stella and Rachel, women who had helped to raise her, fall bleeding to the ground.

The intense fire from the wall slowed the pirates, but their advance continued. Delta ran to Skye's position. "I've sent a team to get heavy weapons, but I don't know if we can survive this until they get here. We have to stop that mortar now. Incoming!" They both dove to the ground as an explosion ripped through the air behind them. The concussion knocked the wind from Skye's chest, grit filled her mouth, and flying sand stung the right side of her face and arm.

She rolled over and looked at Delta. The older woman's nose was bleeding and dirt streaked her face. She spit blood into the sand. "Skye, the mortar is on the far side of the last boat, behind the wheelhouse. We can't get a shot at it with our rifles. Take your bow and arc a flamer high into the air and drop it on those bastards. It may be our only chance."

Skye nodded and then turned to Eagle, who was reloading his rifle just down the wall from her position. She called to him, "Come with me."

He looked at her quizzically. "Are we retreating?"

"No, we're getting offensive."

"Oh good, you had me worried. I thought we were going someplace safe."

She got to her feet and started running in a crouch toward the end of the wall that would take her closest to the target boat. Eagle followed on her heels.

The sound of another mortar shell coming in drove them both to the ground. After the explosion, Skye peeked over the wall. The battle raged and the pirates were getting close to the gate. She could not see where her mother and the captain were through the dense smoke and confusion in the landing area. She swallowed hard. She wanted to try and save her mother but could see an attack in that direction would be foolhardy; besides, she had been given a mission and that was what she needed to take care of.

Skye and Eagle made their way to a spot on the wall above the boat firing the mortar. Along the way, they passed several women they knew, some grievously injured, who continued to shoot over the wall at the advancing pirates. One gray-haired neighbor of Skye's named Elsie looked at them as they approached and said, "What are you kids doing? You should get to the shelters, this is getting ugly."

Skye stopped beside her and peered over the wall. "We're here to help."

Elsie raised a wrinkled brow and said, "It must be worse than I thought."

The mortar fired again; its projectile landed near the gate and resulted in the scream of a wounded woman.

Eagle whispered, "Much worse."

Skye spotted the target boat; there was square wheelhouse on the front and from this angle the stern could not be seen from the wall. Telltale smoke drifted up from the stern, and when another round was launched, Skye was sure it was from the offending weapon. She took a flamer from her quiver and loaded it in her bow.

Eagle watched with squinted eyes. "You think that will work?"

Skye took another look over the wall to gauge the range. "Never tried these in combat before. Top made them for this kind of thing. We light the case on the arrow head, fire it, and two twelve-gauge rounds blow up on impact. Pretty cool."

"Top invented them?" Eagle rolled his eyes. "This is much worse."

Skye ignored him and shoved an igniter at him and pulled the bow string back. "Shut up and light this thing."

Eagle fumbled with the igniter, and after three tries the arrow tip casing sizzled to life. Sparks flew from it and Eagle backed away in a hurry. Skye pointed the arrow to the sky and let it fly. They stared as the missile climbed into the blue, leaving a black trail behind. It arced over the water and fell straight toward the boat, finally hitting dead on top of the wheelhouse. A small explosion sent a plume of smoke into the air, leaving a black hole on the top of the boat.

Skye, Eagle, and Elsie peeked over the wall, surveying the result. Eagle spoke first. "That was lame."

Skye nodded and said, "Needs less trajectory."

Elsie mumbled, "Worser and worser."

Skye pulled another flamer from her quiver. As she did, she saw two figures appear on the wheelhouse of the boat. One was a fat man in ragged camouflage clothes and the other was a heavy woman with stringy black hair with blue streaks. They inspected the damage to the roof of the boat and followed the trail of smoke the arrow left in the sky with their eyes. The man looked directly at Skye and pointed a thick finger at her. The sight sent a chill down her back. Eagle raised his rifle, but the two scrambled off the roof and out of sight.

Skye continued to watch the boat and calculate the angle she needed for her next shot. The mortar fired again and by the sound of the projectile, she knew instantly it was aimed at them. "Get down!"

The three of them dove to the ground just as an explosion went off mere yards from their position. The shock wave sucked the breath out of her, and smoke and dust filled her nose and mouth. She coughed hard and rolled onto her back. Elsie wiped grit from her face and turned her eyes to Skye. "Glad you are here to help."

Skye closed her eyes and visualized the boat and its position. Lying on her back, she pointed her bow to the sky with a flamer loaded in it and called to Eagle, "Light this thing."

"Why, are you trying to really make them mad?"

She gritted her teeth and said, "Light it!"

Seconds later the arrow arced into the air; she held her breath for what seemed a long time. Finally her patience was rewarded with sound of a large explosion. Eagle leapt to his feet and looked over the wall. "Lucky shot! The whole back of the boat is smoking; you must have hit a stack of ammo."

Skye got to her feet and watched as the fat man and the woman frantically drew a hose from the wheelhouse to the rear of the boat. "Luck had nothing to do with it."

Elsie joined them at the wall. "That helps."

Skye said to Eagle, "I have to go help my mother." She started to head back toward the gate at a run when the sound of a heavy machine gun rose above the noise of the battle.

Eagle called to her, "Do you think that is ours?"

She answered, "I think Delta's team made it back with the big guns; if that belonged to the pirates, they would have started off with it." As they ran, a second machine gun started up, this one closer to them. Skye stopped and looked over the wall.

The pirates were retreating back to the boats. Even as they did so, the machine guns ripped into what had turned into a stampeding mob frantically trying to get out of the way of the guns. The intense fire shredded them with gruesome results. Skye turned her head away to avoid seeing the carnage below. She started for the gate again.

By the time she and Eagle reached the gate, the gunfire had subsided and Delta was warily leading a contingent of ten defenders through it. The opening was ten feet wide, and the thick wooden doors were as high as the walls. The blacktopped road that went from the docks into the village had a steep slope that led down to the landing area. Delta and her group paused at the top of the incline to survey the situation.

Skye worked her way to the front of the group of ten. They all had rifles at the ready and scanned the area, looking for movement. The entire landing was strewn with the bodies of pirates, some missing limbs, some nearly cut in half by the effects of the machine guns. Skye forced herself not to back away.

She looked to where she had last seen her mother. Her chest felt hollow when she did not see any sign of her. The sound of the battle had given way to an odd quiet; a few of the women whispered behind her. "My God, what did we do?"

"We had no choice, that's what they wanted to do to us."

"Maybe we could have let them surrender."

Delta spoke over them with a strong voice. "No surrender, no prisoners. You know the way of the lake." Then she pointed to the log pallet and said, "Look there, it's Captain Sharon and Lynn!"

Skye's heart raced and she saw her mother and Lynn step out from the far side of the pallet they had taken shelter behind. Her mother's long gray hair was streaked with soot; she stood tall and held a rifle in one hand; she waved to the group and raised her hand, giving them the halt signal. Skye wanted to bolt to her side but knew better than to disobey. Skye's mother and Lynn approached a fallen pirate slowly.

Skye watched intently as her mother knelt down and whispered to the man. She put her ear nearly to his lips as if he could do little more than whisper. Then without warning, he violently grabbed her long hair and jerked her to the ground, with his other hand he raised a shotgun and blasted Lynn in the chest, blowing her off her feet. Horrified, Skye watched as her mother rolled on top of the man and started to beat him about the face with her fists.

The man reached up to stop her but she was too much for him. Skye took a step to run to her but Delta grabbed her by the shoulder. "She wants us to stay for a reason."

Skye watched in helpless desperation and then saw her mother pull a knife from her belt and plunge it into the pirate's chest. At almost the same moment, the sound of a boat engine came from the far dock. Skye's mother almost leapt off the dying pirate, got to her feet, and pointed to Skye. Even from forty yards away, Skye could see into her determined blue eyes. She shouted, "Skye, none must get away! None! You must stop them."

Skye heard the engine get louder as the pirate's boat kicked into gear. The vessel was at the far side of the dock. It started to move. She could see it was the vessel that had the mortar on it; the stern was still smoking. Skye spotted the people she had seen before, the man and woman dressed in ragged green camouflage uniforms, in the front cabin of the thirty-foot cruiser. She watched as her mother raised her rifle and fired two shots at the boat. The two pirates dove for cover as the windows shattered on the side hatch. Skye and Delta's group were out of position to take a shot as the other pirate boats were between them and the boat that was fleeing.

The man came out from the cabin as the boat backed further from the dock. The woman with the stringy hair pointed a rifle at Sharon and fired three shots, sending her scrambling for cover behind the log pallet. Then the man shook his fist and screamed, "We'll be back, you stupid whores. We'll be back and we'll make you our slaves or kill you all." He pointed to Sharon. "You bitch, you'll be my dog." The engine throttled up and the boat pulled away.

Sharon turned from him and looked up the hill. Skye saw her mother's shirt was streaked in blood, her face was red, and her long silver-blonde hair draped over her shoulders. She raised her hand toward the boat and called, "Skye! None must live. None must get away!"

Skye called back, "I will do my best, Mother!"

"Do whatever it takes. Skye, you must not fail!"

Skye raised her fist in reply.

Delta shoved her rifle into Skye's hands. "You will never stop them with a bow, and the rest of us are too slow to try to catch them. It looks like they damaged our boats, so you will need to race over the ridge to beat them to the choke point."

She grabbed her companion. "Eagle, I cannot slow the boat before it gets to the lookout rock. I may not be able to stop it even then with this small caliber weapon. Bring my Bushmaster with the scope. I will see you there. Hurry!"

Eagle was running even before she finished her sentence. Skye started for the lookout rock.

Skye raced through the trees and caught a glimpse of the fleeing pirate cruiser on the lake. It was faster than she had thought. Stopping it in time was going to be a problem.

CHAPTER TWO

THE BATTLE AT LOOKOUT ROCK

THE SOUND OF THE boat engine echoed off the steep granite mountain walls. Skye's thoughts focused on the enemy. The vision of Captain Lynn slaughtered on the dock made the blood pump in anger through her heart. She vowed to make these pirates pay for their attack.

Skye ran through the trees on the cliffs above the water to keep out of sight from the lake. She cut toward the water and saw the cruiser's progress. She thought she could reach the lookout rock above the choke point before the boat got there, but it was going to be close.

The morning sun sparkled on the blue water, which was fed from the glaciers high in the mountains. Here the lake was so narrow that it had the appearance of a river. Steep mountains climbed on both sides of it and formed a virtual canyon for the thirty miles closest to Stehekin. That was part of the reason her father and his militia had picked the remote village in the first place. When they saw that events in the world might spiral out of control, they put themselves hard to the task of making a survival home for their families.

Her mother had told her the men and a few of the women had met in the army. After their service, some, including her father, had formed a real estate business and made tremendous wealth. None had been particularly political, but they lost faith in the government and decided to protect themselves and their families. As Skye raced to the choke point, she once again marveled at their foresight.

Before the war, Stehekin had been known as the most remote town in what was then called the continental United States. There was no access by road so the only way to reach it was by boat, floatplane, or helicopter. To the north, the village was protected by the North Cascade Mountains and thousands of miles of wilderness that stretched all the way into what had been Canada.

The only practical approach to the town was from the lake. The militia had found the narrowest part within two miles of the village and created a barrier with tons of rocks and boulders blown from the mountainside into the lake. It made a narrow channel in the lake that any approaching craft would have to go through to reach Stehekin. The opening was only twenty yards across with a narrow trail carved into the mountainside above so it could be defended from either shore with a small number of fighters.

Skye's first battle was a defense at the choke point when she was only ten. She mainly loaded weapons for her mother and the other adults, but the experience had shown that a small determined force could ward off what looked like overwhelming odds.

The present problem was different. Something must have happened to the lookouts, who were supposed to sound the alarm in the event a boat came into view. There were only two types of people who came up the lake: pirates and traders. Pirates were the more common.

If they made it past the choke point, it was the goal of the defenders to make sure none left alive. The central government had been close to collapse after the nuclear bombs went off in New York; Washington D.C.; Chicago; and Los Angeles; the militia had decided to make Stehekin invincible and invisible.

No one who came to rob, murder, or steal was allowed to survive. The militia reasoned that if they showed any weakness, they would soon be overwhelmed by the lawless gangs of thugs that had taken to the road in search of food. The first two years had been the hardest. There was still gas for boats and sources of food existed for those who knew where to look and had the means to take it. In the beginning, guns and bullets were plentiful on both sides, and defense of the choke point was a full-time duty.

There were a dozen bloody assaults the first year. After the second winter, the number dropped off substantially. From then on, there were two to three a year. After the men of the militia left during the second year, the task of defense fell to the two hundred women and children who remained behind.

Skye leapt to the lookout rock and glanced to the water below. The lookout post was cut into the side of the mountain twenty feet above the water and gave her a commanding view of the lake and choke point. She gave a quick gasp as she saw the old woman, Hilde, face down in the water, a pool of red encircling her. A sharp pop came from the lake and something snapped past Skye's ear.

Her reflexes forced her to duck, and the sound of a deep laugh came from the cruiser on the lake. She glanced at the lake and saw the fat man on the boat leaning against the wheelhouse, aiming a rifle at her. There was another pop and this time she saw the puff of smoke from the rifle. Another round whizzed past her head, this one closer than the first. She elected not to wait for the shooter to hone his aim, so she jumped to the backside of the rock platform out of the aim of the rifle. The boat was nearly to the opening of the choke point. She needed to act fast.

Skye dropped to her belly and inched up the edge of the ledge she was on. She steadied her rifle, aimed at the man, and fired two quick shots. The boat pitched as it turned toward the opening to the lake, and her shots went wide, plinking off the side of the metal wheelhouse.

The man taunted her, "Nice try, you little heathen! But you're going to be dead yet!" Then he shot back at her, his bullets kicking up chips of rock into her face.

She scooted back on the ledge out of the line of fire. Carefully peeking, she saw the woman had joined him and she was now aiming at her too. They both fired and Skye ducked back behind the cover of the rocks.

Wish I had a bigger gun. Just have to work with what I've got. She rolled to her side, rose to one knee, put her sights on the man, and fired three quick shots. The man fell to the deck, cursing and clutching his knee.

Skye's pulse quickened at her limited success. This was only the start. She needed to stop the boat before it got past the choke point, and it was becoming clear she couldn't do it if the pirates hid inside. *Where the heck is Eagle?*

She rose again to take another shot, but this time both the pirates fired in unison, forcing her to drop back down. The boat was passing through the opening of the choke point now. She got up to shoot again and was startled to see the pirates had gone into the wheelhouse and were peering at her from inside through an open window.

The man's voice boomed over a microphone. "Hey, you little vixen, I'm coming back for you. You can wait up at night because you'll never know when or where I'm coming from. I'll see you …" He laughed with a nasty snort that sent a chill through her.

Then a voice startled her from behind. "What's a vixen?"

Skye greeted Eagle with a command: "Here!"

Without hesitation, Eagle tossed the long leather case to her. She snatched it out of the air and, in one fluid motion, snapped it open and pulled out her AR16A rifle with a 3-9X mm scope. She slammed in a magazine and chambered a round as she brought it to her shoulder. She bit off a breath and brought the cross hairs to the woman's face and focused. She could see the creased features turn to surprise as she figured out what Skye was doing.

"Duck this, witch." Skye squeezed the trigger, her rifle kicked, and the woman's brains blew out the back of her head in a bright red splash. Skye moved the sights to the startled man.

Through the scope, she saw his eyes staring wide at the floor; she put the cross hairs on his temple and squeezed the trigger. She saw a flash of red blow out of his head and he dropped from sight.

She lowered the rifle and let out a heavy breath. She noticed she was panting and suddenly very hot; she wiped her brow with the back of her hand and watched as the boat started a slow turn.

Eagle whispered to her, "How could you do that? How could you kill them like that?"

She was shocked by the question. "You saw what happened on the dock. I had to."

Eagle shook his head and said, "No, I mean with only two shots on a moving target. I don't know if I could."

Skye took a deep breath. "Sun Tzu once wrote, 'The reason troops slay the enemy is because they are enraged.' I hope you never have to be that way."

Eagle shook his head. "I already am and still don't know if I could."

Skye looked down to the lake and said, "The raiders murdered Hilde, and we must retrieve her from the water. She must not have been paying attention, and they shot her from the water. I don't know where the second watcher is, so you will have to stand the watch until a relief arrives." Skye suppressed her tears better than Eagle as they undertook the heartbreaking task of recovering Hilde's body. Skye always thought the woman had been a gentle soul who harmed no one. She hated the pirates even more for what they had done.

Eagle pointed to the boat on the lake; it was turning hard and headed for a collision with the mountains that rose above the lake. It was not going very fast but when it hit the stone, they could hear the sound from two hundred yards away. Metal grated on the rock, and the bow of the boat collapsed inward. The engine kept grinding the boat into the mountainside until it finally tore a screeching hole in the bottom and rolled over onto its side.

They watched for a few moments as the craft started to sink and then settled on the bottom, half submerged. Skye shook her head and said, "None got away."

She looked down to the water and saw the floating body of the lookout. "We must tend to Hilde." After they had pulled the old woman's corpse from the lake and made a temporary resting place for it, Skye prepared to leave. She put her hands on Eagle's shoulders and looked into his eyes. "What has happened is a dangerous thing. We have not been attacked by these numbers in many years. This may be an ill time for us; keep a sharp watch until relief sentries arrive. I will be surprised if we are attacked again today, but the point is not to be surprised at all."

Skye wound her way through the forest on the edge of the lake, headed for the village. She was not concerned that the pirates might return imminently. Their cohorts, if they had any, might not be back for days, or weeks, or months. Sometimes it was maddening to not know what was happening in the world outside Stehekin.

She paused when she came to a small beach at the edge of the trees. Her hands were shaking and a sense of exhaustion overtook her. The cedars and firs climbed hundreds of feet into the sky and made her feel small in their majesty. The lake stretched before her with the sun reflecting brightly off the glacier water. She thought about the woman she had just killed.

She dropped to her knee and prayed for forgiveness. *Please God, make them stay away. Make them leave us alone.*

CHAPTER THREE

CONSEQUENCES

WHEN SKYE REACHED THE gates at the dock, she was greeted by a scene of despair. Twelve body bags were laid side by side on the inside of the wall. Skye was shocked. She had not realized the extent of the damage the pirates had done during the course of the battle.

Women and children wept openly as the bags were loaded one by one onto the back of a pick-up truck. When they saw Skye, they cleared a path so she could pass to the gate.

Outside the gate, on the landing dock, she could see her mother direct defenders to gather the remains of the pirates for disposal. The defenders didn't need much direction as they had done this before, but Skye could not remember when they had done it last. Perhaps two summers ago.

She watched her mother standing at the gate. The sharp features of her face were streaked with perspiration. She called to Skye from the end of the landing, some one hundred feet away. "Did you get them all?"

"Yes, they are dead."

Her mother spoke in a resigned tone. "Gather the children of the watch and see that they are fed. The council will meet tomorrow and decide what to do next. Until then, mind the children well. Tonight the adults will tend to our dead."

Skye could scarcely believe what she heard. She had not had to care for the children for years. It was a duty a defender should not have to perform. "But I can help here. There is much to do."

"Go! Tomorrow night the council will review your actions from today and decide what your future status will be."

Skye clenched her fists at her sides, swallowed hard, and held back a response she knew she would regret. After what she had done, she expected a better response. Surely she must be allowed to join the ranks of the defenders.

Skye knew she had to consult with her best ally in the village. As soon as she had the children fed, she would go directly to Top's cave up on the mountain. Meanwhile, there was domestic work to tend to, even though she loathed it and firmly believed it was beneath her station as an aspiring defender.

She entered the village gate just as the truck with the body bags left the dock area, leaving crying women and children behind. There was an assortment of defenders and domestics in the group, which was unusual except in times of emergency. Both types accepted the value of the other, but generally liked to socialize among their own.

Skye moved through the group and stepped up on an old fifty-five-gallon fuel drum. She cupped her hands around her mouth and shouted with all she could muster, "Children of the watch! Form on me. It is time for dinner."

There was a small commotion as the nearby children quickly came to her. Others who had been busy with different tasks ran down the road to her. She could hear voices calling, "Hurry, form on Skye, form on Skye, she's got the dinner tonight."

The children of the watch got in line at her feet, jostling with each other to get closest to her. Skye was the oldest child in the village, though she no longer considered herself a child, and had special status among the youngsters. That she was admired by the elders, and was said to be a special favorite of Top, made her the envy of them all.

They ranged in age from five to fifteen. The last one was born when

Top was sixty-eight. Most were within a couple of years of Eagle's age. There were two girls at fourteen, Peggy and Heather, born before the food riots and the move to Stehekin.

Ellie, the youngest at five years old, looked up at Skye with inquisitive eyes. "Skye, we heard your gun. Did you get the pirates so they won't come back?"

Skye looked at the red-haired girl and smiled. "Don't you worry, Ellie. Everything is going to be fine." She reached down and stroked the girl's hair. "What's the count tonight, Ellie? Is everybody here?"

Ellie quickly counted noses and reported to Skye, "Thirty-five and one, the children of the watch are all present."

It had been the worst day the village had seen in many years. The loss of so many was hard to take in. Through a stroke of luck, only one child had lost his mother. It was still painful, though, as there were only 197 adults and all were close. Skye reminded herself that now there were only 185.

Once she delegated the dinner preparations, she found a spot in the shade to gather herself. She wanted to clear her head. She desperately wanted to visit Top and was anxious to get there. She watched the kids prepare an open-air fire, though she could tell no one felt much like eating tonight. This was highly unusual, especially for one of their rare group meals, but the events of the day had cast a pall on them all. Her friend Myst approached her.

She wore her usual long dark dress. Her thick black hair grew past her shoulders and outlined her porcelain face. The twelve-year-old had deep brown eyes that seemed to convey knowledge one her age should not have. She said matter-of-factly, "It's over now, isn't it?"

Skye tried to be truthful. "This battle is over; there may be more."

Myst shook her head. "No, not that, there will always be more battles. This place is over. Our life here is over. It will change now."

Skye was puzzled and asked, "Why do you say that? We've survived attacks before and nothing changed."

Myst said slowly, "I know things, Skye. I know things will not be the same. I can see it. Be careful."

A prickly sensation went across Skye's neck. There were some who said Myst had a sixth sense, that she could see the future. Others thought the girl was just a bit off. For the first time, Skye hoped the people who thought Myst was just odd were right. Skye didn't believe that. *Still, the girl was not often wrong about things that were going to happen in the future.*

CHAPTER FOUR

THE HUNTERS

COLONEL JOHN ERIKSON PEERED through the fog, looking for any hint of land. The dilapidated freighter they had dubbed *Homeward* moved slowly, barely making headway into San Francisco Bay. His best friend and second in command, Les Bower, stood beside him on the exposed weather deck. The air was cold and damp, and the smell of rotting kelp filled his nostrils. He recalled another time, another world, when this place had been filled with life. His heart ached at the prospect of what he would find now.

Les stretched his arms, and his wingspan only filled a fraction of the bridge. At six feet tall, he was the same height as John, and his sandy hair was only slightly darker than John's blond. "Damn, I wish we could find some airplanes that worked. I'm so sick of being on this boat for the last month, I could bang my head against the wall."

John smiled and corrected him, "Bulkhead; it's a boat."

Les sat back down and said, "Okay, bulkhead. Yes, if we had some airplanes we could have been here and set up defenses already. Then we'd have a surprise for the bad guys. This is no way for Rangers to travel."

John adjusted his leather jacket, trying to keep the cold off his shoulders. "If we had airplanes, they'd have airplanes. We haven't seen anything in the air since we left Afghanistan eight years ago. Nuclear war kind of screws with the technology."

Les sighed and said, "Ahh, the sand box. Back when we could drive all day and not worry about fuel or where the next meal was coming from."

John answered, "All we had to do was dodge IEDs and hope nobody set off a biological weapon or ranged us with a nuke. Lovely time."

Les whispered into the microphone that connected him to the ship's bridge, "Steady now, we don't know what kind of debris may be in the water. Any sign of other vessels?"

John squinted through his binoculars but they did little more than illuminate the gray. "How's the radar image?"

Les answered, "Getting worse all the time. They are barely keeping it working. Lots of ghost images. Between that and with no GPS capability, they aren't even promising they can keep us near the middle of the channel. Bets are off on getting close to shore without a visual. You sure you don't want to wait until this soup clears?"

John could hear the sound of waves breaking and slowly shook his head. "No. If he's here, we want to get into the bay before he can defend the entrance. I don't think this rusty tub will make it any further up the coast without another engine breakdown. If that happened, we'd be some seriously screwed pooches."

"Yeah, boss, but if Barzan finds us too close to him on the water, we're going to be fucked ducks."

Before John could answer, a break in the fog opened in front of the boat. He stared in shock. They were heading dead on to the base of the north tower of the bridge. He shouted to Les, "Hard port, hard port!"

As the vessel slowly turned, he stared at the remains of the bridge in disbelief. Even though he intellectually knew what was there, nothing had prepared him for the gut-wrenching sight that loomed above them.

Les uttered the same words that John felt. "Oh my God. I thought that after all the nasty shit we've seen all over the world, I'd be ready for this and it wouldn't seem so bad. This is fucked."

John's eyes were drawn to what had been the north tower of the Golden Gate Bridge. The once magnificent structure now bent hideously into the bay, the western part of the tower nearly broken in half, with part of the bridge deck dangling from cables falling into the cold water. He looked at the south tower, and it was bowing into the water as if some monstrous genie had folded it in half. The orange paint was seared black and silver with large splotches of red rust taking on a crimson color in the dim light.

The fog closed back in as quickly as it had opened, once again obscuring the towers. He held his breath as *Homeward* slid by the concrete pylon scant feet away and barely cleared the wreckage that hung from the damaged tower above them. He prayed there was no wreckage from the bridge just under the surface that would rip the hull open. After a few moments, as they passed into the bay, he started breathing again. He looked over the side of the boat, finally satisfied they were clear. He felt Les put his hand on his shoulder. "Welcome home, *Skipper*."

John shook his head and said, "We're not home yet. I just hope we're in front of that bastard and get there first." He took a sip of coffee and watched as Angel Island came into view out of the fog. Les spoke softly. "You know we did the right thing, I mean leaving when we did."

John took a deep breath. "Seemed like the thing to do at the time. I thought we would be gone a year, max. Here we are, twelve years later. The six-year-old daughter I left is eighteen now."

Les said softly, "Do you think they are still there?"

John answered, "I have to. I just have to; it is all that keeps me going. We left them well supplied so they could sustain themselves, and they are in a very defensible location. They are smart women, throw in Top for good measure—hell, they probably rule the West Coast by now."

Les laughed and said, "I wouldn't want to fight them. I need to believe they are still there too. Although sometimes I worry they may be pissed off when we finally show up. Kind of a long break between visits. They may have some pretty long honey-do lists."

John smiled briefly and then a weight settled on his shoulders. "I have to admit that I really thought we could still win the war, that we could keep the big fight over in the Middle East even though the early wars had been going for twenty years. I thought we could make a difference."

Les sighed, "Guess we were kind of naive. That war was just a continuation of a war that has been going on for thousands of years. Who would have guessed that everyone would lose?"

The ship rocked gently under John's feet. "Better go dead slow here, no telling what is in these waters."

Les gave the command and John heard the pitch of the engines change. "Everyone lost but that bastard Barzan. The ancient religions that started all that shit are virtually wiped out by each other, and this guy fills the void by propping up a new deity, the prophet Al-Zar, and terrifying what is left of the population into following him. Believe in him or die."

Les's voice hardened as he said, "I remember when we met the bastard. I didn't really believe in evil until that day."

A surge of anger swept into John's chest. That was a day he knew he would never forget, or forgive. "That day betrayed us all."

John closed his eyes and visualized the day a year before when Barzan had called a truce and held a peace meeting.

John and Les had gone with two senior members of the allied forces to Barzan's temporary headquarters in an estate he had commandeered outside of London. John's palms were sweating and his heart pounded. He had said, half out loud, "I hope we can trust these clowns."

Les answered him, "Not much choice now. Hell, they kicked our asses out of Africa and halfway across what's left of Europe and now they want to talk. You suppose they are going to surrender to us?"

There was a pouring rain and their English-built four-wheel-drive could barely negotiate the mud that filled the bomb-cratered driveway.

Heavily armed guards wearing the long dark robes that the Malsi army used for uniforms watched them warily as they approached.

After being searched for weapons, they were ushered into a large dining room where twenty Malsi officers and two of their priests sat at a table. At the far end, John recognized Barzan, the commander of all the Malsi army. He had short, thick black hair and a trimmed mustache. His skin was tan, his nose had a slight hook, and his black eyes were cold and calculating. He wore a pressed black uniform with large stars on the epaulets and an array of colored decorations on his broad chest.

When John and the others were escorted to the table, Barzan pursed his thick lips into a smile. "Welcome, gentlemen, it is time we finally met face to face."

John gave him a slight nod. It had been previously agreed that John would be the spokesman for the group. Even though the two generals with him outranked him, they mainly came along for show. There was not much to negotiate unless there was something the allied forces did not know. This was considered to be a rare occasion to talk directly to their enemy and maybe find out what his endgame was.

John noted that the room was almost completely bare except for the table and chairs. *Too bad. No handy charts or maps on the walls. That would have been too easy.*

Still standing, he looked at Barzan and asked, "Why are we here?"

Barzan's face remained impassive. "I invited you here as a courtesy; a simple greeting would seem to be in order."

John tried the stifle the annoyance that wanted to creep into his voice. "Very well, how do you do, General? I am Colonel Erikson, this is Major Les Bower, and these are Generals Rice and Westin of the allied Supreme Command. We wish to thank you for your invitation to parlay."

Barzan grinned. "That is more cordial." He waved his hand toward the seated men at the table. "These are my officers; these are the men who have defeated you in battle for a decade and who are about to annihilate the last of your forces unless you surrender."

John felt the muscles in his back go rigid. "You mean these are the men responsible for the slaughter of tens of millions of innocent people." A few of the officers at the table glared at him harshly. "After fighting you for so long," he continued, "why would we surrender now?"

Barzan snapped his fingers and the man next to him produced a small cigar and gave it him. "Don't be foolish. You know your tactical situation is hopeless. We have you outnumbered five to one and you are virtually surrounded. If you don't give in, there will be much senseless killing that will be your responsibility."

John decided not to be baited. "You know that we will never surrender; we won't join the cult of your pretend religion …"

Barzan suddenly stood up. "Do not blaspheme the Malsi way! The priests warned me not to talk to infidels; I'm trying to give you a chance to survive. You only live at my pleasure."

John was slightly taken aback by his outburst. He saw that Barzan was wearing a sidearm but decided to press on anyway. "Why are we really here? Surely not just to listen to you boast of your power."

Barzan lit the cigar and thick smoke rose in a cloud. "I have something to show you." He motioned to the man beside him, who lifted a wooden box that looked to be about a foot tall and wide. "You and your men have been a great nuisance to me. Of all the battles we have fought and all the forces we have faced, your little group has consistently gained our attention. You have been a hindrance to me and have cost me dearly. However, you have had one benefit. When one of your troops fell into our hands, he was very informative."

Barzan reached into the box and pulled out a severed head. John had to steady himself. He fought of a wave of revulsion as he barely recognized the face of Sergeant Ron Hester, who had failed to return from a raid on the Malsi headquarters compound a month ago.

John heard Les say, "You bastard."

Barzan continued to hold the eyeless head at shoulder height. The face was contorted and had a broken nose and numerous lacerations.

"He was quite the talkative fellow. He told us all about your little village, who is there and what you have in those remarkable caves. In fact, he told us so much that once we are done here, I plan to make a visit." He put the head back in the box and spewed smoke from his cigar.

John collected his thoughts and said, "Other than proving to us beyond doubt what we already knew, that you are a complete barbarian, why did you bring us here? Do you intend to do that to us?"

Barzan smiled. "Eventually. My army has chased you and the other forces across the world and defeated you in every major battle. We will defeat you in the one that is coming in the next week. I wanted you to know that once I am done here, we are going to your little village; I hope you will do me the favor of not getting killed because I want to see your face when I gut your wife and daughter like pigs in front of your eyes."

John felt Les grab his arm as he started to move toward Barzan. Several of the Malsi officers rose from their chairs.

"Why don't you just kill us now while you have us?"

Les whispered, "Don't give him any ideas, buddy."

Barzan shoved the box out of his way and sat down in his chair. "Why don't I kill you now? First, you came under an agreement of truce, and I am not the barbarian you want to believe I am. And second, now that you know what is in store for your family, you will get to think about it every day and every night until you die, when I choose to kill you." He stared at John with cold eyes. Then he averted his gaze to his cigar. "We are done; you will go now."

John opened his eyes with a start. A chill air blew in from the bay as Les opened the hatch to the bridge to get a better view of the wreckage of San Francisco. He stood and stared at the gray waters of the bay. He had a sudden chill and was colder than the temperature.

CHAPTER FIVE

TOP

THE MORNING AFTER THE pirate attack, Skye left Peggy and Heather in charge of the cleanup. That way, she was confident things would be done as they should be. They were almost grown now, and when not in training, they took on most of the responsibility for keeping the children in order. If confronted for leaving her assigned task, Skye could report she had left highly competent girls in charge.

The meeting of the council her mother had scheduled for tonight would surely be intense. There would be a review of how the pirates breeched the choke point and got to the docks without warning. Then there would be a vote on whether Skye would be admitted as a full-fledged member of the defense team and allowed on a watch.

No one was ever admitted to the ranks of the defenders without a long line of accomplishments. She hoped that her stopping the pirates from getting away would help her get a positive judgment. Her insides churned in knots at the thought she might not gain the status of a defender. She had trained much too hard and was convinced she was just on the cusp of being admitted to the defense team. She had to think of a way to make them see she belonged with the fighters and not the domestics.

Although everyone shared the tasks of working the fields, tending the herds of sheep and cattle, and fishing, the domestics gravitated toward taking care of the children; most had little interest in planning defense. They took training just enough to get by, but fought hard when called on. The defenders, by contrast, focused on keeping the village safe and, when not working on basic village upkeep, trained at defense incessantly.

Myst's words from yesterday afternoon hung in the back of her mind. They seemed more than a little ominous. She looked up the mountain and turned her thoughts to Top.

When the men went to the war, Top had been the only adult male to remain behind. He was considered too old to go to the fight, something he protested, but to no avail. He had remained behind to help the women and children organize the defense of the village. Only the children called him "Top." They had been taught to call adults "sir" and "ma'am." Once when she was a child, Skye called him "sir," and he had firmly told her, "I was a master sergeant. I worked for a living. Don't ever call me 'sir.'"

Skye had stammered, "Yes, Master." This made him laugh a long time. He instructed her to call him "Top," as in "Top Sergeant." She liked the name and ever since then, that is what all the children called him, except for the ones who called him "Father." The women called him other things.

Skye worked her way up the mountain carefully. The trail was steep, it dropped off sharply on the right, and while a fall might not be fatal, it would probably lead to serious injury. Either way, she didn't want to find out. She had hated heights ever since she fell off the roof of her old home in Seattle and broke her arm. Tight places and heights, she hated them both.

The mountain was on the side of the valley that protected Stehekin from the west. Top had picked his spot because it offered him a spectacular view covering the northern portion of the lake as it snaked through the cliffs to the south.

He had carved out a comfortable cave that was invisible from the water. It was below the tree line, and he never lit a wood fire during daylight, so there would be no smoke to reveal his presence.

The late afternoon sun was hot and made Skye perspire heavily as she climbed. Her blue Pooh Bear shirt clung to her back, soaked by her efforts. Her KaBar hung on her side and a water bottle dangled from her belt. When she reached the plateau that led to Top's cave, she paused for a drink. The water was warm but refreshing, and helped to clear the dust from her mouth.

She looked about for Top and hoped he wouldn't be drunk when she found him. "Yo, Top! Visitor paying a call!"

She had been taught early on not to enter his territory without giving warning. Top had explained it was only polite not to surprise him. She wondered what sort of man thing he didn't want to be surprised about and then removed the thought from her mind.

"Top, Top, are you here?"

She heard a grumbling come from behind the door of the cave as if she'd woken a sleeping bear. Top gave a heavy cough and then said with a ragged voice, "How many got killed yesterday?"

The question was abrupt and caught Skye by surprise. She stood staring at the wood door, thinking how to answer. The door swung open and Top stumbled out, squinting his eyes in the sunlight. He looked like hell.

He had a scruffy red-gray beard that covered a wrinkled face and wore a wine-stained Hawaiian shirt that had probably been clean once. He had on a pair of sweat shorts that barely hung on his hips with a white string swinging in the front. His collar-length hair was unkempt and looked like it had never seen a comb. He had always reminded her of a bear. When he stood straight up, he was a hand taller than Skye, but at the moment he was hunched over and bent like an old man. This was close to the worst she had ever seen him.

He looked at her with foggy eyes and grunted. "Asked you a question. How many killed yesterday?"

Skye didn't like his attitude; seeing him drunk before dark made her feel sorry for him. However, she didn't think it gave him an excuse to be impolite to her. "Which side?" she answered.

He cocked his head, hearing the impudence in her tone. A smile cracked across his dried-out lips. "Which side? Which side indeed? An excellent question. Does the old man give a shit about how our fair village is doing in terms of who of our kind have been lost pointlessly to cut-throats and bandits, or does he care about how well his training served the defenders and how many notches they put on their belts?"

He gazed into the distance as if trying to decide which tally he truly wanted. "Good call, Little One. I should know better to mind my manners around you more than anyone else. Now please tell me, who did we lose?"

Skye reached into her pocket and pulled out the list of names she had written down. She held it out to him and said, "The total was twelve killed. One of them was the domestic, Amora. I believe she was the mother of your son Kyle. I think she is the only one who had that kind of relationship with you. The others were defenders caught by the surprise attack."

Top took the list and read the names carefully. "Amora, she was a good soul, but dumber than a box of rocks. Still a pity to be taken like that. The boy is only eight. Who will look after him?"

Skye walked past Top and took a seat on one of the wooden chairs in the shade of a cedar that offered a view of the lake. "The domestics will sort that out tonight at the council. I'm sure he'll be well cared for."

Top grunted something unintelligible and ambled to where Skye was sitting. "Council? Is there a full council that will include the dames?"

Skye smiled; he had a name for everything and everyone. "Dames" was a variation of "domes," which was slang for "domestics." Only Top and a few of the harder defenders called them dames.

Skye wiped her brow with the back of her hand. "It is a full council tonight. The whole village is to attend, including you. Prior to the attack, I was nominated to be a defender. I do not know what effect the attack will have on my chances. They only nominate once a year."

Top slowly sat in a chair near her, keeping his eyes on hers. "I saw the end of the fight from here. How the fuck did you let those boats into the harbor without warning? Didn't I teach you dumb asses anything?"

Skye recoiled from the comment. She had come seeking Top's advice and was embarrassed when he admonished her as if the whole attack was her fault. She knew letting the pirates past the choke point was a horrendous error that would be difficult to deal with for the whole council, but she had not expected her mentor to have such hostility. He was the one person she thought might be an ally and help them understand what went wrong. That he turned on her shook her confidence to the core.

"Answer me! What the fuck were you all thinking down there? Or, were you? Tell me what happened."

Skye sat stone still and stared at Top. His cheeks were flushed and his breathing was almost a snort. The creases around his eyes seemed deeper than before, and he held his eyes on hers. She could scarcely take a breath. He had never talked to her like this. Sweat trickled down her neck, and she had the urge to bolt, to run back down the mountain, and to keep going deep into the wilderness where no one could ever find her.

"Have you gone mute?" Top's hands started to tremble and they clenched into fists.

Skye stood straight up. "I'll tell you someday when you are sober. Otherwise come to the council and you will find out like everybody else."

She quickly turned and started for the trail. Her knees were shaking. She had never stood up to authority before, especially not to Top, who she respected and loved like a father. She just couldn't stand being lectured about what she already knew was wrong. Before she got three steps, Top's voice boomed behind her, "Don't you turn into a smart ass with me, young'un! If you think you have what it takes to be the lead dog, you better learn how to deal with the mongrels. Get your butt back over here while I'm talking to you."

Skye kept her back to him and her feet moving forward. The hurt was so deep, tears were starting to well in her eyes, and she had no intention of letting him see her cry.

"Damn you, girl, get back here. Don't you make me come get you."

Skye had enough. She broke into a run. In a few short steps, she would be on the trail, down and out of sight of Top. She knew the threat to chase her was an empty one. They both knew he couldn't catch her even if he wanted to. They also both knew he didn't want to. They understood he would never raise a hand to her. His threat, one he had never made before, implied he would not receive her into his graces again. This to her was worse than a physical blow.

She told herself she didn't care and kept running. A hollow feeling crept into her. She needed to talk to a friend. *I have to find Myst.*

CHAPTER SIX

THE COUNCIL

A S DARKNESS FELL, THE women of the village filed solemnly into the open amphitheater. It was a warm fall evening, and the outdoor venue would be more comfortable than the lodge building that was used for school, entertainment, and recreation during the dark winter months.

At the front of the theater was a stage that held the polished wooden council table with twelve seats facing the audience. At the side and to the front of the table was a single chair that faced across the stage so the defendant could see both the council and the audience.

The chairs around the table had originally been soft and covered with fine smooth leather. After years of use, they were now covered with deer skins, which gave the proceeding the appearance of a tribal meeting. The audience sat in a semicircle cut out of the side of a hill. The seats were carved into the hill and lined with smooth rocks. Each woman brought her own form of cushion or blankets to cover the rocks, and over time they had learned to make the seats quite comfortable.

There were six rows going up the hill, with a capacity for nearly three hundred. They had nearly filled the place only once and that had been years ago, before the men had left.

Giant aromatic cedars and tall fir trees towered around the complex, the wind stirring through their branches. Torches lit the perimeter of the circle and electric light powered by the hydro generators illuminated the stage.

The domes took their seats on the top two of the six tiers, and the defenders filled in nearer the bottom, each according to personal preference, although there was an unwritten deference to status. Those who were the captains of the watch took the lowest seats, their lieutenants the next row, and so on.

The women wore a more formal attire than they would for a show or entertainment. There were few furs or old denim garments. Most wore slacks that had been saved for special occasions, with blouses that had been saved for the same reason. There were a few long dresses, most of these worn by domes. Weapons were not allowed and were checked at the entrance.

Once the village was seated, Sharon looked over the theater. She mused that if a stranger from the old days had wandered in they would think they had come across a PTA meeting. Sharon took a heavy breath. She was not looking forward to this. She feared her daughter had not yet gained the grace of the council mainly due to her young age. From her conversations with some of the members, she thought the chances of Skye's quest to join the ranks of the defenders were slim.

Worse yet, this stood as a test for the council. A finding that Skye was not qualified mainly due to age might make the laws appear to be outdated. As she looked at the faces in the crowd, there were none younger than forty. The gap between the children and those approaching adulthood had the potential to cause a serious rift in the way the village was governed in the near future.

The other members of the council filed by her; Sharon entered last, went up the five steps that led to the stage, and moved to the center chair of the table. Dressed in a white blouse with black slacks and low heeled shoes, she had an unspoken air of authority about her.

The other members of the council stood waiting behind their chairs. Sharon raised her hands palms up, and the members of the audience, including Skye, rose to their feet in silence. She spoke loudly and clearly without use of a microphone. "According to the customs of our village, as elected leader, I call this full meeting of the council to order." Then she picked up the gavel that rested on the table and struck it three times on the hard wood. "I invite you to join in the saying of the prayer."

She bowed her head and then everyone joined in the prayer. "Thank you Lord for watching over us. Please help us to be strong in the face of the unknown, please give us the wisdom to follow your path and raise our children well, please give us the strength to protect ourselves from the unrighteous, please take care of those who went to the war and have them safely return to us, thank you for sending us your Son the Savior. Amen."

Then there was a moment of silence. With her eyes closed, Sharon listened to see if any of the doubters would make a sarcastic statement. On the whole, she didn't consider the villagers to be a particularly religious lot. They held to their Christian roots but that was about it. There were a few who had lost all faith, and now and then they would make themselves heard. Sharon was thankful they held their views to themselves on this day.

She looked into the audience gathered before her. "Today we are gathered for a grave purpose. Yesterday we buried twelve of our number who were murdered by pirates from the south. We must understand the failure of our defense so that we are never surprised again. Our first order of business is to determine the fitness for duty of the captain of the watch for yesterday morning.

"Then we must decide the fate of Skye, since she has been nominated to join the ranks. We must determine if she is worthy to become a defender or if she is not yet ready."

Sharon continued from the stage, "Now it is time to determine why we were surprised. As is our custom, we will have two opposing views presented and then the council will decide if the captain of the watch at that time is fit to retain her title or if it should be removed and a replacement appointed.

"Captain Barbara Crane, please approach the council."

Skye watched, fascinated, as the captain stood and smoothed her cream-colored blouse. She was a midsized woman with short brown hair who Skye knew to be fifty-two years old. A lump formed in Skye's throat as the captain went up the stairs to the stage. Skye had only been allowed to attend council meetings since she had turned seventeen. This was only the third one that had been called in all that time and was by far the most serious. It was also her first trial.

Skye knew the captain was one of the most liked by her watch. She also knew that some thought this was a sign of weakness and that she did not keep a strict enough relationship with those in her command.

Crane stopped in front of the single chair at the front of the stage. Sharon remained in her place and faced the captain. "Do you swear by all your principals, and on your integrity, that all you say will be the truth?"

Crane faced the council. "I do."

"Please be seated."

After the captain sat down, Sharon nodded to the woman on her right. Dana Frey, the prosecutor, stood and walked to the front of the stage. Her long black hair was held in a ponytail that trailed halfway down her back. Dana wore a white blouse with khaki slacks and brown shoes. She approached the captain.

"These are the relevant facts of yesterday's incident. First, the Sparrow Watch had the scheduled duty yesterday morning from dawn until three. Second, raiders invaded our dock without warning using motorized boats. Third, the lookouts failed to sound the alarm. Fourth, before the watch responded, over forty invaders attacked our people who were working near the docks, assaulted the gate, and ultimately killed twelve and injured twenty-seven."

Sharon caught her breath as Dana paused. With each sentence she spoke, her words sounded harder. Dana stared at Crane. "Do you dispute any of these facts?"

Crane sat rigidly in her chair. "I do not."

"Were you the captain of the duty watch yesterday?"

Crane barely moved and spoke clearly. "Yes, I am captain of Sparrow Watch and we had the duty at the time of the attack."

Dana faced the council. "The facts are not in dispute."

Dana returned to her place at the table and Sharon rose. "The secretary of defense will state a case for removal of Captain Crane's rank and privilege."

Tracy Morgan, the secretary of defense, headed for center stage. She was a short woman with braided red hair who had the look of an angry bulldog. Sharon knew her as a kind and gentle friend, one who had a quick wit and loved to laugh when she was in the mood for fun. When things got tough, she showed a stiff resolve to sort problems out and had little tolerance for failure. As she approached Crane, her walk was deliberate. She stopped in front of the captain and gave her a hard look.

Tracy's voice cracked with anger. "In your own words, tell us what the failure was that led to the murder of our people."

Crane looked straight ahead. "The lookout was ambushed before she could sound the alarm. We discovered she was felled with an arrow."

Tracy could barely keep her rage under her breath. "Lookout? As in singular? As in one? Is it not our policy to have a minimum of two lookouts posted at all times?"

Crane showed no emotion. "In the past it was our custom, but it has been so long since we have been attacked, we have allowed one person to hold the post during the day."

"We! Who the hell is 'we'? I did not authorize this, the council did not authorize this! Have the captains of the watch started making defense policy on their own?"

Crane's face went tight. "I meant that I authorized it. I do not speak for any of the other captains. It was a day when we needed all the help with the grapevines we could get."

"Since when did anything take precedence over the primary function of the watch? Isn't that your first sworn duty?"

"Yes, it is."

"And who did you send out for this crucial job by herself?"

Skye could see Crane twitch. Everybody knew who the lookout

had been because they had buried her yesterday. She wondered why the question was asked.

Crane's lips tightened. "I sent Hilde Mescal, a member of my watch."

Tracy's anger was nearly boiling. "You sent Hilde Mescal, a doddering old woman, God rest her soul, who was a member of your watch only because of her long standing in the village. She has not been to a drill in two years. You left the fate of the village in the care of someone not physically able to help with manual work so you could speed the harvest. How do you defend this action?"

Crane's back stayed straight. "I made a commander's decision. We have been at peace for nearly two years, and the traders may come in the next few weeks. I felt that there was little risk and that preparing for the trading was of some importance."

Tracy leaned close to the captain's face, nearly hissing. "You were wrong. You violated the rules of defense, you got a dozen of our friends killed, you could have lost the village for us, and for all we know we might still lose it. You are not fit for command."

Tracy turned to the council. "The evidence is clear. Captain Crane took policy on herself and failed to staff the lookout post as prescribed in the orders of the watch. I recommend she be removed from her station and be replaced immediately."

The secretary of defense gave Crane a withering look and returned to her seat. Skye felt her chest tighten. This was going to be hard on Crane; she loved being a captain. Skye could not imagine how she would react to being reduced to a defender.

Sharon stood up again. "Now the secretary of laws will present a defense." Clara Pinto smoothed her long white dress as she took her place in front of Crane. "It is my responsibility to provide you with a defense. What would you have me say?"

Crane spoke slowly with a hint of defiance in her voice. "I have been captain for over five years now. The members of my watch have defended all of you since the beginning. We have never failed before. When attacked this time, my watch fought bravely and was key in repelling the invaders. Four of the dead were members of Sparrow Watch, lost in the defense. I grieve as much as anyone for the loss of all of our friends.

"Yesterday, I posted a competent person on lookout. True, she was not physically strong, but we only needed her eyes and ears. How she was surprised is still unknown. She must have let her guard down. I hold that Hilde failed at her post and that the blame for the disaster lies in the grave with her."

There were several gasps from the audience and a low murmur filled the theater. Sharon banged the gavel for silence. Sharon could scarcely believe what she had heard. The idea that a captain would not take full responsibly for her watch was foreign to her.

The secretary of laws stepped away from Crane. "Your defense, then, is that what happened on your watch was not your fault."

Clara faced the council. "The captain of the watch posted a lookout who failed. That is the sum of the defense."

Clara returned to her seat.

Sharon once again rose in place and spoke to the audience. "As is our rule, the council will vote with the stones. A white stone confers innocence of committing a crime; a black stone indicates a law has been broken. Seven black stones are required to confirm a crime.

"Out of recognition of her long service, if found guilty, the defendant will be reduced from the status of captain but will be allowed to serve as defender first class on another watch, if one will take her. Otherwise she will be removed from all watches and work with the domestics. If found innocent, she will retain her rank and status.

"We will now vote. Members of the council, please rise and make your choice known." The women of the council stood and turned toward the head of the table. The secretary of law placed two boxes on the end of the table. One box held twelve black stones and twelve white stones. The other box was placed on a pedestal that was higher than her head.

The secretary addressed the standing women. "The box on the table contains your voting stones. Pick one and place it in the verdict box above. Handle your vote with care so that your vote is only known to you."

One by one, the council members approached the head of the table and made their choice. Skye could feel the tension in air and held her breath as each vote rattled into the ballot box. She tried to read the faces of the council but they were almost uniformly impassive. The exception was Delta, an outspoken advocate of the defenders. When her rock hit the others, there was a loud crack from the impact, as she had deposited it with great force. The glare she gave the defendant left little doubt as to the color of her vote.

When the council completed the process and took their seats, Sharon stood once again. "I will now count the votes. The verdict will be final and there is no appeal."

Skye watched, fascinated, as her mother reached high into the verdict box and withdrew the first stone. She held it over her head for all to see. Even from her distance and in the dim light of the stage, Skye could see the dark stone. A chill went through her at the thought of Captain Crane losing her status. It had never happened before, and that could mean the council was not prepared to show mercy on anyone.

Sharon reached into the box five more times, and Skye's hopes fell with each new black stone. In her heart, she knew the captain had committed a grave crime. The council had no apparent regard for her past service, and Skye felt her own chances of winning a spot on the guard were reduced with every guilty vote from the single-minded council.

The leader finally reached for the seventh stone. The air on the gathering place was dead still. Crane sat erect in her seat, staring straight ahead. Sharon held the stone vote in her clasped hand. Without looking at it, she opened her fingers and showed the vote to the village. A slight gasp came from the crowd. The polished black rock glittered in the torchlight.

Sharon brought her arm down slowly, displaying the stone in her palm. "Barbara Crane, please rise." The defendant stood up, showing no emotion. "You have been found guilty of negligence by the council. Please surrender your insignia of rank to the secretary of laws."

Crane's lips pressed tightly together, and for a moment Skye thought she was going to say something, but instead she simply removed her captain's pin and walked to the secretary of laws and handed it to her. Then without a word, she turned on her heels and left the stage. She walked crisply into the amphitheater to take a place high in the theater away from the others. Skye was not sure if it was a trick of the lighting or not but she thought she saw a tear on the former captain's cheek.

Skye shifted in her seat. *This doesn't look good. If they are going to throw a captain off the guard, what chance do I have?*

She flinched when her mother hit her gavel on the table, which sounded louder than normal in the hushed chamber. "We have two more issues we must discuss. First, Skye has been nominated to join the defense force. I have thought of removing myself from this process but have decided not to. I will simply tell you that I believe she is an able fighter and has the judgment we would expect of members of the watch. Were I to say more, you would only think I was bragging on myself for raising such a fine child." She smiled and let out a little laugh, as did some members of the audience.

Skye felt heat rise in her cheeks and eyes looking at her from around the room. She studied the toes of her polished white shoes and noticed there was a slight scuff on one of them.

Sharon continued, "I will now open the floor for a brief debate."

Skye cringed as a few members of the audience spoke on her behalf, while others noted her age and doubted her maturity and worthiness. She found it odd to be discussed as if she were an object and not even in the room. She made a mental checklist of who was for and against her.

After a dozen women spoke, her mother raised her hands. "I think we have heard enough to let the council vote."

Top's voice boomed from the back of the amphitheater. "This is bullshit!" Top started walking down the stairs, nearly dragging Eagle like a doll. He had shaved since Skye had last seen him and he had even put on a clean shirt. Even so, he was still pretty scruffy.

Skye's mother scowled at him. "Don't swear in here, Top."

He stopped in front of stage and said, "Sorry, Madame."

"Don't call me Madame."

He said to her in an exasperated tone, "What the hell am I supposed to call you?"

Skye's mother spoke to him as if was an errant child. "Stop it. What do you mean and why did you bring Eagle in here? He is not allowed."

Skye saw him take a deep breath, the kind he did when she had botched a training exercise and was summoning up his patience. "I'm here because I don't understand why there is a debate about Skye's worthiness for the defense team. She's faster and more agile than anyone in this room and a lot better shot. You all nearly got us killed because you've lost your edge. If wasn't for Skye, that last pirate boat would have gotten away and that could have been a complete disaster."

He turned to face the audience. "Ladies, you have to admit, there isn't a person in here, 'cept maybe me, could have done what she did. Running halfway across the mountain and then having the cool to drop two pirates on a moving boat from two hundred yards. Ain't that what she did, Eagle?"

Eagle nodded vigorously. "Yes sir, she nailed them both. Otherwise they'd have got away. Don't forget we, I mean she, took out the mortar too."

Skye tried to make herself small, embarrassed by the outlandishness of Top's behavior.

Top turned to her mother and said, "You need her on the watch. Why is there a debate?"

The room erupted in conversations and the members of the council leaned toward each other.

After a few moments, Skye's mother slammed the gavel on the table again. "You will not interrupt these proceedings …"

Tracy Morgan stood and called out from the council table, "Sharon,

I think the council is in agreement. We would like to suspend the secret ballot and take a vote by voice on this issue now."

Skye saw surprise on her mother's face, and then she hit her gavel again and said, "Highly unusual, but we shall do what the council wishes."

She looked around the council table and asked, "Are you all in agreement on this?"

The members of the council nodded affirmatively. She proceeded. "All who oppose Skye's appointment to the defense, say nay."

Skye's heart leapt at the silence that followed.

Her mother continued, "Those in favor, say yea."

The council stood as one and gave unanimous yea votes. The room burst into applause, and Skye jumped to her feet and wrapped her arms around her mentor.

A minute passed and her mother was at the gavel again. When the room quieted, she spoke solemnly. "We have one more order of business. We must discuss a strategy to confront the fact that the pirates have learned what we have, and they want it. The one who nearly killed me, he told me they know our secret. I'm not sure if that is true or not."

Skye's elation left her and the jubilation went out of the room like a candle blown by the wind.

CHAPTER SEVEN

THE PREDATOR

BARZAN STOOD ON THE upper deck of his makeshift troop transport as it passed into the opening of San Francisco Bay. It had originally been built as a cruise ship for the decadence of the infidels, but his men had converted it to the bare needs of the troops. The crumpled towers of the Golden Gate Bridge stood testament to the madness that had gripped the world at the end. He was not sure who had annihilated who here. He didn't care either.

It could have been the Jihadists attacking, or it could have been the Americans desperately defending, though he thought that seemed unlikely. It occurred to him it might have even been the Chinese who tried to make a power grab as the wars exploded ten years ago. Either way, he was satisfied that the heathens had done a thorough job of blowing up each other's civilizations here and around the world. That was, after all, the vacuum that allowed the great prophet, Al-Zar to rise from the desert and introduce the teachings of the Malsi.

His trusted Lieutenant Ja-Zeer approached him as he turned his attention from the remains of San Francisco. Ja-Zeer gave him the customary hand salute and Barzan touched the bill of his tan general's hat to reciprocate. The lieutenant rarely took his time unless he had something worthwhile to report, and Barzan was ready for some good news. He and his army had been aboard their ships for weeks and he could sense his troops were getting anxious to get into battle again. Despite the constant training and drills, he grew concerned that his men were losing their sharpness.

Ja-Zeer said, without prompting, "I have good news, my commander."

Barzan grunted, indicating the man should continue.

"The radiation detectors have found nothing for us to be worried about here. Some of the shoreline has hot spots but we will be able to find a place to land with little problem."

Barzan considered this for a moment and thought it to be fair news at best. He had little interest in radiation and what it might do to men weeks or years from now. He chose not to share that with his lieutenant. "There is news beyond that?"

"Of course, my commander. The advance scouts report they have found no opposition of any size. Things appear deserted here. There is evidence of ancient riots but there are almost no people here. We have captured several men, but they may be of little use."

Barzan stroked his chin. "Tell your scouts to be wary. The Americans were always deceitful in war and in peace. It is difficult to believe they have all vanished or killed each other."

"Perhaps it was the will of God."

Barzan inwardly winced. He believed his lieutenant was not one of those superstitious fools who could be led around by praising God. Maybe he was just trying to say the right thing. "Perhaps. Remember, there was a decadent power here for many years and it nearly killed us all. Do not take its remnants lightly. Let us inspect the prisoners."

A short time later, Barzan, Ja-Zeer, and several other officers stood on the rear deck of the ship they had renamed *Conqueror*. The deck was wide and flat; it formerly had a swimming pool on it. The pool had been sealed over, and it now offered a place for the troops to train. A reinforced railing surrounded the outer edge of the deck, which at this place was fifty feet above the water. Several guards with rifles at the ready stood on either side of the officers. A dense fog clung to the hilltops at the entrance to the bay and a breeze brought a chill off the

Pacific. Barzan ignored the weather and waited for his prisoners to appear.

A metal hatch opened and Major Ivan Kosomor led two guards and the tracker known as Fielder onto the fantail. Barzan smiled at Fielder's success. He had been dispatched in a launch two days before to scout the shore. Bringing back prisoners was a bonus.

They exchanged formalities and then the guards hauled three mangy-looking prisoners from the hold. Barzan looked them over in disgust. Their hair was long and matted, the clothes they wore were in tatters, and they looked as if they hadn't eaten in a week. The shackles that bound their hands and feet clanked heavily on the metal deck. One had bruises on his face; obviously somebody had started questioning him.

Barzan lit a cigarette and addressed Ivan. "What do you call these? I've seen monkeys that look more like men than this scum."

"Da," Ivan answered. "Not much to look at, less to talk to so far. Say they know nothing about anything."

Barzan let smoke release from his lungs. "Then why did you bring them here? Why do you waste my time?"

A dark look crossed Ivan's eyes. "It was you who called them up here. I require more time to question them." There was a long pause and then Ivan gave his head the slightest of bows, "My commander."

Barzan's heart rate went up. The barely concealed insolence caused him to clench his teeth. If Ivan had not proved so valuable on so many occasions, Barzan would have cut him down on the spot. Even so, there were only so many times you had to pay back someone who had saved your life more than once. He brushed his mustache with his hand. This was not an occasion to take issue with the major; he would need to keep a closer rein on the man though. The immediate need was to remind the men in attendance of his true power.

Barzan brushed past the major and strode to the nearest prisoner. The trembling man stared at the floor. Barzan spoke to no one and everyone. "Why are these men standing in my presence?"

Before the prisoners could move, the guards behind them kicked their knees out from under them and they collapsed on the deck like so many piles of rubbish. Barzan kicked the nearest one in the face with the heel of his boot. "What do you know of the people who live here?"

The man looked down at the deck in silence. Barzan moved to the next prisoner. "Tell me about the army that protects this place." He was met with more silence. A slow burn started to sear his insides. These rats were infuriating him. He could feel the eyes of his officers on his back. This would not stand.

He kicked the second prisoner hard in the ear with his boot heel. The man cried out in pain as his head snapped back under the blow. Blood spilled from the side of his head.

Barzan stood above him. "Tell me about the armies."

The prisoner spat blood out of his mouth. "They ain't here."

"Where are they?"

"Don't know, mister. Please leave us alone. We ain't done nothing to you."

Barzan grabbed the man by the hair, yanked his head up, and hissed, "You live, that is a crime enough for me."

He motioned toward the first prisoner and asked, "Your friend?"

The prisoner blurted a word from his bloody mouth: "Brother."

The third prisoner shouted, "Shut up, fool."

Barzan released the man's hair and turned his back on him. He stared directly at Ivan. "That didn't take long to learn."

He saw the major clench his fist in irritation. Barzan took a satisfied final drag on his cigarette and then crushed it into the rusting steel deck. "Now we can find some things out."

He drew his *jambia*, his prized rhino horn-handled dagger, from his belt. He held it in front of the second prisoner's face. The eight-inch blade gleamed in the sunlight. "You like your brother? You like him a lot?"

The man slowly nodded. Barzan moved to the first prisoner, who was on his knees watching him warily. Barzan stood before the shackled man and tilted his head from side to side. He said to the second prisoner, "Tell me where the armies are."

The second man spit blood on the deck and said, "Told you. Don't know."

In one quick motion, Barzan reached to the first prisoner, tilted his head back, and cut a small slit in his jugular. Blood shot from the slash and spilled onto the deck in a red pool. Barzan grinned as the doomed man's eyes went wild with terror. The prisoner screamed, "Help please, please."

His brother shouted, "Stop!"

Blood surged each time his heart beat, and Barzan backed away to keep from having blood spill on him. He looked at the second prisoner. "How long do you think he will live? Five minutes? Maybe ten? Looks like he has lots of blood to go."

The second man seethed, "You bastard, help him!"

Barzan sneered, "Help him? He is a dead man; we have no way to fix a wound like that. You could help if you wanted." He held the handle of his knife toward the prisoner. "You can help him out of his pain."

The second prisoner narrowed his eyes. "Give me the knife."

"Where are the armies?"

"Give me the knife and I'll tell."

The wounded man was squirming on the deck, writhing in his own blood. Barzan gave a signal, and Ivan took the knife from him and carefully handed it to the second prisoner.

The man took the knife in his hand and shuffled to his dying brother. He put one hand over his bother's eyes and said, "Forgive me." Then he plunged the blade into the struggling man's heart. The mortal wound caused him to let out a high-pitched scream. His body shuddered and then fell still.

The surviving brother recoiled from the body in horror.

There were a few moments of silence. Ivan approached the dead man and yanked the knife from his chest; he wiped it off and handed it to Barzan. "Impressive, but what have we learned, my commander?"

Barzan said nothing but returned to the second prisoner, who was kneeling and weeping on the deck. "Tell me about the armies," he said.

The prisoner shook his head. "I don't know anything, you animal! I told you that, you killed him for nothing!" Then he spit blood at Barzan.

Almost before the blood hit him Barzan reached out and slashed his throat. "As I thought, a common liar."

The prisoner clutched his throat with his shackled hands, falling to the deck in agony. With his windpipe cut, he made a loud gasping sound and his body convulsed.

Barzan approached the last of the prisoners, blood still dripping from his knife. The man looked at him, his eyes wide in fright. Barzan judged him to be twenty years older than the other two. "Tell me about the armies."

"I will tell you what I know."

Barzan lit a new cigarette. "What are you called?"

"I am Owens."

"Do you know of the dog they call Colonel Erikson?"

He watched Owens swallow hard.

"I have heard of one, but it has been some years."

Barzan's heart beat jumped.

"Do you know where he came from? Is it far?"

"A few days by vehicle; I think I can help you find the place."

Barzan blew more smoke in his face and said, "Then I think you might live."

Barzan turned away from him and walked past Ivan, saying, "Feed him. He may be useful, we will question him more later." As he left the deck, he was pleased he had shown his superiority to his men once again.

CHAPTER EIGHT

TRADER RICK

SKYE STOOD ON THE dock with two members of the Cougar Watch waiting for the trader's boat to arrive. She nervously tapped her right fingers against the handle of the sharpened KaBar that hung from her side. Her left hand held her rifle loosely at her side, though not at the ready. She was confident it would only take her an instant to aim and fire if needed.

Delta, second in command of the watch, moved closer to her. The boat was long; she guessed maybe forty feet, heavily armored with steel and thick wooden planks. It looked like it had sustained more damage since it had been here the previous year. There were newer bits of metal around the cabin that glittered in the morning sun. The engine ran unevenly and spewed a foul black smoke from the rear.

The one new feature that made Skye uneasy was the deadly looking gun that was mounted on a swivel above the pilothouse. She guessed the boat could hold thirty people hidden below, and with a gun like that, if this were a surprise, there would be a vicious fight. She scanned the shoreline, looking for a sign of the rest of the watch that she knew was poised to assault the vessel at the first sign anything was amiss. She could not make out a soul and marveled at the ability of the watch to remain concealed.

Delta stepped to the end of the dock when the boat was still fifty yards off shore and called out, "Ahoy, Trader Rick! What have you there?"

Skye shifted her weight to her right foot and moved the left in front. The only sound came from the sputtering engine, and Skye's throat started to go dry. She eased her rifle into her right hand but held it at her side, refraining from raising it in a threatening manner. The boat drew nearer and Delta called out again, this time louder.

"Ahoy, Rick! Let's see you, you old dog!" No response came and Sky started to wonder at the wisdom of standing exposed on the dock with only Delta there with her.

The engine made a sputter and the noise dropped off. At the shift in sound, she reflexively stepped back and raised her rifle. Delta never flinched, and Skye was impressed with her courage. The vessel was nearly to the dock and looked like it might ram it when the engine made a grinding noise then chugged higher again as the armored boat slowed to a near stop.

A tall man with flowing, night-black hair emerged from the pilothouse with a big blue rubber boat fender and shouted, "Grab the front, grab the rail! Don't let it hit!"

Delta ran to the front of the dock, where the boat was about to make contact. She looked at Skye, who had her rifle aimed straight at the man with the fender, and said, "Here, help me. I can't do this by myself."

Relieved, Skye realized the man with the fender really was Rick and not some imposter or pirate. He was one of the few people she knew of who managed to move freely about the countryside, trading goods with all manner of people. Skye put her rifle on her shoulder with its sling as she ran to Delta. Together they pushed the boat as it glided up to the dock and leaned into it as they brought it to a gentle stop.

Rick looked older since Skye had last seen him. His hair was longer and there were deepening crow's feet by his eyes. There was a short new scar on his left cheek but she did not think it detracted from his good looks. His clothes were better too. His leather jacket looked nearly new, and his denim pants had no rips or patches. Judging by the slight bulge around his midsection, he must be eating well also. The pistol hanging on his side was more conspicuous than in the past. Even though he smiled as he handed down the fenders and ropes to complete the docking, she wondered what was below decks and what had brought him back here, to the end of the lake. In the past he had been known to bring marvelous goods that were scarce or nonexistent in the village.

He looked down on her from the deck of the boat, and his smile lingered on her a little longer than made her comfortable. His eyes stared at her in a way that made her back tingle with an unfamiliar sensation.

"Well, Little One, looks like you have grown to be a lady."

Skye didn't quite know what to make of his comment. Nonetheless, she felt her cheeks starting to burn. She stammered out a response, "I've been grown a long time. I'm on the wat … I'm on the reception committee." She nearly bit her tongue for almost revealing the existence of the watch. He had no need to know how the defense was organized.

Skye wanted to assert her worthiness in front of Delta, who was busy tying the boat's stern lines. She looked at Rick and asked with anticipation, "What did you bring?"

Rick gave his head a slight tilt and his smile thinned out. "A surprise for you."

Skye felt a slight shiver go through her. She dropped her hand so it rested on her KaBar. "Me? Why would you bring a surprise to me?"

He glanced at Delta, who was approaching from the stern, and then turned back to Skye and said in a lowered voice, "I'll tell you later. Maybe we'll have a moment alone."

Skye was both alarmed and intrigued by the comment. Her experience with men was negligible, but she had seen some vids of old romance movies and had an idea that Rick might have something interesting, or awful, on his mind. She was fascinated.

Delta approached and looked at her, and then looked at Rick with what Skye thought was a distinctly suspicious manner. She spoke to Rick. "What do you have that we want?"

Rick laughed an honest, jovial laugh. "If you have what I want, I have plenty. I have clothes, I have food, I have hard supplies."

Delta clapped her hands. "It is a good day then. Have you any news?"

Rick's face turned to a slight frown. "Aye, I have news. Not much of it good. But there is time for that later. Will you invite me ashore then?"

Delta queried, "Are you alone?"

"As always. You may look the boat over if you like."

"Your word has always been good but things have been bad of late. You won't mind if I send Skye for a look-see?"

Rick smiled again. "How could I ever mind having the Little One aboard?"

The tingle in Skye's back returned for an instant. Then Skye took his hand as he helped her up to the deck.

That afternoon, Skye observed the trading with interest. Her mother and the others carefully inspected each item Rick had brought to offer. The items were spread the length of the pier and onto the shore. There were boxes of clothes that looked as if they had never been worn. A lot of them had tags that said Wal-Mart. Skye picked up a bright red dress and held it against herself. She heard Rick let out a low whistle and then he gave her a wink. She decided to keep the dress.

Sharon approached Rick and motioned to the boxes of clothes. She said, "These are new. Where did you get them?"

"These, I got these nearly a year ago. Very precious but I've been saving them just for you. Of all my stops, you are the ones who would appreciate them most. Ran across some folks that found a rare container truck full of this stuff. Cost me a lot to get them but I figured you would make it worth my while."

Skye saw her mother shake her head and say, "I hope you didn't spend too much. We don't have any place to wear stuff like this anyway."

She wiped beads of perspiration from her forehead. Skye knew the trading had begun.

She was surprised at how fast things moved along. There was not much negotiation; she surmised this was because neither side had a clear advantage over the other in terms of goods or wants. The village wanted canned foods that were still being mined from old warehouses, clothes, and assorted tools to replace things that had worn out.

She picked up a new axe and ran her fingers over the flat of the blade. It was rough and uneven, not smooth like the machine-made blades the village had originally been stocked with. She caught Rick's attention and asked, "Where did you get this?"

"What is your interest in that?"

She put the axe down and picked up a shovel that had the same type of construction. "These were made after the war. Who did it?"

Skye's mother came to where she was standing and examined the shovel. "Is there civilization out there?" She was breathing heavily and coughed hard. Skye thought her mother was at the beginning of a cold or flu. She had been this way for the last two days.

Rick took the shovel from Skye. "What you need to know, I'll tell you at dinner, if I'm invited. How is that for a trade?"

Her mother picked up the axe and was about to speak when Delta interjected, "You can come to dinner okay, but you have to tell us everything. That's the trade."

"I'll bring a big hunger."

Skye was a little taken aback by Delta's comment. She was one of the most respected defenders, though she rarely put herself forward, preferring to let her actions speak for themselves.

As the sun lowered over the mountains, the trading started to wind down. Sharon and the council had made the bulk of the deals on behalf of the village. The primary good they had to offer was wine. The territory offered itself to growing grapes, and the founders had built great vats and installed them as part of the prewar planning. Some had thought they were daft, but as the years went by, their method proved a huge asset to the village.

The few traders who managed to survive could never seem to get enough of the stuff and were willing to exchange almost anything for it. Skye had learned there were only two commodities the traders wanted more. Besides wine, they were one of the few things the village had in ample supply. Unlike wine, they were the village's deepest secret.

The traders who were allowed to deal with the village in these items had to have something of great value to even get a discussion open on the topic. The few who made the trades were sworn to secrecy. This worked to both sides' advantage. The merchants did not want their source outed and the village desired the source be kept unmentioned. But even those who made these rare deals had no idea of the magnitude of Stehekin's secret.

By sunset, most of the women had left the dock area and Skye lingered behind with her mother and Delta. After the trading for the village was finished, many individuals made deals for various items of a personal nature. When the last of the women were done, Sharon took a seat on a box of clothes, and Delta sat on another box beside her. Skye sat cross legged on the dock. Rick dragged a small chair across the floor and sat facing the two older women. Sharon said, "Is the trading phrase still, what do you gots that I wants?"

Rick laughed, "Yes, they still use that all around. Officially opens the bargain for some. Don't have to use it for me though."

Skye saw her mother smile and say, "Then our bargain is open."

Skye felt her back tighten. Surely they were done; she could not imagine there was something else to bargain for.

Rick leaned back and asked, "What makes you think I have anything?"

Sharon examined her fingernails and said, "'Cause you haven't asked for it yet."

Rick scratched his ear thoughtfully. "I must be getting slow." He nodded toward Skye and asked, "You want to do this in front of the Little One?"

Skye cringed; she could not stand the idea she might be sent away, but she didn't like being referred to as if she was not there. Her mother looked at her and Skye held her breath.

"She is of age now, and she will be useful."

Skye let out a silent sigh.

Sharon put her palms up on her lap. She coughed again hard; Skye noticed that Rick took a short step back as if he didn't want to be too close.

Wordlessly, Rick left the dock and boarded his nearby boat. After a few moments he returned, struggling to carry a plain wooden box almost three feet wide and equally tall. During this time, her mother barely moved, and for the first time Skye became aware of her labored breathing. Perhaps the flu her mother was developing was further along than Skye had thought. She was becoming anxious to get her back to the house and by the fire, out of the cooling evening air.

At the same time, she was intensely curious about what the trader had to offer. Rick checked the area around the dock to make sure they were alone. Two members of the duty watch stood casually at the end of the pier. Other than that, the villagers had returned to their homes for dinner and preparation for the evening's celebration.

Rick opened the lid on the box, reached in, and pulled out an exquisitely carved chest. It was one of the most beautiful things Skye had ever seen. She took in a deep breath and tried not to look too excited. She gently pressed forward to get a better view. The wood was dark and polished to a deep ebony color. Embossed in the top and sides were elephants, tigers, trees, and all manner of things she had seen in pictures of Africa. On the front was a brass keyhole.

Skye asked, "May I touch it?" Rick nodded and Skye reached out and let her fingers glide across the top. The surface was cool as if it had been kept in a cold storage. The figures were rich in texture, and she imagined that she could feel them moving beneath her fingertips. "What's in it?"

Her mother wiped more perspiration from her face as she coughed again and said, "It is a remembrance from before the war. I will open it when your father returns. Was it difficult to acquire?"

Rick ran his thumb along the scar on his face. "Let us just say I've found easier things."

Sharon coughed and smiled. "I'm glad it was no worse than that. It would have pained me if it had been so."

Rick nodded, "Me too."

Skye watched as her mother leaned back and coughed out a laugh. "What do you want?"

Rick's eyes moved to Skye and for a moment she had the distinct feeling he thought she had no clothes on. She folded her arms over her chest and then had a rush of embarrassment as the burning in her cheeks told her that her face was going flush.

Her mother stood up, "There are plenty here who will be more than happy to show you hospitality. What do you really want that you can't get anyplace else?"

CHAPTER NINE

CELEBRATION

MUSIC ECHOED IN THE valley as domes and members of the off watches danced around a bonfire built deep in the forest. Skye watched as the jubilant celebration welcomed the trader for the first time in a year and half. Wine flowed from decorated carafes into crystal goblets that only came out on the most special of occasions.

Skye sipped the deep red liquid in her glass and tried not to show her disgust with the drink. She did not have anything against the others enjoying it, but the bitter taste did not appeal to her. This was the first adult celebration she'd been allowed to attend, and her excitement about being included was tempered by her desire to fit in well and not make a faux pas, as Mother called it.

Delta came by with a full carafe and filled Skye's goblet once again. Skye grinned widely and pretended to take another drink. When no one was watching, she slipped to the edge of the celebration grounds and poured half the glass into the surrounding bushes, just like she had been doing all night.

To the right of the fire, her mother and other members of the council sat on wooden benches in a semicircle, with the trader in the center. He was waving his arms as he talked, and occasionally the whole group would burst out laughing. Around the fire more and more women danced in increasingly unbridled ways. They spun and jumped, some dancing arm in arm and some in a world of their own. Skye knew the intake of wine had an unfettering effect on people, but she had never seen it on this scale. She was amazed there could be this kind of party less than a week after the disastrous pirate attack. She concluded this was part of an attempt to briefly escape the memory and horror of that awful event.

She gazed away from the party and looked at the mountain peaks that jutted into the night sky. Myst's words came to mind, and she felt unsettled in her center. The large party with the trader was a strange act, and she wondered what her mother was up to. A man coughed behind her and she turned to find Top standing by her.

He nodded toward the mountains. "Pretty night."

He was as clean as she'd ever seen him and smelled of wine and some kind of man cologne she had only smelled a few times before. She set her jaw as a chill ran down her back.

He looked at her with clear eyes. "You still mad at me from the last time you were in my camp?"

She chose her words carefully. "I am not mad. I am disappointed that I can no longer trust you."

His eyebrows dropped minutely and he lowered his eyes. "I apologize for the way I acted that day. I sort of hoped getting you help with the council might have made you feel better about me."

"I do thank you for that."

He raised his eyes to hers. "Then why don't you trust me? You've got to trust someone."

Skye let out a breath. "I don't trust anyone, especially men. The only ones I do trust are me and my mother, and sometimes I'm not too sure about me."

"Meaning what?"

Skye licked her lips, not liking what she was about to say. She looked away from him. "Oh Top, I'm afraid that when the time comes, I will not have what it takes to do the right thing. I was scared at Lookout Point; what if I missed the shot?"

Top responded with a firm voice, "Being afraid is part of life. The truth is no one ever knows if they've got it until they are tested. My bet is you'll have it. Don't you trust your father?"

She looked at the ground. "He left us. Sooner or later, everyone lets you down. It is best not to have to count on anyone else."

"Your father went to the war for you."

Skye choked back a sob. "They knew then half the world was at war. On a scale that big, what good could two hundred men do? He should have stayed with us."

Top touched her shoulder with a soft hand. "Sometimes it only takes one person to make the difference. I am afraid your time is coming."

A brief shudder went across her shoulders. "What do you think is happening, Top?"

He shook his head. "I don't know what might be changing. I do know there is going to be a time when this village will have to trust you. That means we will have to trust who you choose to trust. For what it is worth, I trust you."

With that, he kissed her lightly on the forehead and moved back to the party.

Skye took a few deep breaths and a real drink of her wine. Observing the celebration, she slowly worked her way toward the council group. She tried to dance to the electronic music coming from the speakers but she was self-conscious in front of the adults and feared she appeared little more than awkward and clumsy. What she really wanted was to hear the tales the attractive trader had, to find out more about the world outside the village, to hear more about him.

Suddenly a man's voice boomed across the grounds, "There! You there, Little One. Come join us, tell us how you saved the village."

Skye froze in her tracks. Trader Rick was pointing straight at her. Even though the music was loud and the women were still dancing passionately, Skye knew that every eye had turned to her. Her face went white hot; she could not think of anything worse the trader could have said. She wished she could disappear in a magic cloud of smoke. Not being able to do that, she did the next best thing she could think of. She boldly strode across the grounds and stopped directly in front of the trader.

She looked down at where he was sitting. His face shone red in the firelight, and she guessed the wine had gone to his head like the others. His creased eyes squinted up at her as she stood above him. She stood tall, trying to use all of her six-foot height to look as big as she could. "You'll please not call me 'Little One' anymore." Even though the music still played, she could tell everyone was straining to hear what she would say next.

"As for saving the village, which time are you referring to? The time I kept the ants out of the food storage, or the time I kept the coyotes out of the hen house? You see, I've done it so many times I just can't remember them all."

Skye's mother coughed up a laugh. Then some of the others chuckled and turned back to what they had been doing before. The trader lowered his eyes and grinned. "Sorry, I should not have done that. Spend so much time by myself sometimes I forget about being in polite company."

Top spoke up from beside her mother. "Ask her about the time she saved my ass from the bear. Now there's a ripping good story."

Skye gave her mentor a wink. "Top, if you hadn't been drunk you wouldn't have needed saving."

Top slapped his leg and bellowed out a laugh. "If I hadn't been drunk half the kids in this village wouldn't be here."

That produced some laughs and more than a few snickers among the council members who heard it. Skye took a seat by her mother, who said, "Rick, favor us with some tales of your travels."

The rest of the evening was spent listening to Rick and Top telling tales of their exploits. Each story was a little more exciting than the last, and it was not long before fact had fallen away to myth, and by the time the moon set, each man had claimed to have moved at least one mountain and to have slain nine-headed dragons and armies of pirates. The members of the council laughed loud and hard. Skye did not remember a time when there had been so much merriment in one night.

When the stories were finished and the party was over, Skye returned to her home with a pleasantly light head. As she readied for bed, she glanced at her rifle in its place in the corner. The horror of the last attack returned to her, and Myst's words hung on her heart.

CHAPTER TEN

THE GIFT

THE MORNING AFTER THE celebration, Skye shook the sleep from her head and walked through the chilly air to the dock, carrying a hot pot of coffee. The village moved at a slower pace than normal. Only the duty watch had any energy, and they were enthusiastically banging hammers on anvils, dumping aluminum garbage cans, and banging on the sides to make sure they were empty and generally making as much of a racket as they could. Skye figured they were mad because they had missed the party and were letting those with heavy heads know it.

Rick emerged from his cabin on the *Trader Rick* and rubbed his eyes. He looked rougher than she had seen him before. His face had the stubble of a beard and his hair pointed in all directions. He wore the same clothes as he had the night before and squinted at the blue sky as if he hated to see it. He gestured toward the forge, where the sound of a metal hammer on an anvil echoed. "Gripes, what a racket. Don't they ever stop?"

Skye suppressed a smile. "I thought a man of the sea like you would be an early riser. Surely you cannot be upset with a little industry."

"That I can, my dear. And disturbing my sleep is a mortal sin in my book." He stretched his arms, leaned back, and then sat on the deck. "Are you by yourself now, or is one of those watchers hanging in the bushes to take care of you?"

She was a trifle offended by his remark, but it had the sound of an invitation so she let it go. "I am by myself, as I often am. I need no one to look after me."

He rubbed his beard and said, "Would there be a chance you might have some coffee or a morning drink in that pot?"

She held up the container she had prepared just in case she had found him awake. "I do have hot coffee. It is quite rare these days but I've been saving it for a special day."

"You are a remarkable girl. Come up here, Little … I mean Skye, I have something for you."

She hesitated a moment and then decided to join him. She climbed aboard the boat and went to where he was sitting. He staggered to his feet. "Let's go inside and get some cups."

She followed him into the dim forward cabin. On the wall, there were maps and charts of territories she didn't recognize. There were a few leather-bound books and a wooden steering wheel with controls by the side. He unfolded a table from against the wall and produced two coffee mugs from a cabinet. The one he gave to her had a bouquet of flowers engraved on the side, his had a sailing ship on it.

She inspected her cup and it looked clean enough. She resisted the temptation to wipe it out. Rick looked on with hungry eyes as she poured the warm coffee. They gently tapped mugs together in a silent toast. His eyes stayed on her as he took a sip. The small cabin was suddenly getting warmer, and she thought about taking off her light jacket. She watched his eyes and considered that perhaps it was not that hot after all.

He smelled the coffee and savored the aroma. "I have something I brought especially for you."

Skye's fingers were wrapped around her mug, and the heat caused by the liquid spread to her hands. He had promised her a present before, and that was one of the reasons she had arisen so early. She didn't want him to depart without giving him a chance to give it to her. "You're teasing now. Why would you bring me something? I have nothing to trade."

He licked his lips. "You have more than you might guess."

The sense that he wanted something she'd never given gave her a slight shudder. A shudder that was not wholly unpleasant. He disappeared into the lower cabin and quickly returned with a small wooden box that easily fit in the palm of his hand. He placed it on the table and took his seat. She stared at it, not knowing what to do.

He looked into her eyes, "Go ahead, open it."

"But I've nothing to give you in return."

"There may be a time when you might."

She leaned forward and slid the box closer to her. There were hinges on the back, and when she applied pressure to the front, the lid popped open. She was stunned by what she saw. Inside the box was a pendant more beautiful than any she had ever seen. The outside of the pendant was a circle of glimmering stones surrounding a green tree that she was certain was emerald. She pulled it from the box and a long gold chain unfolded.

She stammered, "I can't."

Rick stood and moved behind her. "You must. I got it from a shaman in Evergreen. He said it wards off evil and brings long life, luck, and love." He lifted the chain from her hands and slipped it over her neck. She held the pendant in her fingertips. Rick ran his fingers in her hair and his mouth was near her ear. The warmth of his breath sent hot streaks of pleasure down her neck. She turned her head and their lips were inches apart.

A foul odor came from his mouth and she crinkled her nose. "I think the night was good to you, but at this moment you need a mouthwash and a bath."

She stood and moved to the door, not quite sure why she had blurted out such a rude thing. "Mother wants you to come to luncheon."

Rick's face was quickly turning red. "How about you?"

"Please do. And thank you for this beautiful necklace. I'll find a way to repay you."

"Think nothing of it."

She ducked out the door and hurried back toward her home,

thinking about what might have transpired if things had been just a little different.

As she approached the village, Skye saw Myst sitting on an ancient tree stump, staring at the lake. Skye stopped beside her and tried to see if there was anything on the lake to see. "What are you looking for?"

"I'm trying to see where we are going."

"Who?"

Myst raised one eyebrow. "You and me. We are going on a long journey. I'm not sure if we'll both return. It scares me some."

Skye leaned down and hugged the slight twelve-year-old and looked into her brown eyes. "We are not going anywhere. We are staying put right here. Why would we leave?"

Myst squirmed out of her arms. "You remember I predicted the great blizzard last winter, I was right about the sheep herd being attacked by cougars, and I told everyone that Mary-Ann's baby would be twins, a boy and a girl, long before they were born."

Skye thought, *Blizzards happen in winter, cougars attack sheep, lucky guess. Still, right is right and those aren't the only things she predicted.*

Myst stood facing Skye with her hands on her hips. "Bad things are happening. I can see. I know things."

With that, she picked up a stone and threw it down the hill, causing it to bounce into the lake. Then she ran up the road to the village, leaving Skye feeling just a little creepy. Skye watched the ripples in the water caused by the stone move away from the shore while she rubbed a sudden chill from her arms.

When Skye arrived for lunch, she was surprised when her mother backed away from her.

"Skye, you must not get too close to me. I am afraid my illness is contagious. At least two people who have been near me are showing the same symptoms I have. At lunch, we will sit apart as a precaution, though it is probably too late because we were all close together at the party last night."

When the guests arrived for lunch, the table, which could easily seat ten, was arranged for two groups. Skye sat at one end with Top and Rick. Her mother, who periodically coughed violently into a napkin, sat at the head of the table with Delta, Tracy, and Dana. There was a gap of two chair lengths between the groups. Skye noticed that Tracy's face was wet with perspiration, and she had the same cough her mother had two days ago.

Skye thought Rick looked very uncomfortable in the small house. Top sat beside him, tugging on his earlobe. Her mother took a sip of water and said to Rick, "Tell us of the world outside. What are you seeing these days?"

Rick took a drink of wine and wiped his lips with his sleeve. "You all know that even before the nuclear and biological attacks, things were deteriorating. What was passing for government was barely functioning, and there was not much in the name of law for most of the country, especially here."

Skye saw her mother nod. "That is why we came here, we thought we could ride out the storm relatively out of the way."

Rick continued, "After the nuclear and biological attacks over a decade ago, everything went completely to hell. The nukes were bad enough, but it was the bio-weapons that were the most devastating. Whoever invented those things were some pretty nasty people. Once the viruses started they spread like wildfire, and it did not seem like anything could stop them. The few people they didn't kill tried to go east or south. In the end, the western part of Washington ended up virtually deserted. On the other hand, this place, the north central part of the state, was relatively spared."

Skye asked, "Why was that?"

"It was protected by the Cascade Mountain range to the east, and since there was not much but agriculture out here, it was not targeted by the enemy. However, with no government, things devolved into chaos."

Skye listened as her mother added in, "Yes, that is when the black times started. That was when we stopped taking our boats south of 25-Mile Point and started fighting off intruders."

Rick went on, "Gangs of goons and thugs ruled the area for years. Some were survivors from the west side; others were locals who tried to fight off the outsiders. It was complete madness."

Sharon pressed him, "We all know that history, but it is useful to remember the events on occasion. Tell me, how are things now?"

Rick paused and took another drink of wine. "Things were getting better for a while, the farmers and ranch people banded together in small enclaves and were starting to make some semblance of order, but lately there have been some odd developments. You see, some of the old gangs that have been roaming this side of the mountains since the end have joined up and made themselves stronger than before. Kind of like the meanest ones have taken over the others. They don't mind killing folks and stealing things, and they are not much good at building anything but weapons."

Top interrupted, "That was bound to happen. Brute force usually wins out at first."

Rick continued, "Wasn't so bad when they were all picking on each other, but now there are only a couple around the lake and they're trying to make a truce. They know they'll starve if they don't find more sources of food. Last two years, they started forcing farms to grow for them. They treat the farmers like slaves, leaving just enough for them to survive and stealing the rest. They call it a tax but don't give anything back in return."

Sharon stopped him. "Slaves? Where would they find enough people who know enough to support them?"

Rick took a bite of chicken and said, "There were some small groups that were making villages, trying to grow stuff. That didn't last long once the gangs figured out they could take them over."

Sharon said softly, "You brought handmade tools. Where did they come from? There must be some civilization out there by now."

Rick swallowed a drink of water. "Maybe there is, depending on what you call civilization. First there is Evergreen."

Sharon seemed to perk up. "Evergreen, is that place finally starting to work?"

"It is sort of starting to work. It's a good place to trade. The location is not bad; you remember Chelan City, used to be at the south end of the lake. Well, this place is about twenty miles east of that near the shores the Columbia River. They call it a commune. Everybody is equal, kind of. They built a walled city before the gangs got too strong. They have a militia and laws and their own farms they protect. Maybe a couple thousand people doing all manner of things. They should last against even the gang called Dark Angels for a while. But they are a strange lot. Something not quite right with them. Then there are the people of the mountains."

Sharon interrupted, "We have always heard good things about them. An honorable sort we have been told. We've often hoped we could meet with them sometime."

Rick continued, "Might not be such a bad thing if the time was right. You'd probably get along well with them. A lot of former army up there near old Stevens Pass. They call it New Leavenworth; it's about ninety miles east of here. They think they are defending the interior from somebody. Somebody I don't know about. But they have food and medicine and will share it with you for a story. Good traders too. I'd like to go back. Even I could spend time with them folks. The problem is it's a bear of a trip, dangerous going overland too. I have not been up there for while. I always have to get horses from Evergreen, and that can be a bit of a hassle.

"Then there's this place. You and all the ladies are the most civilized people I've seen since the end. But the gangs know you are here, just not how strong or weak. I'm afraid they might be thinking this would be a fine place to take over and that you would make some pretty good company for them, but in a way you would not like. They also think you've got a pretty big stash of weapons here, makes them think about this place more and more."

Skye's stomach tightened at the thought of someone trying to take over the village. "We'd fight them pretty good. They'd be sorry they came this way."

Rick agreed. "That they might. But that is not your most immediate problem."

Sharon motioned for Skye to stay quiet. "It's not?"

Rick looked first to Sharon, then to Tracy, and then back to Sharon. "You two. You've got the pox. You must have got it from your bout with the pirates. If you don't get the vaccine within two weeks time, you'll be beyond help. Soon after that, you'll be dead. So will a lot more of you."

A chill went through Skye, and she was sure it passed through the whole room. "How would you know?"

"I saw it at Evergreen. Killed hundreds of them. Starts with coughing and sweating and then it just gets worse; your skin will start to turn red and blotchy and then breathing gets harder and harder. I'm no medical man but I think it is related to the old S23 bio-weapon."

Sharon spoke, "Why didn't you get it?"

"I bought the vaccine in New Leavenworth."

Skye winced as her mother coughed again. "Is this the same S23 vaccine they issued before the end? You know, the one the government gave out after the first biological attacks in Europe?"

Rick nodded and said, "Yes, that is the one."

Skye listened as her mother looked straight at her and said, "That is a little good news. When they were giving out the vaccine, Seattle got shorted. Seems everybody east of the Rockies was more important. Our little group got pitifully few doses, less than 100. We gave it to the children. We thought the adults would have a better chance of surviving. We were lucky we never encountered it."

Top pushed back in his chair. "There it is, then. We have to get some more. I'll take an expedition to Leavenworth and we'll buy enough vaccine for the village."

Rick spoke quickly. "You'll never make it. Any group traveling will get the attention of the Dark Angels and be killed or enslaved. You'd have to take a whole army."

Top raised his voice. "We can take care of ourselves."

Rick retorted, "That's not the point. You don't know what's out there."

Skye held her breath as her mother raised her hands and coughed. "Stop it. No one is going anyplace. We can't afford to weaken the defenses by even one warrior. Tracy and I will quarantine and pray that God will take care of us."

Rick drew a deep breath. "It's too late for that. Anyone you have been in contact with who did not have the vaccine before the war is already dead unless they get the vaccine. The symptoms won't start to show for another day or two at the most. Then it will spread like a fire."

Sharon shook her head. "Then what do we do?"

Rick slowly stood. "There might be a way. A troop won't make it, but one or two individuals might be able to move stealthily enough to get to Leavenworth and back. But it would be a great risk. To make it worse, all the old roads have washouts, and some are blocked by landslides. From the Evergreen territories on, you can only travel by foot or horseback."

Sharon spoke softly. "Our boats were damaged by the pirates and are not worthy of the trip down the lake now. Would you go to Leavenworth and help us procure vaccine? We will make it well worth your trouble."

Rick cast his gaze to the floor. "I can take one with me. I need to protect you as my valued clients. But we must leave tonight; there is no time to spare. You will need something to trade. The only assets you have are heavy, so I will have to arrange transport when we reach shore. It won't be cheap."

Top banged the table with his fist, startling Skye so that she nearly jumped in her seat. "Why should we trust him? We don't need no worthless trader. I can leave in the morning. Be back in a week's time no problem." He took a slug of his wine and glared at Rick.

Sharon coughed again. "Thank you for all you have brought and for your news. Please excuse us now. We need to consider all that has been said."

Once Rick left, a brief discussion ensued between Top and Sharon. He blustered about being able to get to Leavenworth without help and how he could do twice the work of any other man. Skye noticed that Sharon and Delta continued to fill Top's glass even though he was already drunk. Near dark, he finally passed out at the table, and Skye and her mother hauled him off to sleep in a goat pen.

Once they had him safely snoring in the straw with a blanket over him, Skye and her mother returned to the house. Her mother went to her room, and in a few minutes she came out, took Skye by the shoulders, and looked her in the eyes. "Skye, someone must go. They must find a way to get the vaccine. I will convene a hearing this afternoon to get volunteers, though I do not think that will be a problem. It is too bad the trader leaves tonight under the cover of darkness; it would be better if we had more time to prepare. Please do me a favor."

Her mother coughed a brutal hack and then took a ragged breath as she gathered herself. She pressed a paper into Skye's shaking hand "Take this to the shelters and draw out these items. Our person will need them for barter. Tell no one."

Skye nodded.

Skye hugged her around the neck, half curtsied, though she didn't know why, and then put on her cloak and headed for the shelters.

CHAPTER ELEVEN

THE SECRET

SKYE CUT THROUGH THE forest on her way to the shelters. The sun had set but she wore only a light sweatshirt and shorts. The new shoes Rick had brought felt good on her feet. They were white cross trainers, and he had said they would do well on all types of terrain. Skye hurried on her way because she did not want to be late for Rick's departure.

She worked her way up the road in the dark by the river, past the rows of hydro generators that kept the village running on electricity. The low hum of the electrical devices gave her a small sense of comfort. Over the years, a couple had worn out and their parts were used to keep the others running. She wondered how long they would be able to depend on the rest as the spare parts depleted. They didn't have the know-how to replace highly specialized machined pieces. She marveled that the founders had thought of so many things in advance, but doubted even they would have expected the dark days to last so long.

She came around the bend that led to the trail to the shelters and caught a glimpse of movement in the trees. She stopped short and moved behind a cedar tree. There should be no one up here except the watch, and they should be at the shelter's entrance, a mile away. She put her right fingers around the handle of her KaBar. The leather sheath that held the razor-sharp blade rested reassuringly against her upper thigh.

Another movement caused her to hold her breath. There was something ahead, but she could not make it out in the night. The possibilities ran through her mind. A pirate? Probably not a realistic threat this far inland. A bear or a cougar was more likely.

She drew her knife and gripped it in a fighting position. Not wanting to reveal herself, she used the old trick Top had taught her and that she'd seen in the old cowboy vids. She found a fist-sized rock and threw it in the general direction of the noise. The rock clamored through the branches and made a thudding sound as it hit the ground. No other sound came back.

Skye's heart thumped in her chest as sweat started to form on her neck. She gritted her teeth and chided herself for being such a coward. It was probably only a stray chicken, but she was spooked now and not sure if she should move forward or retreat and come back with help. *Wouldn't I look silly then? The youngest of the watch turning tail and running from bumps in the night.*

She swallowed hard and made up her mind. She would make her own noise and advance, figuring it was just some wild animal like a deer that would flee at her presence. She took a deep breath and boldly jumped out from behind her tree. At that instant a figure appeared close in front of her in the dark. She let out a combat shout and then kicked the legs out from under her attacker.

In a heartbeat, she had the figure pinned on his back with her forearm across his chest and her knife to his throat.

"Skye, Skye! Wait, it's only me!"

Skye sucked in a breath and saw that it was Eagle who was under her blade. Furious, she held him in place. "What are you doing following me?"

"Let me up!"

"Why are you here?"

"I wanted to talk to you to find out what is going on with the trader. Everybody has been acting weird since your mother's lunch broke up. Let me up, you scared me."

Her heart was just now beginning to slow down. "I scared you? Glad to hear it. What do you mean by jumping out of the dark like that?" She stood up and sheathed her knife. "I must go."

Eagle stood and dusted himself off. "Where? What are you doing up here this time of night? "

Skye ran her hands through her hair, trying not to look prideful. "I have official business; I need to go to the shelters."

Even in the thin moonlight, she could see Eagle's eyes grow wide in envy. "You're going to the shelters? Let me go with you, please!"

Skye pondered this for a moment. Most of the village knew of the shelters but few had any idea of the full extent of what was within. She knew because her father was a founder and architect of the village. She had been in and out of them since she was a child. Even from the beginning, the true intent of the shelters was kept to a few key members of the village. However, Skye had the capacity to allow an assistant to join her. The instructions her mother had given were explicit in that. Skye had originally thought of enlisting a member of the watch but she wanted to see the size of the load before she bothered anybody.

She considered Eagle's pleading eyes and his strong shoulders. Allowing him to see a small part of the shelters probably would not do any harm. Beyond that, it would increase her stature in his mind. Maybe it would help her to get some respect so she could better keep him in line. "It is agreed. You may accompany me on two conditions."

Eagle nodded enthusiastically and said, "Anything."

"First, you must not breathe a word of this to anyone. Second, from now until we are done, you must do everything I say."

Eagle gave a slight bow. "As you say, my commander."

Skye could not be sure if he was being sarcastic or just trying to please her. Either way she felt committed. "I have your word of honor?"

He spit on his hand and held it out as a sign of his loyalty.

She grabbed his wrist above the spit line. "I will hold you to this."

The two members of the watch at the entrance to the shelters were hesitant to let Eagle pass with Skye. Even though Skye showed them the letter from her mother, the leader of the council, they wanted to call the captain of the watch to confirm it. The prospect of having to explain Eagle's presence did not appeal to her. After a brief discussion, she convinced the guards they would look foolish questioning what were obviously clear and lawful orders from the council, and the guards let them pass.

Skye paused before the small cave opening that served as the front entrance to the shelters. Eagle whispered from behind, "What are we waiting for?"

Skye closed her eyes and said, "I hate this part. I hate small places." She thought back to a time when she was exploring a cave with Top and the ground had collapsed under her, sucking her into a six-foot-deep pit. Dirt poured in on her and she could barely move; she thought she was going to suffocate. *Lucky Top was with me or I would have died for sure.* She looked at the narrow entrance again and shook her head and took several deep breaths. "Let's go."

She led Eagle through the tiny opening, ducking so as not to hit her head. Her undersized lantern barely illuminated a small portion of the cave. There were two turns to the right, and each was darker than the one before. She felt along the rough rocks with her hands to guide her. The darkness started to claw at her and the walls seemed to close more so than she remembered. She loathed the darkness; even so, she told herself she must continue.

Eagle's voice came from behind. "What kind of a shelter is this? I've been in better caves by the beach."

The question was a welcome distraction. "After the shelters were built, the founders made this false entrance to keep them secret. The idea was that visitors would not guess the extent of the construction it conceals or guess what it might contain. This entrance can easily be made larger if needed; it is part of the design."

After another turn, she breathed easier. The faint glow of the first inner chamber was finally visible ahead. The rough rock face gave way to a smooth concrete surface and the ground flattened out under her feet. A few steps later, they entered a giant cavern and stood between two gleaming steel doorways that towered on either side of them. Each was ten feet high and eight feet wide.

Blue neon lights bathed a white glow on the rocky ceiling twenty-five feet over their heads. Skye watched as Eagle's mouth opened in awe. He looked straight up, and then left and right, slowly turning in place as if there was more than his mind could take in. He finally stammered, "What is all this?"

The sound of his voice made a faint echo in the cold silence of the chamber. Skye rubbed her arms to ward off the chill of the room. She had forgotten how cool it always was in here.

Skye tried to sound matter of fact. "This is why we survive. When the founders foresaw the war, they built this place so some of us could live. A few of them were awesomely rich, and they had huge construction firms build these. They contain the essentials that helped to keep us going in the early years. We don't use the things in here except when we need to. But when we need it, we really need it."

Eagle fixated on one of the steel doors. "What's in here?"

Skye thought he had been told plenty so far. She decided to get to the job at hand and leave it at that. "I'll show you a little bit of what is here."

Beside the giant door that had been on their left as they entered the chamber was a normal-sized door made of the same material as the big ones. There was a handle and above it, a black pad with numbers on it and a red LED screen. She positioned herself between the lock and Eagle so he could not see the numbers she punched into the pad. After putting in the code, she turned the latch, which opened with a satisfying click. She was pleased she remembered it on the first try. One time when there was a power interruption after a storm, she had seen Top use the manual override. She was glad she didn't need it at the moment.

She cracked the door and then paused, saying, "Look at this."

She swung the five-inch-thick steel door open and watched as Eagle's eyes widened more than she'd ever seen them. "Whoa ... we've got all this?"

Skye motioned for him to follow and then quickly entered the armory. The warm dry air felt good against her skin. The humidity- and climate-controlled hall was a welcome change from the outer chamber. She quickly closed the door behind them. Overhead neon lights flickered on as they moved deeper into the room that stretched out before them for what she knew was another fifty yards. It was ten yards wide in the center, and each wall was encased in thick Plexiglas. It was what was behind the glass that had provoked Eagle's reaction.

Behind the protective glass were hundreds of firearms of a wide variety of types. There were automatic pistols, assault rifles, light and heavy machine guns, sniper rifles, antitank rockets, and grenade launchers. Each class of weapons occupied a particular cabinet and was set three feet above the ground.

Eagle wandered up and down the armory, staring into the cabinets. "Is there ammunition for these?"

Skye nodded and said, "Plenty."

She checked her mother's instructions and went to cabinet 21. Behind the glass were stacks of M40A1 sniper rifles, good for long-distance stealth shots. She applied the code and the glass slid gently to the side. After she lifted the lowermost weapon from its rack, a soft electronic ping sounded. At the bottom of the case, a mechanical dial turned. There were two lighted blue readouts: **Issued: 2. Remaining: 2.**

Eagle read the dial. "Says two; where's the other one?"

Skye slid the cabinet shut and said, "In my room."

She knelt down below the cabinet and punched in the code on the lock on the drawer. When she finished the combination, she pulled the drawer open. Inside, boxes of bullets were laid out in trays. She withdrew four boxes, and like magic, new boxes slid into place. A counter, like the one in the rifle cabinet, moved mechanically. **Issued: 200. Remaining: 39,600.**

Eagle opened his mouth but Skye cut him off. "In my room."

She locked the drawer and then went to a cabinet containing M240G machine guns. She opened the window and withdrew two. Eagle whistled as she pulled them out. The counter turned, **Issued: 51. Remaining: 149.**

Eagle raised his eyebrow. "In your room?"

Skye stooped to open the ammo drawer. "Except for the ones we used in the last attack; the rest went with the men who went to war. Maybe they will help to bring them back someday. Maybe." She withdrew ten metal boxes that contained long belts of ammunition. The counters moved, **Issued: 400. Remaining: 8,400.**

She watched as Eagle ran his eyes over the growing load. He asked her, "Why are we getting this stuff out? Is there another attack coming?"

Skye told the truth, thinking everyone would know by morning anyway. "Someone is going with Rick to trade for meds; they need this to barter."

His voice sounded astonished. "Someone is leaving, with all this? This must be bad."

The boxes were heavier than she had anticipated; it made her glad she had brought Eagle along. Skye loaded as much she could onto Eagle, who staggered under the weight.

To fulfill the list her mother had given her, they repeated this process two more times with other weapons. They gathered four M16A1 rifles and a trunk of automatic pistols with ammo. When she thought they could carry no more, Skye slung a machine gun over her right shoulder and the sniper rifle over the left. They lifted the heavy bags they had filled onto a hand truck, and she glanced at Eagle and said, "Time to go. I have a lot to do."

CHAPTER TWELVE

THE FEW

As NIGHT FELL, A storm blew in from beyond the mountains. Skye labored under her load from the shelter when the rain first started falling. She dropped her burden from her back on the porch of her house and locked the brake on the hand truck she had been pushing. She half wished Eagle was still there to help her but she had felt compelled to send him home; he already knew more than she wanted. She entered the house to get a drink of water. She heard her mother coughing in her bedroom and went to see her.

Sharon was pale and her face damp from her own perspiration. Skye's spirits fell, watching her mother shaking in the bed. Skye gave her some water and pulled her covers up to her neck. Sharon closed her eyes and took Skye's hand. "You're a strong one, Skye, like your father. We'll need to defend the village against the coming attacks, and I know you'll do well. Still, this time things seem worse. The trader warned that the Dark Angels have grown strong. Even though we have good defenses, our numbers are small. I wish there was a place we could get help."

Skye knelt beside her and said, "Maybe there is help. Maybe our emissary can persuade the people of Evergreen or the mountain people to help us."

Her mother's eyelids opened a fraction. "I am afraid our emissary may not survive the journey. Skye, I love you. Remember, our way is to take care of ourselves. I hate to ask this but I have to. You are young, nimble, and fast, and I have come to trust your judgment. Will you please go with the trader and act as our emissary?" Then her eyes closed and she fell asleep. Skye put a cool cloth on her burning forehead and kissed her cheek. She left the room and instructed the dome who was acting as nurse and housekeeper to keep a close watch on her mother.

Skye entered her own room and put together a traveling pack. Satisfied she had the essentials for a long journey, she strapped on her KaBar, took her bow and rifle, and then went outside. She heaved part of the load from the shelters onto her shoulders and, using all her strength, pushed her overloaded hand truck toward the docks.

Thunder crashed overhead and lightning split the purple sky. As she approached the dock, her guts clenched when she didn't see the *Trader Rick*. Missing the boat could mean the difference between life and death for those with the pox. It would take days to traverse the length of the lake on foot or by paddling a small boat. Lightning flashed again and she breathed a sigh of relief when she saw the boat.

The boat had only moved to the end of the dock, and the lines were still in place. She carried her load to the end of the pier. Rain was coming down hard now but she was protected by her long cloak and hood. The wind was kicking up, and cold waves were starting to splash up onto the dock. When she reached the boat, she called out, "Ahoy on the boat! Permission to come aboard!"

In a moment, Rick appeared on deck in a leather coat and broad-brimmed hat that warded off the rain. "Who goes there and what is your business?"

Skye pulled the hood of her cloak off her head. "It is me, Skye of the Cougar Watch. Today you offered to give passage to the mountain city; is your offer still good?"

More lightning streaked across the night, and she could see a look of surprise on the trader's face. "You? I thought maybe someone more experienced."

"My experience is my business. I will pay for your trouble. Is your offer good or not?"

He slowly shook his head back and forth, and Skye thought he was refusing her. She persisted, "I hear your engines running. We must leave soon; help me with these bags." She took one of the bags off her shoulder and swung it onto the *Trader Rick*. She heard him grunt at the weight.

"What are you hauling Little One, rocks?"

She glared at him and started to heft another long bag when Rick leaned down and took it from her. Then he reached for her hand and pulled her aboard.

A wave slammed the boat into the dock and she grabbed him for support. He wrapped his arms around her. She could not see his eyes in the dark but his grasp was strong and comforting. Even the rain that pelted them did not seem to matter. Her breath was tight in her chest, their lips were close once again; this time a hint of cinnamon briefly touched her nose. She closed her eyes and then heard a voice.

"Hey, you up there. You need any help?" It was Eagle calling to them from the dock. For the first time ever, she cursed him under her breath. Rick's embrace relaxed and he turned her loose.

Rick shouted to Eagle, "Throw those last bags up here and then tend to the lines. We have to get out of here before it gets any worse."

"We? Is she going with you?" Skye thought he did not sound surprised. She also noticed he had on a backpack and carried his bow.

She shouted in exasperation, "Just load the bags and let the lines free and go home."

Eagle nodded. After he heaved the last bag aboard, he ran to the stern. A wave washed over the dock and nearly knocked him off. He untied the line and threw it to Skye. Rick went to the cabin and gunned the engine; the stern started to swing away from the dock. He yelled out the door, "Get the bowline, hurry!" Skye and Eagle raced the length of the boat, he on the pier and she on the boat. He undid the line as a gust of wind hit Skye and almost threw her down on the pitching deck. He tossed the line at her and grabbed the rail on the bow. "Help me aboard."

"No, you can't! You mustn't come with me."

The engines roared and the boat jerked backward, pulling Eagle off the dock and leaving him hanging on the rail. "Help me, Skye!"

She grabbed his left wrist with one hand and clung to the rail with her other hand. She braced her feet against the base of the boat's rail and pulled him until he was able to climb up the rail. With her pulling on him, he was finally able to plop onto the deck as the nose of the cruiser swung toward the channel. She fell, gasping, to the deck. "You should not be here."

He panted back, "You'll be glad I came along."

She glared at him as lightning lit their faces. "Not likely."

The vessel shook under them as Rick sped the engines up. Waves splashed over the sides and gave Skye a blast of ice-cold water in the face. It did not do anything to improve her mood. She scrambled to her feet, pulled Eagle up, and half dragged him to the cabin, where they would at least be out of the elements.

The pilothouse was distinctly quiet compared to the wind and rain outside. Skye closed the hatch behind them, water still dripping from her face. Rick had one hand on the wheel and one on the throttle. His attention was focused on the narrow channel ahead of them that led to the choke point. The boat pitched abruptly, nearly knocking Skye off her feet. She grabbed a handhold by the wall and called out to Rick, "We have to go back!"

Rick gave her a questioning glance. "What?"

She pointed to Eagle. "We have to take him back. He can't go with us."

Rick was focused on the churning waters in front of them.

He didn't look at her but said, "What us? He's with you, Little One. You are in charge of your group. That's my deal. As for him, he can do what he wants, but we're not going back. It's much too rough to dock and I can't wait for this storm to blow over. Don't have time."

Skye tried to keep the anger out of her voice. Suddenly the trader was talking like he barely knew her, like she was a mere passenger to be dumped at the first opportunity. She resented his attitude, and worse than that, he had embarrassed her in front of Eagle. "We have to go back. He's too young to go and the village will miss him. The council will not look kindly toward you on this."

Rick looked at Eagle and then back to Skye. "He looks plenty old. And the ladies council is the least of the things I have to worry about."

Skye was about to press her argument when the sound of someone pounding on the hatch to the aft deck startled them all. Eagle was standing closest, and he opened it slowly. Skye could not keep her mouth from opening in surprise. A small, cloaked figure stepped through the doorway, dripping water. She pulled her hood back, and Myst smiled at them.

"I'm glad we are finally getting going. I've been waiting in the hold since this afternoon after Delta told me we were sending someone for help. I knew it would be you two."

Rick gave her a sideways look. "Pardon me for holding things up. Are we expecting anybody else or does the rest of the village have other plans for tonight?"

PART TWO

CHAPTER THIRTEEN

STRANGE WATERS

I N A DENSE FOG, the *Trader Rick* tugged gently on its anchor chain rolling back and forth, causing the wine in Skye's glass to flow from side to side. Seated beside Rick, she watched him eat a bite of his dinner. The yellow cabin lights gave the small galley a warm glow, one that matched the sensation the wine gave her inside. The baked chicken dinner Rick had prepared had been surprisingly good. She was embarrassed and a little angry at the way Eagle had wolfed his down and asked for seconds. She thought it reflected poorly on the entire village, she and Myst included. She elected not to call him on it in front of Rick and Myst. He was sensitive to things like that. She would definitely talk to him later.

Besides, Rick appeared to appreciate the boy's appetite, and they were all having such a pleasant time. This was in great contrast to his frustrations earlier. He had cursed the fog loudly and been quite beside himself at having to stop. He kept muttering things like, "This'll get me killed." But he refused to elaborate further. He finally stated that trying to continue on with zero visibility was as much as suicide and one way of dying was as bad as the other, so he had cut the engines and dropped anchor. Skye was happy that dinner and wine had mellowed him considerably.

She finished her second glass of wine and considered another.

Before she made up her mind, Rick picked the green bottle up from the crowded table and poured the red liquid into her glass until it was nearly full.

"Sorry I don't have proper wine glasses, Little One, I mean Skye. I don't have that many visitors aboard the ole *Rick*."

The boat seemed to be rocking more now than when dinner had started, though she saw no change on the small bit of lake she could see through the porthole beside her. Skye wondered if Rick was trying to get her drunk. Even if he was, she figured nothing would come of it as there was certainly not much chance for privacy on this boat. "Think nothing of it. These glasses are just fine with me. It's what's inside that counts."

"Aye, you have that right. The ladies outdid themselves this year. This is some of the best I've had in a long time." Rick took a deep drink from his glass and placed it back on the table.

Skye sipped her drink. "I've never really been fond of it, though I do admit it is growing on me."

Rick leaned close to her ear and whispered, "Let it grow. The more you drink, the more you'll like it." It was something in the way he said it that made her shiver slightly in an ever so unique way.

Eagle put his fork down on his metal plate with a clang and belched. "That was good. Can I have some wine too?"

Almost in unison, Skye and Rick answered, "No, you're too young."

Skye almost laughed at the pouty look that crossed his face. He narrowed his eyes defiantly. "Who says? You ain't my mom. I ain't that much younger than Skye."

Before she could reply, Rick responded, "I'm the captain of this vessel. I'm in charge here and I make the rules."

Eagle wiped his mouth with a cloth napkin. "You're no captain. You're just a trader with the same name as your boat. *Trader Rick*, that's kind of funny. Did you name yourself after the boat or the boat after you? I bet it's not your real name."

Rick sipped his wine and scratched his chin. "You are right about that. Before the war, I had another name. Doesn't matter now. I named the boat after a bar in San Francisco, kind of my little joke. After a while, when people saw me coming around the lake they'd call me the guy from the *Trader Rick*; eventually they just started calling me Trader Rick. So maybe the joke is on me, and I am named after the boat."

Eagle laughed in a tone Skye thought was a little derisive. "Named after a boat. Sure does not make you a captain."

The boy was starting to irritate Skye in a way she was not familiar with. She squirmed in her seat at his attitude toward their host.

Eagle reached for the wine bottle. Before he got it, Rick slapped his hand away. "Law of the sea, boy. It's my boat and I'm the captain. You don't like it, you can go for a swim anytime you want. Long as you are onboard, you do as I say."

Skye saw crimson start to come to Eagle's cheeks. She put her fork on her plate and folded her hands in her lap, glancing back and forth as the two males stared across the table at each other. She noticed Myst was sitting very still and her face looked more pale than normal.

Rick took another drink of wine. "Eagle, now that's a funny name. That your real name?"

Eagle shot back, "It's not funny. It's a brave name."

Rick persisted, "What's your real name?"

"Just call me Eagle."

Maybe it was the wine or maybe it was because Skye thought Eagle was being impudent to his host; she found she could not resist telling Rick the truth. She blurted out, "Marvin Howard Petty."

Rick looked at her and asked, "What?"

"That is his given name."

Eagle shouted, "Shut up, Skye!"

Skye took a drink of wine and giggled. "We used to call him Marvy for short. Right, Marvy?"

Rick laughed out loud. "Marvy? Ha! How did you get to Eagle from that?"

Eagle said nothing, he just glared at Skye. She thought that if eyes were lasers, they would bore a hole through her. He looked so mad it made her laugh. "When he was a little boy, he loved to watch the eagles fly. Told his mother he wanted to be one. She said he could be whatever he wanted and she started calling him Little Eagle. It caught on around the village and after a few years, when he got older, he just became Eagle."

Rick laughed again. "So it's not like he earned it or anything, didn't kill a bear or slay a dragon or anything like that, right, Marvy?"

Skye could not help but laugh again at the silliness of it. Eagle pushed himself away from the table. "I'm going on deck. I'll get you for this, Skye."

Rick looked at him with a forced sternness. "Remember, Eagle, I'm the captain; do as I say or you'll be Marvy the rest of the time you are onboard."

Eagle glared at him. "Yes, sir. Thank you for dinner, sir. Can I go now?"

Skye suppressed a giggle. It was hard to see him embarrassed even though he had brought it on himself; still, he looked so mad it was comical. In fact, everything seemed comical, and she laughed out loud, not even sure why.

Suddenly, Myst stood and said in alarm, "Someone bad is coming."

Rick gave Skye a curious look, raising his eyebrows. "Is it anybody worse than those of us who are already here?"

Skye and Rick both laughed at the comment.

Eagle pointed to Myst and said, "You should know better than to poke fun at her. It's one thing to make fun of me, but Myst's done nothing wrong here. By now you should know to listen to her, Skye. Maybe if you two weren't drunk, you'd pay attention."

Rick took a long drink of his wine. "We ain't drunk, least not yet. How would she know if someone was coming anyway, good or bad?"

Skye saw Eagle touch the handle of his knife that hung in a leather scabbard from his side. "She knows things. I'm going up on deck for a look."

Rick waved his hand toward the hatch. "Go ahead, you aren't going to see anything in that fog anyway. Nobody is going see to us either."

A trickle of unease crawled across Skye's shoulders as Eagle and Myst went out onto the deck. As she left, Myst glanced at her with what Skye thought was a look of disappointment.

Skye's head throbbed as she lay on the cramped bed in the forward cabin of the *Trader Rick*. She opened her eyes to near pitch-blackness and tried to focus on who was in bed with her. She was crammed between the bulkhead and a large sleeping person who was breathing heavily through his nose, making a dull snoring sound.

In a flash she realized it was Rick, and she was instantly awake. He had his arm around her shoulders, almost pinning her to the bed. She tried not to move because she didn't want to wake him up. She searched her memory for what had happened last night. At the same time, she slid her hand down her front, happy to discover that all her clothes were still on and in place.

After Eagle and Myst had gone on deck, Rick had continued pouring her wine and telling outlandish stories about his travels. She could not recall how she got from the galley to his stateroom. She prayed she had done nothing to be sorry for. If this was the result of her first hangover, she was certain there would never be a second one. Though she could not remember how she got here, she had no doubt that she needed to get out. She had a pressing need to relieve herself, and if she waited any longer, something would happen she knew she would be sorry for.

As delicately as she could, she dislodged Rick's arm from on top of her and climbed over his reclined body. The space above was tight and she had to slither over him. Because of the pressure in her bladder, she had to use less caution than she wanted. His body was warm against her, and the inside of the cabin was cool in the dank night air. Her face went close to his and his breath was thick with wine and garlic. She crinkled her nose reflexively and was happy he was heavily passed out.

She slid off him, her bare feet finding the wooden floor colder than she thought it would be. Using her hands in the dark, she impatiently felt her way to the head, afraid she may not make it in time. When she finally took her seat and closed the door, she knew another moment longer would have been a disaster.

She managed to make the flushing work and then stood and braced herself as she flicked on the light. The dull light assaulted her eyes and made her head pound even more. There was scarcely room to stand in the tiny room, and she had to bend down to keep from hitting her head on the ceiling. She bent over the sink and washed her hands and splashed cold water onto her face. It was refreshing until she looked in the mirror and saw the bloodshot eyes that looked back at her. Reaching into one of her pockets, she retrieved two of the painkillers she always carried and swallowed them with a drink of water.

Checking the mirror once more, she shook her head. "Not doing this again."

She turned off the light and opened the door. Squeezing into the dim hallway, she saw someone sitting on the steps leading to the deck. From his profile, she saw it was Eagle.

"That just you, Skye?"

"Yes, who else would it be?"

"I don't know. From the sounds of things I thought there was a horse pissing in there."

Skye was glad it was dark so he could not see her face go red. She wanted to get off the defensive and at the same time soothe relations with her friend. "Funny. What are you doing up?"

Eagle stretched his arms as if he was warding off sleep. "I'm being the lookout. Somebody needs to be."

Skye wanted to offer to help him but the ache in her head made her think twice. "Rick says there is nothing to worry about out here while we are in the dark and the fog."

Eagle leaned back with his elbows on the stairs. "Myst thinks there may be someone coming. Doesn't hurt to keep your guard up. You know that."

Skye couldn't argue with his logic. She was also apprehensive and being on this strange boat made her feel exposed. "You're right, wake me in two hours and I'll spell you."

Eagle stood to go back on deck. "You sleeping with him?"

A trace of guilt clenched her throat. "Not really. We just …"

He cut her off. "Didn't think you were like that."

Then he disappeared up the stairs before she could respond. She said to the empty hallway, "I'm not."

She had an urge to follow him but her head hurt so much all she wanted to do was put it back on a pillow. She swallowed hard and went into the cabin next to Rick's. The small bed was unmade so she wrapped a blanket around herself and lay down and fell hard asleep.

Skye awoke with a warm breath blowing on her ear. She opened her eyes, puzzled by her surroundings for a moment. A low light filtered through the cabin windows, and she realized she was not alone. The pain in her head was gone and had been replaced by something different. She was lying on her side and Rick was pressed up behind her, caressing her arm.

He whispered softly, "You awake, Little One?"

She didn't answer. He continued to stroke her arm. The sensation was soothing but she felt tenser than she ever had. He breathed on the back of her neck, and a tingle went all the way down her spine, causing her to reflexively quiver.

"So you are awake. Good, seems like we fell asleep before we got started last night. Looks like you got confused and ended up in the wrong bed." He stroked her arm again and this time let his hand continue down to her thigh.

She turned her head to look at him, and he kissed her cheek. The stubble of his growing beard was scratchy against her face but not altogether unpleasant. He moved his hand to her arm again and then led it down to her inner thigh, rubbing her softly.

She took a deep breath, and a longing within her started to grow. She rolled onto her back and looked him in the face. He smelled of cinnamon again, as he had when they were last close. His hair was freshly combed, and his brown eyes seemed gentle and inviting. He kissed her cheek again. A wave of desire filled her, and almost without thinking, she turned her lips to his.

The kiss was awkward, and her inexperience made her feel clumsy. He didn't appear to mind because he kissed her again, pressing his lips hard to hers. She felt his hand moving to her shirt and realized he was working the buttons. She was exhilarated and terrified at the same time. She whispered, "No." His fingers moved from the buttons but his hand caressed her breasts; her heart pounded in her chest.

Passions woke in her that she had never known before. She let the sensations flow through her body, more excited than she'd ever been with another person. He kissed her again as he slid his hand down toward her shorts. He started to slip his fingers under her belt when something in her mind screamed, *Stop!*

She grabbed his wrist and said out loud, "No." He kept his hand where it was and said, "It's okay. Everyone is nervous the first time."

Even though she was a little surprised by her own change of mind, her resolve grew. She said firmly, "No, this is not what we are going to do."

He breathed softly in her ear again. "Come on, Little One, you'll not be sorry."

She closed her eyes and the physical sensations of arousal filled her mind. He slowly started moving his hand down again. She put her hand on his and held it still. "No!"

Abruptly there was a pounding on the deck above. She heard Eagle shouting, "Pirates! There's pirates coming! Everybody up!"

Rick sat up and banged his head on the ceiling. "Bastards, they could have waited a while." He gave her a quick kiss. "If we survive, we'll come back to this."

She covered her breasts with her hands over her shirt, feeling very exposed. She did not respond to him and found that a part of her had never been happier to hear that pirates were coming.

Skye quickly slipped her dagger in its sheath over her shoulder with its strap so that it rested on her side by her left elbow. She strapped on her knife belt, grabbed her rifle, and put on her cloak as she hurried to the bridge. She emerged onto the deck, apprehensive about what she would find. The fog had almost cleared to the east and the mountaintops were still in the clouds. The sun was a pale white circle that could barely be seen. The water was flat and calm without a ripple crossing the surface. Rick stood behind Myst and Eagle on the bridge, looking over the bow. She followed their eyes looking south and saw that in the distance there was a fleet of small boats emerging from the lingering fog there and heading toward them. She counted an even dozen.

Myst looked at her and said, "They're bad."

The brisk air was sharp on Skye's bare legs and face. She loaded a magazine into her AR16A, knowing that if all the boats attacked at once, there would only be a slim chance of survival for those aboard the *Trader Rick*.

Rick hit the start button and the engines groaned, refusing to turn over. Skye heard him curse, "Damn old diesels take forever to fire."

He hit the ignition again with the same result. Skye entered the bridge and received a look of reproach from Eagle. "Told you we needed a watch."

She chose to ignore the comment and spoke to Rick. "Will you be able to get this thing going? It looks like they have superior numbers."

Rick tried the ignition again. Skye recognized the sound of dying batteries as the engine slowly cranked but didn't start. Rick said, "This isn't going to fire soon enough. I'll have to change batteries but by the time that happens, our guests will be here."

Skye asked him, "What's your plan?"

Rick glanced out the window. "There is only one gang out here with that many boats. We'll just have to wait, and maybe they'll give us a jump. Too bad I owe these guys money. I knew we should have been out of here by now."

Skye picked up the binoculars that were stored by the wheel. She focused on the boat that was closest. It was an overloaded skiff with four men in it but they were too far away to see their features. "We need to prepare our defense. With my rifles we can probably hold them off until the batteries are changed. Maybe if we kill a few of them, the rest will get scared and go away."

Rick said, "Whoa, Little One. We aren't killing anybody. Those are some of my best clients, even if I do owe them. Just because Marvy here says they are pirates, that does not make them hostile."

Skye was shocked by the trader's response. She leveled the binoculars on the skiff again and she saw a crimson flag whipping in the wind above the lead boat; dread locked her stomach. "They are flying the same colors as the pirates who attacked us."

Rick took the binoculars and said, "I thought you didn't get out much."

Skye shifted her bow in her hand. "The leader of that raid told my mother they were going to kill all of us."

Rick let out a low whistle. "When you make an enemy, you don't fool around. The head of this gang is the one they call Digger. He is one nasty hombre, kind of a sicko too. I'm pretty sure I don't want him finding you on my boat."

Skye touched his shoulder. "Then you will fight with us."

Eagle gave her a short look. "He's no fighter."

Rick lowered the binoculars. "You got that right, Marvy, but I have not survived out here by being stupid either. You two go out that side door so nobody sees you. We have to get you out of here."

Skye protested, "You promised to take us to the mountains."

Rick hustled them to the door. "I promised a lot of people a lot of things and mostly I hold true. This is something I can't change. If we don't get you kids off this boat, those bad boys will probably do like you said: they'll kill us all. Or worse."

Skye felt a twinge of resentment at being called a kid. She saw Eagle swallow hard. He murmured, "Worse?"

Rick almost shoved them through the door and said, "You don't want to know."

Skye glanced over her shoulder at the approaching boats. She guessed they would arrive in just a few minutes. She, Eagle, and Rick scrambled along the deck of the *Trader Rick,* staying out of sight of the approaching fleet. Rick led them to the stern, where a great blue tarp covered most of the deck space.

He pointed to a rope that held the tarp down. "Cut this."

Skye drew her KaBar and sliced the line. Rick pointed to two others, and she quickly cut those. He pulled the tarp back and revealed a small gray zodiac. "Help me get this in the water."

In a few moments, the three of them had the vessel splashing into the lake alongside the bigger boat. Skye's feet took a big dousing of the frigid lake water. Rick looked at Skye and Eagle and asked, "Either of you know how to run an engine and steer a boat?"

Skye nodded. "Of course, we live on a lake."

"Better hope you're good." Rick jumped into the boat and said, "This is how you start it." He shifted levers as he talked. "Motor neutral, throttle at start, pump the fuel bulb, and then yank the rope." He pulled a rope on the motor. Nothing happened.

Skye could hear the sound of approaching engines. Rick pulled the rope again. Nothing. Skye turned to Eagle and said, "Get Myst and our stuff, hurry."

Rick yanked on the rope but the boat wouldn't start. She jumped in the boat beside him. Rick pulled and pulled until he was sweating in the cool air and turned red in the face. Eagle and Myst dragged Skye's bags and their personal gear to the edge of the deck.

Eagle dropped a heavy bag with a clunk. "They're almost here. We better get ready to fight."

Rick pulled on the rope again. The motor refused to fire. Skye could hear other engines getting louder. Her chest started to tighten. "We may have to battle and we're losing any hope of a tactical advantage."

Eagle was getting excited. "They're nearly on us."

Rick glared at him. "Shut up or I'll choke you!"

Skye shouted, "That's it! The choke, where's the choke for the motor?"

Rick let go of the rope. "I can't believe I'm such an idiot." He reached under the engine and pulled out a small slide button. He yanked the rope again and the motor sputtered to life. He grabbed the rail of the *Trader Rick* and vaulted onto the deck.

Skye saw Rick sweep Myst off her feet and nearly throw her into the zodiac. He looked to the other side of the boat, and Skye could see a look of panic cross his face. He shoved Eagle and yelled, "Get in, get in!"

Eagle helped Rick toss the bags on board and then jumped in the zodiac.

Rick opened a wooden chest that was bolted to the side of the boat and pulled out a pistol. He started talking fast. "Get out of here, Little One! Go south to the end of the lake. When you start walking, stay off the roads. Your best bet is to head to the mountains. Don't trust anyone in Evergreen; avoid the place entirely. Try to find someone to buy horses from. We'll meet again sometime, Skye; we'll have some catching up to do. This is important: don't pay attention to what I say after you pull away. Now go!"

Skye pushed off the *Trader Rick* with her hand and turned the throttle. The zodiac jumped more than she expected, knocking Eagle backwards into Myst. The two were tangled on the bottom of the boat but she couldn't do anything about it; she pointed the bow straight away from the *Rick* and cranked it up to full speed. Behind her she heard a shot and Rick's voice shouting, "Come back, you little rats! Come back with my boat, you thieves! When I catch you, I'll kill you!"

There were several more shots that she knew she didn't need to worry about.

CHAPTER FOURTEEN

HOSTILE SHORES

EAGLE SPOKE JUST LOUD enough for Skye to hear him over the zodiac motor. "I don't like this place," he said.

Skye couldn't agree with him more. Dusk was falling on the lake, and the shoreline had changed from steep mountain walls to a flatter area that was littered with burned-out houses and abandoned buildings. There was no sign of human life, and Skye could only wonder at what had become of the people who had lived here. Even though she had not been here for fourteen years, she remembered the place had been called Wapato Point. She had heard it had been destroyed; even so, she was still dismayed to actually see the extent of the devastation caused by the gang wars.

She looked over her shoulder again to be sure no pirates were in pursuit and was relieved that none were in sight. It was a small comfort, however, because the lake twisted and turned so she could only see half a mile behind. She was thankful the zodiac was much faster than the boats that had started to pursue them when they escaped the *Trader Rick*. For the moment, she was content to cruise at half throttle to conserve fuel. They had been traveling all day and guessed they were still an hour from the south shore. The surface of the lake was mirror smooth, and the boat felt like it was gliding on the water.

Skye pulled the hood of her cloak onto her head to ward off the cold that was creeping in with the setting of the sun. She watched Myst staring at the shore. Myst had scarcely said a word since they made their escape. Skye knew Myst was usually quiet and soft spoken, so it did not concern her heavily, though she wondered what the girl was thinking.

Skye had considered taking the two younger ones home but had elected against it. Time was too precious to spend a couple of days back tracking. She had only a vague idea about how long it was going to take to get to the mountain city and get back with the vaccine. The thought of her mother and the others suffering weighed on her.

There was also the issue of the pirates. They were between her and the village now, and getting past them would be something she would have to think about for the return trip. As it was, going ahead appeared to be the best course of action.

Myst sensed Skye's gaze and turned around to face her. Her pale skin seemed to glow white, as it was highlighted by her long black hair and the dark hood of her cloak. Her large brown eyes were set off by a petite nose. Skye thought she was quite beautiful.

Myst pointed to the shoreline and said, "There is danger there. We must hurry."

A shiver went across Skye's shoulders. She looked to the edge of the lake and asked, "What? What do you see?"

"I don't see anything, but there is danger."

Skye strained her eyes. There was a half-collapsed building that she recognized as a hotel she had stayed in with her parents once. This had been one of the resorts that had been on the lake before the war. Then she saw it. A small boat was coming out of the old marina, and it was coming fast.

She recognized it as a bass boat, so it probably had a bigger engine than the zodiac. She remembered zooming around the lake with her father in a similar-style boat when she was little.

The black hull was flat and the gunnels close to the water line. It was an ideal craft for the lake. She counted four figures on board; it seemed to have its course set dead on the zodiac. A flicker of fear crossed her heart. There was no place to hide out here. She called out to Myst and Eagle, "Hold on."

She twisted the throttle to full open, causing the boat to surge forward. The propeller bit into the water, making the craft skim across the lake as if it was levitating. The wind ripped her hood back off her head; the engine screamed; she looked over her shoulder and shuddered. The black boat was gaining at an alarming rate.

The sharp report of a gunshot came from behind. She looked again, and as darkness started to descend on them, she saw the flash of another shot. Eagle shouted above the wind, "Skye, what are we going to do? They're going to catch us!"

Skye searched the shoreline for a place to land but nothing looked remotely promising. Here the shore had turned to a boulder sea wall. Even if they got to shore, they would be no better off than they were now. The black boat would be on them before they could get ashore.

Another shot sounded, so she cut a turn to the right to change the angle for their assailants and create a harder target. She also wanted to make the other boat cross her wake and destabilize the shooter. She raised her voice so Eagle could hear her. "Eagle, hand me my blue pack."

He fumbled in the cramped space and managed to get the pack to her. She continued to zigzag the boat but their pursuers were still closing. "Eagle, stack all the bags up in front of you and Myst. Take my rifle."

Eagle started to stack the bags as more shots came from behind. "What are we putting these up front for? They're shooting at our backs."

Skye shouted, "Just do it."

Myst cried out, "Oh no!"

Skye's heart leaped; she was afraid the young girl had been hit by one of the shots. "What's the matter?"

Myst pointed up the lake. Skye strained to see in the darkness that continued to fall. Then she made it out. In the distance, she could see half a dozen pirate boats. Her insides went cold. A bullet splashed in the water near her, forcing her attention to the immediate problem. She gritted her teeth in resolve.

Reaching into her pack, she pulled out a 9mm automatic pistol. It was awkward but she was able to cock it without taking her hand off the throttle. Eagle's eyes went wide. "What are we going to do?"

"We are fortunate this man is a poor shot, but they are almost on us and he may get lucky. We can't run anymore."

Eagle sounded scared. "What are you going to do, Skye?"

She looked back and the black boat was only fifty yards away. She had to act now. "We are going to attack. Get behind the bags, use my rifle, and aim for the driver."

She turned the tiller as hard as she dared without flipping the boat and set a course straight for the bow of the bass boat. As soon as they were headed dead on bow to bow, she raised her pistol and fired three shots at the man in the forward seat holding a rifle. She did not think she could hit him but the maneuver and surprise had the desired effect.

The pursuers turned suddenly, throwing the shooter off balance. Better yet, it brought the black vessel broadside to the zodiac. Skye steered for the stern. She could see the shocked looks on their faces as the boats closed at a terrifying rate. She held her breath, hoping this would work. "Eagle, fire!"

Eagle braced himself on one knee and fired a shot with the rifle. The men on the bass boat dove for cover. Skye leveled her pistol on the biggest target she could see, the outboard engine of the bass boat. She fired four times from only yards away and heard at least three bullets hit metal. Eagle shot again and a man's agonized cry cut the air.

Skye didn't have time to look. She turned the zodiac away, heading down the lake again at full speed, away from the bass boat. Myst turned around, staring behind them. Skye looked at her and asked, "What do you see?"

Myst smiled. "I see smoke coming from their boat. They're not moving."

Eagle crept back to her. "You're completely crazy, Skye. That was awesome."

Myst nodded in agreement.

Skye tried not to feel too prideful. It was really the only thing they could do. "You guys are great too. Excellent shot, Eagle. Now we have to get off the water. We're almost out of lake to run on."

As they neared the shore, Skye cut off the engine. The zodiac glided smoothly toward the brush-covered shore. She had chosen this spot because she thought it offered the most opportunity for cover. It was hard to make things out in the dark, and she hoped fervently that she had made the right choice and that she was not steering them into worse trouble than they already had.

In the falling darkness they had lost sight of the pirate boats behind them, but she knew they could not be far behind. After the encounter with the bass boat, she had steered to the southwest until they could no longer make out the pirates. After that, she turned to the east in the hope she could buy at least a little time with the misdirection.

Her ears were cold from the wind of the night air, but she resisted the temptation to pull her hood up because she wanted to hear everything. The trees that loomed ahead threw shadows across the beach and onto the water; it was difficult to make out any shapes beyond the waterfront. There were no sounds other than the chirping of insects and a dog barking someplace far away.

She fingered the pistol in her hand and saw that Eagle was ready with an arrow in his bow. The silence of an arrow would be handy if there were others about. The beach was only a few yards away now; her shoulders were tightening as they drew near. She knew this was where they were most vulnerable should there be an attack from shore.

The zodiac stopped abruptly, startling Skye and throwing her forward into Eagle's back. She banged her knee on the plastic seat, sending a surge of pain up her leg.

Eagle whispered, "Ouch, what the heck was that?"

Skye shushed him as she regained her balance. Her pulse rate quickened and she scanned the area around them, looking for danger. Not seeing anything, she regained her seat and then looked into the water by the engine. She let out a breath of relief. She whispered to Eagle, "The propeller grounded in the sand. That is why we stopped. I forgot to raise the drive."

After a couple of moments of fumbling in the dark, she found the release and tilted the engine up, freeing them once again. They started paddling the short distance to the shore when the faint sound of a boat motor made her blood go cold. She leaned forward and said, "Hurry, we must get off the lake."

She put her paddle down and swung her legs over the side of the zodiac. She jumped into the water and found it was little more than knee deep, and incredibly cold. She knew the glacier-fed lake was always cold, but it was easy to forget how cold it could be. She grabbed one of the lines that was attached to the side and started pulling the boat to the shore.

Eagle jumped out and pulled the other side. They quickly splashed to the shore and, with Myst's help, carried the zodiac off the beach into the tree line. Exhausted by their burst of energy, they sat on the ground, gasping for breath. All of them looked at the dark lake, trying to see if anyone had followed them. She hoped the half moon rising above the mountains would reflect some light onto the lake as darkness fell.

The sound of the boat motor that carried across the water was slowly getting louder. Skye listened intently. There was something different than before. She could hear a dog baying in the distance but there was almost nothing else. Not even a cricket chirping nearby.

She realized their danger and almost called out in alarm but then heard the sound of a man's voice sneering "Howdy:" from behind her. She spun around and was greeted with a cackling laugh coming from two men standing ten feet away in the last light of dusk.

She held her breath when she saw one had a rifle pointed directly at her. The other held a pistol directed at Eagle. The man with the rifle said to the other man, "Whats we got here, Jimmy-boy? We got us a girlie and a pup."

Jimmy-boy just tilted his head and laughed, "Got damn, we got 'em good, Bud."

The sound of his voice made Skye's skin crawl. Her pack was too far to reach. Even if she could get to it, the guy would have to be a moron not to be able to shoot her from this range. She stayed frozen in place, trying to think of what to do. Eagle sat like a stone on the ground. She couldn't see Myst. She hoped the men couldn't either.

The two stepped closer and Bud said to her, "Better stand up, girlie girl. Got to get dem hands up where I sees 'em, that one too, I thinks." He nodded toward Eagle.

Skye slowly got to her feet and raised her hands palms out, shoulder high. Her mind raced, trying to think of a plan, but the terror in her heart held her motionless. Eagle didn't move. She whispered, "Eagle, get up."

Skye winced as Bud snarled, "Got to shut the mouth, girlie. I tell you what to do is what I think."

She held her breath as he stepped to Eagle and gave him a vicious kick in the ribs, making Eagle sprawl on the ground. "Told you to get de fuck up I thinks."

Eagle scrambled to his feet, and Bud shoved his rifle barrel under the boy's chin. Skye stayed frozen as Bud mumbled to Eagle, "Got to know what I does wit girlie but don't know 'bout you. Maybe make you my slave. Work you for myself or sell you to a farmer. One thing sure, you does what I sez or I blow you fuckin' head off I think."

Bud swung the rifle back to Skye. Jimmy-boy laughed like an idiot behind him. He moved closer to Skye until only the rifle barrel separated them. A flicker of moonlight gave her a good look at him for the first time. His stringy dark hair was matted on the sides and tangled around his shoulders. His nose was crooked as if it had been broken, and his cleft chin had a jagged red scar that went across his lips. His skin clung to his cheekbones as if it was stretched as tight as it could possibly be; it was sprouting patches of short whiskers. A shiver went through her as she realized this was the foulest human being she had ever seen. He stunk too.

Skye felt Bud run his eyes up and down her. "Got to be takin' that robe off, it only get in de way I think." He called over his shoulder to Jimmy-boy. "Got to be havin' sum fun tonight, Jimmy-boy, dis a fresh one I think."

A shiver ran down her back at the sound of Jimmy-boy's lustful laugh. *I can't believe I'm so damn helpless.*

Skye tried to keep her knees from quivering. The stinking man in front of her had the barrel of his rifle almost on her chest. Her mind raced for a way out of this. A few feet away, Jimmy-boy had a shotgun pointed at Eagle's head. Even if she found a way past the filth talking to her, she could not help her companion.

He said again, "Girlie girl, don't make me ask agin. Got to git dat cloak off 'en. I aims to have you right now I'm thinking."

Skye shuddered; a trickle of sweat went down her neck. "Yes mister, I know what you want and I'll gladly give it if you will let the boy go."

Bud laughed in a nasty way. "Got to know you'll give it all right. Da boy be givin' some too for Jimmy-boy, he likes 'em young I think. Got to get the cloak off now I think!"

He pressed the barrel to her chest. Skye was horrified at what might befall Eagle. This was all her fault; she never should have let Rick bring him along. She should have made him turn back when she had the chance. The gun on her chest convinced her there was no way out of this predicament. She'd have to go along and hope for an opening later. She lowered one hand to unbutton her cloak.

Even in the darkness, she could see the features of the slug standing in front of her. Her insides were nauseous at the idea of what would happen next. The slime with the gun was drooling. Then, over his shoulder, a movement caught her eye. In the moonlight, a small fist raised behind Jimmy-boy's head. *It's Myst!*

Skye's heart raced in hope.

She tried not to stare, which would give her friend away. She swallowed hard as one finger sprang up on Myst's fist; Skye read the signal immediately. She moved her hand from the button on her cloak to the slit designed to allow her to reach the dagger in her inside pocket.

A second finger sprung up. *Careful, Myst. Not too fast.* Skye felt the handle of her knife and undid the snap. This was going to be tricky. She'd have to get it out without tangling on her cloak and move the barrel that was pointed at her in one motion. No second chances. An instant before she was ready, the third finger went up.

Myst shouted, "Hey mister."

Skye saw Jimmy-boy turn, and Myst smashed him in the face with a stout branch.

Bud looked to see what happened, and Skye drew her dagger from its sheath. In one motion, she knocked the gun barrel away from her chest with her forearm and slashed the throat of her assailant.

Bud stumbled backward with a shocked look on his face. Skye pressed her attack, yanked the rifle from his hands, and jammed her knife into his gut. She heard him gurgle in pain as he fell to the ground.

To her side, she saw Eagle tackle Jimmy-boy, causing the shotgun to go off with a deafening roar. The big man screamed in agony and grabbed at his wounded leg. He squirmed away as Eagle wrestled the gun from him. Jimmy-boy got to his feet and ran into the woods with a limp. Eagle started after him but Skye called him back, "Leave him go. We have other business."

She looked at the mortally wounded Bud at her feet. He looked up at her, and she could barely make out the gurgled words he said: "Got to think you killed me, girlie girl."

Skye looked into his dying eyes. "Got to think."

The sound of a motor drew Skye's attention to the lake. Boats were coming; she guessed they were drawn by the sound of the shotgun blast. A spotlight illuminated part of the shore. It started to sweep along the beach and then pointed into the tree line. Her jaw tightened at the thought of having the pirates so close to them.

Eagle came to her side. "What do we do?"

Skye had only one notion. "We get out of here, fast."

Skye's pulse raced as she and the others gathered their bags and slung what they could over their shoulders. The bags she had brought for trading were particularly heavy. She half staggered under the weight. She wished Rick was here with the transport he had promised. She took a few steps and then waited for Eagle and Myst. "Hurry!"

Checking the lake, she saw that the pirates were shining their light only fifty yards down the shore, but they were headed toward her. Eagle stood, his knees almost buckling under the packs he bore. Myst shouldered two small bags, and Skye led them through the darkness into the forest of ponderosa pines.

They had only gone a few steps when she heard men yelling behind them.

"Skye, I think they spotted the zodiac." Eagle was already panting.

She worked to form a plan. "That means they'll be right behind us."

Eagle drew even with her as they half stumbled through the forest. "We may have to drop some of these bags."

Skye shook her head. "No, we must have them to trade for the vaccine and to barter our way."

Eagle said, "They won't do us any good if we get captured by those guys."

She knew he was right but she was not willing to give up so easily. The trees gave way to a small, dimly lit clearing with a cooking fire and a camp light hanging on a tree. A gutted deer was hanging from another tree. She pulled up quickly, alarmed that they had come upon a hunting camp. Eagle and Myst froze beside her, and then she saw him.

Jimmy-boy was across the opening but what he was doing was what made her gasp. He was trying, without success, to strap a saddle on a horse. She shouted, "We're coming to get you, fat man."

Jimmy-boy turned to them. Skye dropped her bags, drew her pistol, and started charging across the clearing. Jimmy-boy whooped and limped as he ran wildly into the forest. Skye caught the horse by its reins and then saw another horse tethered to a tree.

Eagle and Myst hurried up to her. "These two guys must have been hunting. They probably heard the zodiac before we cut the engine so they were waiting for us when we came off the lake. That explains why they were right there."

Eagle stroked the horse's neck. "This thing is kind of thin."

Skye agreed, "It looks like they didn't take very good care of it. The one over there does not look much better. They'll have to do though. Help me get the saddle tight."

Skye stroked the animal's nose, and it shook its head and snorted. "Seems like this one is a little feisty. I'll ride her with Myst, you take the other."

Eagle's voice sounded incredulous. "You mean to take these? They aren't ours. That's stealing."

Skye moistened her lips with her tongue and hefted one of her bags onto the horse's back. "The way I see it, we probably just killed the horse's owner, and his dim friend is running around the woods like a fool. We have many miles to go and pirates on our tails. If somebody wants us to pay for these mounts, they can bill me."

She was going to continue but Myst grabbed her arm. "Skye, we have to go. Now!"

Skye looked at Eagle. "Any questions?" He shook his head no. "Now get the other horse saddled!"

Skye swung her other bag onto the horse and quickly secured it with a rope from her pack. She balanced the weights of the bags so they would not throw the horse's balance off.

Eagle hustled to the other horse and threw the saddle that was on the ground onto its back. Myst helped him secure it, and then he untied it and mounted it, still wearing his packs. Skye threw the last two of the four heavy bags over its back and secured it as she had on her horse. She could hear movement in the forest behind them and guessed the boat had already landed. A flicker of light slashed through the trees, shooting a jolt of fear through her. The pirates were closer than she had thought.

Skye mounted her horse and reached down and helped Myst up behind her. She saw Eagle was ready. "Let's go."

"Where?"

Myst leaned forward, pressing against Skye's back, and pointed to a narrow opening in the trees. "That way."

Skye heard a voice behind her shout, "There they are!"

She didn't wait for another second. She kicked her heels firmly into the horse's sides and had a surge of relief when the animal broke into a gallop. Myst held her tightly around the waist, and they rode headlong into the dark woods at the south end of the lake.

CHAPTER FIFTEEN

MARCHING NORTH

BARZAN SAT AT HIS field table by the side of the road as his army marched north. He used his fork and picked at a piece of chicken that he had long ago lost interest in. His mind was concentrating on the news the scouts had brought him. It was strange information and had the sound of either a minor annoyance or a well-laid trap.

He looked at Ivan. "Show me on the map."

With a nod of his head he signaled the servants to clear his dishes and make room for the major. He wiped a bead of sweat from his forehead. This place they called California was hot, not like his home had been in Aden, but it was hot enough to be a nuisance, especially to an army that had to travel at the pace of the slowest troops on foot. He firmly regretted not having enough vehicles for more than a quarter of his men. Fortunately they had found water enough so far, but if that changed they would have to review their strategy.

Ivan spread the map and Barzan's four top commanders, and Lieutenant Ja-Zeer, surrounded the table looking at it. Ivan pointed to a spot halfway up the page. "We are here on this road marked I-5. As you know we have only come across a few gangs of bandits and they have been dealt with, no problem."

Barzan wished he'd get to the point. "Go on."

Ivan continued, "Five miles beyond the head of the column is a town of some sort. The scouts report they see about fifty buildings. It does not appear on this old map. They have seen men, women, and children but have remained undetected. There is a small wall around the perimeter but it seems inadequate for a strong defense."

Barzan interrupted, "As if it is an invitation to attack?"

Ivan nodded. "Perhaps a test of our strength."

Barzan scoffed at him, "By who? We have seen no signs of an army."

Ivan stepped back. "What is your command, my general?"

Barzan licked the inside of his cheek. "I like invitations. Have two lead companies attack and burn the village. Keep anything useful as usual. Hold the rest of the army out of action."

Ivan spoke slowly. "If our companies are attacked?"

Barzan answered, "Let them fight on their own. We will judge the enemy's strength by this. It is a test of their will. If two hundred men are not sufficient, then we will reinforce from the main body. With four thousand men in the field, I do not believe we will have a problem."

Ivan followed with another question, "What of the people in the village?"

Barzan was feeling hungry again and was getting tired of having to close every detail. "Question them, find out if they know anything of our quarry, and then do what you will with them. They are spoils of war. After that destroy them, I do not want to be bothered by prisoners."

Barzan stood up from the table and then froze in place; his heart jumped when the sudden rattle of a snake caught his full attention. Ivan leaped up from the other side of the table and drew his sidearm and fired four times before he killed it.

Barzan kicked at the five-foot-long serpent. "Deadliest thing we have encountered so far. How many have we lost to these vile things?"

Ivan answered, "Six so far. This whole place is infested with them. The men are terrified of them."

Barzan looked to his major. "It is no wonder, we have no antivenom and the death is excruciating. Excellent job, thank you for your swift action."

Ivan saluted, and he and the other officers departed. Barzan called to a servant, "Bring me something sweet."

CHAPTER SIXTEEN

FOLLOWING

JOHN ERIKSON CREPT TO the top of the timber-covered hill and peeked through an opening in the trees. From here, he could see across the open valley that he guessed was a mile across. His spirit sank at the sight of the huge encampment made by the Malsi army.

Next to him, Les let out a soft whistle. "Man, that's a lot of bad guys. How many you guess there are?"

John couldn't see a way to count the men. The dusk was pierced by what looked like thousands of campfires. Each fire was ringed by four pitched tents of varying colors. He focused his binoculars on a fire that was close by the edge and made out ten figures around it. Smoke from the fires hung low in the still air, lightly stinging his eyes. The heat was oppressive so he figured the fires must be for cooking. The odor of burning wood and some meat he could not identify reached his nose.

He counted the number of fires in one corner of the camp and then estimated how many areas that size were in the valley and multiplied by twelve. The math made him dizzy. "There must be a few thousand."

Les nodded in agreement. "At least."

John and Les dropped to their knees and started crawling to the edge of the tree line to get a better look at their adversary. They stopped behind the cover of some thick junipers at a place that offered a full view of the valley.

Les spoke softly, "Looks like they brought a whole damn army. What the hell do you suppose they want here?"

John suspected the answer was all too obvious. "I think they came to finish the job they started in Europe and Asia. One world, all bowing to the prophet of the Malsi in Baghdad."

Les snorted, "Nice little religion, if you can call it that. Worship with us or die. Death to the nonbelievers."

John scanned the perimeter of the camp. He noted there were sentries posted in pairs of two, spaced about fifty yards apart going around the outside of the camp. He focused on a pair at the base of the hill he was on. They seemed bored and more interested in talking with each other than in looking into the forest for attackers.

Les said, "What do you think? Looks to me like the guards are window dressing. Probably just the lower echelon officers trying to impress the higher-ups they are on the job."

Crackling brush on the ridge caught John's attention. Someone was coming toward them on the hilltop. His heart pounded hard, and he and Les started crawling back into the trees trying not to make a sound.

He was startled to hear a shout from close by in a language he didn't understand. Les whispered, "Come on," and jumped to his feet and bolted into the woods; John followed close on his heels. The sound of gunshots cracked in the air and bullets snapped past his ear.

John said half out loud, "That's some window dressing."

Les cut to the right and John kept up his pace. They were sprinting hard, trying to get trees between them and their pursuers. There were men yelling behind them, and they could hear the pursers charging through the woods.

John heard another bullet zip by his ear. *Damn, that was close.* He pumped his legs harder, racing through the trees as fast he could. Small branches slapped at his arms; the uneven terrain threatened to trip him up or snap an ankle. Just ahead of him, Les tore his way through the underbrush, crashing through low scrub brush, breaking branches as he went.

John pulled his pistol from its holster and fired two shoots over his shoulder. He hoped that would slow down the guys behind him.

John panted heavily. The hot air made him sweat, and his shirt stuck to his back. The attackers continued in dogged pursuit of them. The situation was getting seriously worse. He knew the tree line ended in less than half mile, where they would reach a cliff rising up from the river by the Malsi camp. If they kept going the same way, they would be trapped.

He shouted to his friend, "We got to cut left or we'll be pinned in."

Les didn't say anything, and John was about to call again when Les veered away from the river. Now they were going downhill, which made the footing even more treacherous. Les stumbled, rolled head over heels, and then staggered to his feet and kept running.

They ran until they came to a steep ravine that cut across the route toward their camp. John paused, breathing hard, and saw Les double over, putting his hands on his knees to catch his breath. John could not see any place to go except straight down the rocky cut or back the way they had come. "So much for turning left."

Les pointed into the gap. "Look."

John didn't see anything but had to hurry because Les didn't wait for him. He slid down the side of the hill, waved for John to follow, and then vanished under a rock overhang. John clambered after him, scraping his elbows on the rock as he skidded down under the outcropping.

John held his breath even though his lungs were demanding oxygen. He and Les were standing precariously on a narrow rock ledge, which was the only thing that kept them from tumbling nearly a hundred feet straight down a rock face. A stone outcropping covered them from above; John knew if they were discovered they would be toast.

Between gasps of breath, he whispered to Les, "Are you nuts? We're sitting ducks here."

Les nodded his head toward the top. "We'd be dead ducks up there."

John froze as some rocks clattered and skittered down the steep slope right beside them. He and Les slowly pointed their pistols at the direction they had come from. He could hear faint voices above him speaking in a language he could not make out. It sounded vaguely Middle Eastern.

John could feel his pulse pounding as he wiped sweat away from his eyes. He hadn't been this scared since the Malsis had overrun the fortress of London. He, Les, and half his men had been lucky to escape on that day. It was the last time Westerners had made a serious stand against the overwhelming army from the East. Since then, his troops had barely been able to stay out of the way of the conquering masses.

Les touched his arm, motioning with his eyes above them. Rocks fell off the overhang as if someone was trying to reach over or climb down. Adrenalin pounded through his body. Suddenly, he heard a sharp scraping sound and a man cried out. Directly in front of his eyes, boot-clad feet dangled over the rock ledge. John and Les recoiled, pressing back against the rock wall. If this guy on the rope was lowered any further, the game would be up.

There was loud cursing from above, and the feet kicked furiously. Obviously the climber was not too happy about his assignment. Then he was lowered a little so his knees were visible. John searched for an idea, and then it came to him. He reached into his pocket and pulled out the rattle they had removed from a snake the day before. He held it high and shook it for all he was worth, praying these guys knew what a rattlesnake was.

Immediately, there were loud shouts back and forth, some angry, another more panicked. In a few moments, the feet were hauled up and out of sight. The sounds of men cursing and then laughing came down the hill. John guessed the guy on the rope was giving his cohorts a little what-for.

John breathed a sigh of relief. He looked to Les and saw he had his hand over his mouth, suppressing a laugh. "Glad you think this is funny. I just hope they don't drop a grenade."

Les straightened up; his gaze went to the ledge above. "You always have such pleasant thoughts."

The sound of men moving on the ridge soon subsided. John thought it best to wait until darkness blanketed the countryside before they left their perch.

When they finally made it back to camp, John and Les welcomed the warm water Trevor handed them. He was a British marine who had joined them after the disaster in London. John thought the black-haired man looked like a pit bull in a uniform. He considered him one of the best men in what remained of the outfit, though sometimes he could be a bit peculiar in his mannerisms.

"I'm telling you, sirs," Trevor started. "It's not right for you to be traipsing about the countryside by yourselves, sneaking around the enemy camp like that. What if they'd caught you? A big blooming mess that would be. Who'd take over here?"

John let the metal cup of water warm his hands. "Anyone here could take over. You all know what to do. Everyone is ready to take over any job here."

Trevor served him some fresh rabbit he had no doubt just snagged. John admired how fast the men learned to live off whatever the lands they passed through gave them. "I don't understand why you couldn't a' let me or some other blighter go for your look-around."

John took a bite of the rabbit. It was succulent with a hint of garlic on it. He wondered how Trevor managed to keep spices on hand even after all this time. "We needed to figure out their strength. We have a pretty good idea where they are going but with the numbers they have, I don't know how we'll stop them."

ONE MORE TOWN

F ROM A HIDDEN VANTAGE point on a mountain above the town that
the Malsis were preparing to attack, Barzan used a telescope and
looked down with interest. He saw a bent and rusted road sign that
read WEED 2 MILES. He sat on a platform that was set on top of the
bed of his command truck. He mused that there was a certain irony
in sitting atop an American-made Humvee getting ready to attack
Americans in their own homeland. How differently things had turned
out for the world than what the West had expected. Especially the
arrogant U.S. politicians.

He put the thought away. There would be more time to enjoy these
thoughts later. Right now, he needed to focus on getting past this place
and on to Erikson's village. It would be a double pleasure. He'd get to
kill the infidel's family, if they were still there, and then gain the prize
that would make him more powerful than anyone.

The head priest of the expedition, Musafa al-Jost, joined him. He
wore the red robe of his office and had a long black beard that billowed
to his chest. A thick mustache almost covered his mouth, and black-
framed spectacles sat on his cragged brown nose. A hood covered his
head, and his dark face contrasted with the robe. He said, "We will
ensure the believers will be anointed before the battle."

Barzan clenched his teeth, took a deep breath, and asked, "Does the emperor desire to delay our entire advance?"

Musafa spoke in what Barzan thought sounded like a hiss. "The Emperor Prophet would not like what he is seeing with this command. The believers have started to stray; the long voyage on the ship diminished morale. Men are weak and need to be reminded of their duty to the emperor. Do you not agree?"

Barzan looked into the valley, sweat started to trickle down his neck. "How could my men stray? Your priests follow their every move."

Musafa gave a slight nod and said, "It is for their own good. We have already found one blasphemer since we landed. He was attempting to get several others to desert into the countryside. If not for my watchers, we could be less many men instead of one."

Barzan rubbed the back of his neck. "What became of him?"

Musafa answered, "He is being educated."

Barzan took a cigar from his pocket and put it in his mouth, unlit. "Go ahead, anoint the troops. But we must attack tonight."

Musafa leaned close and whispered, "As you command." Then he descended from the truck and left the command area, followed by a trio of other priests in dull orange robes.

Barzan watched them leave. *Ignorant religious fools. If they did not have the ear of the emperor, I would get rid of them all. Still there is the paradox, they help keep the sheep in line. And the emperor is still the true power, for now.*

Barzan returned his attention to the town below. It looked like little more than a collection of wooden shacks and barns. The workmanship was crude and rudimentary. There were few people about, some men and a couple of children playing in a dusty street. He surmised most of the occupants were staying out of the blazing sun.

His attention was drawn to what looked like the center of the village. There were four two-story buildings that stood above the others. Through his telescope, it was easy to see these buildings were better crafted than the others. He focused on the largest and caught himself smiling. This one would drive his men into a frenzy. He almost pitied the townspeople now.

"My commander, the men are almost ready to attack." It was Ivan speaking to him from the road where the command car was parked.

Barzan graced him with a nod. He noticed the man had found time to get the insignia of general on his uniform. Promoting him after the incident with the snake was a tactic that would show the others that bravery and loyalty would be justly rewarded.

"My commander, are you sure you do not wish to wait until dusk or dawn? It is so hot now, men will tire easily."

Barzan stretched his neck and signaled to his servant, who was sitting in the back passenger seat of his Humvee, to pass him a cold drink of water. He looked at Ivan with an impassive expression. "If I wished to attack at another time, I would have ordered it so."

Ivan nodded. "Yes, my commander, but your presence surprised us and has moved our time table up by several hours."

Barzan accepted his water from the servant and took a long drink. He kept his eyes on his new general, noting the sweat soaking through his Western-style tunic. This set the man apart from most of the army. The majority of the converts from conquered countries conformed to the dress of the Malsi high priests. The flowing robes were practical in the hot climates, and in the colder countries they could be layered to add warmth. Aside from that, most captives wanted to blend in with their new masters and try to be like them as much as possible. The multicolored robes offered a clear signal they were converted to Malsi.

He considered for a moment the Malsi religion. It was simple at its heart. A few skillful men could rule all the others by promising them everlasting paradise if they strictly followed practices prescribed by the priests. Pray twice a day at midnight and noon, hold the Emperor Prophet as the holiest on Earth, and do the bidding of the priests without question. To keep strict control of his followers, the emperor occupied them with a war to rid the world of nonbelievers. Making them all learn the common language of English was another way to control them. Even if they only spoke a little, it gave them all something in common. But it was the war that was most useful for keeping people organized in the rigid hierarchal order required of an army. *Ordinary men are so stupid. It is good to be commander.*

Barzan took a moment to examine the insignia of rank on Ivan's hat. It was a source of pride to him that the Emperor Prophet of the Malsi people had agreed years ago to Barzan's recommendation that the army have one practical type of head cover. He disliked the tall ornamental hats of the former royals as pretentious and impractical. Turbans and things that allowed men to cloak their face were too easy a way for assassins and thieves to hide their identity. They also looked too much like the attire of the conquered peoples of the past.

He convinced the emperor that a hat with a long bill in the front, an option to drape a cloth over the neck and ears, and an insignia of rank on the front would be the most practical type of garment. After all, one did need to know who was in charge at any given time. Barzan licked his lips at the recollection. It had helped that he had presented the emperor with a gold emblazoned cap of his own to help sell his case.

"You should hope, General," he stared at the officer to make sure he had his full attention, "that I am the only thing that surprises you today."

"Yes, my commander."

The man gave the slightest of bows. Barzan could not quite tell if this one was insolent or just lazy. Either way, he would remember it. He sharpened his tone. "Attack within the hour." He did not add that he wanted to get back to the main camp and his air-conditioned tent.

Lamont Wilson hefted a bag of corn off his cart in front of the blacksmith's shop. The afternoon heat almost sucked the strength from his arms, and he barely managed to get the bag on his shoulder. In the process, he scratched the back of his hand against the sideboard, reopening a scab just above his wrist. He cursed softly as deep red blood started to flow across his ebony skin. He hoped it wouldn't lead to an infection. Since the meds ran out, he had seen more than one man suffer awfully from seemingly inconsequential wounds like this.

His nine-year-old daughter Latoya scampered into the smithy's open yard. The sound of the hammer hitting the anvil stopped and was replaced by his little girl's giggling. Orlando Wilson was one of Latoya's favorite uncles, and he always managed to have a treat for her. Lamont had long ago stopped trying to figure out how he kept coming up with such things as girl's toys that looked new, sweets that were better than anyone else's, and handmade trinkets every woman in the village vied for. Lamont suspected Orlando had a secret stash someplace near the river but he never questioned his brother about it. One of the main rules in town was to keep out of other people's business.

He shifted the bag of corn on his shoulder and passed through the front gate of the low picket fence that surrounded the yard. He went past the residence around the corner to the work area. There, beside the anvil, Latoya was jumping up and down, trying to reach something Orlando was dangling from his raised hand. She pleaded, "Please, Uncle O, please, let me see it."

Orlando pretended to be stern. "I don't know that you are old enough to see such a fine thing. This is for big girls."

"But Uncle O, I'm big. I'll have ten years before Christmas."

Latoya jumped again, her black hair bouncing wildly on her shoulders. Lamont noticed that her patched pants were wearing thin around the knees and that her favorite blue tee shirt was getting too tight around her shoulders. He would have to get at least another load of corn to the spinners so she could have some better clothes. Now that the fall harvest was coming in, he would once again be able to pay for new goods. He dropped the bag of corn he was carrying onto one of the smithy's sturdy tables with a grunt.

Lamont admired his brother as the big man finally allowed his niece to grab ahold of his massive arm and bring it down. He stepped closer to see what was in his hand, and even he had to gasp at the ornate stickpin Orlando revealed. On the end, there was a white cross with a sparkling stone in the center.

Orlando pointed to the stone with a calloused finger. "The shining stone represents the light of the Lord."

He smiled as Latoya gently lifted it from his hand; she said, "It's the most beautiful thing you've ever made, Uncle O. May I wear it for just a little while?"

Orlando bent down and gave her a kiss on the cheek. "I would be pleased if you would take it as your own and wear it any time you wish to."

He saw Latoya's eyes light up in delight and she leaped up and threw her arms around his neck. "Thank you, Uncle O, thank you! But why? There's no holiday and my birthday is still months off."

Orlando held her in a hug and looked in her eyes. "Let's just say it's a beautiful day and a beautiful young woman like you should always have something beautiful to wear."

He put her on the ground and watched as she ran back and held the pin up to her father. Lamont admired the detailed work and said, "How can a man with such big hands make such a delicate thing? Brother, thank you. It is very kind of you to give her such a marvelous gift. Be sure to come over for dinner tonight. I'll be adding a little spice to the roast just for you."

Orlando nodded, his wide smile showing true warmth. "I'll be happy to, Lamont. I'm glad we're finally getting to some fresh meat again."

Lamont started to respond when a loud explosion shook the ground. He turned and looked to the south; a column of smoke drifted into the air near the edge of town. Sounds came that shocked him to the bone. Rapid-fire guns were going off and automobile engines were discernable in the distance.

Latoya asked in alarm, "What's that, Daddy?"

He didn't have time to explain. "Run! Run the back way to the church as fast as you can and tell everybody else, give the alarm! Get in the church! Go, go now! Orlando, come get your gun."

Orlando and his brother rushed into the house as Latoya hurdled the back fence on her way to the town center. Orlando raced to his storeroom. He pushed the door open and then quickly unlocked the big cabinet at the end of the short room. Opening it, he reached in and pulled a rifle off the rack and tossed it to Lamont. Orlando opened the drawer that contained loaded magazines; he took one out, jammed it into his rifle, and then chambered a round. He put two more magazines in his pockets and then gave three to Lamont. All the while he could hear sporadic gunshots that were getting closer and closer.

Lamont went to the front door and stopped beside it to peer out the window at the road in front of the house. His cart was still there; nothing seemed out of the ordinary. A still silence hung in the air. The heat was stifling, causing sweat to trickle down his neck. His pulse raced, as he tried to determine where the attack might come from.

Lamont moved to the door, slowly turned the knob, and cracked it open. He stepped on the porch just as an open truck full of men in dark robes skidded around the corner. Before he knew what was happening, gunfire erupted from the vehicle. Lamont was blown back through the door, bullets ripping into his head and chest.

Orlando threw himself to the floor as more bullets tore through the windows and walls. He was almost face to face with his dead brother, whose features were shattered in a grisly mess. His stomach churned and he almost threw up from the loss and horror of seeing his brother dead. He held his breath and listened. The truck didn't stop.

Tears welled into his eyes as he kissed his fingertips and pressed them against his brother's forehead. Taking two deep breaths, he drew himself to his feet, clutching his rifle; fearing the worst, he bolted out the back door and started running toward town. "Latoya."

Ivan watched in disgust as the truck ahead of him closed on a woman who had been unlucky enough to be caught out in the open. She was wearing a bright red dress, which made her stand out against the brown dirt road. He could only guess what the barbarians in the front truck would do with her. Some just liked the killing. Others had more savage ideas.

He adjusted the goggles over his eyes, trying to keep sweat from seeping in and obscuring his vision. Damn, it was hot here. Abruptly, he was almost slammed into the dashboard when his truck skidded to a stop. He yelled at the driver, Francois, "What are you doing?"

The driver pointed out the windscreen and said, "The pigs!"

The Humvee in front of them had stopped; it was just as Ivan had feared. Two robed men had jumped out of the truck and were chasing the woman on foot. They caught her in a few steps; the closest grabbed her blonde hair and yanked her to the ground. He knelt down on top of her and ripped the front of her dress open. She screamed in terror.

Ivan's stomach turned. Despite countless years of horrific battles and conquests, few things sickened him more than this. He slammed his door open, grabbed his rifle, and leaped onto the road. He covered the distance to the laughing men and the screaming woman in seconds. "Stop it!" he yelled.

The fighter who was standing turned to look at him but the one on the helpless victim continued to tear at her clothes. Ivan shouted again, "I said stop it!"

The attacker glanced at him with a sneer and then ripped open the bottom of her dress. She was sobbing now, begging for help. There would be no prisoners, but at least Ivan could save her something. He stepped to her side; her face was covered with tears and dirt. He took aim at her forehead and pulled the trigger.

The man sitting on her howled in anger. Ivan stepped back and raised his rifle at him. "I told you to stop it." He pulled the trigger again, blowing a hole into the man's chest where his heart was. The impact blew the attacker off his feet; he barely twitched when he hit the ground.

Ivan turned to the other man and the hostile faces that looked at him from the trucks. Pulse pounding, he shouted to them, "He disobeyed my order. We don't have time for individual pleasure; go!"

The fighter closest to him growled, "He don't speak no good englise."

Ivan stared at him and said, "He should have learned."

The men didn't move. Ivan fingered the trigger on his rifle again.

The sound of an engine revving caught his attention, and his truck sped toward him. He raised his weapon but the vehicle stopped between him and the other Humvee. The passenger door swung open and Francois called to him, "Get in."

The attack proceeded quickly and intensified in viciousness. Ivan's command vehicle passed burning houses and dozens of mutilated bodies on the way into the main part of the village. By the time Ivan arrived at the town center, the advance elements of his strike force were already there. As bad as it was, he was surprised there was not even more evidence of the village's destruction. There appeared to have been little resistance but his gut told him something was amiss.

A Malsi sergeant Ivan recognized as Abib signaled for the command vehicle to stop. Ivan and Francois dismounted from the truck and Abib approached Ivan excitedly.

"General, you may never have believed these if not seeing with your own personal eyes."

Ivan sorted through the pidgin English to grasp the meaning of what the man had said. Though he was fluent in three languages, it still took him time to decipher another person's attempt at a language that was not native to him. "Tell me what is the situation. Do we have control of the whole town? Are all the occupants dead?" Behind Abib, Ivan heard shouts of the attack party punctuated with occasional gunshots.

Abib's face was streaked with black soot marks; his hooked nose dripped sweat under the bill of his uniform cap. He answered slowly, seeming to choose his words one at a time. "My general, those who live here are the worst kind of scum on the earth. They hide in a place of blasphemy. They make a trap."

Ivan's sense of danger kicked his heart into a higher rate. Falling into a trap would be disaster. Even if the attack element survived the fight, that bastard Barzan would blame the commander for any failure, which in itself had been fatal to more than a few of his officers. "Explain yourself. Show me."

Abib bowed and said, "Yes, General, this way."

Abib waved his hand down the road and then took off at a trot. Ivan followed him on foot with the Frenchman at his side. Black smoke billowed from every building they passed. Malsi fighters took time out to carry away anything that looked like it might have value. He saw several men herding cows and sheep toward the back of the advance column. Whatever trap these people had laid, it didn't appear to have the troops too alarmed. Or maybe they were just ignorant peons, as he had always thought.

They came to a burning structure on the edge of the town center. Three men were crouched by the corner of the building, not willing to look beyond it. Abib motioned for Ivan and Francois to stop. "They are evil. See place they hide. Walls so strong make bullets not get through. Malsi are angry. Nonbelievers are they."

Ivan started to look around the corner but Abib grabbed his shoulder and yanked him back. "They will blow off your head." He pointed to the ground at a Malsi corpse laying on the road; the fighter had a gaping hole where his brain used to be. Ivan gave Abib a nod of thanks. He dropped to his knees and crawled to the edge of the wall. Peering around it, he almost laughed at what he saw.

The Malsi attack force was stymied by a Christian church. A great white cross stood above the building, gleaming in the afternoon sun. No wonder the troops were shouting rude things at the structure. It represented all they had been taught to loathe. These villagers did not worship the Emperor Prophet and needed to be destroyed.

He pulled back, slightly cutting his hand on a broken shard of glass. He cursed, flicking the offending sliver off. A spot of blood seeped to the surface of his palm. He confronted Abib. "It is only a building with a superstitious sign over it. We have burned many of these over the years. Why are your men afraid of it?"

Abib snarled at him, "Not afraid. Don't care about sign. Building built like a fort. Not like the other buildings here. They shoot out, have kill fields. We can't get close."

Ivan looked at his hand and licked his wound. "Then burn it."

Abib nodded and said, "Yes, tonight we burn it. At twelve, the Malsi will burn the nonbelievers as the emperor has written."

Ivan sat on the ground, leaning back against the wall of the burning building. He nodded to Abib, who took his leave to make preparations for the night. Francois sat beside him.

"Why do we not burn it now? Dis will take forever. I could go to camp and sleep on my mattress."

Ivan rolled his head, stretching his neck to relieve tension. "You know these idiots. When they find a religious place, they have to do the Emperor Prophet's bidding. Burn them at midnight or miss your trip across the river to the great reward."

Francois took a metal flask from his pocket. "Did they not figure out that after Mecca, Jerusalem, and Rome were obliterated in a matter of days that religion is nothing more than superstition?" He took a drink from his flask and handed it to Ivan.

Ivan took a long drink. The whiskey stung his mouth and warmed his insides as darkness enveloped them. "These warriors of Malsi, look at them, most were born after the end or just before. Like armies in the past, they are little more than children. The religions of the past are another generation's memory, not theirs. They only live for the prophet and the opium he keeps them doped on. You know that." He gave the flask back to the Frenchman.

"Oui, I know that. How did you end up here?"

Ivan wiped sweat from his forehead with his hat. "Years ago, the command I was in was trying to stop the Malsi advance in Germany but we were losing badly. We were on the verge of being overrun and my commander surrendered our troop. Barzan gave us the choice: join or die. I chose to join. I saw many good men who refused to join get massacred. I don't know how they could be that brave. How about you?"

Francois said, "It is much the same. I did not like the alternative to joining. Now I go to the prayers twice a day and pretend I care. I keep my head down and do what I'm told."

He paused and then asked, "You know what I miss most about the old world?"

Ivan didn't care but decided to humor him anyway. "What?"

"Champagne."

CHAPTER EIGHTEEN

EVERGREEN

Skye rested her horse in a stand of poplars. A small stream bubbled down the hillside, and they watered the animals while they rested. They had ridden through the night, guided only by the moonlight and a small path that wound its way between the trees. It was little more than a game trail, and she had constantly had her arms and face swatted by low-hanging branches.

They had traveled as fast as she dared. After their initial gallop into the woods, the horses were hesitant to go much faster than a trot. She let her animal seek out water. It acted like an intelligent creature and was responsive to her commands. Though she could feel its ribs under her legs, it had a strong gait, giving her hope it would take them all the way to the mountains.

Because of the pirates, they had landed far away from where Skye had planned to land based on the old road map her mother had given her; now they would have to pass through the territory of Evergreen, which is why she had stopped before they left the trees. Myst's grip around her waist had been tight all night, and Skye was ready for a break. Eagle's horse drew next to hers and continued drinking from the stream.

Myst whispered from behind her, "Can we get down now? My bottom hurts."

Skye nodded in agreement and felt Myst slide off the horse. Then Skye crossed her leg over the beast's mane and dropped to the ground herself. Her knees almost gave way, surprising herself with how sore they were. The first gray hints of dawn started to break through the tops of the trees, and she welcomed the day with a little hesitation. She looked forward to the warmth the sun would bring, but they were far from home and she had only a vague notion of where they were headed or who they might meet. At least the black of the night had offered some concealment.

Eagle got off his horse, kneeled, and rinsed his face in the stream. "That's cold. Are we going to rest now or do we keep riding?"

Skye ran her hand down her horse's neck, feeling the sweat that was soaking her. "We need to rest these animals and give them a chance to drink. I think we need to eat ourselves. I am famished."

Eagle moved away from the stream, looking back down the path they had come up. "What about the pirates? Do you think they are still following us?"

Skye stretched her arms, trying to loosen up the tension in her back. "They might be but I do not think they could have traveled as fast as us."

Eagle kept looking into the woods. "What if they have cars?"

Skye massaged her neck with one hand, trying not to let alarm creep into her voice. She hadn't considered that. "If they had autos, they surely could not have come the way we did. Rick told us to stay off the roads, and the cuts on my arms testify to our following that advice. Let's set the horses to feed and have something ourselves. We will pause till mid-morning and then continue."

Myst patted Skye's horse on the shoulder. "I think we should name them."

Skye smiled at the young girl. "A fine idea; do you have any in mind?"

Myst put her hand on her chin. "This one is strong, she carried us all night. Perhaps we should call her Midnight. It matches her black color."

Skye nodded and stroked a white splash of hair between the horse's eyes. "This patch almost looks like a light in the sky. Perhaps we should call her Midnight Star."

Eagle spoke up and said, "A fair name indeed. I think I shall call this brown mare Sunchaser. Because I believe we will always be chasing the sun."

Myst let out a short laugh. "Can we get any further apart?"

Skye mocked, sounding wounded, "I like these names, what's the matter with them?"

Myst undid the ropes securing the packs on Midnight Star, and they fell to the ground with a clunk. "The names are fine, maybe I just see too much into them."

Skye decided to drop the matter. "Let's eat, and then we can sleep in shifts. No fires, though, we still don't know what is around us."

After a meal of cold jerky and water, Skye tucked Myst into a blanket resting on a bed of soft pine needles. It was not long before she and Eagle were hard asleep. Skye pulled her cloak around her arms and put the hood up around her head against the morning chill. She opened her eyes wide, trying to ward off the fatigue that was overcoming her.

She checked Midnight Star and Sunchaser to be sure they were secured and had access to water and grass that grew near the stream. As the morning light filtered into the forest, she made an assessment of their location.

Creeping to the east of the brook, she found they were well hidden from view from the mountains that rose steeply a few miles away. She climbed a short way up a cottonwood tree and saw they were near the crest of a small hill. To the north, the direction they had come from, she saw a thick forest that went all the way to the lake, which shimmered in the distance.

Dropping from the tree, she almost turned her ankle, which sent a spike of pain up her leg. She crossed the stream again and started for the top of the hill when a movement caught her eye. A rabbit scurried into a wall of brush just ahead of her. Her curiosity urged her on, and she followed where the furry animal had gone.

It was not her intention to go down the rabbit hole but before she knew it, that is exactly where she found herself. There was no sign of the rabbit, but she had slid into a small cave almost big enough to stand in. The adventures of Alice came to mind and she muttered, "Curiouser and curiouser."

The cave was cool and dry with just enough light coming in to keep it from feeling closed off. She wondered if it had been an old Indian hideout. She'd have to come back with some light.

Climbing out was not as hard as she had feared; there were small footholds dug out of the entrance. When she got out and turned around, the entrance was again nearly invisible in the brush.

As she moved up the hill, a cold wind blew into her face. The dawn had turned gray and low clouds were piling up against the snow-capped mountains. She slowly approached the edge of the thicket and looked for a place to peer out unnoticed should there be anyone out there.

She found a place behind a wall of blackberry bushes that allowed her to look into the valley below. A twinge of fear and excitement passed through her. The forest gave way to a vast plain stretching to a wide river to the west. A great blacktop roadway ran nearly straight to the river, disappearing down a gorge with no visible end. On the edge of the road, almost to the river, stood a walled city. From Rick's description, she realized it must be Evergreen.

The plain was dotted with people working in fields that were arranged in big circles. She surmised these must be the crops that Rick had talked about. Great plumes of water shot into the air, coming from spindly steel contraptions making the plain look as if it were populated by fountains in the crops. She caught herself not breathing as she took in the spectacle.

Skye stayed where she was, fascinated by the open space. The road was mostly deserted, but here and there horses pulled wagons. She did see one automobile traveling at high speed, weaving around the wagons. She was too far away to hear anything but from their gestures she got the impression the wagon drivers were not too fond of the auto driver.

She watched as long as she could keep her eyes open, and then knew she needed to get some sleep. She returned to her companions and shook Eagle until he groggily opened his eyes.

"What? What do you want?"

"It is your watch now; my eyelids will no longer stay open."

Eagle rubbed the sleep from his eyes. "Very well. I will take the watch as my duty. You can depend on me."

Skye touched his shoulder. "It is important we are not surprised. I believe our greatest risk is from the east. I have spied a city there and farmers in their fields. Be alert to all but be aware of that direction. I think we are safe here for now. Wake me when the shadows move to here."

She placed a stick in the ground, indicating a spot she thought it would take the shadows two hours to reach.

Eagle's eyes widened and he said, "A city? Are we going there?"

Skye yawned, wrapped her cloak around herself, and then lay down by Myst. "We will make a plan. Do not be seen." She closed her eyes and welcomed sleep.

CHAPTER NINETEEN

SEND THEM TO HELL

JA-ZEER PACED BACK AND forth on the road in front of his vehicle. Barzan had been most unhappy with the delay in the taking of this pitiful little town. After the massive battles they had fought in Europe, an inconsequential skirmish such as this one should be executed swiftly and without delay. Ja-Zeer had been sent to the battle to make sure Barzan's wishes were carried out. Ja-Zeer agreed with him in principle, but things were different now. He needed to find a way to balance his commander's orders with the reality of the situation they faced.

Smoke from the burning buildings shifted on the wind and caused his eyes to water up. He wiped his face with the sleeve of his black robe. He checked his timepiece and sighed when he saw it was still another hour to midnight. The door to the general's Humvee swung open, and Ivan dismounted. Ja-Zeer greeted him with a salute.

Ivan returned the gesture and said, with an air of exasperation, "Have the priests finished yet?"

Ja-Zeer hated the answer he was forced to give: "No commander, the truck with the sacraments was delayed, and the men have not been fully anointed."

Ivan spat on the ground. "You mean the dope hasn't kicked in yet?"

Ja-Zeer stepped close to the Russian and lowered his voice. "You must be careful, my commander, the priests have ears everywhere. To be heard blaspheming them could lead to your undoing. They have more power now than ever before."

Ivan squinted at Ja-Zeer in the dark and said, "There was a time when we could conduct our battle plans without interference. We didn't have to stop and make the slaughter of a few helpless people a religious experience."

Ja-Zeer knew Ivan was right; even so, he wanted to avoid any hint of his own doubts of the faith. "The people we will attack tonight are a special kind. They have taken refuge in a church under the sign of the cross. It is as bad as hiding behind a five-pointed star or the banner of Islam. They do not believe in the Emperor Prophet as the priests have taught and they are condemned to their fate as is our law."

Ivan waved him away and drew a packet from the pocket of his trousers. Opening it, he offered Ja-Zeer a hand-rolled cigarette. Ja-Zeer accepted it gladly. "These priests are taking their power too seriously. It is bad enough that we have to stop everything twice a day on the twelves so the prayers can be offered. It is even worse that we have to conform to their schedule for the completion of our job."

Ja-Zeer flicked a match and lit the commander's smoke and then his own. The tobacco was dry and the taste was harsh. He didn't mind, though; this was a rare treat. "It is better not to speak of such things, my commander."

His thought was interrupted by the sound of shouts and gunfire coming from down the street. "The ceremony must be complete. Pity the townspeople who are still alive."

In a few moments, he watched as three priests arrayed in orange robes led the troops up the street. The priests held torches high in the air. The men fired random shots into the sky, and many waved torches as they chanted a prayer in unison. Ja-Zeer knew the words were said to be handed down from the prophet and that only the holiest could understand them. He suspected they were little more than random chants that had a simple cadence the opium smokers could mutter without thinking.

The sound got louder as the men came closer. Each time the refrain started, it grew in volume and intensity. By the time the priests turned the corner toward the church, the men were almost shouting the lines.

Ivan started toward the men. They were packing the street now, marching as a mob toward the church. There was only one more turn until they would be in the city square, and then Ja-Zeer knew the gates of hell would be opened. He hurried after his commander.

"Sir, what are you going to do?"

Ivan blew out smoke as he walked. "This is where we take charge." His lip trembled. "Otherwise the idiot priests are going to get good men killed for no reason."

All Ja-Zeer could do was nod.

In the next moment, he saw the priests peel off from the front of the pack. The chant broke and was replaced by screams of anger and rage.

Ja-Zeer stood fascinated as Ivan strode to front of the mob and raised his hands. The mob quieted down under the orders of platoon commanders.

Ivan shouted, "Form the attack phalanx, now!"

The mob shuffled itself into order until it transformed into a box ten across and ten deep. The last rank was filled with men with mortars and RPGs. Ivan shouted again, "Forward, now!"

They marched in order, and as they reached the corner and turned toward the church, Ja-Zeer could hear a few gunshots coming from the square. Ivan let the troop pass and fell in step behind them. Ja-Zeer ran to catch up with them. Gun flashes came from the slit windows of the church, cutting down a few of the lead men.

Ivan shouted again, "Attack! Attack! Rear ranks fire!"

At the command, the phalanx broke into a run and started screaming again and returned fire at the church. The last rank hesitated, creating space between them and the main body, and then set up mortars and started hurling rounds at the church. A few took aim with RPGs, and Ja-Zeer watched the fiery trails of two rockets as they streaked to the church and exploded against the walls.

When they got close enough, the lead element started hurling torches at the building. If a man with a torch was felled, the torch was picked up by another of the demented troops and advanced further.

Ivan approached Ja-Zeer as the church started to burn and hissed to him, "Needless slaughter. There is no reason for this."

Ja-Zeer could only parrot what the holy men had been preaching. "The nonbelievers must die by the new ways. They must be exterminated from the earth and burned into hell."

He watched as two more torches hit the walls of the church, adding to the funeral pyre for those inside.

Ivan turned away from the scene. "It was not like this when we fought in Europe. Then the priests gave us support. Now they seem to mock us."

Ja-Zeer watched, fascinated, as the church was rapidly engulfed in flames.

The next morning, Ivan stood with Lieutenant Ja-Zeer waiting for Barzan to finish his breakfast. It irritated him that the man could be so rude as to let his officers stand and watch him eat without so much as offering a seat or cup of coffee. The inside of his mouth was pasty with dust and smoke from the night before. His eyes were red and dry. All he wanted to do was seek out his shelter and get some sleep, though he knew he dare not do anything until he gave the commander his full report.

Barzan wiped some crumbs from his thick graying mustache with a white linen napkin. Ivan glanced around the inside of the opulent tent, which was ridiculous in its finery. Over the last couple of years, the commander had taken to traveling like some kind of ancient royalty, a regular sheik of the burning sands, as one of the Brits had once whispered.

The entire floor was covered with plush Persian carpets, so guests were required to take off their footwear prior to entering. An array of tapestries depicting Arab warriors from another time riding into battle covered the walls of the tent. Barzan sat at a highly polished mahogany table, surrounded by fifteen leather chairs. When he used it for meetings, the chairs were arranged with two on each end, six on one side and five on the other.

Barzan always took the center seat on the far side, showing his power in the old Japanese way. Around the tent, there were dozens of brightly decorated pillows for sitting and lounging on. When the commander entertained, this was how most visitors were seated. Ivan also imagined that was where Barzan was entertained by the troupe of consorts that had been traveling with the army the last several years.

Nobody knew much about the man before the end; some said he had been in jail in Africa when the wars started. Ivan had heard that he was born in Baghdad and had been a small-time smuggler and assassin. None of that mattered now. No one cared what you were before. It was what you proved to be now that was your worth. Barzan had proved to be a shrewd, brutal, and loyal servant to the Emperor Prophet and was rewarded accordingly by being put in command of the Malsi European army. Ivan sucked on his dry lower lip; he hated keeping the bastard happy but it was the only way to stay alive.

Barzan interrupted his thoughts when he let a heavy silver knife drop to his porcelain plate with a clang. The general looked at him in a way that made the lower part of Ivan's back cringe. "Were there any survivors?"

One servant in a white coat took away Barzan's plate and another filled his coffee cup. Ivan's mouth felt pasted together. "No, my commander. There were none."

Barzan gently blew the heat off the top of his coffee. "Have you eaten? Are you hungry?"

The question was so incongruous, Ivan didn't know how to answer. He chided himself for not being able to read the man better. He didn't want to eat with him, not now anyway, though the coffee was tempting. "No sir, I have not."

"Then you should take better care of yourself. How can you lead the troops if you do not nurture yourself? Look at me, the sun is barely over the horizon and I have completed my meal and am ready for the day and what it will bring."

Ivan kept his hands from clenching noticeably; at least he hoped he did. "As always, what you say is true, my commander. I should have had a bite as we drove back from the battle this morning—then I would be more prepared. I had foolishly planned to wait until I could get to the officer's shelter and have something warm."

Barzan pointed his finger at him and said, "A man in your position should know better. You are a key officer to me. I cannot afford the luxury of you running yourself down. Have some coffee."

He turned his finger to Ja-Zeer. "You too. Now sit, both of you. Tell me what you know of this village."

Ivan gratefully took a seat and the coffee that was immediately brought by a servant. He nearly burned his mouth on his first sip, so he put the cup on the table to let it cool. Ja-Zeer spoke first. "With your permission, my general."

Ivan nodded his consent.

He was well aware how close the lieutenant was with Barzan and wanted to appear to have trust in him.

Ja-Zeer recited the particulars about the attack, noting now and then how Ivan had kept the raid on track despite minor setbacks. Ivan knew the guy was a good suck-up but this was better than he had expected. After he summed up, Barzan started asking questions.

"There are two matters that concern me. You say the village was easily overrun, but, when attacked, the center of town showed strong opposition. You say that the church was like a fort but was easily burned. What did you miss?"

Ivan watched as Ja-Zeer's back stiffened.

"There was nothing to miss. They all ran for the church like scared rabbits to a hole. We surrounded it and stayed there until it burned. No one came out."

Barzan rubbed his chin; his black eyes went cold and he turned them on Ivan. "Did you count the bodies?"

Ivan felt the chilled air pumping from the air conditioner hit the back of his neck. "It is still too hot to sift through the ashes. I will have it attended to as soon as it is possible."

Barzan leaned forward. "Do it now. Put the fire out yourself if you must. I want to know how many bodies there are."

CHAPTER TWENTY

WHO ARE THEY?

JOHN MOVED SILENTLY THROUGH the night, keeping low so his profile would not be revealed against the backdrop of the three-quarter moon. Les and two other Rangers followed him, each carrying a rifle at the ready. An orange glow on the horizon had lit the sky the night before, and John had felt compelled to investigate. It was from a different direction than Barzan's encampment, and John's gut told him it was an ominous sign.

They moved cautiously below a ridgeline that paralleled an old road. He would have preferred to go cross-country but the uneven terrain in the foothills of the Syskiyous made that alternative impractical. The bridges for the road were still intact and they made for an easy crossing of the deep ravines and fast-moving rivers along the way. Even so, they presented a threat; each bridge crossing caused the men to be exposed should there be something on the other side intent on stopping them.

He paused and took cover behind a rock outcropping when he came to the opening of another deep chasm in the hills. A sharp cliff fell away from the road, dropping to a stream he could hear hundreds of feet below. His shoulders tightened while he focused on the roadway that followed over a graceful arched structure to the other side.

Les stopped behind him. "Used to drive this road at eighty-five miles an hour. Never realized how many bridges we went over."

John wiped his brow with his sleeve. "Damn well didn't think I'd ever be hiking this thing. After all that time on the boat, my ass is starting to drag."

Les chuckled, "Whew, I thought it was only me."

John could see his friend smile in the dark. "Let's take five and keep a watch on the other side."

Les motioned to their companions to take a break. Without a word, the men took up positions that allowed them to survey all avenues of approach to their location and promptly sat down to take a load off. John admired the discipline the men showed. They had been at war for nearly twenty years, yet the Rangers still responded to every situation in textbook style. They were never sloppy and refused to let their guard down. John briefly closed his eyes, thankful the team's continued professionalism had kept so many of them alive despite the odds they constantly faced.

In spite of all the battles they had fought together, John's mind was nagged by apprehension. He needed to get home before the bastard got there. If home was still there. He opened his eyes lest sleep catch up with him. There was something different about the fight now. Before it had been trying to keep the Malsi invaders out of what had been North Africa, and then Europe. Then as the ranks of the conquerors grew, it had turned into a matter of survival for his small troop. Now it was personal.

He had not expected to have to fight this enemy in his own homeland. He had been surprised when the news of Barzan's sailing reached him in the fortress in Scotland after the disaster in London. They had been lucky to get a vessel in working order to be able to beat the scourge of the Malsi leaders across the ocean and through the canal in Panama. That had cost a lot. The gang there did not see too many ships these days, and the tribute they had demanded put a serious dent in the Rangers' supplies. It had taken more than a little gentle persuasion to gain safe passage.

He knew the further north the Malsi army went, the closer they would be to what he and the others had left behind. He had no idea if what they had left was still there but prayed every day that by some miracle it would be. He choked back a laugh. *There's the irony. We went off to keep the enemy away and now we're racing it home.*

He stared down the road. *I've lost a lot of battles to you, Barzan. This time you can't just keep throwing bodies at us. This time I'll stop your ass. Somehow.*

From his concealed spot, Les quietly whispered to John, "Movement on the bridge."

John slowly crawled to Les's vantage point and squinted at the roadway below them. Two figures were crouched at the far end of the bridge, apparently surveying it. The moonlight exposed them, and John could see them almost as if it were daylight.

He softly asked Les, "What do you think? Does not seem like Barzan's guys, no robes. Those guys were using vehicles and driving around like they own the place."

Les nodded and said, "These two act like they are on the lam. Maybe they're one of the gangs that are around and had a run-in with Barzan's army."

John considered the thought. "Makes sense. Nobody else is out here that we know of. Look, they're coming across."

As he spoke, two men, dressed in dark clothes, started to trot across the bridge. Each carried a rifle and wore a small backpack. The one in front wore a baseball cap and the one behind a small brimmed cowboy hat. John was glad it was not he and his men who were in the glaring light being watched by someone on the other side.

The two men reached the halfway point of the quarter-mile bridge and stopped. They knelt down, peering in the direction of John and his troops. He leaned over and whispered to Les, "Did they make us?"

Les's reply was barely audible, "Don't think so. Something else? Wait, here they come."

The sound of an engine reached them. Looking far across the chasm, John could see the faint glow of headlights coming down the road. The men on the bridge looked behind them and then started to sprint toward John's end of the bridge.

Les whispered, "Looks like they don't want to stay and play with whoever is coming behind them."

John watched, fascinated, as the men ran as hard as they could. He found himself rooting for them, though he was not sure why. *Come on guys, hurry up or they'll be right on top of you.*

The runners were nearly at the end of the span when the vehicle came around the corner, approaching the bridge with its lights glaring on the blacktop. The men reached the end of the railings and jumped off the road, scrambling under the end of the structure just as the Humvee turned onto the bridge and raced across it.

John held his breath. He recognized the paint scheme as being that of Barzan's army. The truck passed over the bridge without slowing and then sped past him on the road below. Relieved, he slowly let out his breath. He tapped Les on the shoulder. "Let's go find those guys. Maybe they know something useful."

John led his men carefully down the hillside toward the base of the span. They moved quickly, using hand signals to minimize their noise. He had no idea what to expect from the two runners, so he chose to treat them as hostile until he knew otherwise.

Les went to his right and his other two troops fanned to the left. He had kept his eyes on the place the runners had hidden but had not seen any movement since the truck had passed. With the moonlight painting the dried grass white, it was difficult to stay hidden as they moved. Sweat soaked his shirt and he wondered if the men they were after might have him in their sights.

His question was answered when a voice came from behind him: "Freeze mother fucker or I'll blow your head off."

John stopped in his tracks and froze in place. His heart leapt in his chest and a shiver of shock and fear swept down his back. *I can't believe I walked us into this.*

"Get your hands where I can see them."

The voice was deep and hard; John slowly raised his hands, keeping his rifle in his grasp with his hand away from the trigger.

"Turn around, slowly."

He did a quick search of the area. Les and his troops were not in sight. He was the only one who was cornered. He turned around and saw a tall black man wearing a faded San Francisco Giants cap holding a silenced rifle on him from about fifteen feet away. The guy in the cowboy hat was a few feet to the right with an automatic weapon pointed John's way.

The guy in the Giants hat asked, "Who are you and what are you doing out here?"

Before John could answer, Les's voice came from out of the dark, "Let him go or you'll both be dead before you hit the ground. We've got you surrounded."

John was glad to hear his friend's voice but was not too happy about the timing. It would have been nice to wait until he didn't have two guns pointed at him. The sound of a distant engine got his attention. That must be the reason Les had chosen now to make his challenge. There was no time to wait. In this position, they were all very exposed to the road.

The guy in the Giants hat didn't move. "I'll get this guy before I fall. Give it up. I don't believe there's more than one of you."

Almost simultaneously, John's troops shouted, "Here," on either side of the standoff.

The truck noise was getting closer. Les called out again, "You going to wait out here for the car to go by?"

The big man's voice sounded less sure now. "Is that part of your group?"

John thought it might be prudent to chime in. "They aren't with us. They are our enemies, and we know they aren't with you. We saw you hide from them. How about we all back off and get the hell out of sight?"

The man in the Giants hat shifted his weight slightly and said softly, "The enemy of my ..."

John heard the loud pause and filled in, "enemy is my friend."

The big man added in his deep voice, "For the moment."

John thought the guy might be wavering and needed reassurance;

he said, "My name's John. The guy out there with the gun on you is Les. What's your name?"

The big man sighed, "I'm Orlando." He motioned his head toward his companion. "This here is Jessie. Let's get the hell off the sky line."

CHAPTER TWENTY-ONE

DETOUR

SKYE WAS STARTLED AWAKE by the feel of something shaking her arm. She opened her eyes to see a dark form in the dim light towering over her. Instinctively she recoiled away and then, with relief, recognized that it was only Myst nudging her awake. A couple of heavy raindrops hit her face in what she was sure was a prelude to a heavy downpour.

She sat up and gave her eyes a rub. "What do you want?"

Myst put her fingers to her lips in a shushing signal and motioned for Skye to follow her; she trotted to the eastern side of the tree line, the one that was closest to Evergreen. Skye didn't like what she saw. Eagle was hard asleep, sitting on the ground and leaning with his back against a tree with his hood pulled up on his head. She got out from under her blanket to follow Myst. She wondered how long she had slept. She was anxious to get moving because getting meds in time to stop the pox was crucial.

She took a moment to stretch her sore arms, and Myst looked back at her, impatient for Skye to hurry up.

"All right, I'm coming. Can't a girl even wake up around here?"

A layer of thick gray clouds hung in the treetops, and the rain started coming down in earnest. Skye went past Eagle without disturbing him. There would be time for that later. Myst kept trotting and she had to hurry to catch up with the girl. As they neared the crest of the hill, Myst stopped and turned to wait for her. Skye caught up, and Myst gave her a hand signal to stay low. Advancing to the top, she carefully peeked over the ridge that offered a view of the plain below. Skye's heart jumped at the sight that greeted her.

A group of men on horseback were galloping across the valley. It was easy to see that if they kept on a straight line, they would ride directly into their camp. She counted ten riders and guessed they were only minutes away.

She could not imagine their little group had been discovered, or what the men might want if they were found. *I will not wait around to find out either.* She pulled her hood up to keep the rain off her head and quickly went back down the hill to wake Eagle. She patted Myst on the rump as she passed by her. "Good girl."

When she reached Eagle, she gave him a not-so-gentle kick in the thigh. His eyes popped open in surprise. "Hey, cut it out."

She was completely dismayed by his irresponsibility. "You are quite lucky it is only me. Fortunately for us, Myst has some sense about her. Get up and gather our things. Strangers are approaching fast, so we must ride."

Eagle lifted one of the bags of trade goods and groaned. "Frick, these are heavy. I wonder how far these horses can carry them."

Skye lifted one of biggest bags, once again feeling its weight. She opened it up and withdrew three Kevlar vests; they were kind of large but they would have to do. She tossed one each to Eagle and Myst. "Put these on under your cloaks; I'm afraid we will need them."

Eagle picked his up and examined it. "Body-armor, nice."

She made a quick decision. "We can't take these bags with us for now. We don't know what we will find next, and we cannot afford to be robbed. We must have these to trade for the meds. We will hide them here and thus travel lighter and faster. We will come back and get them later."

Eagle's face scrunched up into tight wrinkles. "We can't just leave stuff lying out."

She walked her pack to the brush in front of the little cave she had found earlier. "Of course not. We will hide them here."

She slid the pack into the brush. "Bring the others."

Skye took another bag from Eagle. "Quickly gather the horses. We must fly."

Eagle yawned. "How did we get so popular?"

Skye shoved the bag into the brush and heard it slide down the smooth rock to the cave. "What do you mean?"

"People are always chasing us."

Skye waved him off. "Hurry, get the animals. Myst, you break the camp. We want to make it look like nobody was here."

Skye slid down the smooth rock into the cave and pushed the bags into a corner where they were not visible from the entrance. Using a leafed branch for a brush, she erased the marks she had made in the dust. She emerged from the cave, happy to see Eagle was mounted on Sunchaser and Myst was waiting with Midnight's reins in her hand.

Myst held the reins loosely. "Can I steer?"

Skye took the leather lines from her. "Later."

Myst pouted, "You get to have all the fun."

Skye called to the boy, "Come on, Eagle, we have to get out of here. We can't afford to get caught by anyone. We don't have the time to spare."

Myst spoke up and said, "I got a feeling."

Skye looked to the young girl. "Time to go?"

Myst rolled her eyes. "Do I have to say it?"

Skye mounted Midnight and pulled Myst up behind her.

Skye waited for Eagle to bring Sunchaser even with her and then gave Midnight a nudge with her heels. The horse burst into a gallop down a narrow trail that led into the forest and away from the valley she had seen. Myst held Skye's waist tightly as they went deeper into the woods.

Even though it was daylight, the tall firs and clouds filtered the sun, causing the forest floor to be a dark path flickering with specks of muted light that played tricks with the dim shadows. Skye could scarcely make out the way between the trees. Beneath her Midnight moved with a grace and confidence that gave her comfort. "I hope you know where you are going, lady, because at the moment I am somewhat disoriented."

It was not easy trusting the horse to lead the way. Skye reasoned that since the main thing she wanted to do was to get away from the camp, and the riders, it really didn't matter where they were going in the next few minutes as long as it was away from anything that would endanger their mission.

She hated the thought of having to take the time to circle back for the weapons, but avoiding capture was paramount.

After they had covered a good distance, Myst tugged at her from behind. "I think we're okay now. We can slow down."

Skye pulled gently on the reins until Midnight slowed to a walk. The morning air was crisp, and the gallop had been invigorating. She was glad it had stopped raining and drew in a deep breath of the pine-scented air. She looked over her shoulder at Myst. "You okay back there?"

Myst loosened her grip slightly. "I'm fine. Where are we going?"

Skye closed her eyes briefly, enjoying the rocking motion of the ride. "We have to go past Evergreen to find the road to the mountain."

Myst answered matter-of-factly, "There is great danger there."

Skye sighed, "I think we'll find that is true every place we go."

Myst gave her a hug from behind. "I like hanging out with you. It's never boring."

Eagle pulled up beside them on Sunchaser. "What are you two talking about?"

Myst smiled at him. "Girl stuff."

Eagle spit on the opposite side of his horse. "Must be pretty dull then."

Skye pulled Midnight away from Sunchaser. "You're such a boy."

Eagle mumbled, "What do you expect?"

They rode in silence for an hour until Skye thought they had gone far enough to evade the riders. She had wrestled with the idea of trying to watch them from afar to discern their intentions but ultimately decided distance between them would better serve her purpose. *I don't have time to play cat and mouse with every group of riders that comes along.*

Late in the afternoon, they came across a stream that looked as if it had come from one of the fairy tale books Skye's mother had read to her. A warm glow came from the sun that filtered through the branches of the great trees that lined the water. The stream rushed and gurgled down the mountainside to the valley below. There were small waterfalls just above the trail, and she could trace the flow of the stream for mere yards above and below her. The water came out of the lush green forest of firs and hanging moss, briefly showing itself under the grand canopy of giant trees and then disappearing again into the forest below.

Skye and Myst dismounted and let the horse free to water herself and feed as she would. Eagle slid off his mount and stretched his legs.

Skye watched as her companion dejectedly sought out a place on his own away from her and Myst. After splashing in the water for a few minutes, Myst made a bed of pine needles and fronds and promptly went to sleep.

Skye washed in the refreshingly cold stream and knew she had to address the situation with Eagle. *I guess I've been a little hard on the boy. I need to resolve this so it does not distract us from our purpose.*

Skye dried her face and walked to where Eagle had thrown his cloak on the ground and was sitting in a spot of shade. "Hello Eagle, may I join you here?"

He looked at her with an air of defiance and sneered, "You can do whatever you want, you're in charge."

The words stung, as she was too aware of the way she had been forcing her will on him. "It is true I am in charge by default, but I never planned for you or Myst to even be here. Without repeating everything we have gone through I can only assure you I'm doing my best to get us all through this. I hope we can improve our relationship."

Eagle cocked his head. "And that means what?"

She reiterated her original question, "Do you mind if I sit with you?

He motioned with his hand as if addressing a monarch. "Please sit and join your humble servant."

She bit her tongue and ignored the sarcasm. Taking a seat on the ground beside him, she tried to lighten the conversation. "This might be the most beautiful place I've ever seen. Don't you think?"

Eagle yawned, putting his hand over his mouth. "If you say so."

Though discouraged by Eagle's hostility at her every remark, Skye pressed on with her mission to right things with her friend. "Things have happened on this brief trip that were both unforeseen and unfortunate. I have said things that should not have been said, and I'm afraid they were found clever by others at your expense. I thought they were funny at the moment, but now I realize I wronged you and did so without thinking. If I have offended you, I apologize and ask your forgiveness and understanding. We have been places and in situations I've never encountered before, and I'm still learning my way."

Eagle turned his head to her with a cold eye. "You mean you're saying you're sorry for making an ass out of me on the boat with that thief?"

Skye's neck tensed at the slur toward Rick and elected to let it pass.

"Trader Rick was not a thief. He kept his word and delivered us as far as he could."

Eagle spoke with his lips thin, his face shading red. "Well, you made an ass out of me; why, I don't know. Apology accepted."

Skye wanted to breathe with relief but knew there was something missing from Eagle's statement. "Thank you."

Eagle licked his lips. "No problem; of the two of us, I came out looking the better."

Not wanting to hear but still puzzled, Skye took the bait. "Meaning?"

Eagle smirked, "I came off looking like an adolescent fool. You're the one who came out as woman trash."

Her hand moved before her brain kicked in. Her palm shot out from her body and slapped Eagle across the face with a blow that knocked him on his side. She stood over him, putting her foot on his chest. "You will never, never speak to me like that again!"

Eagle's eyes were wide with fear and hurt. "What will you do if I do?"

At that moment, Myst's scared voice came from across the trail, "We have to go!"

Eagle looked toward Myst. "I hate it when she says that."

Even if there was immediate danger, Skye wanted to drive her point home; she pressed her foot harder onto Eagle's chest and said, "We will discuss this more later, but no matter what happens, we cannot let our differences interfere with our mission."

Eagle grabbed her ankle but did not try to move it. "Whatever."

Myst called out again, "Come on, hurry!"

Skye held her place and glanced in Myst's direction. She had collected the mare and was leading it toward Sunchaser. A flicker of doubt crossed Skye's thoughts. She dismissed it. Safe would be better.

She took her foot off Eagle and extended her hand to help him up. He refused it and stood by himself. Together they ran to the horses and in moments were mounted and galloping up the narrow trail they had been following all afternoon.

After a short ride, Myst clenched Skye's arm. "It's okay now. We can slow down."

Skye didn't change pace. Midnight was running easily, and it made sense to move fast while it was still light. Eagle was a little behind her, and Sunchaser appeared to be running with ease. Putting distance between them and anyone following was a sound course of action. Myst tugged on her arm again.

"I said you can slow down now."

Skye said over her shoulder, "I want to get away from whoever was coming."

Myst answered quietly, "There was no one."

Skye could scarcely believe what she had heard. "What?" She

slowed Midnight to a walk and turned as best she could to face the young one. "What do you mean?"

Myst wiped a tear from her eye. "I lied, I didn't mean to but I did."

Skye knew the answer. "You lied because you saw me fighting with Eagle and it was the only way you knew how to stop us."

Myst nodded. "I'm sorry."

Skye gave her an awkward one-armed hug. "Well done. Just never do it again. I have to be able to believe what you tell me."

Myst squeezed her tightly. "I promise. Please don't fight with him anymore. You two are all I've got out here, and I'm kinda scared."

Skye reined Midnight to a halt. "Me too."

Eagle pulled up beside them. "What's going on?"

Skye made a show of taking the map from her cloak. "I think it's time we change directions. We must turn toward Evergreen soon. I believe it best to approach soon after dawn on the morn of a new day. Travelers may be better received then than at the start of night."

Eagle looked puzzled. "I thought Rick said to avoid that place."

Skye answered, "He did suggest that and that has been our plan. However, it is clear we need a couple more horses to transport us and our goods. If we make ourselves known, perhaps they can direct us to safe passage so that we don't have to run from everyone we see."

Eagle nodded. "You're the boss."

Skye wanted to say something to try and soothe things. She regretted that the right words eluded her so she simply put her eyes to the map. She could not make out any landmarks from their location in the woods so the map at this point was of little value. She announced, "We'll have to go east to get out of this forest. Once we are in the open we'll have a better view and be able to make a course to the city."

Following her compass, Skye nudged Midnight off the trail into the woods. The horse seemed to sense what she wanted and picked its way through the trees carefully. The afternoon turned hot, and the moist forest floor gave off a light mist, creating a greenhouse effect. The muggy air caused Skye to pull off her cloak and Kevlar vest and stow them in her bag. Riding in her short-sleeved leather top and khaki shorts made her a little more comfortable, though it left her arms exposed to branches when they passed too close to a tree.

A brief shower passed over, adding to her overall dampness. She didn't mind the rain, however, as it refreshed her spirit.

After an hour of winding their way down the hill through the thick trees, Skye noticed the forest was opening up in front of them. Abruptly they reached a distinct edge to the trees and nearly stepped out into a vast opening outside the trees. A road cut through the forest, and the sun created a shiny glare on the wet surface that was nearly blinding in its brilliance.

Skye pulled Midnight to a halt so quickly that Sunchaser almost ran into them. The horses circled nervously in place, and Skye could feel Myst's hands tighten on her waist. She peered through the edge of the trees, trying to make out what was beyond them.

Skye saw Eagle had to wrestle with the reins to keep Sunchaser in place. Eagle looked at her with a question in his eyes. She whispered (although she could not have said why), "There's a road out there. We need to see where it goes."

Eagle nodded and she saw him prod Sunchaser out of the trees. Skye's heart leaped. "No! Not like that!"

She watched Eagle turn to answer when a loud shout from nearby took her attention.

"There they are!"

Skye looked in horror as five men on horseback only fifty yards away kicked their animals into a hard run, heading straight for Eagle. A gunshot echoed against the trees, and Skye saw five more mounted men just off the road north of the first group.

Sunchaser whinnied in surprise and rose up on her back legs. Eagle lost his grip and fell hard to the ground; he didn't move. Sunchaser settled and brushed Eagle with her nose. The riders were fast approaching. One kept shouting, "Stop or we'll shoot again. Stay where you are and you won't get hurt."

Skye, still in the tree line, reached behind Myst and drew her rifle from its scabbard. *I can't leave Eagle behind.* She put her rifle to her shoulder and took aim at the lead rider. Suddenly, Myst grabbed her hand and took the rifle off target. Skye jerked the weapon back angrily. "What are you doing?"

Myst said quickly, "If you shoot him, they'll kill us all. This I know. If we let them take us, there may be a chance."

Skye didn't like it, though she recognized the logic and knew it didn't take a psychic to figure it out. Now the riders were almost on top of them. She reluctantly put her weapon away, straightened her shoulders, and watched from the trees as the men approached.

When they reached Eagle, he was still lying on the ground. Sunchaser stood over him, not allowing the men to touch him. Skye shouted to the men near Eagle, "Leave my man alone. I will tend to him when I may."

The other riders cautiously approached the trees. One held a rifle and the others carried short swords. The one closest to her was tall with long black hair that flowed over his large shoulders. Like the others, he wore a billed cap with the symbol of a fir tree stitched on the front. It resembled the necklace Rick had given her and which she now wore around her neck. She could not quite make out his features. She did note all the men wore identical green shirts and pants. They appeared clean and in good condition.

The long-haired one looked at her squarely from a distance of twenty yards. "Call your horse off. I have a man of medicine in my troop, and he will give your companion care. Now you must come forward or risk injury to yourself."

Skye knew the odds of escape were negligible, and she could not leave Eagle in any event. Still she had no intention of appearing weak. "By whose hand would I be injured and for what reason? We have caused no harm to anyone."

"Your injury will come from those behind you."

Skye took a look behind her and was startled to see two men in green with rifles standing scant yards behind her. Midnight stepped forward nervously, and Skye had to rein her back.

The man with the black hair spoke loudly as if he had authority. "I will take you into my custody for trespass on the lands of Evergreen without permission of the House of Commons."

Skye retorted, "I have seen no sign that this is the land of Evergreen, and having never been there, I have been deprived of the opportunity to inquire of the House of Commons if we might pass this way."

The response came back quickly. "Flippant words will not serve you well with me. I am Armstrong, captain of the outriders of Evergreen, the guard of the city. I am tasked with bringing all strangers in our lands to the city for questioning. Should they be unwilling to come on their own, I am charged with subduing them or killing them, whichever I see fit."

Myst tightened her grip on Skye's sides and whispered, "This one is okay. I can't tell about the city."

Skye said in near silence, "Why didn't you tell me they were here?"

"I never said I could see everything. I don't know why."

Skye sat as tall on Midnight as she could and whispered to Myst, "Sit straight."

She gently tapped the mare with her heels and rode silently to the captain. She squinted when she reached the bright sunlight and got her first clear look at the leader of the guard. His hazel eyes were clear, his features were sharp, and his face clean and smooth. She guessed he was only a couple of years older than herself. She found she was suddenly short of breath.

The captain touched the bill of his hat in greeting. "We have been aware of your presence for a nearly a day now. News of strangers in our lands travels rapidly. It is unfortunate you chose to elude us. It was not my desire to have to use weapons against your party. Will you please call your horse off so my man can tend to your companion?"

Skye called to Sunchaser, and to her mild surprise the horse backed away from Eagle, who was still lying motionless on the ground. One of the outriders knelt over the boy and after a moment looked to

Armstrong. "The injury is superficial. Lucky for him he has body-armor on. He must have hit his head when he fell. He is just a little dazed."

Skye's relief at the news helped her sit straighter on her mount. It was as if a weight had lifted from her shoulders.

Armstrong looked at one of his men. "Tie their hands. We will return to the city at once."

Skye stared at him in anger. "There is no need to tie us. Certainly your band of strong men are capable of escorting me and these two children without bonds about us."

Armstrong answered her flatly, "You have run from us for some hours now; why, I do not know and do not care. When you are delivered to the Commons, your fate will be decided by those who are equal to all. Until then, you are my prisoners, and all of my prisoners are bound."

Skye could feel her face starting to flush, her checks burning. "Must you tie the little girl too?"

Armstrong paused for a moment before answering, "These are strange times and there are accusations flying about that give me cause for concern about strangers of all stature. After a thorough search, you will each be secured, but we will make every attempt to make you comfortable."

As he spoke, the man by Eagle helped the boy to his feet. Eagle was clearly dazed and the man quickly patted his hands over Eagle's person, including his private areas, and took away his knife and short sword. In an instant, his hands were tethered and two of the outriders hoisted him onto Sunchaser.

Skye watched as the rider closest to her dismounted and approached Midnight. She guessed he was over six feet tall. He had a large frame and long red hair that almost reached his shoulders. When he looked up at her, she noticed pockmarks on his tanned face. He said, "Please dismount, miss. It is my duty to insure you are not armed."

Skye looked directly at Armstrong. "No man will search me. I will freely surrender my weapons but I will not consent to being touched."

The man at her feet sighed, "I tried to be polite. You know, I don't need your consent." He reached for her knee. Before his hand touched her, Skye slashed the reins across his face. He fell back a few steps, holding his face in pain. Armstrong and the other outriders laughed, and this clearly made the would-be searcher angrier.

Skye spoke to Armstrong again. "This is your fault. I have no quarrel with your man but he must not try to touch me again."

Laughing, Armstrong looked to his man. "What's the matter, Corporal Hicks? She too much for you?"

Hicks spit on the ground and snarled, "I'll get you searched to the skin, you witch."

He charged and grabbed her knee and started to pull her off Midnight. Skye slammed him in the face with her backhand. He held his grip on her and with the leverage of his weight, he succeeded in pulling her off the horse.

Skye hit the ground hard but she was able to break the fall with her hands and instantly jumped to her feet. Hicks had fallen too and was slow to stand. Skye took advantage and delivered a swift kick to his midsection. He groaned and collapsed in the grass. She could hear the other men laughing at their companion's problem though she chose not to listen and focused on her immediate adversary.

One of the riders shouted, "Hicks, do you need some help with this big bad girl?"

Skye whirled, expecting another attacker. She was relieved the others seemed content on watching the show.

Hicks got to his feet, holding his side. "I don't need no stinking help. Miss, you're just making this hard on yourself. When I'm done with you, you'll be riding into town in nothing but what you was born in."

He looked bigger from her position on the ground compared to when she was looking down at him from the horse. She estimated the outrider was almost twice her weight and a several inches taller than she. *He's one big boy; better remember all those rounds I put in with Top.*

She backed up a few steps to give the appearance of being afraid.

Hicks took the bait and charged at her like a bull. When he was almost on top of her, she sidestepped and delivered a kick to his knee.

The man screamed in pain and toppled to the ground again. She ran to him under a shower of laughs from the others. She knew she could have crippled the man had she intended. This was a delicate game of winning, yet pulling punches so as not to truly injure her adversary and outrage her captors.

As Hicks tried to regain his feet, she delivered a kick to his shoulder that pushed him straight down onto his stomach. In a swift motion, she knelt down and put one knee in the middle of his back, pulled out her KaBar, yanked his head up by the hair, and put the long blade to his throat. "Who you going to search now, big boy?"

The laughing suddenly stopped and was replaced by the sound of weapons being drawn. Skye tried to slow her breathing. She looked to Armstrong. He shook his head with a wry smile. "If you will kindly let the corporal go, I give you my word there will not be a search of you, or the little one, if you consent to surrendering your weapons."

Skye took a deep breath to center herself. She drew the blade away from Hicks's throat and stood up. She walked to Armstrong, still holding the knife. She could feel the weapons pointed at her and knew that at any moment she could be struck dead. The captain held his ground and looked down on her from his horse.

When she reached him, she looked up into his eyes. From what she knew of the world, he looked to be a man she could trust. She held the knife up toward him and then, with a flick of her wrist, flipped it in the air and caught the blade so that she was presenting him the handle. "I place myself and my companions under your protection. I trust we will be treated justly."

She heard a collective sigh of relief from the other riders. Armstrong took the KaBar from her and nodded. "It is my duty."

Then Skye, in succession, handed over her pistol, her cutting knife, and a throwing star she kept for unforeseen events. She did not offer up the small dagger she kept close to her heart. Being completely defenseless made no sense.

Skye returned to Midnight and allowed a member of the guard to tie her hands together in front of her. The man was quick and the bonds were noticeably loose. When he finished, he winked and smiled at her and drew away as if he expected her to leap from the horse and do him in.

While this was happening, she watched as the defeated Hicks approached the captain. "You going to let her get away with that, Cap'n? She made a fool of me."

Armstrong responded, "She made a fool of us all. Don't think about it. You're lucky she decided not to kill you and a bunch of us with you just to be spiteful. I don't think we've ever seen the likes of her around here. We better hope there aren't more like her, wherever she came from. More importantly, we better hope those idiots in the House of Commons don't trifle with her."

CHAPTER TWENTY-TWO

NEW FRIENDS

JOHN CROUCHED UNDER THE bridge between Orlando and Les. The Humvee passed over the span, accelerating as it went. The men around him nervously fingered their guns, though John thought there was little chance the vehicle would stop. *I wonder how much those bastards know. There's one sure way to find out.*

He spoke out loud, startling the group around him who had been intent on total silence in the night. "Let's pick the next one off and take some prisoners. We need to know what these clowns are planning."

Orlando peered at him in the darkness. "Didn't you get what I said? There's thousands of 'em. They burned our whole town down. Ain't but fifty of us left and that's only 'cause we built the church over an old mine shaft just in case some'in' like this happened."

John answered with a measured response. "You don't believe they came all the way across the ocean just to visit your town. They have a bigger design, and I need to know what it is so we can warn everybody else."

Lamont let out a deep laugh. "You ain't been paying attention. There ain't anybody else. The Sierras were wasted by some damn bio-diseases that killed most everything and everybody came into contact with it. Everything south of old Frisco is contaminated by nuclear fallout. The central valley has been dead for years, and most people there starved to death. Without irrigation, the place has gone back to desert. My people lucked out and we managed to survive up there by Shasta 'cause I guess it was off the target list of whoever was throwing nukes and bio-shit at us."

John remained unconvinced. He rubbed his arms to ward off the chill from the early morning hours. "What makes you think you are the only ones on the whole West Coast that survived? Have you been exploring? Have you tried to contact anyone else?"

Orlando talked with sadness in his voice. "At first we just tried to survive. There was a family up here and they had some property in an isolated valley. We'd thought they were nuts for years but they'd stocked up food for the end of the world. Never dreamed they'd been right.

"Then we had to sort out who we could trust and who we had to avoid. When things collapsed, we learned people can be awful nasty when they're hungry and desperate. We laid low for a long time, discovering that being invisible was the best defense against the gangs and hoods that roamed the countryside for the first few years. Eventually most of them went away. Don't know why, maybe they starved or maybe they killed each other off, doesn't matter which. We was just glad they was gone.

"We started planting crops, and now and again a few small bands of people would show up looking for a safe place to be. If they agreed to work with us, we'd set them up with the things they needed to survive. Most of what we know came from them. Your question was, did we do any exploring? My answer is we just kept trying to get by and stay out of sight of outsiders. Worked for a long time until these bastards showed up."

John took a drink from his canteen. "My point exactly. You probably aren't the only ones who made it. There may be others who we could warn about the Malsi army that is here now."

Orlando stretched his arms behind his back. "I have heard stories about other survivalist groups who were ready for the war. One I've heard about a couple of times from travelers, really wanderers what ain't got no home, is 'bout a place up to Canada way. One said there's some old army outfit survived and made a city in the mountains."

John almost jumped to his feet. "Where? In Canada or the States?"

Orlando recoiled at John's reaction. "Not sure, man. The guy was pretty sick when we found him. He had the pox and we didn't want to have much to do with him. He just said it was up north."

Les leaned in between them. "There's another vehicle coming. I think we ought to take it out and find out what the hell is going on."

John looked to Orlando. "You and your people with us?"

Orlando shook his head no. "I don't even know who the hell you people are."

John knew he had a point. "We're what's left of a company of Rangers that set out to help fight the war against the radical Islamists. Funny thing is they collapsed from within and were replaced by a new power. The Malsis have taken over most of what's left of the world and are aiming to complete the job. We're trying to stop them from succeeding here."

Orlando lit a hand-rolled cigarette. "We just likes being out of sight."

John put his face close to the big man. "Kind of late for that, don't you think?"

Orlando inhaled and then let out a cloud of smoke. "I figure so. Guessing you're right; me and Jessie will help. Bastards murdered my brother. I can't say for the rest."

Minutes later, John and Les peered from behind a boulder, watching the approaching headlights of one of Barzan's vehicles. They had set a classic trap: rocks piled on the road to cause the truck to stop and shooters on either side to provide a seamless killing field. John just hoped everyone remembered that the whole point was to capture someone who could give them information.

Taking out a truck had its potential downside. It would alert Barzan that there were enemies about. John could only hope he would chalk it up to bandits or one of the gangs that still managed to carry on.

The truck came over the bridge at a relatively high speed. The headlights lit up the road block, and the driver slammed on the brakes. The Humvee skidded sideways. Everybody held their fire, waiting to see what the occupants would do. A door swung open and a man stepped onto the road. He was only a few yards from John's concealed location.

John's chest tightened in anticipation. He yelled as loud as he could, "Freeze! You're being taken prisoner."

The man on the road looked into the darkness.

John shouted again, "Put your hands up!"

The Malsi slowly raised his arms.

Les called out, "Everybody out of the truck."

Without warning, the Humvee bolted forward, the engine revving loud. The truck veered off the road onto the rocky surface of the field. The soldier stood stock still even as John's troops fired on the vehicle. The truck kept going but the withering barrage blew out the tires and windows until it hit a deep hole and flipped side over side.

John ignored the wreckage and ran to the guy standing on the road with his hands up. As he drew close, he saw the prisoner had fair features, unusual for most of the Malsi army. "You speak English?"

The man answered directly, "Oui, I do. Thank you for rescuing me."

CHAPTER TWENTY-THREE

CITY OF STONE

SKYE RODE WITH HER back as straight as she could make it. They passed vast fields of crops tended by people of all manner of description. The water that shot from pipes above the ground and shimmered into great showers over the crops mesmerized her. She tried to comprehend how they worked but more than that was fascinated by the beauty of the flowing water and the greenery beneath it.

She eyed Armstrong as he brought his mount close to hers. He motioned toward the city and said, "It took us a decade to build the walls. It was done mostly by hand, we started with a small, defensible position first and then expanded over time to what you see now. There is rich irrigation here; our engineers have been able to tap the hydroelectric power of the dam where the glacial run-off from the lake spills into the Columbia. It also provides electric power for our city."

Skye acted unimpressed. "My city has electricity also. It is not such a rare commodity."

Armstrong bowed slightly. "Excuse me, I did not mean to imply that you would be ignorant of such things. It is rare that we encounter a traveler with knowledge of these items. Where are you from?"

Skye refused to look at him, still angry that her hands were tied. "That is not important."

Armstrong leaned close to her. "Soon I must turn you over to the

House of Commons and you will be beyond my help. You are a strong person yet your inexperience with our ways may betray you. When you deal with these people, be careful what you say and how you act. Deference to their power will work to your advantage much better than confrontation."

Before she answered, he reined his mount away from her.

They approached the great walled city. She estimated the rock walls stood five times her height. Towers rose above the walls at even intervals around the entire complex. Dark burn marks stained the fortifications here and there, and she imagined they were the result of battles fought in the past.

They reached the arched entrance to the city of Evergreen, and Skye was sure she had never seen a structure so immense. Across the top, carved in stone, was an inscription that read ALL ARE EQUAL.

Myst asked from behind her, "What does that mean?"

Skye responded, "It means the people who wrote it are either liars or insane."

Corporal Hicks, who was riding closest to her, added, "Or both."

Inside the gates of Evergreen, the scene was one of complete tranquility. Rows of neat stone structures, which Skye took for residences, lined the walls as far as she could see. Each building was identical except for the decorations on the wooden doors. There was one window on either side of each door and a brick chimney in the center of each sloped roof.

Her tactical eye noted that the roofs gave easy access to the walkway on the city wall and thus would give defenders ample places to get to the defense of the city. Each house had a neat plot of land in front and was fenced in with identical railed fences. All of the yards grew some type of food; she recognized tomatoes, corn, and peas in the plots closest to her.

Across the street from the houses against the wall were nearly identical buildings with the exception that these were clearly larger. They featured two windows on either side of the door and a larger garden. As the riders passed the second row of houses, they came to another street and observed that the next row of houses was progressively larger. With each street they passed, the pattern stayed the same, and as they moved toward the center of the city, the houses became quite large.

Armstrong led the group, sitting tall and straight on his gray mount. One of his lieutenants rode beside him; Skye kept Midnight close behind him, with Myst clutching her shirt with bound hands. Eagle rode beside her, and Corporal Hicks and another of the guards brought up the rear of the small column. The rest of the guards had left when they entered the city.

The sun was still above the walls, and the heat was oppressive. Skye kept looking for people and only caught fleeting glimpses of faces peering out from windows or behind corners. The horse's hoofs made loud clacking noises as they deliberately made their way through town, causing her to wonder if the city dwellers were afraid of the animals, or the guards, or both.

She said to Armstrong, "Where are all the people?"

He turned and looked at her. "The citizens make themselves scarce at the sound of our approach. It is rare that the guard comes into the city. It normally means there is to be an arrest, and those are often without warning. Digressions from the rule of the Commons are not tolerated and many times are reported by anonymous persons."

Skye was not quite sure what she had just been told. "What would get someone arrested?"

Armstrong slowed his mount slightly so that he rode abreast of Skye. "Violence of any kind and theft were the things that caused trouble in the early years. The sentence for violence is simple. Anyone who commits those crimes is put in a box and buried alive."

The thought of being buried alive sent a chill through Skye's insides.

Armstrong continued, "The sentence for theft is simple also. Persons guilty of theft lose all their possessions and are forced to live in a house by the wall until they prove they can be trusted. The crimes of violence and theft have almost vanished from the city in recent times."

Skye was still puzzled. "If those things are gone, then why do people still hide from you?"

The captain looked around to see if there were unwanted ears about. He lowered his voice and said, "Impure thoughts are what the guard is most called for these days."

She was incredulous. "Impure thoughts?"

He leaned closer to her. "This society is based on equality. Words or actions that do not conform to that notion are deemed to be a threat to the common good, and those who utter them are arrested and brought before the House of Commons. Often people are arrested without knowing they have even been accused."

A knot started to form in Skye's stomach. This House of Commons was sounding less appealing all the time. She needed to ask one more question. "What is the punishment for impure thoughts?"

"It depends on the gravity of the situation. It can be anything from being held in the public pillory, to banishment to the outside, which often can mean death at the hands of the wild ones."

Skye cringed. "We call them gangs or pirates. It would certainly be an unpleasant fate."

Armstrong looked up and down the seemingly deserted street they were on. "We near the House of Commons; ride in silence from here on." He resumed his place at the head of the column.

Skye took a deep breath to try and shake off the wave of apprehension that enveloped her. *We have got to get out of here.*

She gave Midnight a pat on the neck, more to comfort herself than the horse. They turned a corner, and Skye was startled to see a large open square in the middle of the city. On the far side, which she guessed was a hundred yards away, stood a towering stone building. On the corners were turrets that gave the inhabitants a commanding view of the city. By their height, she imagined they could see outside the city also.

Myst peeked around her side. "That's a scary looking castle. Nothing good for us will happen in there. We must get out of this place."

Skye tried to keep the alarm she felt out her voice. "It can't be that bad. These are people of civilization. They have laws. We will explain our circumstances, and they will surely let us go on our way."

Skye looked at the foreboding structure. Her wrists were sweating where they were tied. *This is bad. Once we get out of here, I will never lose control of our fates again.*

They approached the great wooden doorway that was the entrance. It was large enough that four riders could enter side by side and twice the height of a man. Two guards stood on either side, each shouldering a short rifle.

They came to a stop in front of the closed doors. One of the guards approached Armstrong. After a brief exchange, the man went to the door and spoke to someone on the other side through a small opening in the door. A few moments later, the doors swung outward, opening from the middle. Armstrong led them inside as Myst tightened her grip on Skye's shirt, constricting the fabric around Skye's throat and nearly causing her to choke.

Skye gave Myst a nudge with her elbow. "Let go."

Myst let up on her grip slightly. "Sorry."

The inner courtyard was covered in a blanket of grass, except for the roadway that ran down the middle. It was noticeably cooler behind the walls, as a fabric canopy covered the entire opening from above. A waterfall cascaded down the far wall that stood about fifty yards from the entranceway. A small brook ran the length of the lawn. The space was as wide as it was long, and the walls were covered with blooming honeysuckle.

Multicolored rhododendrons bloomed, and red and white roses grew near the walls, softening them and giving the place the feel of a sculptured garden. To their left was a platform with two big padded chairs that Skye thought looked a little like thrones. There were no people visible, and when the doors closed behind them, a wave of apprehension went down her neck.

Armstrong signaled his men to dismount. They quickly dropped to the ground, and the lieutenant came to Skye's side. He reached up to help her down. She considered giving him a good kick in the face and realized it would serve no purpose. She allowed him to assist her even though she could have easily gotten off in spite of her hands being tied. Myst soon stood next to her, and Eagle took a place at her side.

Her knees were sore from riding so hard the last two days, and she gently flexed them. They faced the podium on the sidewall with two guards behind them and Armstrong and the lieutenant flanking them. From the ground, the platform was more intimidating. The top of it was at Skye's eye level, so she could see straight across what amounted to a stage to the two padded chairs. A large wooden door swung open on the right of the chairs, and four uniformed men marched in unison across the platform, stopping at the edge of the stage and standing directly above Armstrong. Their uniforms were more ornate than the captain's, with a swirling design on the arms and shiny metal emblems on their collars.

The one closest to Armstrong spoke while the others eyed Skye and her companions in a way that made her uncomfortable. She wished she had her pistol. "Captain of the Guard, I am ready to relieve you of your prisoners."

Armstrong answered, "If it is possible, I would like to accompany the prisoners to the Commons. I have some experience with them and their circumstances and have information that may be of interest."

The man on the stage shook his head. "Thank you for your offer. You will be summoned if it is deemed you are needed. Now it is time for you and your troops to retire from the city."

Armstrong nodded, and he and his men mounted their horses. Without further words, they turned to the gate. The three new soldiers hurried down the stairs to Skye and her group and quickly hustled them up across the platform to the door they had entered through.

Skye's stomach tightened, and she cast a glance back to Armstrong, who was waiting for the gate to open. When she noticed that Armstrong's men were also leading Midnight and Sunchaser away, she nearly had to bite her tongue to keep from crying out in protest. She had the premonition that she had been better off with him than these new men.

They passed through the door and entered a tunnel-like hall that appeared to go on forever. Electric lights dimly lit the walls, and their steps echoed as they walked at a rapid pace down the passageway. Skye noticed doors evenly spaced on either side and wondered if the place was full of apartments or meeting rooms.

Myst complained from behind, "Why do we have to go so fast?"

The guard nearest Skye snarled, "Shut up and keep up, otherwise we'll drag you."

Skye said evenly, "Leave her alone."

Not slowing down, the man looked back at her. "You shut up too, or you'll learn fast who is in charge here."

The guard on her other side mocked his companion, "You need to be careful with this one, Sergeant. The outer guard reported she is quite the demon fighter. She might eat you if you don't watch yourself."

The sergeant let out a rude laugh. "I'll give her something to eat all right. Hey little girl, you hungry for me?"

Without missing a step, Skye dropped her shoulder, moved to her right, and jammed her elbow up under his chin and smashed him into the wall, choking and clutching his throat. Before the other men could react, she kicked him in the groin so hard she felt the wall through his body. He let out a piercing scream and doubled over in agony. She looked down at him. "No, I am not hungry now. But if I ever desire some skunk, I'll come looking for you."

She turned to face the other guards. *I've done it this time, these guys are going to kill me.* She raised her tied hands in the best defensive posture she could manage.

To her surprise, the men just stood there looking at her, slowly raising their weapons as if they expected her to attack. The one closest to her, a young-looking fellow with blond hair and a peach fuzz mustache, had a look she could not decipher. His lips trembled. Behind her, the sergeant let out another groan.

The blond man smiled and then laughed out loud. Soon the other two guards joined him in what quickly turned into riotous laughter.

Myst whispered to Skye, "These are strange people. They laugh whenever you best one of them."

The humiliated sergeant moaned, "I'm going to kill her. I need a healer."

This brought more laughter from the other guards. The lieutenant who was in charge took a step toward Skye. She tensed and readied to defend herself. "He had no just reason to be rude to me," she said. "He only got what he deserved."

The lieutenant wiped tears from his eyes and nodded. He motioned for her to put her hands down. "If anyone ever deserved a thrashing, it is that one." He pointed to the man still on the ground. "It is not our custom to treat prisoners in his way. As you say, he perhaps deserved what you gave him, but I must warn you another attack on one of us will result in your being bound tightly about the hands and feet."

From behind the sergeant moaned, "I need a healer."

This brought more laughter from the lieutenant and his men. Skye was not sure what to take seriously, though the notion of being completely bound sufficiently convinced her that another attack on a guard would not be to her advantage.

The lieutenant pointed down the hall. "We must go, please hurry along with us. The representative of the Commons waits, and he is an impatient man."

Skye nodded and they started hurrying down the hall, leaving the sergeant behind. The lieutenant looked at her and said, "The outer guard sent word that you were a capable person. We truly had no idea what to expect."

CHAPTER TWENTY-FOUR

EQUAL

THE GUARDS HURRIED SKYE and her companions through the corridors, and they finally entered a great room with wood panels on the walls. The place looked like a courtroom Skye had seen in old videos, with a large, highly polished judicial bench looming in the front. There were a dozen empty wooden chairs on either side of it, and she imagined that was where a jury might sit.

Behind the bench, a bearded man with white hair wearing a white robe sat in such a way that only his shoulders and head were visible to her. The soldiers took her and the others to the front of the room, where they had to look up at the man. The lieutenant of the guards said, "This is Claudius, counsel to the chancellors of the House of Commons."

The guards backed away, leaving Skye, Eagle, and Myst standing before the bench. The man squinted down at them. "Why are you here?"

Skye swallowed hard. The truth may not be the best answer but it was what it was. "We are here because your soldiers brought us here."

Skye looked at the bearded man, wondering if he would think her flippant. His eyebrows narrowed and his jaw set tight.

"Your answer, while direct, is not a suitable response. You were caught trespassing on the land of the people of Evergreen, and I want to know where you are from, why you have come to our territory, and what your intentions are."

Skye had no desire to tell him anything that he wanted. She didn't want to reveal her village at the end of the lake; she certainly did not want to let him know they had been exposed to the pox and were searching for the vaccine. She summed up her thoughts, *I don't want to tell this man anything that is the truth.*

Her back muscles tightened as she looked up at him. "I am called Skye. My companions and I are free citizens of the world. Our travels take us to lands that we are unfamiliar with, and we came to be in your territory quite by accident. We are surprised we have been taken prisoner simply for being in your territory. We have no ill intentions and will be thankful if you will kindly let us on our way."

The representative of Evergreen stroked his beard. "You are vague and your answers are evasive. What is your business?"

Skye didn't care for the tone he had adopted. It was condescending and he clearly enjoyed wielding his power. She licked her lips and said, "I have certain items that I am able to trade for goods."

"I am told that when you were taken prisoner, you had naught but your backpacks and your clothes. What is it that you trade in?"

He raised a white eyebrow and pushed his cheek out with his tongue as if he was contemplating something delicious. Skye's mind raced, debating if now was the time to reveal one of her bargaining chips. Playing her limited hand at the wrong time could result in a bad outcome for her and her party. "Are you a person in authority to make deals?"

Claudius leaned forward and stared down at her. "I am a person who can have you locked up for as long as I choose. What do you have to deal with?"

Skye looked him square in the eyes. She noticed they were brown and ringed with wrinkled skin. She saw no pity in them; her hand was forced. "Your soldier has my pack. If he will bring it, I will show you."

Claudius nodded to the guard, and the man cautiously approached

Skye and held the pack out. It was a little difficult with her bound hands but she managed to reach into her pack. As she did, the other guards stepped closer to make sure she was not pulling out a weapon. Claudius waved them back. Skye's fingers found what she wanted. Before she withdrew her hand from the bag, she asked, "What do you have that I want?"

The representative didn't blink. "I have the power of your freedom. What do you have?"

Skye pulled her hand out of the pack and stepped to the bench. She extended her full fist and then dropped eight bullets on the desk in front of him. "I've got these. Bullets with brass cases."

She heard one of the soldiers gasp. Claudius's eyes widened and he asked, "More than these?"

"Lots more."

"And guns to go with them?"

She nodded, barely breathing, waiting for his reaction.

He picked up one of the bullets and examined it. "Perhaps there is a deal we can make. I will speak with our leaders, and we will discuss the matter. You may have something we are interested in. Until then, you will remain in our custody."

Skye tried not to let the disappointment she felt creep into her voice. "When will that be? We are in some hurry to reach our destination."

"Since you have refused to tell me your destination, I am inclined to believe you may be going to deal with our enemies. We will meet again at the convenience of the House of Commons. Perhaps two days from now."

She was horrified. "No, we cannot wait that long!"

"You can and you will. However, I will share your concern with the Commons."

He looked at the lieutenant and ordered, "Hold them in the tower until I return."

CHAPTER TWENTY-FIVE

ACCUSED

SKYE STARED OUT THE window of the room where she had been imprisoned. Many floors below was the courtyard she had seen when they rode in with the guards. The waterfall and stream that meandered through seemed to mock the harshness of those who dwelled here. She wanted desperately to get out, to get to the people of the mountain and the vaccine, but could think of no way out of her current predicament.

As the hours dragged on, she grew increasingly impatient. They had been delayed nearly two days now, and she felt time was wasting. She found staring out the window of the small quarters did no good to relieve her mind. She turned from the opening to talk with Myst and Eagle again. She wanted to review their story one more time to make sure they all had it straight.

Hard knuckles banged on the door, and the warning knock made her jump. The wooden door swung open. The guard she recognized as the sergeant she had fought with earlier stepped in. She had learned he was called Matt. She braced herself to fight.

The sergeant said, "You are summoned to the Commons. You have five minutes to collect your belongings and make yourselves presentable." He then exited and closed the door.

Skye's heart leaped. "Quickly, gather your things. Maybe they're going to let us go."

Myst shook her head. "I don't think so."

Four guards tied their hands and then led them from their room through a labyrinth of hallways. Skye noticed that Matt kept a distance from her and barely looked at her. They finally emerged into the courtyard. This time, the podium was occupied by twenty people dressed in flowing green robes, standing around an equal number of tall wooden chairs flanking the throne. The large chair on the left was occupied by a small man with cropped black hair. His face was pale, and the sleeves of his robe were adorned with stitched gold leaves.

In the other chair, a woman with long white hair sat upright. Her robe was a royal green, and she also had gold leaves stitched onto her sleeves. She had a flower wreath on her head that Skye thought looked like a crown.

The soldiers took them to the center of the stage, where they stopped and all faced the couple in the center seats. The pale man motioned to Claudius, who was standing to the side. Claudius spoke to Skye. They were only ten feet apart, and she was startled by how loudly he spoke and how his words resonated against the stone walls. "The House of Commons has summoned you before it to consider your fate. Our way is peaceful, and if we can have your word you will remain calm, you will not be shackled for the proceedings."

The idea of being bound in chains gave Skye a shiver. There was no reason not to be calm, though she knew in fact she was trembling inside. "Our way is peaceful. There is no need to apply restraints to us anymore than you have."

Claudius looked to the sergeant. "Take your places."

The guards quickly moved to the center chairs, and two each took stations on either side of the couple in the middle. At the same time, the other people on the podium took their seats in the wooden chairs.

Claudius spoke again, this time directing his comments to the man in the center chair. "If it pleases Your Honor, these are the trespassers of whom we spoke. They are here so you may interview them and decide in your wisdom the proper disposition of them. They claim to have goods to trade."

Skye was liking this situation less every moment and was pretty sure she did not like the idea of being dispositioned. Especially by someone who looked like he had set himself up to be king.

Claudius looked at Skye. "These are the chancellors of the House of Commons of Evergreen, their Honors, Picard and Sills." He moved aside and took a seat with the other robed members of the Commons.

Picard had dark eyebrows that stood out on his pasty white face. His nose was sharp and his cheeks drawn. He did not appear to care for the sunlight, or at least had not been in it much lately. Skye wondered if he might be sick. His eyes darted from her to Eagle, to Myst, and back to her. He was silent for what she deemed was a long time. *He's just trying to make me nervous and he is doing it.*

When he spoke, she had to strain to hear his words. His voice was low though confident. "Why are you in my lands?"

Skye answered clearly, "We are simply traveling to another destination. This land was between where we started from and where we wanted to go. We intended no harm and have no ill intent."

Picard kept his eyes on her. "Where are you from?"

This was a question she had known was inevitable and one she still did not want to answer. "We are free people from the north."

Picard's face didn't change. "North where?"

She didn't like lying yet could not think of an alternative. "Beyond the mountains and some miles past."

The chancellor let silence fill the courtyard again. "I have not heard of a civilized tribe or village being in that area, or anywhere for that matter. Forgive me if I appear too inquisitive. We are always curious about the people we find."

Skye responded, "We are also curious about who inhabits the lands. It has been some years since the end, and we are trying to learn about the world around us."

Sills snapped at her loudly, "For what purpose?"

Skye was taken aback by the implication raised in the woman's voice. She answered quickly with an even tone, "We hope to find those we can trade with."

Sills retorted, "Trade with or steal from?"

Skye's stomach knotted. The sun started to peek over the wall in front of her, causing her to squint into the shadows where the chancellors sat. "It is not our way to steal. We are simply on a peaceful journey."

Picard stared at her in a prying way. "Where did you get that necklace with the symbol of Evergreen about your neck?"

Skye swallowed hard, thinking of the jewel Trader Rick had given her. "It was a gift from one who has traded with your city."

Picard spoke flatly. "A gift of that value would come at a high price. Did you give him favors, or did you kill him for it?"

Skye took a step back. "No! It was a gift. He said it was for good luck."

Sills stood up. "You say you are on a peaceful journey yet you will not tell us where you are from, where you are going, or why you are here. I submit that you are spies looking to scout our lands and learn our weaknesses so you can attack later."

The accusation made her rock back on her heels. She had not anticipated this hostile a reception. "These charges are unfounded. We are but on a benign expedition to develop trading relationships with villages we do not know yet. We are in your territory quite by accident."

Sills took two steps toward her and hissed, "We are told you have murdered at least one man, you arrived here on stolen livestock, and you personally have savaged two of my soldiers. This is not the behavior of someone on a benign journey."

Skye's heart leaped in her chest. This was a confrontation she had not imagined, and for a moment she found herself speechless. *Jimmy-boy! Armstrong's troops must have found him. That's how they knew.* Sills took another step toward her; this time she pointed a long wrinkled finger directly at her. "What say you to these accusations? Do you have some way to defend yourself?"

Skye heard her own voice stammer, "I see no witness against me here. Is it your custom to accuse people without benefit of the accused knowing who has charged them?"

Sills's voice rose in volume and intensity. "You will not question me! I am the power here and you are but a trespasser in my land. You will answer my questions and I will determine what will happen next."

Skye took in a deep breath; something close to the truth would need to be said. Arriving on Midnight and Sunchaser, horses they did not own, could not be denied. Defending her position as to how they came to have the horses seemed logical. "I admit that a man died at my hand."

The chancellor nearly shouted, "Then you are guilty of murder!"

Skye shot back with a rising anger, "I said nothing of the sort. I acted in defense of my companions and myself. Our lives were threatened at gunpoint. It is only by good fortune I was able to defend myself, which unfortunately resulted in the end of one of our attackers. After that, his companion showed his true courage by running away. We took possession of the animals left behind so they would not be tied and abandoned in the wilderness, where they would be prey to wild creatures."

She struggled to pace her breathing and remain calm. Sills let a sideways grin cross her face. "So your motives are entirely altruistic." She quickly pointed to Eagle and asked, "And what do you say, young one? Does she speak the truth?"

Eagle took a half step back. He hesitated a moment and then blurted out, "Yes, what she says is what happened. It was dark and we were being chased and they scared us all."

Sills paused for a moment. Skye could feel the sun warming her face now as it edged over the wall of courtyard in front of her. *Uh oh, our being chased is not going be helpful.*

Sills clasped her hands together in front of her. "You were being chased, how interesting. By whom?"

Skye almost shouted before Eagle could speak, "A deadly gang! We had crossed the trail of a band of them, and they took to following us.

We thought we had lost them the day before but dared not stop as we feared they may catch up with us at anytime. We were in the woods when we ran into the men with the guns."

Sills's voice sounded skeptical. "Is that so?"

Eagle and Myst nodded vigorously.

Sills pursed her lips. "Your story is interesting though I find it somewhat convenient. The facts are similar with what I've been told, so I do not discount it outright. I am still unconvinced about your motives and wonder why you attacked my soldiers."

Myst spoke for the first time. "They were mean to us. Especially to her." She motioned to Skye. "They're lucky she didn't do worse to them."

Sills laughed. "Okay, young one. I may take that into consideration."

She turned her back on them and went to Picard, who was still sitting in his chair. Skye tried to ignore the tension in her back. This had not gone particularly well, and a knot of worry clenched her stomach.

The chancellors conferred with each other for several minutes. Skye could not make out the words they were saying. Sills's gestures were quite animated. Picard did not appear to say much, though he nodded his head constantly. Suddenly he shook his head twice and then pointed to Sills's vacant chair. She stepped back and then stalked to her seat. Once there, she cast a look at Skye that made her shiver.

Picard walked halfway from his chair to where Skye was standing. He looked slowly around the courtyard and the assembled people as if to be certain everyone was listening to him. "Skye, Eagle, and Myst, you have traveled from a place you will not disclose for a purpose you refuse to divulge. In Evergreen this is no crime and you will not be charged thusly."

A brief thought of relief flitted through Skye.

"On the more serious matter of killing and stealing, the facts are equally murky. Your version of events are consistent with things that have happened in the past but we have another account that contradicts yours. Therefore, we are compelled to investigate further. To do so will take several days; as a favor to you, we will allow you to work in the fields so you do not add more debt to that which you already owe us. In three days time, you will return here and we will pass final judgment on you."

Skye's throat tightened; three days was much too long. "This cannot be. We are in much need of continuing our journey without delay. And I do not know what debt you speak of; we owe nothing here."

Picard scrunched up his face. "If you are on an exploratory journey, this should not be a problem for you. As to the debt you owe, I think you are wrong. Have you not been in our company almost two days and been given ample food and drink?"

Skye let out a breath. "Against our will."

"Nevertheless, everyone is equal in Evergreen. That is the basic rule of our laws. You eat, you work. There are no exceptions. By allowing you to work in the next three days, we allow you to be able to pay off your stay in as few as six days total. I am not normally this generous."

Skye could not think of a civil thing to say. *Six days! We'll never get back in time, and that is if they don't find me guilty on this outlandish charge of murder.*

Beside her, Eagle said excitedly, "We can't wait six days, we have to get back with the …"

Skye cut him off. "Quiet!"

Picard took two steps toward them. "With the what?"

Skye said the first thing that came to her: "The maps to the new lands."

The chancellor raised his hand to her. "Silence." He stared at Eagle; Skye could see her friend's knees shaking. "With the what?"

Eagle murmured unconvincingly, looking at the ground, "Maps."

"Don't lie to me."

Eagle looked up and then pleadingly said, "The vaccine. We need to get the vaccine back home. Please let us go."

Those who heard him let out a collective gasp. Picard took three steps backwards. Skye's spirit plummeted in her chest.

Picard nearly yelled, "The pox! Your people have the pox! Are you trying to kill everybody?"

Skye stood tall. "You should really let us go. The sooner the better for you."

Picard stood with his mouth open; he sucked in a deep breath. "No, you are all too young. Your parents would have vaccinated you before the end or when you were born while there was still vaccine. This is another of your lies. This changes nothing. We will decide your fate in three days time."

Skye blurted in desperation, "What about our trade?"

Picard's lips turned up in a sneer. "I don't think you have enough of what we want to be worthwhile."

Skye stammered, "But you don't know …"

Picard shouted, "Enough!" And waved them away.

CHAPTER TWENTY-SIX

CAPTIVE

SKYE THREW HER HOE down in disgust. Dust filled her nose, and her parched mouth tasted of burnt rubber from the garbage pile that was smoldering across the strawberry field she was working in. *This is stupid. We have to get out of here.*

One of the guards at the edge of the field eyed her warily. She went past Eagle and Myst, who were also clearing weeds from the patch, and stopped at the water barrel. Filling the ladle, she poured water on her face and let it run down her neck. Even though it was lukewarm, it refreshed her. She filled her mouth and then spit it on the ground to try and cleanse the nasty taste that was in it. After that, she took a drink.

The guard nearest the cooler started to come toward her. He was slower this time. She'd been watching the guards all day and was starting to figure out which ones to look out for and which didn't really care. Since she and Eagle and Myst had left the House of Commons the previous afternoon, they had been put to work in the fields of Evergreen. This particular field, she had learned, was considered light work, and she was advised by the others in the bunkhouse they shared she should be glad to be there.

Surveying her surroundings for the umpteenth time did not reveal anything she had not already seen. The flat treeless terrain ran on for miles in each direction. Along with a dozen other workers, they had been delivered to work in a cart drawn by four swayback horses. These people had said they were free citizens of Evergreen, though they had made some small infraction of the rules of the Commons and were moved to the outer village to tend the fields. They had no idea when they would be allowed to rejoin the community and most did not seem too upset at that.

Though she could make little conversation, as the others did not seem to want to be seen near her, Skye gathered information as she could. She detected a clear undercurrent of fear. More than one person told of rumors of an approaching huge gang of Kanuks coming from the north. She frequently caught the guards looking to the mountain pass in that direction.

This only increased her desire to leave this place but she could not make out a viable escape route. If they ran, there would be no place to hide. She was confident she could outlast the guards around her; however, that still left two problems. Eagle could probably keep up but Myst would not have much of a chance. The bigger problem was the guards in the outer fields. Keeping raiders out of the fertile croplands was one of the biggest challenges Evergreen had to face. To do this, they had gone to considerable trouble to fortify the fields, and they were heavily patrolled at all times. Running away from one field would only run her into the next set of guards.

"Come on, back to work, the next break is in twenty minutes." This guard sounded more bored than anything. She surmised he had to say something, otherwise the other keepers would think he was not doing his job. She took another drink and deliberately walked back to her place in the field. They would have to make their escape under the cover of darkness. At the back of her mind, she knew time was running out for the people in Stehekin with the pox. She decided to make the escape tonight even though she wished she had more time to make a plan.

Dinner that night was just like breakfast and the midday meal had been: a mixture of fresh boiled vegetables with a piece of fruit. She had noted there were not many heavy people in Evergreen. The fullest ones she had seen had been the robed members of the House of Commons.

They had passed herds of cows and she had seen numerous chickens and pigs. However, none of them had so far shown up on their plates.

After the evening meal, she gathered Myst and Eagle in a quiet corner of the bunkhouse. The other occupants sat near the fireplace and played assorted games on boards or with cards. They had been invited to join and had politely refused. Myst sat on her bed, looking sleepy. Eagle sat beside her, his head hanging low. Skye sat on her bed, facing her two friends.

"I need your help," she said.

Eagle lifted his head and Myst yawned. Eagle said, "Why my help? It seems like everything I do or say is wrong."

Skye was grateful for the opening. "That is not true. You have been a tremendous help to us all along. I myself have made some poor judgments, and these have caused grief for us all. I have also been unfair to you in some instances and can only ask for your forgiveness."

Eagle cocked his head. "Do you mean you won't treat me like a child anymore?"

She looked directly at him. "It was never my intention to do so, though if that is how you feel, then that is how I must have been perceived. In answer to your question, I will treat you as an equal, as you deserve. I will consult you on things that matter to us; however, I do retain command of our group and my judgments are final. Is this okay with you?"

Eagle nodded. "I guess I have said and done things that were not helpful or polite. I will do my best to earn and keep your respect from here on. I agree to this arrangement."

Skye looked to Myst. "This okay with you?"

Myst let out a deep breath. "It's about time you two stopped fighting. Let's get out of here."

Skye glanced around the bunkhouse to make sure no one was paying attention to them. "I'm glad that is settled. I am afraid we will not get a favorable judgment from Picard or Sills in the House of Commons. They do not strike me as either fair or honest."

Eagle nodded. "I agree, this is a regular animal farm. It must be nice to be a pig."

Myst laughed lightly. "I didn't think you were that smart."

Eagle wrinkled his brow. "Thanks for the compliment, I think."

Myst just smiled and said, "You are welcome. I think Skye is right. I don't trust these people."

The muscles in Skye's neck tightened. "All the more reason for us to get out of here. Escaping will be a difficult task to execute. There are guards and soldiers seemingly every place. Getting away in the daylight will be impossible so we will have to leave in the darkness.

"I have noticed that the guards here are not very attentive and that we are allowed easy access to the yard around the bunkhouse and the outer facilities. It should be an easy matter to get out. That is when the problems will start. We will have to make our way in stealth all the way to the forest before daylight breaks. It is a long distance to cover on foot. You must each get some sleep as soon as possible. I will wake you at midnight and we will leave. Prepare your things right away."

She was interrupted when the main door banged open and four guards came in, their weapons rattling. "Where are the three outsiders? Chancellor Sills has summoned them."

Skye and her companions scarcely had time to be certain they had gathered all their belongings before they were manhandled out the door and put on large, snorting warhorses. These were not the kind of farm animals she had seen before; these were tall beasts with muscles and spirit, the kind the soldiers of the outer guard had ridden.

This time Myst was given her own mount, which made Skye a little nervous. The girl was not very large, and Skye did not recall Myst ever doing a lot of riding at home. The guards did not bother to tie them and barked orders at them in a tone that suggested they would have no tolerance for any missteps.

The lead rider kicked his horse into a gallop, and Skye's animal bolted after him. The saddle was smooth against her legs, though the stirrups did not match her height. She grasped the reins and held on with her knees as they raced through the night. A slight rain started to fall, and a cool wind blew into her face. She looked around in the dark and could make out Myst hanging on tightly due to the furious pace.

Myst had her hands on either side of the horse's neck as if she were talking with it. Eagle rode behind her, and the three guards from the bunkhouse pressed close behind. Squinting into the darkness, Skye made out another half dozen riders behind them. This was an escort that did not plan to let them get away. Skye wished she could talk to Myst, to see what she felt. As for herself, Skye thought, *This just gets uglier and uglier.*

They rode at full speed toward the lights of the city. On their approach, the great city gates opened; they passed into the inner walls and clattered down the streets and into the courtyard of the House of Commons. The horses had barely stopped when Skye was hoisted off the panting animal by a giant-sized soldier and deposited on the ground. Eagle and Myst were similarly put down with her. On the podium, she could make out Picard and Sills in their chairs, now covered by a great awning that kept the rain off the entire podium area.

The soldiers took the horses and withdrew, leaving four of their number behind. The members of the Commons again flanked the center stage, sitting still in their chairs.

High torches that cast a flickering light over the whole scene surrounded the podium. She was curious why they would use firelight when electricity was in ample supply.

Skye drew her hood over her head to keep the drizzle off her face. She could feel Myst standing close at hand and sensed Eagle was directly beside the girl. Her heart was still pounding from the ride, and she focused on catching her breath.

Claudius walked up the center of the stage toward them, light bouncing off his pale skin. He was dressed as he had been the day before, which Skye thought seemed to have been a long time ago. She could not read the language of his face, though his shoulders were squared and imperious. He strode to the edge of the podium and stared down at her. She kept her eyes lowered, caring to neither look up at him nor view the bottom of his robe and sandals, which were at her eye level.

He spoke from above with a loud voice, clearly intended for the ears of all present. "The one called Skye, you offered to make a deal. Is that still your intention?"

The question caught her off balance. She had heard nothing about her offer since it had been made and had come to think it had been in vain. She answered in a measured tone, loud enough for only him to hear. "It is true I made an offer of a trade. Given the right bargain, it is still open."

"You have precious little to bargain with. What makes you think you have any choice for what we are willing to trade?"

Skye kept the same tone. "You do not know how much or how little I have. Your ignorance detracts from your ability to make a bargain with me."

Claudius raised his voice. "Do not be impudent with me. Your freedom is at stake."

She added a note of defiance to her voice. "As is the security of Evergreen."

Claudius was getting agitated and stepped toward her. For a moment, she thought he might decide to leave the podium and strike her. She crossed her arms in front of her chest and patted the silver dagger she had managed to retain in its sheath under her leather vest. The guards had never brought themselves to search her very closely.

She hoped the rumors she had heard in the fields were true, saying, "A large gang of Kanuks is in the outlands, and they have begun to challenge the outer lands of the village. These are people like you have never seen before, and some of them are better armed than your troops. What I have will help to make you equal."

Claudius waved his hand. "Rubbish! Ignorant street talk."

"As you say. Now I must ask, why did you bring us here? It is wet and cold and we need to prepare for tomorrow's work so we can earn our freedom."

She raised her eyes just enough to see that while they were talking,

Sills and Picard had slipped up close to Claudius, and she surmised they had heard a fair amount of the conversation.

Behind Sills, Skye saw one man leaning on a cane. His face was a ghastly white, and a clumpy stubble beard punctuated his drawn features. Her heart jumped as she recognized Jimmy-boy. Sills spoke to her with ill-concealed contempt. "Is that what you want, to go back to the fields? You will be fortunate if you live long enough to see them again."

Skye's thoughts swirled; the change in tracks was hard to follow. First they were making a deal, now she was being threatened. Her fear at seeing Jimmy-boy started to turn to burning anger. "I require to know who is in charge here? Am I dealing with Chancellor Picard or this woman, who has behind her a pirate and a murderer?"

Sills said, "You are the one here accused of murder and should best watch your tongue, lest it be separated from you." She looked to the man behind her and spoke to the man in the shadow. "Is this the band of cutthroats that surprised your partner, killed him without regard, and stole your horses?"

His voice answered, "Yup'em, I'm guessing them's the ones alright I thinks."

Myst whispered to Skye, "That's the guy that got away, the friend of the one that tried to kill us."

Skye nodded, her chest tightening. *This looks bad. Better go on offense.*

"Who are we accused by? A brigand and a dullard! How dare you use this vermin to accuse us. Your borders are in danger, and I have the means to arm twenty-five of your men with powerful weapons that may save your pathetic village. If you trouble me further, you may have the satisfaction of disposing of me, but you will never find my trade, and my people will find this rotting excuse for civilization and make a hole in the ground out of it."

Sills shouted, "You cannot make empty threats on us! I do not accept it."

Eagle stepped to the front. "You must listen to her. My people prefer to be secluded but no one has attacked us without paying a high price." He pointed to Jimmy-boy and said, "Look what happened to him when he crossed us."

All eyes turned to the man leaning on the cane. Skye tried not let her knees shake visibly while they waited for a response. Her bluff was thin, and she felt the outcome would weigh heavily on the words of a man whose companion she had been forced to kill.

Jimmy-boy growled from behind, "Them are evil ones. They got guns and bullets from what I hear. With the Kanuks coming down the river, we gonna need all them guns we can get. I sez we take her guns and make them stay and help us."

Skye raised her voice. "No deal. We trade for freedom only."

Sills held her hand up. "Agreed, no deal." She turned to the guards. "Take them to the tower. The old one will be put in a box and buried in two days time, and the other two will be remanded to the fields for life."

Skye's breath left her. *A death sentence. This can't be.*

Two guards approached her warily. As they reached her, the sound of hoofs galloping through the gates drew everyone's attention. Armstrong and several of his men drew up in front of the podium. He addressed Picard in a hurried voice. "Chancellor, I bring news of an attack on the outer village. I am told a gang of foreigners has breached the outer defense. They have weapons more powerful than ours, and even though our men fight bravely, they are being overwhelmed. We must call a retreat into the walled city at once."

Picard went pale, the color draining out of his face. "When did this happen?"

"It happens as I speak. A wounded messenger made it to me just as I was riding out of town."

Picard straightened up and squared his shoulders. He spoke to one of the guards on the podium. "Light the warning fires and sound the alarm." The guard immediately ran to the door.

Picard looked at Armstrong and pointed to Skye. "Take this one and she will lead you to a cache of weapons that may be our salvation. We will keep the other two here to make sure she cooperates."

Skye glared at him. "What of my sentence?"

Picard smiled. "If you perform well, it will be commuted."

Skye flattened her tone. "I do not go without my companions."

Picard made a slashing motion with his hand. "Enough of you. You will go now or in the next instant I will kill one of your friends in front of your eyes."

Before she could speak, Armstrong reached down from his horse and swept her on to his mount in front of him. She was so startled, she could not get a word out. She heard his voice shout, "Get them." Then he kicked the horse into a gallop.

Looking over her shoulder, she saw Hicks snatch Eagle up into his saddle. Another rider swung Myst up into his saddle, and in seconds they were all out the courtyard doors, charging into the night.

They rode for twenty minutes before Skye could think of a way to ask her questions. At first, she was half in shock at being picked up. As they passed further into the outer fields, a sense of relief crept into her. This was clearly a rescue and not a kidnapping. She allowed herself to lean back against Armstrong's warm chest. He wrapped an arm around her to hold her steady. For the first time in days, she felt just the slightest hint of being secure.

He slowed his horse to a walk. A light rain started but she tried to ignore it. It was cold on her arms and face. The scent of the man who held her was pleasant in a new sort of way. She turned her head to speak and found her lips almost on his. "Why are you doing this? Will this not put you in peril?"

Armstrong dropped his eyes to meet hers. "You were in great danger, as is Evergreen. The politicians play silly games while the survival of our city is at stake. They would rather be self-important in front of each other by making an example of you instead of taking advantage of what you have to offer."

She could not figure out how Armstrong knew so much since

he had not been in the courtyard. "You have spies in the House of Commons?"

He looked far away into the night ahead of them. "Survival depends on knowledge of your surroundings."

She turned around, looking forward again, a twinge of disappointment unaccountably crossing her chest. "What are your intentions for me and my companions?"

Armstrong waited a moment to answer. "It would suit me if you were to stay here and join arms with us. If you would take a place by my side and perhaps consider spending more time in my company, it would be pleasing."

Skye's pulse quickened, and her cheeks started to warm in spite of the cold rain.

He continued, "It is unfortunate that I know this is not possible. You have your mission to finish, and I must stand in battle against invaders from the north, though I still need your help."

At the words "this is not possible," the air left her. Deflated, she knew he was right. She inhaled deeply and said, "I am willing to make the deal I offered Picard. I will give guns to arm twenty-five in exchange for our freedom, the horses we came on, our kits, and some food."

His arm squeezed around her just a little tighter. "I would offer nothing less."

Dawn was breaking steel gray when she returned to Armstrong's company, which was waiting near the edge of the outer fields of Evergreen. They had made a small cooking fire and she could smell bacon frying as she drew near. It made her mouth water.

She approached with a grinding nag of doubt. As part of the bargain, Eagle and Myst had gone with her to retrieve the goods, but she felt it best to leave them hidden in the forest when she made her delivery. If the guard turned on her, she would have a hard time escaping them. That would leave Eagle and Myst to make their way home alone through the wilderness. It would be the end of the journey.

She stretched her neck. She had made her choice to trust Armstrong, and she urged Midnight on.

Corporal Hicks was the first to greet her. "Yo, Skye, I'm happy to see you arrive. We are grateful for your trade. There was some said you wouldn't return, but I knew you would."

She waved to the corporal. "Thanks for your faith, Hicks. Thanks for grabbing Eagle. I know the captain thinks you are a good man, as do I."

Armstrong got up from his place by the fire and approached her. In the morning light, he stood tall, his shoulders broad and his hair tucked neatly under his uniform hat. She looked for a sign of something in his face though she was not sure what. He raised a hand to her in greeting. "You made good time, I am pleased. That will help us get to the fight sooner."

She dismounted and pulled two large bags off Midnight that fell heavily to the ground. "As I promised, fine weapons to arm twenty-five, and ammunition to sustain them if they aim true." She opened one bag and withdrew a hinged black box as long as her forearm. Other solders gathered around to see what she had brought.

She opened the top of the box and showed the contents: five automatic 9 mm pistols, each secured in its own place. She reached in and drew one out. "This is how you operate it." She pulled back the slide, inserted a magazine she had already loaded, and then quickly turned and shot nine pinecones off a tree fifty feet away.

The sound of the shots made the men step back, and the smoke from the gun turned the air around her blue. Armstrong picked up one of the spent brass cartridges. "These we can use again. This is good. We now have a chance against the Kanuks." He looked to Skye and said, "You have kept your part of the bargain; you are free to go."

She peered into his eyes. "For this, I thank you." A thought of guilt crossed her. She knew she should have trusted him. "Here is a special gift for you." She reached into the bag again and withdrew a rifle with a long barrel and a telescopic sight mounted on it. "With this, may you keep your enemies at a distance."

Armstrong took the weapon in admiration. "I will put it to good use." He looked into her eyes. "I look forward to the day when we may meet again."

"I will look forward to that day as well." She resisted the temptation to hug the captain and forced her eyes away. She put the pistol back in the box and mounted Midnight. She was readying to leave when Hicks came through the crowd with two fine horses in tow.

"Warrior Skye, you a have long way to go and I'm guessing a heavy load. Take these so each of you will have a ride and a pack animal as well. The Cap'n says it's okay."

Armstrong rode near and spoke softly. "I hear the men of the mountains are honorable, but wary of strangers. We may need help to repel the invaders from the north. If the people of the mountain are willing to consider giving us aid, we may make a good alliance. Tell them Armstrong, captain of the Outriders of Evergreen, sends them greetings."

She caught Armstrong's eye, and he nodded slightly. "It is four days' hard ride to New Leavenworth, and there are many dangerous men and creatures between here and there. Follow the river and stay off the roads for two days. On the third day, turn up the mountains and head to the spires. You will know them when you see them. Good luck to you."

She nodded to him. "And luck to you."

She took the reins of the new animals from Hicks. Kissing her fingertips, she touched them to his forehead. "You must take care of our captain." She reached into her cloak and withdrew the dagger she carried under her vest. "Take this and hope you never need it. If you do, use it well."

Hicks took the blade, his mouth falling open. She nudged Midnight and headed for her rendezvous with Eagle and Myst.

CHAPTER TWENTY-SEVEN

THE RIVER

LONG SHADOWS FROM THE trees cast themselves on the swirling water of the river called the Columbia. Over the tips of the shadows, the sun's light reflected white on the blue water. The temperature was oppressive, and Skye longed to tie the horses and dive into the cold water. She knew better though.

There was no telling what kinds of poisons still washed from the contaminated mountains into the water. She had seen no signs of life in it for the last day and a half and could only imagine that whatever could have survived in it would be loathsome and dangerous.

The trail they were on widened, and Myst brought her horse, which she called Phoenix, up beside Midnight. "You're troubled."

Skye stroked Midnight's neck; the mare was hot and sweat matted her hair. "Yes."

They continued in silence for a few moments. Myst spoke again. "Are you going to share or should we play guessing games?"

Skye looked at the young girl and half laughed. Myst's long dark hair fell almost to her waist. She rode with a sleeveless tunic under her Kevlar vest and wore khaki shorts, but kept her skin shaded from the sun with her dark cloak. She sat with admirable posture on Phoenix, who seemed a little big for such a small passenger. She had black boots that went halfway up her calves, and she loosely gripped her knees against the horse.

What made Skye smile was the outlandish sunglasses the girl wore. They had thin silver plastic frames and mirrored lenses that covered half her face so Skye could see herself looking back at herself. Though they all wore sunglasses left over from before the end, Myst's were clearly the most distinctive. Skye recalled when Myst had first showed them off to her years ago. They were much too big for her then, and the girl had put them away until this last spring. Wanting to lighten things up, she said, "Tell me again where you got those?"

Myst self-consciously adjusted the glasses. "They were my uncle's. Do they look funny?"

Skye shook her head. "No dear, you look marvelous."

"Don't patronize, it isn't becoming."

Skye tried to convince her. "I would not deceive about something like that. I think they look great. You look like a movie star." She called to Eagle, who rode a few yards in front of them, leading the pack horse, "Hey Eagle, don't you think Myst looks great in these shades?"

Eagle turned around and raised an eyebrow. "She looks very mysterious, kind of like the mysterious person that she is." Then he turned to the front, apparently not really interested in the subject.

Myst touched her glasses again. "I think I might like that. Now tell me what troubles you."

Skye shrugged. "What is not to trouble? Our progress is slow, we have been on this journey six days now and are still two days from our goal, if we are lucky. Even if the mountain people have vaccine and will share it, we still must return home with it before fourteen days have gone. That is when people in the village, including my mother, will start to die."

Myst nudged Phoenix closer. "We do not know that fourteen days is the limit. You only got that from what the trader said."

Skye wiped some perspiration from her forehead. "It is hot here. Perhaps you are right, though that is a chance we cannot take. I fear the bad luck that has plagued us will be the undoing of our village."

Myst shook her head. "No, you are wrong. Our luck has been wonderful."

"What?"

"Our luck has been wonderful," Myst said. "We escaped the pirates on the lake, found horses when we landed, made allies with the guard of Evergreen, and were provisioned by them too. You have made great good luck for us, Skye, and as long as you keep making our luck, then we will succeed."

Skye thought, *I'm glad somebody's glass is half full, mine is about three-quarters empty.* Then she said to Myst, "It is kind of you to say such things. We would not have gotten this far were it not for you and Eagle. We are a good team together."

Myst smiled. "It's like that guy on the old vid said, 'We're marvelous, simply marvy.'"

Skye smiled and said, "Just don't let Eagle hear you say that." Skye sat a little straighter. She was comforted somewhat by Myst's confidence. They rode on into the deepening gloom of a canyon as afternoon drifted toward evening. The water near the shore of the river moved slowly here, and the air was still. There was an old road on the top of the cliffs that grew above them, but Skye had followed Armstrong's advice and stayed off of it. Looking at the steep walls that now towered above them, she wondered if she had made the right choice.

Skye brought Midnight abreast of Sunchaser as they followed a turn in the jagged canyon wall. Midnight stopped abruptly, her ears going forward. Skye's chest tightened as she saw two black bear cubs less than ten yards in front of them. She heard the alarm in Eagle's voice as he said, "Uh oh. Where's the mother?"

Before she could answer, an adult bear rose on its hind legs to the left of Eagle only a few yards away and let out an angry roar. The creature was taller than the horse, and Sunchaser rose onto her back legs, kicking in the direction of the bear with her front hooves and sending Eagle sprawling to the ground. Midnight tried to bolt but Skye fought to keep her in place. Sunchaser and the pack horse ran the opposite direction from the bear, leaving Eagle helpless on the ground.

Skye shouted, "Back!" at the top her lungs to scare the beast but the animal charged anyway.

Midnight bucked three times to get away from the bear, and it was all Skye could do to stay on her mount. She could hear Myst screaming to scare the bear, which was now on top of Eagle. She saw him roll into a ball and cover his head with his hands while she brought Midnight under control fifteen yards away and reached for her pistol.

Myst fired shots into the air, and the bear looked at her with what seemed like curiosity and roared again. Skye finally got her pistol out and fired four rounds into the air. The bear was unmoved and started to paw at the motionless Eagle.

Cold fingers of fear gripped Skye as she made the choice that she was going to have to kill the beast to save Eagle. She feared that if she only wounded it with the pistol, it would intensify its attack on the boy, so she holstered the pistol, dismounted so she would have a steady aim, and drew her rifle from its scabbard.

As she hit the ground, the bear left Eagle and started to charge her. Before she raised her rifle, she heard Myst fire four shots and saw the animal stagger. Skye quickly took careful aim to make sure she missed Eagle. The animal kept charging, and its head filled her sights. Holding her breath, she fired five quick rounds at the bear. She took two steps back as the animal tumbled to a stop almost at her feet.

The next morning, dawn crept through the camp smoke that filtered into the sky through the leaves. The stream made a pleasant sound as it ran down from the mountains to the river, which was some miles away. After the battle with the bear, they had found a secluded clear space at the base of the mountains and made camp to regroup.

Skye moved beside Myst, who had been watching over Eagle all night. Skye placed her hand on his forehead. It was still warm. "You made some pretty good luck yesterday."

Myst nodded. "Imagine that, me making luck and it turns out kind of good."

Skye kneeled by Eagle. "Has there been any change?"

Myst yawned. "He mumbled a few things during the night, but nothing I could make out." She stroked his head. "He is still in there, it is hard to know how badly he is hurt."

Skye moistened a cloth from the bowl by his side and placed it over his brow. "Perhaps we should not have moved so far from the beach. The journey may have made things worse. It would be something if he was bleeding more but I think his bad injuries are on the inside, and I have no knowledge of such things."

Myst touched her arm. "We had no choice, we could not stay anyplace near the river with such monsters about. There were more than the one, this I know. We have a good shelter here. The trees offer shade in the day and our tarps are hidden and secure from the rain. We can stay here undetected for a long time unless someone stumbles onto us."

Skye stood and took a deep breath. "You are right. We can be safe here. However, I cannot stay. I must press on to the mountain people. Perhaps they will offer aid. If they don't, I will return for you in a few days' time." She braced herself for an argument.

Myst stood also. "It is as I thought. It is agreed that you must go. I have loaded supplies and some trading samples onto Midnight. She is ready once you load your personals. I hope you will return soon."

Skye was not sure what to say. A feeling of warmth toward her companion filled her chest, and a tear made its way to her eye. "Thank you." As an afterthought she added, "If I am not back in five days' time ..."

Myst pursed her lips. "If you are not back in five days' time, we will assume the mountain people are not our friends and make our way home. We have good horses and are well supplied and know how to live off the land. The two of us should be able to travel in stealth."

Or the one of you, if only one is still alive. Skye tried to push that thought from her head.

Skye checked her gear and fingered the new dagger she had taken from her pack, strapping it under her vest; she wondered what would become of Hicks and his captain. She had a quick breakfast, kissed

Eagle on the cheek, hugged Myst, and then took Midnight by the reins.

With care she picked her way out of the hidden camp with Midnight close behind her. She took a look back and was pleased she could see no signs that anything other than poplar trees and sage bushes were against the mountainside by the stream.

She mounted Midnight and leaned to whisper in her ear, "I will be demanding and I am sorry. We must be swift, I need all you have." Before she even sat back, Midnight burst into a gallop, and they swept up a sun-filled hillside into the new day.

PART THREE

CHAPTER TWENTY-EIGHT

A NEW KID IN TOWN

COLONEL SEAN MOORE CLAPPED his gloved hands together to ward off the chill. An early cold front had unexpectedly swept into the mountains during the afternoon, dropping the temperature to near midwinter levels. There was only a dusting of snow so far, and he hoped there would not be an accumulation of any sort. There were still patrols in the eastern valleys, and they would have a difficult time returning if the pass was deep with fresh snow.

He drew in a cold breath, enjoying the freshness of the mountain air. Stamping his feet to increase his circulation, he wondered if he had been overzealous in taking this post. By his rank, he had no business being here; this was a job typically performed by any of the soldiers in the fort. On the other hand, by taking the duty now and again, he demonstrated that he was willing to do all required jobs, and the message was not lost on his officers or men.

It also gave him a chance to get out of the fort and get away from making decisions all day long. Being commander of New Leavenworth was taxing him, and now that more civilians were coming, some of the rabble-rousers were talking about starting a representative government. As if he had time for that distraction. It was hard enough just keeping the place safe from the gangs and mutants that came up the mountains to try and steal food and kidnap women without having to deal with subversion from within.

His post was perched above the east valley pass that eventually wound up to the gates of the fort. This was the only approach to the fort from the east, and in his position he was below the skyline and could observe the pass virtually unseen. *Damn, it's cold.*

He lifted his binoculars to study the valley floor again. The mountains swept open and down to the east so that someone approaching from that direction would be funneled into the small open space that led up to the start of a thick tree line. The open space was half a mile across and two miles long and walled in by steep rock slopes on either side. An old blacktop road went down the center of it, though it was buckled and parts were washed out.

Visibility was fair, and he was startled to see a rider burst from the trees to the east and race full speed into the valley. The horse looked strong and the rider wore a hooded cloak. He swallowed hard. He had seen this before. The rider was only a few strides into the opening when three more riders came out of the forest, hot on the tail of the cloaked figure.

The colonel looked to the west end of the valley. He scanned the narrow opening with his binoculars. It only took him a moment to see the two creatures lurking near the narrow opening. He felt a pang of sorrow for the poor bastard in the cloak. He was being driven into a trap from which the colonel had never seen anyone escape.

Skye pressed her head down almost to Midnight's neck. She glanced behind and saw the three men were not gaining on her. The shock of their sudden appearance had worn off, and now she needed to make a plan. Racing into the valley had been her first and only option. The men had surprised her when they came out of the trees and demanded she dismount and surrender to them. By their ragged look, she took them for a band of thieves and gave no thought to giving into them. Instead she charged Midnight into the valley to buy herself time to think.

Now she had that time and knew there was not much. *This is too easy. They could have surrounded me and taken me down without this chase.* She heard a loud POP and heard a bullet whiz by her ear. A crimson stripe tore open on Midnight's neck as the shot grazed the mount. Skye looked ahead to the trees near the far end of the open space. Something moved. *Uh oh. Figures to be a trap.*

Behind her a voice yelled, "Don't kill her; I want to know if she knows what the hell she's doing out here. Maybe she's got something we want. Wee ha!"

Another voice called, "I get to ask her first. Come on, horse, run faster, damn it!"

A cold tremor went though Skye's body. She wrapped her fingers around her pistol. *Time to get offensive.*

Another shot was fired from behind. "Hey girl, better stop before you make us mad." This was followed by a wheezy laugh that made Skye's lips curl in disgust. *Now is the moment.*

Skye pulled her pistol out and then yanked sharply on Midnight's reins; the animal stopped so abruptly she almost went over its head. She spun around to face the three attackers, who were so shocked they nearly collided with her and went several yards past her before they could stop. Skye wheeled Midnight around to face them and took aim at the one closest to her, putting a bullet in his chest. The attacker was blown off the back of his horse and hit the ground with a groan.

Skye didn't watch the impact. The next closest guy's horse reared up and kicked his front legs in the air, sending the man flat on his back to the ground. The third attacker fought to get his spooked horse under control while he attempted to take aim at Skye with a rifle. She leveled her pistol and put two shots into his shoulder and neck. He slammed into the ground with blood gurgling through his teeth.

The guy who had been thrown from his mount staggered to his feet and jumped for Skye's foot. For his trouble, he took a heel in the face that sent him staggering back. Skye fired again and the man collapsed in a heap on the ground. Skye moved the horse a few yards away and drew to a halt.

Midnight stood motionless in the clearing as Skye swept her pistol from each motionless form on the ground to the next, watching to make sure they would not get up. She took a deep breath and realized her hand was trembling. She patted Midnight on the neck, relieved to see that the bullet wound looked to be superficial. She gave a thought to collecting the extra horses but decided to forget about it because there might be others around.

Oh no! There are others, you idiot! Just as she turned to look behind her, she was shocked when a huge arm wrapped around her waist and yanked her off of Midnight. She hit the ground heavily on her shoulder, the impact jarring the pistol from her hand. She rolled to her back and tried to stifle her terror as she looked into the wild eyes of an enormous, seven-foot-tall man with matted hair and tattered clothes. His face was streaked with dirt, his nose was crooked as if it had been broken and never mended, and he had an overwhelming stench.

She turned and saw another man holding a long pole that was attached to a chain that wrapped around the monster's neck; he looked at her from behind the beast. He had a shaggy beard and sunken eyes that were squinting in malice. He spoke a command to the giant: "Kill him. Kill that man that shot up the partners. Killed 'em all he did. Do what I sez."

The giant didn't move. The little man rapidly turned a crank on the side of the pole and the giant grabbed the chain around his neck and howled in pain. "Do what I sez or I'll do it again. Kill him, I sez!" The huge one looked to the man as if he wanted to attack him. The man pointed the pole at the giant and held his hand on the crank. "Do what I sez." He gave the crank a half turn, and the big one shuddered in pain. Then he turned his eyes to Skye and took a step toward her.

Skye rolled to her left and gained her feet just as the beast got to her. She took two quick steps and reached for her gun. Just as she grabbed it, the giant snagged the back of her cloak. She tried to move away and found she was no match for his strength. With her left hand, she released the clasp on the cloak and spun out of it, falling back to the ground.

The sick-looking man holding the chain cried out, "Looky, it's a girl, a blondie. Don't matter, kill her, do what I sez."

Skye was too busy to see it, though she heard the huge one scream in pain and guessed the weasel with the crank had notched up his torment of the creature. She tried to get back on her feet, and the giant pushed her hard in the back. Her face slammed into the grass and snow, and instinctively she rolled to her right, barely avoiding a crushing stomp to the head by the giant's foot.

His calloused bare foot was right in front of her nose and emitted a foul smell that turned her stomach. She pointed the pistol up at the man that loomed over her. She pulled the trigger even as the beast kicked at her sideways, almost lifting her off the ground. She let out a moan as the wind rushed out of her lungs. The sound of the shot startled the giant, and he backed off a step. She crawled on her hands and knees, desperate to put distance between herself and the creature.

Midnight charged the beast and hit it with her shoulder. Skye watched in horror as the giant hit the horse on the side of the head with a huge fist. Midnight staggered off in a daze.

Skye scrambled to her feet and turned to find the huge one almost on top of her. She fired a wild shot, hoping to at least scare him again. This time, the bullet went wide, and she heard a scream as the little man with the crank fell to the ground, clutching his shoulder. The giant knocked her across the shoulder, spinning her back to the ground, the pistol flying from her grasp once more.

She rolled over once, knowing the monster would soon be on top of her. She pulled her dagger from her vest, hoping to get one plunge to the giant's throat when it closed on her. When she stopped on her back, she was startled to see the huge one standing in front of her with a curious look. Behind him, the little man whined in pain.

"She shot me. The girl shot me. Kill her. Do what I sez! Do what I sez!"

The giant slowly turned from Skye to the little man, who lay on the ground several feet from the pole with the crank. He took a small step toward his tormentor. The man's eyes went wide with fright. He shouted, "Get back, I sez! Get away, I sez!"

The giant took another step closer, and the pitch in the man's voice raised as his terror engulfed him. He started to crawl for the metal pole with the crank on it, and the giant moved with amazing speed, bounding to the pole in a few steps and snatching it from the ground. The man rose to his knees and tried to sound firm. The quaking in his voice was almost pitiful. "Now Dummy, you gives that to me, your ole buddy Dan. Give it to me, I sez. I sez."

Skye slowly got to her feet as the two antagonists faced each other. She eased toward the pistol. At the same time, the giant moved closer to Dan, who held his hands out for the beast to give him the pole. "Come on Dummy, give me the grinder, I sez. You always do as I sez. Now do it, I sez!"

The giant stopped just short of Dan, whose shaking hands revealed his fear. In a quick move, the huge one jabbed the pole into Dan's stomach, doubling him over in pain. Then he raised the pole over his head, screamed a hideous cry, and brought the pole down across the man's back, driving him to the ground.

The giant went into a frenzy, beating Dan again and again, jumping and screaming in rage until his body was beaten to a bloody mess. Skye took advantage of the distraction, picked up her pistol, and started slowly backing up toward Midnight. The giant finally wore himself out and stopped pounding the body. It dropped the pole, raised its fists into the air, and let out a wailing sound as loud as any Skye had ever heard come from a living being.

Then the giant's dark eyes fell on Skye. Even though he was twenty yards away, a chill ran through her that caused her knees to almost buckle. She tightened her grip on the pistol and wished it were a higher caliber. She also wished she could remember how many rounds were left.

The creature moved toward her with slow steps. The pole on the end of the chain dragged behind him. His hair was missing in clumps, and though he had a large frame, he was thin to the point of emaciation.

She could see cuts and scrapes all over his exposed arms, and there were bloodstains on his ragged shirt and pants. Overall, she thought he was a wretched-looking thing. Skye stared as she backed up in the general direction of Midnight. The horse was standing motionless thirty yards from her, and she hoped to get to it and secure a more powerful weapon.

The giant took three quick steps and closed the gap by almost half. She raised the pistol and pointed it at his face. "Stop, I sez!" She hoped "I sez" was the command phrase, and it couldn't hurt to try, even though it had not worked all that well for the weasel as of late.

To her surprise, the giant stopped and stared at her. He let out a low moan and held his hands up to her, palms out. After a pause, apparently satisfied she was not going to shoot him outright, he placed his hands on the chain around his neck and tugged at it, moaning again. He opened his mouth and winced; she saw he was nearly toothless and only had the stub of a tongue.

For the first time, she saw the bloody red ring around his throat that the chain had caused. The skin was raw and dotted with dried blood. He pulled the chain away from his neck as far as he could, which was only a couple of his finger's widths, and pointed at it.

"What are trying to tell me, big guy? That chain is hurting you, I can see that. What do you want?" *This poor guy is not all there in the head.* It occurred to her that talking to a giant, one that moments ago had nearly killed her, was one of the more curious things she had ever done.

The giant took a slow step toward her and held part of the chain in his thick fingers. Then she saw it. It was the clasp to the chain, a small bolt that was recessed and too tiny for the giant's fingers to manipulate. He held it toward her as best he could and moaned again. A bit of pity formed in her as she could see he had been badly abused. The wariness in her kept her in check for the moment.

"Off, you want me to take that off?"

She was not totally surprised when he nodded and gave out a low moan.

"Then what? Then you kill me?"

The giant shook his head vigorously in the negative and whimpered woefully.

Skye swallowed. He sure was a pitiful-looking thing. She took a deep breath. The giant dropped to his knees, put his arms out to either side in a position of surrender, and moaned. A light snowfall started, and flakes began to stick to his hair.

"Okay, I will get it off. If you do anything foul, I will feel quite stupid."

Keeping her pistol leveled at his face, she slowly approached him. When she was within arm's length, she paused; he moaned that pitiful sound and put his hands behind his head the way a prisoner in surrender would. She took one last step and was right next to him. Keeping the pistol aimed straight in his face, with one hand she tried to undo the clasp with the other hand. "Sorry to say it, big guy, but you stink."

He let out a sigh and the stench of his breath almost made her back away. She started to work on the lock but after a few moments, it became apparent to her she would not be able to manipulate it with one hand. She tried to unscrew it several times but it spun and needed to be secured. This job needed two hands.

She looked at the giant with his hands on the back of his head. If he swung his arms at her, she guessed she might not get a shot off anyway. She looked into his sunken black eyes and said, "You be good."

She lowered the pistol and put it in her holster. With trembling fingers, she turned the latch, and in a few seconds the clasp came free, allowing the chain to fall clanking to the ground. Startled, she jumped back, and the giant suddenly stood. He touched his neck and shrieked with what sounded like joy. He jumped in the air and then loped off into the forest.

Skye watched him go and let herself smile. "You're welcome." She watched the giant disappear into the trees as an exhausted sigh left her. She picked up her pistol and automatically reloaded it. Viewing her surroundings, a sudden chill shook her. What had been a light snow

now began to fall heavily. There were four dead men in close proximity, and the new snow was stained red near their bodies.

She guessed the whole battle, if she could call it that, only took a few minutes. Even so, she was completely spent. She gathered her cloak and pulled it over her shoulders against the icy wind. It did not help much. The cold she felt almost seemed to be coming from the inside. She knew she needed something to eat, though she was not sure her stomach could handle anything. *Later.*

Darkness was creeping into the valley, and she had the uneasy sensation more nastiness lurked in the trees surrounding the valley. She went to Midnight and took a close look at her companion. The horse had glazed eyes and a trickle of blood coming from its ear. On her neck, the skin that had been grazed by the bullet was black with dried blood but did not look as awful as she had feared.

Skye patted Midnight on the side, took her reins in her hands, and started walking to the west end of the valley. *Surely we can't be too far from the mountain city. It's our only hope.*

They kept just off the old blacktop road to keep Midnight's hoofs from clomping in the gloom. Even with the wind picking up, the sound echoed off the mountain walls, and she wanted to pass as quietly as possible. She recognized that if anyone was looking into the valley, or had heard the gunshots from the fight, she would be easily discovered. There was no need to announce their presence to anyone who might have missed all that.

Snow started to accumulate, and soon they were making tracks in the soft white powder. They entered the tree line of Ponderosa pines and discovered a small stream running close to the road. Midnight drank for a long time; Skye envied the horse, as she could not force herself to take in anything.

They continued on, and Skye studied the road ahead. The valley was narrowing quickly in the darkness, and she got the impression the road ran straight into the mountain. Figuring her eyes were playing tricks on her in the dark, she kept walking forward until the wall closed in front of her completely. She almost walked square into it.

This can't be. She scraped some snow off the road and saw that the road indeed ran into the mountain, or more likely, she realized, a massive rockslide. She let Midnight go and paced from one sheer wall to the other, looking for an opening, her heart wrenching as she discovered there was none. Panic started to well in her chest. They were in a box canyon with no way out except the way they had come in.

She thought of her mother and the sickness in her village. In a sobering instant, it came to Skye that her journey might come to an end against a cold rock wall on a freezing mountain far from home. The realization that the failure of her quest was nearly on her hit her like a punch to the stomach. Her strength left her, and she dropped to the ground, burying her hands in her face. *Got to think of something.*

CHAPTER TWENTY-NINE

DRIVEN

JOHN WOKE WITH A shiver. It took him a moment to realize Les had given him a hard shake. The cold ground had been uncomfortable; even so, he had been valuing the sleep. Ever since Francois had confirmed his worst fears, that Barzan was trying to get to Stehekin, he had been on edge.

Les whispered, "Someone's moving out there, moving like they want a look-see at us."

John looked past Les and could make out Orlando and Francois peering into the dark with his night vision binoculars. They were kneeling behind a giant cedar log that offered both concealment and protection. He rubbed the sleep out of his eyes and got to his knees. "What do you think?"

John watched as Orlando moved to them, keeping a low crouch so he could not be seen from afar. "There are lots of them. I counted at least twenty. They're moving military style, leap-frogging past each other. None of the gangs we've seen have that discipline. These guys do."

John's back tightened. He had deliberately set out with only a small group, eight of his best, in three vehicles they had off-loaded from the ship, to try and reach what civilization he might find before the Malsi army found them. He had counted on moving quickly and quietly and avoiding significant confrontation. It was becoming clear that someone else had other plans.

He went to the log and used the night vision binocs to look through the darkness across the open field before him. In a moment, he spotted two men about a half a mile away, cautiously moving toward him. After a few steps, they stopped and dropped to the ground. In a moment, two more men got up and did the same thing. "Orlando's right. These guys are pretty well trained."

Les said in a low voice, "Good thing we have a good defensive position. The mountain shields us from behind, the river has our left flank, and we have two escape points. Maybe we should use one of them."

John always appreciated Les's ability to not mince words. "You don't think they've covered them?"

"I'm guessing they have the front door pretty well nailed shut. They may not realize we have a back door."

John scanned the field again. More dark figures moved across the wheat-colored grass. There were definitely more than twenty. "Keep the field covered with two machine guns. Get everybody else loaded up. I don't think these guys are coming to borrow a cup of sugar, so I'm pretty sure once we start the engines, they are going to open up on us. We'll have to go like hell."

Les went to carry out the instructions. John took a position by Francois. "Think they are Malsi?"

"No, they are too quiet and move with too much deliberation. The Malsi are only force, by force of numbers. They have no finesse like these guys."

John spoke more to himself than anyone else. "I wonder what the hell they want."

The Frenchman looked at him quizzically. "Is it okay if we don't stay to find out?"

John rubbed his arms to ward off the cold. "It is okay."

Two minutes later, everyone except for the two machine gunners were loaded in the vehicles. Les gave a hand signal, and the drivers started the trucks. The first Humvee fired immediately, breaking the silence of the night with the rumble of its big engine. The 4X4 behind it started quickly, but the second Humvee cranked and failed to start. The driver furiously cranked it again; this time, the engine caught, allowing John to let out a breath of relief.

Almost immediately, the sound of gunshots came from the field. The two machine gunners sprayed the field with two long bursts from their automatic weapons. John stood in the doorway of the first Humvee and shouted, "Let's go!"

The gunners jumped to their feet and raced to the waiting trucks, bullets zinging around them. A round hit the hardened side of the Humvee and pinged off. John's driver hit the gas, throwing John back against his seat. The truck jolted, trying to get up to speed with what John thought took an incredible amount of time. Rounds pinged off the side as they pulled onto the old highway and accelerated.

He looked behind and guessed the 4X4 was taking hits too. It was not armored, and his chest tightened at the idea of how exposed the men in the truck were. They went around a curve that took them away from the field up toward the mountains. It was the only place they had to go, and a sickening thought crept into his mind. He called to Les in the back seat, "We're being driven!"

"What?"

"We're being driven like game animals!"

Les's eyes shot wide open and he yelled, "Stop!"

John was almost slammed into the windshield as the driver braked hard. His stomach took a dive as he looked down the barrel of a cannon mounted on a main battle tank.

CHAPTER THIRTY

PLANS

BARZAN MOVED THE UNLIT cigar from one side his mouth to the other as he stared at the map on the field table. A gust of wind blew in when Malik, the general in charge of intelligence, came through the tent flap. The other officers around the table nodded in recognition as Malik gave the customary salute to the commander.

Barzan gave him the slightest of nods in acknowledgment and then returned to looking at the map. He used the cigar and tapped a spot on the map that read Sultan.

"This is a strange name for a place in this country, is it not?"

Nobody spoke. Candles cast light and played with the shadows on the faces of those around him, helping to mask their expressions.

He looked at the intelligence officer. "Why are we not there yet?"

Malik stood stiffly and cleared his throat. "I beg your forgiveness, my commander, but I am not in charge of logistics and maneuvers. I only provide the …"

Barzan cut him off. "Intelligence?"

Malik swallowed hard. "I do my humble best, my commander."

Barzan turned his look on his general. Malik was a slight man who wore the Western-style uniform the high staff preferred. He had a graying mustache and dark brown eyes. Wrinkles creased his skin, which looked as if it had been worn in the sun too many times. As

Barzan glared at him, he could see sweat beads starting to form on the man's small forehead.

Better to let him sweat for a few more minutes. In the old days, he would have just had the general shot for incompetence. However, over the years, he had learned that if he killed all of the people who failed him, he would soon be out of some of his best performers. These could be hard to replace, and everyone else was so scared all they would do is nod and say yes to everything he said. While that had its advantages, it killed imaginative thought, and in a war that was undesirable.

Being magnanimous on occasion could bring long-term rewards. "I concur that your best has been humble most recently."

Malik's eyes blinked in worry.

Barzan went back to the map. "Tell me again why we are not yet in this place called Sultan."

The general edged up to the map table and drew his finger along the lines that indicated the widest road. "The prisoner Owens told us that we would find the infidel fortress in this mountain pass. It is called Snoqualmie, which is the name of an indigenous tribe the Americans murdered in the old world."

Barzan tapped his finger on the map. "I do not care about the history of the failed peoples. Why did you think the fort would be here?"

Malik continued, "Other prisoners we have found have been of some little use. We have pushed the army hard for over eight hundred miles since making landfall nine days ago. Most of the prisoners we have found have been thieves and members of unorganized gangs. We also captured a few small villages that have managed to withstand the thugs."

Barzan put the cigar between his teeth. "There is a point you are getting to?"

"Yes, my commander. Across this vast distance, we have had many independent accounts of a sizable force that has retreated into these mountains. From the descriptions, I believed that this major road would be the likely place for them to make their fortress. As we now know, I was wrong. My deepest apologies, my commander."

Barzan watched as Malik bowed his head. "And now I am led to believe you have new information."

Malik kept his head down. "Yes, my commander."

"Do I have to ask or are you going to tell me?"

Barzan's mouth was getting dry as his patience was getting thin.

"I have new prisoners, and they are very specific about the location of the fortress. It is as was reported to you."

Barzan took the cigar from his mouth and inspected it. The end was becoming worn from his biting on it. He looked back at the map. "I can see why you might have thought the fortress was at this Snoqualmie Pass. There is easy access and troops could be moved in and out with ease. That is also why it is a poor choice tactically. A fortress by its nature is a place you want to restrict access to. That is why the remnants of an army trying to survive would pick a place that would be difficult for a large force to get to."

"Of course you are correct, my commander."

"Of course I'm correct. We have wasted two days with this Snoqualmie place only to find it blocked by landslides, and now it is starting to snow in the mountains." He addressed the rest of the staff. "Do any of you have any ideas?"

One general spoke up. "Yes, my commander. We can get back down the mountains, turn north, and reach the Leavenworth fortress in a day's time."

Barzan nodded. "The fort that blocks the only pass to the east side of the mountains. The only pass that we assume is open that will get us to this Stehekin place. And you believe the good general's new intelligence that a sizable force exists there?"

Malik made a brave voice. "It is there, my commander."

Barzan looked at the map. "Are you sure? Would you bet your life on it?"

Malik stammered, "Why, umm, yes, my commander."

Barzan looked at him and smiled. "As you wish."

He then said to the group, "We will disengage from this Snoqualmie place immediately. Make plans to turn the advance force north and make an assault at this Stevens Pass. I will bet that the coalition is in this place called Leavenworth.

"I want to have reliable information so we can start the attack within thirty-six hours. I want to extinguish this nuisance so I can advance to Stehekin."

He chewed on the cigar again. "Does anyone have a match?" Four matches appeared and lit almost instantly.

CHAPTER THIRTY-ONE

I Had a Feeling

MYST HELD HER HAND over Eagle's forehead. She didn't need to touch it to know it was burning. His face was red and swollen, and he had not opened his eyes for a full day. She was losing him, and her helplessness gnawed on her insides. She kneeled and put her mouth next to his ear. "You are truly ill, my friend. I will not leave you, though I must go out to try and find some remedy. I know about some of the things they used to use in the village, and it may take me awhile to find them. Don't be alarmed if you wake up and I am gone. I will be back for you."

She stood and pulled his blanket up to his shoulders. Now that dawn was breaking, she hoped to have the chance to search for the herbs and roots she had learned could ward off a fever.

When she exited the shelter, she was careful to trace her way back to the road they had turned from two days prior. From the cover of the forest, she looked up and down the road to make sure no one traversed it.

The morning shadows cast dark places along the near cliffs, and she sensed nothing out of order, so she stepped onto the old blacktop surface. She did not care to be exposed like this but her predicament was dire. In the days since Skye had left, Eagle had never fully recovered, and last night a fever had set in. *Suppose I should have thought of that before and found some meds in advance. I wish Skye were here.*

Myst started up the slope of the road. She examined plants as she went and looked for the leaves that would lead her to the roots she sought. She spied a promising specimen: two stout stalks of phlox with faded purple flowers on them. Without warning, a cracking in the bushes caught her attention.

She fought off an unsettling feeling in her stomach. *Someone is near.* She dropped to her knees and took cover behind the weathered brush that filled the valley floor. Low voices came from the road. The sound of boots on the blacktop made her hold her breath in the hope that if she made no noise at all, whoever was out there might pass and not notice her.

"He was over there, by the low tree. Fan out, watch yourselves." The voice was strong and commanded respect. Her heart skipped a beat. She'd been discovered. "The tree" must refer to the very tree she had been standing by when she found the plant she had been looking for.

What had been a cool morning had suddenly turned very hot. The sound of men working through the brush grew louder. She started to crawl away from the road as quietly as she could. The ground was covered with uneven rocks that dug into her hands and knees. Some of the plants had thistles that poked into her arms and sides. She had to be extra careful to avoid painful stinging nettles. Worse, the dry brush made an unmistakable sound as she moved.

"Yo, somebody is in there. I see movement." It was a different voice, and much closer than the first. A knot of fear formed in her neck. She froze, not sure what to do. So far, they had not met any friendly people except for Armstrong and his guard, and they were outsiders to their own leaders.

"Hey, you in the weeds, stand up and be seen."

What would Skye do? She looked around herself and could only see more sagebrush and dried tumbleweeds. There was no place to hide and no place to run.

"I said stand up. If you are a friend, there will be no harm."

A friend to who? All manner of ill thoughts ran through her head, especially the encounter with the bad men by the lake their first night ashore. She shivered at the thought of them.

"Show yourself or I'll take you for a hostile and fire into your place. I give you ten seconds."

Myst closed her eyes and breathed deep. Her feelings were mixed. She knew staying hidden was clearly not working but standing and showing herself did not seem desirable either.

"Five seconds."

Myst clenched her fingers around the knife under her cloak and slowly stood up. A man in a camouflaged uniform stood not twenty feet from her. He held a short rifle, and when he saw her, he pointed it directly at her.

He shouted, "Check your fire! I got one here."

She looked around and saw people in similar uniforms spread in a semicircle around her. All had rifles pointed at her. That two of the six were women she found to be a small comfort. By their uniforms and demeanor, she had the hope they were not a gang of cutthroats.

The one closest to her shouted, "Raise your hands over your head where I can see them."

She let go of the knife and slowly complied with the command.

"How many of you are there?"

Myst considered her answer. She could lie and say there were a thousand of her closest friends and warriors just behind her, though she doubted these people with the guns would see the humor in the statement.

"How many?"

He was growing more impatient by the moment. She answered with a soft voice, "There are no others."

The woman closest to her had braided red hair that fell out the back of her billed hat. "It's a little girl." Myst winced at the description of herself.

A man near the center raised his rifle slightly so it no longer pointed at her. "What are you doing out here by yourself?"

The group closed around her with caution. They warily eyed the area behind her as if they expected something more than a little girl to suddenly pop out of the weeds. Myst took a page from Skye's book. "What concern is it of yours as to my purpose in being here?"

The man who first spotted her said loudly, "Don't be smart, kid, or I'll smack your ass silly." He moved toward her as if to strike her. Myst backpedaled in defense, and then the red-haired woman ran between them.

"Knock it off, Carver. You aren't smacking anybody."

The man backed away, glowering at her. "Have it your way. But find out where the hell her people are and what they are up to. She isn't out here picking flowers by herself."

The woman turned to Myst. "Don't be fooled because I wouldn't let him hit you. We'll not put up with nonsense or disrespect. This place is much too dangerous for all of us to screw around with you or anybody else." Her tone was firm.

Myst could feel the resolve in the woman's manner. She maintained what she hoped was an impassive face. *I know what comes next. Tell me who you are and where you are from.*

The woman said, "Tell me who you are and where you are from."

Myst looked into the woman's green eyes and was reminded of her own mother. She saw kindness that was guarded by a tough exterior. "I am Myst of the Long Lake."

Carver seethed behind the woman, "She's the mist of the lake? What the hell kind of answer is that supposed to be? Let me slap some sense into her." A few of the men snickered as if they agreed.

The woman turned to Carver. "That's not what she said, you idiot. She said her name is Myst and she comes from the Long Lake; she must mean Chelan." The woman looked to Myst with a raised eyebrow. "Right?"

Myst nodded and the woman smiled. "What are you doing here?"

Her arms were growing weary of being held up for so long, and the point of it was wearing off. After all, she was surrounded by six armed adults. "May I put my hands down?"

The woman nodded. "Of course, Myst; sorry. My name is Shelly. I am of the army of New Leavenworth. Our mission is to patrol this region for intruders. Now why are you here?"

Myst could hardly believe her luck. She decided not to stray too far from the truth, though she did not want to reveal everything. She sensed little danger from these people if she cooperated with them. They did not appear hostile. Desperate to get aid for Eagle, she decided to gamble and seek their help. "My companions and I set on a journey to find the people of the mountain, to find you. We came upon some people and creatures with ill intentions and are much the worse off for the encounters."

Carver raised his voice. "You said you were alone."

Myst kept her gaze on Shelly. "As I stand here, I am alone. We started on our journey as three. My leader forged ahead when my other companion was seriously wounded by a bear we surprised. He now lays in hiding with a fever taking over his body. I am here scavenging what meds I can find to try to cure him. As for my leader, I fear for her fate."

Shelly slung her rifle over her shoulder. "Lead us to your companion. We will take you both to the mountain fort. I have a lot of questions about why you are looking for us and why such young people would be sent on such a journey. There must be good reasons but I will wait to find out. These days are short, and we have discovered there may be trouble coming down the river. We must leave here now."

WHO DO YOU TRUST?

JOHN TOOK HIS PLACE in the line-up as his captors had demanded. Les was on his left and Francois to his right. The other members of his team were being held in another part of the camp. He recognized some of the insignia on the uniforms of the men holding their guns on him. They were old U.S. Army, just like the kind he had once worn. He had a growing hope that these men would be the allies he so badly needed. On the other hand, they could be his worst nightmare.

A man with the rank of major entered the tent and immediately started quizzing the sergeant in charge. "What's their story, Sergeant Tully? More gang bangers from down south or are these local types?"

Tully, a big man with a thick black mustache, kept his eyes on John as he answered his superior. "These are weird ones, sir. They act like military types. This one here," he gestured with his gun toward John, "says he is the commanding officer and won't talk to anybody but our CO."

The major looked at John with slight sneer on his face. "That so?"

"At's what he sez, sir."

The major had short black hair with silver streaks in it. His face was soft and pudgy as if he had too much to eat and not enough time to do something about it. He was wide in the waist, and his trim uniform bulged in an attempt to keep him in it. He approached John, and the smell of alcohol made John turn his nose. "So you are the commanding officer?"

John played it straight. "Yes sir."

The major pursed his lips. "Of what? A roaming gang, a band of thieves, a troop of girl scouts?"

At this, the guards and Tully burst out laughing. John knew his face was going red. He took deep breaths to keep his cool, though he felt his temperature soaring. This pompous fool was going to be hard to deal with. He needed to get past this guy and talk to whoever was in charge. He forced himself to smile as if he appreciated the joke.

"You are too kind, sir. Certainly one must be careful of those strangers met in the wild. We are neither thieves nor girl scouts. I lead a small band of men who wish to join forces with the elite group that has captured us. We honor strength and integrity, and clearly your troops have both. We wish to ally with you to overcome a dangerous peril that comes from beyond your shores."

Tully spoke first. "What the hell are you talking about?"

The major rubbed his jaw with his hand. "Yeah, what the hell are you talking about? There ain't a shore within sixty miles of here. Where you boys from?"

John tried not to let his irritation come out in his voice. "We are from here and from everywhere. It is extremely important that I be allowed to talk to the officer in charge of your group, or army, or village, or whatever it is you are. A grave danger follows us, and if you are not ready, it will overwhelm you before you know it."

The major leaned toward John and thrust his finger at him. "You threatening me, boy?"

John could hardly contain his frustration. "Of course not, sir." *You idiot.* "I'm trying to tell you that we are just a small team who has learned of a significant threat to all those who inhabit this land. We bring warning, although it is almost too late already. I implore you to let me speak with those in charge so that you might prepare a defense."

The major straightened his back and stood as tall as he could muster. "If this is so damn important, why don't you just tell me and I will pass the message along, if it is worth repeating."

While he tried to think of a way to describe the Malsi army, he was surprised to hear Francois speak up.

"He just told you, you stupid fool. We have fought our way to zhis place to warn you of the evil army that even now marches toward you, and you waste our time with zeez stupid questions. You should treat us like ze heroes who come to save your asses."

Tully shouted at Francois, "Watch your mouth!" Then he smashed him in the face with his fist. The Frenchman went down to his knees, blood trickling from his mouth.

Les stepped in front of Francois. "Leave him alone, Sergeant. Just 'cause your drunken major is a dumb ass doesn't mean you have to be one."

Tully raised his fist again. "Shut your mouth or you'll get some too."

John said sharply to Les, "Knock it off. Our man was out of line." He looked to the major, who was seething. "My apologies, sir. My men are tired from our trip and have seen little rest in days. If you could let me speak with your superiors, or at least take them my message, it would only do you good."

The major shifted his shoulders back and presented himself in the best stature he could manage. "I will not bother my leaders with the nonsensical drivel of a band of passing thieves. Your lack of manners and discipline reveals you for who you are: common trash, that from time to time tries to infiltrate the fort with plans to wipe us out. No, I will not bother my leaders with your preposterous tale of the monstrous invasion you claim is being launched by an imaginary army. Instead I will tell them of the execution of just another outlaw gang that has entered our territory."

John's heart dropped in his chest. He could no longer contain his anger. "My man was wrong when he called you an ignoramus. He was much too generous. You are a complete fucking moron, and you've let your pitiful ego put your entire command in grave jeopardy. The battlefields of Europe were littered with the bodies of men wasted because of peons like you. I can't believe you are allowed any responsibility here. Those in charge will deserve whatever fate they get for allowing a low-life like you to be in the chain of command. I only pity the innocents who will be lost because of you."

Two guards grabbed John by the arms to keep him from getting close to the major. Satisfied that John could not get to him, the pudgy man put his face with his stinking breath in John's face and said, "It will please me to watch you squirm when you die tomorrow. Most of our firing squads are very accurate, but others are not. Sometimes I find it amazing how slowly men can die from gunshot wounds."

The major turned on his heels and left the tent, with the guards still holding John tight. Tully barked an order, "Take 'em to the hoosegow. Major says we shoot 'em at dawn."

John caught Tully's eye. "Surely that man does not have the authority to assign capital punishment, especially without a trial."

Tully shook his head. "We been at war for twenty years; all field grades have the authority."

A cold spike of fear slid down John's back. He took one more shot. "Sergeant Tully, please, please listen to me. I have to talk to someone in authority besides that idiot. You guys can shoot me in the morning, hang me, draw and quarter me if I get you in trouble, but unless you let me tell my story to someone who counts, you might as well shoot yourselves 'cause you won't be alive by the end of the week."

Tully licked his lips. "We've been through an awful lot, buddy. It's going to take a lot to wipe us out."

John pleaded, "Sarge, what's the downside? I hurt somebody's feelings? You get a stripe taken away? Give us a break here, give yourself a break."

Tully ordered his men, "Get 'em out of here. Take 'em to the lockup."

CHAPTER THIRTY-THREE

IN

SKYE LAY SHIVERING ON the ground, clutching her cloak around her shoulders in a vain attempt to keep off the cold. She had slept fitfully for what she guessed was the last couple of hours. She had managed to eat a little and put a blanket down for her bed, knowing it would offer scant help in this weather. Unfortunately, it offered less help than she had hoped.

After her initial failure to find an opening, the despair she felt had almost overwhelmed her. Once she regrouped from her disappointment, she spent several hours searching in the dark around the slide area again to see if there was another way up. She became convinced there was no other way; exhausted, she had to submit to trying to get some sleep.

She tried to focus on a new plan of action, hoping she would come up with something or fall asleep trying. Out of the night, Midnight let out a loud whinny. Skye didn't open her eyes. The horse had been slow since the blow it took from the giant, so she had taken the unusual step of tethering her to a tree before she went to sleep. The horse whinnied once more, this time louder. Skye put her arm over her ear.

Just when I thought this night could not get any more miserable, Midnight starts making a racket and now something stinks.

A jolt of recognition shot through her, and she opened her eyes and confirmed her fear. The giant was standing right in front of her.

She rolled away hard, her blanket and cloak tangled around her in the process. She tried to reach her pistol and was horrified to find that her arms were pinned by her own clothes. The huge man stepped toward her.

Skye struggled to get her hands free from the tangled cloak and blanket that held them. The giant was only a few feet from her, and she could not even stand, much less reach a weapon. Terror gripped her insides. She feared the beast would attack at any moment. She willed her hand to move against the clothes that bound it as she tried to reach her gun.

She had a breath of hope when her fingers reached the pistol butt. She tried to free the weapon and had almost succeeded in drawing it out when she was puzzled to see the creature back up two steps and hold his palms out to her.

She managed to get herself loose from her entanglement and decided to leave her pistol undrawn. She got to her feet with the giant watching her every move. Not sure what to do, she said the first thing that came to mind. "Hello, what are you up to today?"

The huge man turned his head a little sideways as if he was pondering a question he did not understand. He did not show any hostile intent; in fact, she reasoned, if he had been hostile he would have already done her in. Perhaps there was a chance he was only curious. Taking deep breaths, she carefully knelt next to her backpack and reached in and pulled out an apple.

He looked at it with some interest. Skye extended her hand, offering the fruit to the giant. He held his huge hand out, gently took it from her, and then made a soft sound.

Skye was almost certain the sound he made was a word. "Why, you are most welcome, Mister what should I call you? How about Lucky, because clearly you aren't."

Lucky did not reply and instead put the apple in his mouth and devoured it in one bite. Skye thought she detected a smile as it wiped its mouth with the back of a big hairy arm.

Gaining ease with the presence of the giant, she took out another apple and took a bite for herself. Talking between chews, she puzzled out loud, "You're a big fella and I bet you have been around here a long time. I do not suppose you know the way to the fort of the mountain people?"

Lucky tilted his head again, "Moort."

"Sure, fort, moort, anything you say. Do you know where there are more people? I mean good people, not like the ones you knew before."

"Moort."

Skye finished her apple and tossed the core to the ground. The giant startled her by bounding to it and hungrily scarfing it down. She realized the man was nearly starving yet had not made a move toward her or her pack while she had leisurely munched her own apple. She went into her pack again and dumped out the last two she had.

"Hey, Lucky. This is all I have, but you are welcome to them." She gently tossed the two apples to him. To her surprise, he did not pounce on them. Instead he took one and tossed the other back to her.

"You are a sharing creature. I find I am kind of liking you."

After the two finished their snack, Skye thought it was time to go. She stood and put her pack on her back as the giant eyed her. "Lucky, it has been marvelous chatting with you but I do need to be on my way. If I do not find a way to the mountain people by midday, I fear I will have to return to my friends who I left down in the valley."

She started walking to the face of the mountain to search again for a way to Leavenworth. Behind her Lucky bellowed, "Mort ..."

She turned to him. "Mort?"

He waved his arm, beckoning toward the east, "Mort."

He took a few steps in the other direction and then looked to see if she followed. Reluctant at first, Skye took a couple of steps in his direction. He took a few more strides and she followed with more assurance. *Been that kind of week.*

The giant turned away from the rock face of the mountain and instead headed into the scrub brush and trees beside the old road. Skye followed and wondered where the man was taking her. The sun came over the crest of the peaks in the east and streaked yellow rays through opening clouds.

As they traveled, she looked in vain for Midnight but only saw hoof prints dusted over by the new snow. *Probably bolted when she sensed the giant hanging around. Do not blame her for that. I need to learn how to tether better.*

The thin snow cover glowed white on the ground, and each breath she produced came out as a frosty mist. Ahead of her, the huge man produced what were almost cloud banks when he exhaled. They passed into the thick trees, and Skye recognized what looked like a well-traveled path, even under the snow. Her heart leaped a little as her hope grew that the giant might indeed have an idea as to how to find the fort.

In a short time, they were once again facing the steep face of the mountain, which loomed above looking as impassable as ever. "Mr. Lucky," Skye started, "I thank you for your time. Unfortunately, I do not believe we have communicated well. I am perfectly capable of not finding the fort by myself. I proved that yesterday."

The disappointment at finding a dead end turned her stomach, and she sat down in the snow and put her face in her hands. *This is hopeless. I think the giant meant well but did not know what I needed. I should have known.*

The sound of the giant moaning made her look up. Lucky was pointing up the mountain and saying, "Mort, mort, mort."

Skye looked up the side of the uneven rock face and tried to figure out what he was doing. She got to her feet and dusted the snow from herself. Going to where the giant stood, she looked at the rock face closely. Even though she was not a tracker by trade, she could see it was evident that the rocks here had been scarred by men. She ran her hands over the marks and was both excited and disappointed. "Lucky, I see that there must have been a way up here before. I'm afraid that path is long gone, probably a rockslide like everywhere else."

"Mort!"

She was taken aback by the loud cry of her guide. The giant pointed high again and this time cradled his hands in a gesture she didn't understand. He lifted his interlocking fingers up the mountainside and then pointed to her and repeated the motion. After a moment, it dawned on her. *He wants to give me a boost up the cliff!*

She looked up again and didn't see anyplace to be boosted to, though she could imagine there might be a slight ledge that was not visible from this angle. The giant implored her with his eyes and lifted his hands again, saying, "Mort."

Skye took a big breath and said, "Okay. I'll give it a try."

She moved to the side of the cliff where the giant waited. He cradled his massive hands again, down around his knees, and Skye put a tentative foot onto them. Slowly he lifted her upwards. She leaned against the rock face, trying to keep her balance using her hands, and then had to grab Lucky. "Whoa, buddy, slow down."

The giant lifted her higher and higher until her feet were level with his shoulders. She was twelve feet above the ground and once again found herself questioning her own judgment. Her alarm increased when he moved one hand, grabbed her ankle, and put it on his shoulder. Her face pressed hard against the rocks when her other foot was placed on the opposite shoulder.

She reached above her as high as she could; her fingers only met smooth, cold stone. She was shocked when she felt big hands pushing on her body where no other hands had been before. The giant had reached up and pressed his palms on her bottom, inching her even farther up the cliff.

Her heart was pounding and her freezing fingers still could find no hold. "Lucky. I think we're done. There is nothing here I can find."

Without warning, two hands grabbed her wrists from above and started to pull. She blurted, "What the …"

A male voice shouted, "Use your feet, and climb on his hands. You'll be okay. I won't let go."

With a total of four hands on her bum and wrists, and balancing between the cliff and a hard fall, Skye knew she was not in a place to bargain. Nonetheless, she was not ready to give in to the unknown.

"Pardon my asking, who might you be?" Visions of the scoundrels that had been abusing the giant were still fresh in her mind.

She looked up and saw the face that was attached to the hands holding her wrists. The man wore dark glasses and had creased temples and a bushy moustache with black and gray streaks. "I'm a friend to those who come here in peace."

The giant's hands were slipping on her rump and were inadvertently slipping to places they surely did not belong. She looked to the man above her and said, "Pull!"

He gave her a yank, and she managed to get one foot on the giant's hand and then, balanced by the hands above, put her other foot in the other upraised hand. Between the giant pushing, and the man pulling, she was shoved and dragged onto a narrow ledge above the valley floor.

Perspiring and panting from the effort, and glowing red from the indignity of the moment, she took a few breaths to compose herself. She looked to the man, who was also breathing hard; she guessed he was in his fifties. He wore a uniform and made no move to her; even so, she put her fingers around her gun. "I'm sorry; I did not hear your name."

He held his hands up. "Don't worry. I'm Colonel Moore of the fort. You are safe with me. May I inquire of you?"

She relaxed her fingers. "I am Skye from the Long Lake. Pleased to meet you." She extended her hand and shook the colonel's.

A loud cry came from below. The colonel looked down the cliff, and Skye crawled over so she could see the giant too. Moore waved and called, "Good job, my friend!" Then he tossed Lucky a bag of apples that had been sitting on the ledge. He looked to Skye and said, "He is a pitiful creature but a kind one. I wish he would come back to the fort but he prefers the wild. You are fortunate he found you."

The giant took the bag and then trotted across the valley. Moore pointed up the road that had been carved into the side of the mountain. "This way."

Skye followed the colonel warily. Wanting to trust him was one thing, actually trusting him was quite another. After all she had been through, it was hard to believe anyone she didn't know, and it had been a while since she had been around anyone she knew. "Where are we going?"

The colonel kept his brisk pace on the mountain road, barely turning his head to speak to her. "We're going to get warm and get something to eat."

The thought of getting out of this dreadful cold was certainly appealing. "I have some questions for you."

Moore left large footprints in the snow that were much farther apart than Skye's stride. She had to hurry to keep up. "I need to get my horse."

Again he hardly acknowledged her. "It'll be along."

"How can that be? She won't get boosted up here by a giant and there is no other trail."

This time, the colonel stopped and gave her a look she could not read. Snow danced around his face and a little clung to his thick mustache. A few flakes dotted the bill of his green camouflage hat. His sunglasses hid his eyes, and she could see her own tiny reflection staring back at herself. "Miss, you seem to be a bright young woman. Just because you didn't find the trail up here does not mean there isn't one. Your animal will arrive here when it is needed. Meanwhile, we need to get inside."

He looked at the steel gray sky and the clouds that were lowering over the mountaintops. "A storm is growing, and you are not the only stranger who has come into our midst. I fear a change is coming, and I am not sure that it is a good one."

Skye brushed the snow off the sleeves of her cloak. "How long have you been at New Leavenworth?"

A smile creased his face. "We don't call it that anymore. When we first moved here, we had hope that we could start anew. Unfortunately, the world was not ready for that." He slowly shook his head as if recalling a sad time. "Now we just call it 'the fort.'"

Skye's stomach tightened; she could tell there was remorse in calling the place the fort. "I have news that may have some consequence for you."

A slow rumbling thunder echoed across the valley. Moore looked to the mountains. "Thunder in the snow. Unusual, almost as odd as finding a woman from afar who can deal death to a gang of men who have ill intent."

Skye took a sharp breath. "You saw that?"

He nodded and said, "Most impressive. I saw that yesterday and came out this morning in the hope that by some stroke of luck you would find your way here. Come, we must go. I will hear your news of consequence over a warm bowl of soup and then you will tell me what you want." He started walking again.

Skye called to him in wonder, "How do you know I want something?"

His answer, though a little muffled by a gust of wind, was crystal clear in its meaning. "No one comes to the fort unless they want something. And most want more than they have to give."

CHAPTER THIRTY-FOUR

LOCKED UP

JOHN STARED AT THE stone walls of his prison. He and the others from his advance team were being held in a cave carved into the side of a mountain. He had not slept all night. The sunlight creasing into the cold room through a slit window on the door was filtered by gray clouds. He tried to keep his mind clear. *There has got to be a way out of this.*

Les leaned over to him as if reading his mind. "We're in some kind of a jam this time, boss. I just know you're working on a plan that will get us out of this fix."

John let out a sigh. "Right, I'm on it. You'll be the first to know when I get it worked out."

The sound of men approaching came though the wooden door. Les whispered, "Anytime will do now, John. I don't think this is room service."

The lock turned with a metallic grate, and the heavy door swung open with a bang. Two men entered the cell, leveling automatic weapons on the prisoners. Sergeant Tully stepped between them and pointed to John. "That one first."

The man nearest John motioned with his rifle barrel for John to move. He swallowed hard and found his mouth was dryer than he ever remembered it before. He looked at his best friend Les. Their eyes met for what John thought would be the last time. "Sorry, buddy, fresh out of ideas."

Les smiled. "A fine time you picked for that. It's been a pleasure traveling the world with you."

John nodded. "Been an honor for me." He looked at the rest of his men and added, "An honor to serve with all of you. Sorry about the ending."

His troops stood as one, causing the guards to step back and point their guns at them. John's men saluted their leader in unison.

Tully put a pistol to John's ear and said, "You guys are going to make me cry. I'm all choked up." He said to his guards, "Let's get out of here."

Tully put his arm around John's neck and, keeping the pistol pointed at his head, backed him out of the cell. The other guards backed out as well, clanging the door shut behind them. The door was hardly closed before Tully jammed John against the wall, jabbing the pistol into his neck and pinning him against the cold rocks with his body.

Tully put his lips almost to John's ear. "Tell me your story again, mister. You know, the one about the bad guys coming to town."

John talked through pursed lips. "It's not a story. I told you everything I know last night after your drunken officer finally got out of here. We left Chelan twenty years ago to fight the war. As you can see, we lost. Since then we've traveled all over Africa and Europe, fighting the Malsi every place we met them. They are here now, not far behind us."

Tully said, "So the evil Malsi are coming to get us. But why do they give a rip about us?"

John said in exasperation, "I told you, they don't give a rip about you, your fort is just in the way to what they want."

Tully retorted, "Right, they came halfway around the world to get the pot of gold at the end of the lake."

John pushed his point. "Even if you kill me, you've got to warn your higher-ups."

The sergeant shifted his weight off John a little. "I don't have to."

"Don't be a fool."

"I don't have to 'cause you are going to. After that episode last night, I sent two patrols out to look for your bad guys. Neither one came back. If you are lying, you will regret ever being born."

John turned his head to look at Tully. "How long ago were your patrols sent out?"

Tully leveled his brown eyes on John. "About ten hours. They should have been back at dawn."

"Are they mechanized?"

"Yes, they had fast vehicles so they could cover max distance."

John looked at the pistol the sergeant held. "We better hurry. The Malsi force is mechanized too, and they travel fast."

Tully lowered they gun. "Are they as bad as you say?"

John nodded slowly.

Tully stepped back and put his gun in his holster. He motioned to the two guards with him. "Let's go. We need to get this guy to the fort, pronto."

The guard on the right shook his head. "The major isn't going to like this."

Tully replied, "The major is a drunken idiot. There is a reason he was assigned this little back door command. Nobody ever thought a force in strength would come this way."

CHAPTER THIRTY-FIVE

CLOSING IN

BARZAN SCANNED THE MOUNTAINS ahead of him with his high-powered binoculars. He could make out the road ahead for about two miles and then it disappeared into the trees and mist. This was a cold and desolate place, and he was anxious to finish his task and move on. Earlier in the day, he had been able to see the snow-covered peaks and the places where roads had been cut into the forest for the old loggers. He mused that they were extinct now. Gone with the rest of the civilization that had once lived here.

He listened to the sound of the wind rocking the treetops of the giant fir trees that towered over the road. The silence made him unsettled. He was accustomed to the rhythm of the convoy and the continuous noise of an army on the move. Clanking weapons, thousands of men going forward with purpose, orders shouted above the roar of the engines of the caravan.

His decision to accompany this small scouting party had taken his men by surprise. Though he missed the noise and comfort of his command force, it was exciting, almost exhilarating, to move with stealth and speed. It reminded him of his younger days when he would lead attacks, not just direct them from the rear. Abruptly the men in the truck ahead of him started shouting and motioning to the side of the road.

With quick precision, the team of four trucks of scouts turned off the road and disappeared into the trees, two on each side of the road. The men moved into defensive positions and covered the approach with their automatic weapons.

Ivan took a place beside Barzan. He spoke in a voice much lower than the commander thought was needed. "Another patrol approaches from the north. Our point men signaled from ahead. It is probably from the fort like the two we destroyed yesterday. They let it pass so you could decide what we should do with them."

Barzan grunted. He didn't want to make this choice, which is why he had lower echelon officers. He wanted to evaluate his men in combat. Up the road he could see two vehicles approaching at a cautious speed. Seeing the heavy guns mounted on the tops of the trucks sent a trickle of sweat down his back. The knot of fear and excitement in his stomach made him take a short breath.

He calculated that it had been several years since he had last exposed himself to hostile fire. Directing his conquests from the rear had been his mode of operation ever since a bullet grazed his head outside of London. At that point, he decided there were plenty of troops to do the line work. Over the years, he had taken his share of wounds and had scars on his shoulder and legs to prove his mettle.

That one shot, though, the one that was purposely aimed at his head and took off a piece of his lower ear, had taught him he was mortal. The notion that he was a breath away from meeting his end focused his mind quite like never before. Barzan closed his eyes for a moment and visualized the scene.

The campaign in England had lasted for months. The combined armies of the Europeans had been decimated by diseases and biological weapons they were not prepared for. But here, his troops had been stopped by the determined and now desperate enemy they had chased halfway across Europe. The foes were in the defenses before the Malsi army arrived to lay waste to London, the last of the major surviving cities of the nonbelievers. They had refused his offer to let them surrender, so he led a raid on the foremost defense, an ancient castle that had been reinforced by the infidels.

The artillery blasted a hole in the front wall, and his men poured in the breach. Once inside, they spread out to sack the castle as the defenses crumbled. Barzan entered the grounds and was greeted with the sight of dozens of bodies scattered like so much broken wood in the vast courtyard. His men continued to shoot high up the ramparts at an enemy that rained death on them from above.

Bullets flew and the steady sound of explosions rocked the battle. Smoke poured from open windows and the acrid smell of gunpowder mixed with the stench of burnt flesh. Men screamed in agony, and officers tried to bark orders over the chaos. Barzan's attention was drawn to an upper turret. Then he saw it.

A familiar face was pressed into the side of a rifle aimed directly at him. In an instant, he recognized the commander of the troops from America and knew he had been drawn into a trap. The muzzle flashed a micro second after a large explosion jarred him almost off his feet. He later realized it had probably saved his life.

That day, his men withdrew from the castle in defeat, one of the rare times he tasted the bitterness of failure. In the end, the weight of the Malsi army overwhelmed the enemy and won the war against England, as they had every place else. From then on, most of the battles were little more than slaughters of those who did not join them.

Barzan opened his eyes; he wondered if the American Erikson still lived. He had led a company of the ones called the Rangers, and they had been a hindrance to him for years. It had always seemed they acted almost independently of the coalition armies. They disappeared after the battle for London. Barzan never could convince himself they were destroyed. He wondered if they could have made their way back to their home. Back to his target. That would be satisfying.

He turned his attention to the pending action. Yes, there were plenty of troops to take on the enemy up front. Barzan's talents, he knew, were needed to lead one of the three Malsi armies to conquer and wipe the nonbelievers from the planet. When this was done, the

Emperor Prophet had promised him he would rule a vast empire of his own. Beyond that, Barzan had ideas of his own; to achieve those, he needed what was at the end of the long lake.

Ivan whispered to him, "What is your command? Do we let them ride on or take them down now?"

Barzan's tongue was dry, and he took a drink to quench his thirst. The wind gusted with a chill he was not accustomed to. "We take them now. Let no one escape. Try to get a prisoner. You will direct the attack."

"As you command."

Ivan made a hand signal to the men hidden on the other side of the road. The two green-painted trucks drew within twenty yards of their location. Suddenly one veered to the right and made an abrupt turn about in the grass on the side of road. The other turned the opposite way, and both ended up speeding away from Barzan's men. "They've seen us! Get after them!"

The Malsi Humvees roared out of the woods and onto the road behind the green trucks. A machine gun opened fire from in front, and the first Malsi vehicle careened off the road and then rolled over twice. The men were thrown like rags from the Humvee, and Barzan held his breath as he saw one of the men's legs torn off.

The Humvee in front of him returned fire with an RPG. The rocket ran true and flew straight into the back of the trailing green truck. The explosion ripped the back of the truck apart and blew off one of the wheels. The truck skidded sideways and then flipped over the hood onto its top. A second RPG hit it as it laid on the ground and sent a huge plume of smoke into the air.

The attack column passed the crash in close pursuit of the other fleeing green truck. Barzan saw Ivan turn to him and smile. Barzan nodded in agreement. The trap was well laid, something they learned from those damn Rangers years ago.

The truck that survived rounded a corner and that took it out of sight of Barzan and his men. A moment later, a huge concussion tore through the air and sent a black cloud of smoke hundreds of feet into the air. The force of the blast stripped branches from the nearby trees and caused Barzan to wince at the sound.

The Malsis slowed and went around the corner with their guns ready. Barzan quickly saw there was no need. All that remained was flaming bits of shredded metal burning at the side of the road.

The vehicles came to a stop, and the men looked over the scene. Two troops came out of the woods and waved in recognition. One held an explosive detonator over his head in triumph. Some of the men from the Malsi trucks greeted them with whistles and cheers. Barzan spit out the window to clear the taste of diesel smoke from his mouth. "Effective, though inefficient for catching prisoners."

Ivan nodded. "Very effective for keeping anyone from escaping. Let's go back and check the other truck."

The driver gunned the engine, and in a few moments, Ivan and the three troops that were accompanying him had a badly wounded man sprawled in front of them. Barzan thought it looked like he had a broken arm, and one leg was bleeding profusely. Barzan listened as Ivan tried to question him. "How many are you?" The man only moaned.

Barzan moved Ivan out of the way and knelt beside the prisoner. "Your wounds are not so bad. We can help you." He looked to one of his men. "Water, quickly!" He took a canteen and offered a drink to the wounded soldier.

"Why did you run from us?"

The man's eyes were bloodshot, and his eyelids were half-closed. "Thought you were bad guys; guess we were right."

Barzan ignored the comment. "Where were you running to?"

The man sighed, "Away from you."

Barzan stood and put his foot on the man's broken arm. "Where were you running to?"

The injured man's eyes got wide. "Piss off."

Barzan applied pressure to the arm. "Where were you running to?"

The man screamed and Barzan let up on the pressure. The man panted, "The fort, back to the fort."

Barzan left his foot on the broken arm. "The fort? Is it far?"

The injured man said, "Maybe twenty clicks."

Barzan asked, "How many defend it?"

The prisoner shook his head no. Barzan pressed on the arm again, and the man screamed in agony and passed out. Barzan splashed water on his face but there was no response. Barzan turned to Ivan. "Prepare an assault; we will attack at dawn tomorrow." His eyes went to the prisoner. "Kill him."

CHAPTER THIRTY-SIX

QUESTIONS

Skye lay on the bed she had been given and stared at the ceiling. The room was smallish with no windows and was decorated with paintings of deserts and oceans—no mountains in here. A dim yellow electric light washed the colors out of everything. She wondered if she were a prisoner or a guest. They told her she was a guest though they were very specific about what she could do (and mostly what she could not do). Though night had fallen, she did not feel like sleeping.

She thought about her conversation, or rather interrogation, with Colonel Moore and his staff. She had learned he was the commander of the fort and that his rule was law. Little else had been disclosed about the nature or composition of the garrison and other inhabitants of the city. She had detected a clear air of disdain for some of the population from the officers. She was curious about the source of the issue.

She had started with Armstrong's message. "The captain of the Outriders of Evergreen sends his greetings and an offer of alliance with the people of the mountain."

Moore tapped the wooden table they sat around. "Then Evergreen is under attack. Armstrong is a good man; we have crossed paths. The leaders there are something else. They would only ask for our help if they were desperate. We will consider this but, I'm afraid, without enthusiasm. We have many concerns of our own."

After that, she mostly answered questions.

"Where are you from?"

Skye sighed, "I get asked that a lot. I am from the Long Lake, you may know it as Chelan."

Moore asked, "Where on the lake?"

"It's not important."

"Why won't you tell us?"

Skye found her mouth going dry and asked, "Why should I trust you?"

"Why don't you?"

"Since I left home, I have not met many who could be trusted. Am I a prisoner?"

Moore leaned back in his chair. "There is no doubt the wild is full of nasty people. Of course you are not a prisoner."

"Then I can leave if I want?"

"I advise against it. These are dangerous times."

"I'm aware of that; after all, you did see what happened yesterday."

"How many in your party?"

"We were three."

"What happened to the others?"

"I'm not certain. One was gravely injured and we made a camp not far from here. If I do not return to them shortly, I expect they will start making their way back home."

"To Chelan?"

"To the Long Lake."

"Why are you here?"

"My village needs help. I was told I might find it here."

"What kind of help?"

Skye paused and looked around the room. Besides Colonel Moore, there were three other officers. Two were men who looked lean and fit with weathered faces and clear eyes. The other was a woman with short red hair. She seemed not much older than Skye and spoke very little. Skye assumed she was the lowest ranking person there.

Skye wondered how they would receive her request. In a lowered voice she said, "My village needs meds. The vaccine for the pox."

None of the officers so much as raised an eyebrow. After the reaction she had received in Evergreen, Skye found the lack of reaction here quite surprising. The colonel tapped his chair with his finger.

"What makes you think we have vaccine here?"

"I was told this by a traveler who came to our village."

Moore stared at her intently. "There is no vaccine here."

Skye's heart fell in her chest. Her journey was a failure. She dropped her eyes to the wooden floor. There was no hope. She heard herself whisper, "Then I was misinformed."

She looked up to see the officers shift uneasily in their seats. "I am afraid many in my village are doomed. I must return at once." She stood up from her padded chair and found her knees were barely willing to support her.

The colonel said softly, "Please sit. I have a few more questions."

Skye bit her lip and tried not to show her discomfort. "Please, sir. I would like to be on my way. There are people waiting for my return with hope about what I may bring. Now it is evident it is but a cruel false hope, and I must in fairness let them know that."

Moore took a drink from the mug on the table by his side. "I encourage you to wait until morning. We will feed you and your animal, and you will be stronger for it."

Skye's pulse quickened. "You have my horse?"

Moore nodded. "It was picked up by one of my patrols. It is stabled now and being fed."

Skye's relief was tempered with anxiety. "Thank you for finding my animal and for taking care of her. May I ask what has become of my belongings?"

Moore's lips pursed into a thin smile. "You travel heavy for one so slight."

She answered, "I'm certain that I do not know your meaning."

Moore's jaw set in a way that made her think he did not believe her.

"You have food enough for only a short journey but you are armed like a combat soldier. Curious for someone only looking for vaccine.

Skye countered, "The wild is full of nasty people."

Moore persisted, "Do you have other intentions?"

Skye's back tightened at the implied accusation. With nothing to hide, she told the truth. "I carry the weapons as a means to bargain. I had hoped to trade them for the meds I need. I would not ask for such a thing without offering a worthy payment. Guns are what I have to trade. Good ones too. The guns I carry with me are but a sample of what I have to trade. I trust my weapons will be returned to me."

The colonel gave a slight nod. "Of course. Would you be willing to trade still?"

With the mention of the guns, she had sensed a slight change in the officers' attention. If human ears could perk up like an animal's, she was certain she had seen their ears perking up. "What do you have that I want?"

That had been the end of the conversation, and now Skye lay on her bunk wondering what had really happened. She sat up and took a bite out of the bread roll that had been left with the plate of food in her room. They had fed her well, and she was grateful for it. They had also allowed her to soak in a warm tub and scrub off the grime from the road.

She stood up, put on her freshly brushed hooded cape, and walked to the wooden door out of curiosity. She reached for the latch when suddenly it turned and swung open. To her complete surprise and delight, Myst stood in the doorway. Skye's mouth fell open, and she dropped the roll to the floor. "Myst! How did you get here?"

Myst looked at her with dark eyes. "I am glad to see you too."

Skye put her arms around her friend. "Are you well?"

Myst returned the embrace. Skye found the feel of her friend's arms around her comforting. Myst's voice was muffled by her pressing against Skye's chest. "I am fine, and you?"

Skye could hardly keep back tears of joy, and her voice cracked in response. "I am well also. What of Eagle?"

Skye heard a sob, but it was not one of happiness. "I fear for his life. They brought him here and he is with their doctors. I am afraid he will pass."

Skye stepped back and grabbed her friend by the arms, looking into her eyes. Thick tears streamed down Myst's face. "I tried to find meds in the fields but none were close. When I ventured too far, these people captured me. I had no choice except to ask for their help. They had other business and our journey here was slower than it needed to be for Eagle.

"When they captured Midnight, I was terrified that you had been hurt, or worse. I was much relieved when we entered the fort and I realized you were alive."

Skye wiped her nose. "Where is Eagle?"

"He is down these stairs and in the next building. They sent me to bring you to him."

Skye lowered her voice. "And the heavy guns?"

Myst whispered, "They remain hidden."

Skye entered Eagle's room, afraid of what she might find inside. The room was large with a dozen empty beds against each wall. White lights glared on the sterile walls and green tile floor. Aluminum carts filled with medical instruments were parked in intervals between the beds. What caught her attention were two women and a man in long blue gowns gathered around a gurney at the far end of the room.

They barely looked up as she approached. When she saw Eagle, a wave of nausea rolled through her. He was nearly as white as the sheets he lay on. His eyes were hollow and sunken in his face, and purple rings drooped under them. Skye went to the bedside and touched his matted hair.

The woman closest to her said softly, "Are you the one he asked for, the one called Skye?"

"I am."

"He kept asking for Skye, at first we thought he was delusional. If it wasn't for the girl here," she nodded toward Myst, "we wouldn't have known what he was talking about."

Skye could not take her eyes off of Eagle. "How is he?"

The woman shook her head. She pulled back the sheet that covered the boy and revealed his chest. The muscles on his shoulders sagged, and his skin was crossed with ugly red lines. The woman replaced the sheet. "Come with me."

The woman led Skye away from Eagle's bed and walked to the other end of the room, where they were joined by the other people in the blue gowns. The woman extended her hand to Skye and said, "I am Doctor Janis, and these are Doctors Choy and Bates."

Skye shook the doctor's hand, which had a firm grip with a soft feel. "Please tell me how my companion is."

Janis squinted her eyes slightly and brushed her dark hair away from her face with her fingers. "He is not good. His body has a massive infection, and I am afraid there is little we can do to prevent it from spreading further."

Skye tried not to show her emotion though her insides were churning and she knew the blood was draining from her face. "You said there is little you can do. Does that mean there is something you can do?"

Janis's lips grew tight and she looked away, shifting on her feet. Choy said in a barely audible voice, "There is one thing that would help."

Janis answered in an equally low voice, "It is not allowed. Especially for outsiders."

Skye was bewildered. "What? What can you do?"

Choy raised his voice a bit. "Only the chief surgeon can request it, and it must be approved by the colonel or by a vote of the Command Staff. They have never granted it to an outsider."

Skye's neck started to tighten and her pulse quickened. "Tell me, what do I have to do to make this happen? Who do I have to appeal to?"

Janis answered, "I'm afraid you will find it a vain pursuit. The meds we have are in limited supply and only used for the most dire of emergencies."

"What kind of meds?"

Bates spoke for the first time. "We have antibiotics and vaccines from the old days …"

Janis broke in, "That's enough!"

Skye said in wonder, "Vaccines? But I was told by the colonel that you didn't have any. Did he lie to me?"

Janis pressed her hands together. "Not according to our laws. You see, these meds are so valuable, and in such short supply, our laws say they cannot be used on outsiders. So as far as you are concerned, for practical purposes they don't exist."

Skye's cheeks started to burn in frustration. "Doctor Choy just said there could be exceptions."

Janis waved her hand dismissively. "There's never been one, and I hardly think one will be made for, excuse me as I mean no disrespect, a teenage boy who has made no contribution to the city."

Skye's jaw went slack. She couldn't think of what to say. She stammered in her disbelief, "You can't just let him die."

Choy spoke again. "I asked the chief surgeon to intervene already. He declined to elevate the issue. Unfortunately, even if we administer the antibiotics, there is still only a small chance they will be effective enough to save him. The surgeon believes it would be a waste of the medication."

The doctors all seemed to have found something of extreme interest to look at on the floor. Janis said, "Please believe us, we are quite sorry. I wish there is more we could do."

Skye kept her voice steady. "I wish you would do something instead of nothing. What kind of place is this where you have the means to save a life but choose not to?"

Janis sounded apologetic. "It is not our choice."

The door to the infirmary burst open, and two men in the uniform of the fort strode in. They quickly approached Skye and the doctors. The taller of the two addressed Skye. "Good day, I am Lieutenant

Jackson and this is Lieutenant Eyer. We have orders to invite you to an emergency meeting of the Command Staff that is convening now."

Still reeling from the discussion with the doctors, Skye's senses were jolted by the sudden change in topics. "Is this an invitation or a summons?"

Jackson gave her a smile and a slight bow with his head. "An invitation, ma'am, and one I am certain you will want to accept."

It was clear to her that this was indeed a summons. *So lucky to be among such polite people.* She looked at Janis. "Is this the Command Staff that can release the meds?"

Janis nodded. Skye looked at Jackson. "Let's go, and hurry."

Minutes later, she was ushered into a large room deep within the fort. In the center was a big round polished wooden table surrounded by twelve leather chairs. The walls were covered with maps she recognized as the local area. Lieutenant Jackson invited her to take a seat and then left her alone in the room.

Skye dropped her pack by the chair. She found that it swiveled, and she took a spin just to look around. Besides the maps, there was little else on the walls, just curtains that covered the unfinished bare wood. The light was dim, and she imagined it could be brought up if needed. The ceiling had miniature spotlights that she saw could be pointed at different angles by a control panel on the far side of the table from where she sat. There were also two large desks in opposite corners that had two chairs in front of them and pads of papers stacked on them.

While she sat, a man in a white uniform coat carried in a tray with cups of water on it. He moved around the room in silence and distributed the water in front of eight chairs, including Skye's, and then put a bottle on one of the desks and left without a word.

When the door opened again, four men and three women entered, each glancing at Skye as if she were some kind of strange animal they had heard about but never seen. Three of the men and one woman were in uniform. The last to come in was Colonel Moore. Uncomfortable that they were all looking down on her, Skye stood and made eye contact with Moore. He gave her a nod and motioned for her to take her seat.

Once all the others had taken their seats, the colonel introduced Skye to the group as the person he had told them about. In a quick manner, he named those at the table for her. She pretended to grasp them all and smiled and nodded.

With introductions done, he got to the point of the meeting. "The reason I have assembled the staff is to discuss a matter of great urgency. We have captured a group of men who claim they would be our allies. However, we do not have a way to verify if the story they tell is true. I have invited one of them to address the Command Staff so we can listen and decide if we believe him. I have also invited our guest, Miss Skye of the Long Lake, as she may have some information that will be of value to our questioning of the prisoner."

Skye had not the slightest clue as to what she could possibly know that would be of value to them in regard to a prisoner. In spite of their problems, there was one thing for certain she wanted to make sure got on the agenda. "Colonel Moore, sir. May I address the staff?"

Moore raised an eyebrow in question and then gave a nod of approval.

Skye steadied herself to speak to this intimidating group. "Thank you, sir." She looked at each individual around the table and then focused on the colonel. "I came to this place on a mission from my village. We have always believed there was still a place in the world where justice prevailed and where people were trying to build a new world where life would be fair and valued.

"We have heard many tales of the people of the mountains, so much so that perhaps we made those people into a myth of what we wanted them to be instead of what is true. In my small village, we survive by stealth; we have little contact with the outside because we have found it to be almost universally hostile and unkind to the weak. Still, the few contacts we have allowed have always spoken of this place as one that held the value of human dignity.

"Prior to this meeting I went to see my companion, who was

horribly injured on our journey here. Your troops were kind enough to bring him here and offer care. Unfortunately, your doctors tell me that without antibiotics, he will surely die. I am told this staff can allow the use of these meds to an outsider." She paused to take a drink from the water that was in front of her and hoped the others did not see her hand tremble as she put the water back down. She continued, "I implore you, I beg you to please release the meds he needs. Please help him."

All the eyes that had been locked on her turned away. She held her breath as everyone looked to the colonel. His face was tight. He met the eyes of each person on the staff. Skye could not discern what passed between them. Moore turned to her. "Thank you for reminding us of something we had forgotten. The purpose of this fort has always been to save the innocent and protect those who could not help themselves. Sometimes we lose track of what we are about."

Lieutenant Jackson had taken a seat at the desk near the door. The colonel called to him, "Lieutenant."

Jackson stood. "Sir?"

Moore said with authority, "Tell the chief surgeon to take all measures possible to save the boy. All measures. Am I clear?"

Jackson replied, "Crystal clear, sir. Crystal."

"Quickly, Lieutenant."

Skye wondered if Jackson heard him, as he was already halfway out the door.

After the lieutenant left, Moore turned his gaze to Skye. Her relief at knowing Eagle would get the best help available was tempered by her concern about why she was here at all. She took another swallow of water to buy time to collect her thoughts.

One of the women who was not in uniform spoke next. Skye recalled she had been introduced as Miss Baxter. She had short black hair and a pasty white complexion, making her appear as if she had not been outside much. Her features were sharp, and she wore a white sweater with a leaf pattern emblazoned on it. When she talked, Skye found her voice to be somewhat shrill and irritating.

Baxter stood and gave the members of the staff a withering look. "It is about time that someone noticed we have lost our purpose. I too would like to thank Miss Skye for pointing out our glaring deficiencies."

Skye saw Moore's jaw go tight, and the uniformed members of the council rolled their eyes in a "here we go again" manner, while those not in uniform nodded in agreement.

Moore replied in an even tone, "Miss Baxter, now is not the time for this discussion. We have an urgent matter to discuss concerning the prisoner we have captured and the news he claims to bring."

Baxter did not back down. "It seems there is never time to discuss the fact that we live in a virtual military dictatorship. We need to decide when the next elections will be held. Our people are tired of being told what they can do and what they can't do. The history of our civilization is based on freedom and the rule of the people. We need to reestablish that here and now."

Moore's look was one of contained rage. "Miss Baxter, this government was voted in to preserve our civilization. It was decided new elections will be held in the four-year vote. That is not due for another sixteen months. The newer people that have moved to this town are here by the good graces of the troops that fought to hold this land and freely offered to protect them from the thugs, gangs, and criminals that prowl the outlands. They are free to leave anytime they are so unhappy with their protections that they cannot stand it anymore. No one has ever been prevented from leaving, and in fact I encourage those so inclined to do so."

Baxter slapped the table with her hand. "That is not the point. The issue is that the wild times are over; you are living in a past that is no longer there. The gangs are gone; the outlands are not nearly what they were even a few years ago. We all owe a huge debt of gratitude to you and your brave troops, but face the new reality. This town is no longer just a military encampment struggling to survive from day to day. It is a place of peace and stability, and we need to accelerate the vote so we can adapt to our changing circumstances."

Moore slammed the table with his fist so hard it made the cups rattle. "It is you who is failing to learn from the past. The outlands remain dangerous and there is no reason to believe we are safer now than at any time in the last fifteen years. It is true we have not been attacked in the last few years, and that is only because we deal with the world from a position of strength and unity. The outsiders know that and find weaker targets to deal with. Without a firm central command, we could fall prey to those who want what we have."

Baxter sneered, "This regime is like a dictatorship. The people are restless and thirst for rapid change."

Moore shot back, "The people are safe and thirst for protection for their families."

A knock on the door broke the conversation. Moore shouted, "Enter."

The door opened, and a guard stepped into the conference room and saluted Moore. "I have the prisoner here, sir."

Moore returned the salute. "Very well, keep him outside until we call for you."

The guard backed out of the room and closed the door behind him. Skye still wasn't sure why she was here, and the argument between the two leaders was unsettling. She guessed Baxter had never been in the outlands. She had an urge to tell her details of her recent journey, though she thought she would be well out of place in doing so. She decided silence was probably her best course of action.

Moore took his seat and sat in silence. Baxter looked around the room and after what Skye thought was a long pause took her seat as well. Moore said with a flat tone, "Miss Baxter, the issues you bring up are valid and certainly in need of further discourse. However, I believe those discussions need to wait for a different time. The prisoner claims to have news that may sway your opinion to agree with me on this point."

Baxter snapped, "You always want to have this discussion at a future time. When will we decide that the future time is here?"

Moore almost came out of his seat. "When I damn well decide!"

Baxter smirked, "My point exactly."

Skye squirmed in her chair; this was something she had never expected and she was pretty sure no one had intended that she learn of the animosity between members of the Command Staff. She then mused that the term "Command Staff" was very generous. It implied that more than one person was making the decisions. Apparently there really was only one member of the staff that counted, and it was Colonel Moore. She was not sure if she liked that or not.

The man had saved her, and then he had lied to her. He chose to help Eagle though would not discuss sharing freedom for his people. *He at least seems to know the way the outside world works.*

Moore stood up again. "Enough of this. We need to address the issue of the men who were captured yesterday. There were eight of them, and they put up little resistance. They were pretty much driven into our hands, from what we're told. You have all seen the debriefing documents. The major in charge of the defense team was going to have them executed. One of the sergeants thought their story was of enough importance that it should be considered at a higher level. We are here to decide if he was right."

Colonel Moore turned his attention to Skye. "I know most of you are wondering why Miss Skye is here."

Skye nodded in silence. *I sure as hell am.*

Moore continued, "The senior prisoner, the one we are about to talk to, has made claims about his origins that no one in the fort has any way of verifying. He claims to have been a resident of this area, once in Seattle and then places east, at the time of the end. He further claims that he led a company of militia who went to the Middle East just before the end. Their aim, he says, was to join the coalition forces against the terrorists."

Baxter interjected, "Lots of soldiers and would-be soldiers went to the Middle East at that time. Most were mercenaries trying to cash in on the war before it spiraled out of control."

The officer who had been introduced as Major White, a man with deep black skin, a ramrod posture, and sharp eyes, interrupted, "You will recall that there were a lot of patriots who joined the war effort too."

Baxter scoffed at him, "Too few. The real patriots were the ones who demanded the war end before it started."

White looked at her with a grim face. "If not for them, the enemy wouldn't have been encouraged and the whole outcome might have been different."

Moore rapped the table with his knuckles. "We are not going to reopen this debate. At least not now."

Baxter muttered under her breath, "Of course not now. Now never seems to exist in your world."

The colonel said to Skye, with an air of resignation in his voice, "Miss Skye, please excuse our squabbling. If you please, do you recall the period before the end?"

Skye sat straight. She recalled it all too well. The terrifying journey from Seattle to Stehekin, her brother being murdered, the desperate battles to save the village. Sweat trickled down her back. "I do, sir. I was very young."

Baxter let out a gasp of exasperation. "What good is she? How old are you, girl? Were you even out of diapers?"

Skye resisted the urge to fire back at her. She clenched her teeth, remembering her mother always taught her to maintain composure under pressure. She was startled when the colonel snapped at Baxter, "You will not disrespect our guest again. In fact, one more word from you and you will be dismissed from this meeting."

Baxter shot him a nasty look, folded her arms across her chest, and leaned back in her chair without comment.

Moore softened his tone. "Miss Skye, please tell us if you know of any men from where you lived who might have gone off to the war."

Skye leaned forward and spoke in a firm voice. "I was young, it is true, but my memories are vivid. The men of our village believed the war was going poorly. Allies had deserted us and our troops needed help. They had formed as a company of soldiers, most had been in the previous war, and they answered the call from the government to join the effort.

"All of our men left, that is except for one, and he does not really count."

Moore asked softly, "What became of them?"

Skye pondered the odd question. She assumed everyone knew. "What became of them? It was only days after they departed that the end started. We never heard from them again."

She brushed away a tear that was forming in her eye. "I am sorry if I am not much help."

Moore prodded her further, "Do you think you might recognize the men, or perhaps their names, if you were to see them again?"

Skye was unprepared for this question. It represented a hope she had suppressed for most of her life. A hope that somewhere, somehow, the men of the village, including her father, had survived and might be on their way back. On their way home to the wives and children who waited for them. She drew in a deep breath as the air seemed to be leaving the room. She whispered, "I believe I would."

Moore called to the guard, "Bring in the prisoner."

The door opened, and a thin man in a slightly tattered uniform was led into the room. Skye stood in shock. Her knees almost gave way under her. The man squinted in the light, and then after a long moment his eyes met hers.

She stammered, "Father?"

He paused, and then whispered, "Skye?"

CHAPTER THIRTY-SEVEN

PREPARATIONS

IVAN STAMPED HIS FEET to keep the circulation going in them. It was cold, though not the bitter cold of his homeland. It had started snowing at midmorning and steadily increased all day. Evening was now on the advance team he was commanding, and the gloom of the afternoon had given way to a dark night filled with blowing white streaks. He waited impatiently while the last of the trucks in his direct command eased through the small pass the road followed through the mountains. He hated mountain fighting.

After the truck passed, he left his spot on the side of the road and walked behind. The column of ten vehicles made thick tracks in the wet snow, and he used them as a makeshift trail. He was careful not to slip as he looked as far up the mountainside as possible. He knew before he looked that he wouldn't see much. He didn't. He cursed the night and his commander in the same breath. *They will never expect us to attack in this weather. Only fools would try it.*

He wondered what had become of Francois. He had not seen him for a day and a half. *Maybe he deserted and is going to try to live off the land or find a village we have overlooked. That is an idea that has a great deal of appeal to it, as long as you don't get caught.*

Even though the truck ahead of him was gunning its engine loudly as it strained up the slope with its cargo of men and equipment, he heard a new engine come from behind. He turned and had to shield his eyes from the bright lights of a command car that approached at a reckless speed. He waved his hands and realized it was doing no good, so he hurried off the road and slipped in the process.

Ivan went face down into a snow bank. The car missed him by inches. He jumped to his feet in anger as the car skidded to a stop. Furious, he approached the vehicle to admonish the idiot driver. The door swung open, and he was startled to see Lieutenant Ja-Zeer, who he knew had unusual influence with Barzan, emerge from the driver's seat; he also saw a priest in the passenger seat. A large grin crossed Ja-Zeer's face that did not improve Ivan's disposition at all.

The lieutenant said in rapid bursts, "I knew Russians liked the snow. I just did not know you enjoyed to kiss it, my general."

Ivan resented the sarcasm in the lower ranking officer's demeanor but decided to hold his temper and brush it off, for the moment. "With respect, Lieutenant, we will kiss most anything if it will keep us alive. Getting out of the way of a speeding car can make strange things your friends."

The lieutenant kept a wide grin and spoke with the arrogance of someone more important than his rank. "I see. And I am able to trust that you are not injured other than in your pride. Perhaps not a bad thing; pride should be injured from time to time to help a man know his place."

Ivan took his hat off and used it to brush snow from his trousers. "And I am able to trust you did not come to the front simply to injure my pride?"

The lieutenant grinned again. "A truly perceptive man. No wonder the commander holds you close to the top."

Ivan could not quite decide if Ja-Zeer was toying with him or not. He waited for him to continue.

"My, I think you use the term 'comrade,' it is a glorious day for the Malsi army."

Ivan tried to guess at his meaning. "Yes, the day before a battle is always glorious. We give the troops the drug and all are happy to do our will."

The lieutenant let his smile go. "The spiritual elixir is the motivation for our brave warriors. It has served us well for many years; you should be glad we have such a potent weapon. This is not why I came here. I bring great news from the commander."

Ivan put his hat back on. "Isn't all news from our commander great?"

"Your attitude is only tolerated because of your strategic capabilities. Now here is the news. There were prisoners captured by our scouts in the afternoon."

Ivan shook his head. "This is not news, and they were all killed this morning. I saw them myself."

The lieutenant's grin came back. "You do not know what you think you know. Yes, there was an attack this morning and our great commander led the assault. All of the infidels were killed as you saw. There were other separate incidents later that resulted in the capture of prisoners. One small group knew details of this fort we approach. They saw they were well outnumbered and surrendered with no fight and have already given us information we could never hope to get otherwise.

"They have revealed approaches to the fort we would not find in a hundred years. Even now, Barzan has updated the attack plan. We will crush the enemy before the sun comes to the hour of noon."

Ivan was skeptical. "This seems very convenient. Is there no worry of a trap?"

Ja-Zeer climbed back into his vehicle and spoke through the open door. "Barzan is planning an attack. He would not do so unless he was confident of victory. Here are your orders." He handed Barzan a leather pouch.

Ivan put the picture together in his mind. "We will make a decisive strike on the fort at dawn with the main body. The main force will attack from the front and at the same time we will launch an attack to the rear on what can only be a small force. This indeed may be a glorious day. With the fort out of the way, then we can find Barzan's main target."

Ja-Zeer closed his door and said to Ivan though the open window, "It is better than that. I believe the attack on the fort is only part of his plan. The prisoners told us of a path around the fort over the mountains that vehicles cannot traverse. We have troops exploring it now. We will get to Barzan's target one way or the other."

CHAPTER THIRTY-EIGHT

GETTING ACQUAINTED

JOHN CROSSED THE ROOM to Skye, and the two gently clasped hands and then wrapped their arms around each other in a fierce embrace. It had been over a decade since she had last seen him. The joy that filled her was almost beyond containment. She wanted to leap into his arms, ask him a million questions, cry on his shoulder, and much, much more. She knew it would be out of place to do these things now, which only made suppressing them harder.

When he left, she had been but a small girl, yet she remembered his features and his build as if it were yesterday. Of course he was older now, his once black hair was peppered with gray streaks, and it was a little longer than before. His face was thinner, as was the rest of him. He was trim, and from what she could tell, his muscles were firm. His face had a dark tan, and there was a slight scar on his left cheek. His deep blue eyes had the same intensity she remembered as a child, and his smile was like no other she had ever known.

The embrace was warm, and she felt the firmness in his touch she had held only in her memory. It surprised her how much she had missed it. She stifled her tears when he whispered, "I have missed you so. How is your mother?"

She almost choked on the answer. "I have missed you also. I am afraid I must tell you Mother is not well. That is what brings me here."

Colonel Moore spoke from across the table. "It would seem you two are related. How delightful. With the staff's permission I believe we can dispense with the planned questioning and inquire about what information Colonel Erikson has brought us."

The staff nodded in agreement. Skye was relieved to see even Miss Baxter did not object. Colonel Moore sent the guard out, gave brief introductions, and invited John to sit. John took a seat beside Skye at the staff table, and she tried to get her mind around the idea that she was actually sitting next to her father. She wanted to rush him out of the conference room and find out everything about him. As it was, she tried not to fidget in her seat.

Colonel Moore put his arms on the table and put his hands together. "We are told you have news of a potential threat to our city."

John leveled his eyes at him. "With respect, sir, this is not a potential threat. This is a force that will make every effort to wipe you out, without warning, without mercy."

Moore raised an eyebrow. "Where do they come from and why have we not seen them before?"

"You have not seen them before because they have only recently arrived on these shores. My men and I, the remnants of the coalition that started to fight the war on terror, have kept them occupied in the Old World, if you will, until just recently."

Baxter broke in, "You mean to tell us you're still fighting that war? That was done a decade and a half ago."

Skye sent her a hard look that she realized went unnoticed.

John nodded. "That is correct. The fight we have been in has been a different struggle entirely."

Baxter responded, "If the war on terror was over so long ago, who won?"

John cocked his head as if he had not heard the question right. "Who won? Well, obviously they did. They set out to bring down

Western civilization, and they started the chain of events that caused it. However, they got waxed too."

Colonel Moore interjected, "Please forgive our ignorance. From our vantage point, when the end came, it was swift and nearly without warning. Once the world communication links went dead, we heard virtually nothing except what we learned from occasional travelers, and we have not seen many of them. Please tell us what happened."

John rolled his shoulders as if trying to relax them. Skye recalled him doing this even when she was a child and realized she had adopted the same mannerism. John looked around the table and said, "I fear you do not take the threat facing you seriously or realize how close you are to extermination. My time here will be futile and wasted if I cannot convince you what an ungodly menace you face. Perhaps if I can keep my remarks brief, I will be able to tell you our story and you will then take measures to protect yourselves.

"In this event, I will offer myself and my men to your services. However, I will do this under one condition."

Moore nodded. "Go on."

"If at the end of my story I am not convinced you take this threat to heart and will take every action you can to stop it, then you will release me, my daughter, and my men so that we may avoid your fate."

Skye had to add, "And Myst and Eagle, my horses and ... enough vaccine for my village." She looked at her father, wondering how he would react to her brashness.

John kept his eyes on the colonel, adding, "And what she said."

Skye's heart raced, and she noticed the room had become very warm. That her father agreed with her without question sent a rush of satisfaction through her.

Moore leaned back in his chair and rubbed his chin with his fingers. He was silent for what Skye thought was a long time. Moore said, "I agree to everything but the vaccine."

Skye reached over and squeezed her father's hand and whispered, "We must have the vaccine. Mother and the rest need it desperately. I have a sample of automatic weapons to trade."

John did not change expression. "If you do not believe me, you will have no need for vaccines, or anything else for that matter. Our conditions stand."

Baxter broke in again, "You seem somewhat pretentious, Colonel Erikson. You offer up a story that may or may not be true. Then if we don't satisfy you by running around and getting ready for what we can only guess is a war, you waltz out of here with all your men and all of our precious meds. What if we do not agree to your outrageous demands?"

John looked at her with the same steady gaze he maintained throughout. "We don't want all of your meds, only enough for our small village. We will trade fairly for them. Beyond that, if you do not accept my offer of life for your village and life for my village, all of us here will die together."

Baxter opened her mouth to speak but Moore cut her off. "We will consider your offer with the following addition. Your daughter came here with the sole purpose of gaining our vaccine. She told me she was willing to trade goods for them. If we let you go with the vaccine, we retain the goods she brought to trade."

Baxter snarled, "What does she have that we want?"

Skye's blood pumped through her veins in aggravation. She jammed her hand into the inside of her pack, reached in, and grasped a handful of high caliber bullets. Drawing them out, she slammed them on the table so they scattered across the polished surface. "I have these, and lots of them."

There was a low whistle from Major White. He stood and walked to Skye's place. Standing over her, he picked up one of the rounds and examined it. "You have anything to shoot this out of?"

Skye nodded firmly.

White held the bullet up to the light so all could see it. "She's got what we want."

The others moved to examine the bullets with brass casings scattered on the table. John leaned to Skye and whispered in a barely audible voice, "Is everything intact at home?"

The question startled Skye. Years of being isolated and living in secrecy had made her suspicious of all questions regarding the village. She hesitated and found herself embarrassed to find a morsel of distrust toward her father. She answered, "Yes, why?"

Before he could answer, Moore rapped the table with his knuckles to get everyone's attention. Leaning forward, he looked at John. "Well, Colonel Erikson, seems like you two drive a hard bargain. For our sakes, I hope your story is unconvincing. Unfortunately, I'm afraid that will not be the case. Please tell us what happened to the world."

John faced the staff of the fort. He took a sip of the water that had been placed in front of him and tried to frame the story he was to tell. It had started so long ago that he found he had a difficult time putting it all into perspective. It was a story he decided that had to start from the beginning, or at least near it.

"You may recall when the Soviet Union collapsed in the late 1980s and early 1990s, there was a great relief in the Western world, and the idea of a large conflict seemed unimaginable. Those who wished for peace chose to see this as a time of great opportunity and a time to scale down the armies that had kept the peace in the years of the cold war.

"The Europeans were especially anxious to stop paying defense bills and put their money and energy into business and social programs. A period transpired when the United States was the greatest power on the planet, both in economic might and military prowess. The thing few people in the West recognized was the raw power of the poverty and hatred that had festered in the African and Arabian world for years.

"While the first Gulf War looked like a clear win for the coalition forces, in reality it only served as an insult to the many who practiced the religion of Islam. A great Arab country was reduced to rubble in a few hours, and Western forces annihilated one of the largest armies in the world in a few days.

"This set the seeds of resentment, which coupled with the West's continued backing of Israel made it easy for radical clerics to recruit men who were willing to die to save their sacred ground. The leaders of the West ignored the warning signs, the bombings and murders, and words coming from the East, and did nothing to prevent it from spreading.

"After the terror attacks of September 11, 2001, it became clear to some of us the world was not as stable as we once thought it was. The history of the twentieth century is really the story of major wars. Two world conflicts within a few decades of each other, numerous small wars around the globe mostly between proxies of the United States and Russia, and these two countries each had their own costly wars in Vietnam and Afghanistan.

"The terrorists, fundamentalists, whatever you want to call them, had two goals. One, to rid their holy lands of all infidels, and two, to bring the West down by collapsing its economy.

"A small group of us became convinced that the United States and the West were far too vulnerable to the loss of oil from the Middle East to not take personal preventive action. We purchased land in a small village well away from any population centers. We selected the members of our group by their moral orientation. We wanted people who would be able to contribute to a group by their skills and dedication. Above all we wanted people who were just and who believed in freedom.

"It was essential that several members of our group had almost unlimited funds, and we were able to secure the things we needed to stock our village for what we thought would be dark times. We had no idea we would be so correct in our assumptions. The locals only tolerated us at first, but eventually most of them joined us; the others left for even remoter places.

"When the last oil war started, none of us were truly ready for it. You may recall that the Afghanistan war had dragged on in various forms for over a decade. When the Iranians developed their nuclear weapons, the change in the balance of power in the region was striking. Once the hard-line Islamists had the bomb, we thought it would only be a matter of time before they would be willing to share it with the fundamentalists.

"It is hard to say there was one event that triggered the end, there were so many pieces in place: the West's total dependence on foreign oil, the outsourcing of core jobs and technologies from the United States to foreign shores, the arrogance of the West, the ability of the Islamic fundamentalist to be able to sell the war to their impoverished people as a religious struggle, the weakness of the Europeans.

"If there was one event, it was probably the fall of the house of Saud. We were still in Seattle when that occurred. The Wahabies, who the Saudis had nurtured for decades, finally turned on the royal family during the hajj. The security forces were no match for the millions of pilgrims who were whipped into a frenzy by a firebrand cleric named Laden.

"The impact was almost immediate. The richest oil fields in the world were shut down overnight. The uprising swept across the Arab lands, and in short order virtually all oil production came to a halt. The global economies came to a standstill. In a matter of months, food riots started breaking out across the globe as farm goods could not find transport to the metropolitan areas. We had to flee Seattle as the infrastructures started to collapse.

"With our families secure in our hideaway, we had to determine our next move. As part of our organization, we were all reservists in the Army Rangers. With the situations in Afghanistan and Iraq deteriorating, we volunteered to join our forces there.

"By the time we got there, almost all the coalition forces had been withdrawn to Europe. What we found on arrival was appalling. Every moderate government in the Middle East had been overthrown.

"Things are a little less clear after this. I don't know which happened first. At this point, it does not matter. We got word by radio that a nuclear device went off in Jerusalem, wiping it off the map. In short order Mecca, Tehran, and Damascus were obliterated. Then the Vatican in Rome was attacked in the same way.

"We had reports come in from all over the world, and in the space of a week, we had lost all satellite communication with any of our forces anywhere. Pilots who came during that week reported mushroom clouds all over Europe, static in their earphones on every channel, and no signals to guide them."

John stopped and took a drink of water. Colonel Moore broke a long silence. "What happened in Europe?"

John shook his head. "Bio-weapons devastated the populations. What antidotes that were available went to coalition forces. The same with available oil reserves.

"Then a new enemy emerged, the Malsi." John shook his head again. "The Muslims at least believed in something. Once Mecca with the sacred Ka'ba was obliterated, the clerics lost their hold on the people. Over the course of the next several years, a new 'religion,' if you will, led by someone called the Emperor Prophet, channeled the energy of the masses of the people in the region. The priests and their army strictly controlled food supplies and freely gave out a narcotic. They taught that all nonbelievers must die. I'm still not sure what they believe, but they are real damn adamant about it."

Baxter whispered, "What did you do?"

"We tried to hunker down and build defenses but with little infrastructure, day-to-day survival was our biggest problem. The coalition spent the next five years fighting across Europe, mostly retreating, dodging nuclear hotspots as we could, until we ran out of places to be. It was pretty grim."

Moore asked, "How did you get here?"

John answered, "We discovered one of their most ruthless commanders planned to assault Stehekin. What is left of the coalition released us so we could return home and prevent him from succeeding. We were able to get a cargo ship going, and we arrived here just as he and a sizable force arrived."

John saw Moore sit up in his chair. "Stehekin? What the hell does he want there?"

"Two things. First, he wants revenge on me for problems we caused him. More importantly, he wants what is there."

John saw Moore's right eyebrow raise. "What's there?"

John paused and looked at the faces around the room. He took a deep breath. "Six tactical nuclear weapons."

An insistent knock came from the door. Moore called, "Enter."

Lieutenant Eyer came in. "Sir, it looks like we are about to be attacked."

"Where?"

"The south gate, and movement has been seen across the approach to the front gate."

Moore said, "Rally the troops."

John asked, "So we have a deal?"

Moore nodded. "We have a deal."

John turned to Skye. "Can you take them to your goods?"

Skye answered, "My companion Myst can, she knows the way. I prefer to stay with you and prepare for the fight."

John nodded and then spoke to the entire staff. "The Malsi, especially Barzan, like to attack at dawn. The sun will be up in a few hours. I suggest you prepare for your defense."

CHAPTER THIRTY-NINE

NOT HUMAN

IVAN MADE HIS WAY to the front of the column, which had come to an unplanned halt on the road. He found Hassan, the advance team leader, and asked, "Why are we stopping? We need to be in place by dawn, and it is almost midnight now."

Hassan pointed up the road. "There is a house we must pass in front of. It is occupied, and they will surely see us. My orders are clear that we must move to this new attack point undetected. What would you have us do?"

Ivan kicked at the snow that was covering his boots in frustration. The latest attack plan from Barzan was very specific. "Our orders from the commander only say that no one must know of our arrival. Surround the house and take those inside prisoner. Let none escape."

Hassan protested, "This will slow us down, and then we will have to use some of our men to watch the prisoners. We have few enough as it is."

Ivan glared at the man, though he knew the full effect was lost on him as Ivan's eyes were covered by goggles and the coat of his collar was pushed up around his mouth. "Do not question me. I know full well that we have few enough men for this mission. If you attack the house, your weapons and the lights from them may tell the enemy of our presence. Take this place quietly, and we will just have to deal with the prisoners. They may have information that is useful to us." *Everybody else's prisoners have been helpful.*

Ivan took a position on a hill just overlooking the house. Yellow lights shone from the windows, casting a reflection on the snow that surrounded the place. The house was in a clearing with trees all around it. He guessed it was a farmhouse. There were two levels and a space in front that he thought must be a yard. For a moment, he thought of the house he had been raised in outside Odessa. It had been a warm, secure place where he always felt safe. He pitied the people in the house in front of him.

Even with his binoculars, he could not make out any movement around the place. Just as he was beginning to wonder how long Hassan's men would take, five figures emerged from the woods, running fast. They covered the clear space in seconds and in silence made it to the broad porch that ran in front of the house. The first man crossed the porch and with one kick burst the door open. The others raced inside, out of Ivan's sight.

Ivan stood and brushed the snow from his legs. In a few moments, the men came back outside; this time, they pushed three other people in front of them. Ivan raised his binoculars again. There was one small boy, perhaps seven or eight years old. His face was a mask of terror. The other two were women.

They were dressed in long white night coats that flowed around them. He focused on the first. She had long dark hair that went to her shoulders; her face was that of an adolescent and carried a horrified expression. He looked at the other. She had shorter hair, and he figured she must be the mother. As he watched her, she suddenly pushed at the soldier closest to her and let out a loud scream of anguish.

Ivan shifted his view and saw what caused her to cry out. The boy's body lay bleeding in the snow, and one of Hassan's men held the child's severed head high in the air. Ivan's stomach lurched in revulsion. He let his binoculars down so he could see the full picture.

Two of the men grabbed the mother, and two others held the girl. More men came from the woods, and one of them ripped the gown off the girl. Ivan yelled to Hassan, who was standing near him, "Make them stop! I want the prisoners!"

Hassan answered with disdain, "Why should you have all the fun? The commander has always said the spoils of war are ours."

Ivan looked at him. "Idiot." He started to run down the hill to the house through the foot-deep snow. "Stop!" He tripped on a covered branch and fell to his knees. Even as he got to his feet, he could see the men were having their way with the girl, and they forced the mother to watch. One of them tossed the boy's head to her and she recoiled in horror; it dropped at her feet.

Ivan ran as best he could and then discovered that a stream he had not seen cut between him and the house. The air was filled with the sounds of the screams of the women and the malevolent laughter of the men. Ivan stumbled down the steep slope to the stream and splashed across the shallow water. The far side was steep and slick with snow-covered mud. He clawed his way up on his hands and knees.

When he finally got to the top, the screams of the girl had stopped and the mother was sobbing. It was joined by the sound of the crude laughs of the drugged men's shouts of victory. Ivan stood above the stream bank, and the gruesome sight in front of him sent another wave of revulsion through him.

The heads of the boy and girl were mounted on the front porch of the house, side by side. The mother lay in the snow with several of Hassan's men all around her and one on top of her. Ivan shouted, "Stop, I command you." He heard his voice trail off into near nothingness. He knew they could not hear over their own laughter. He started to run again. His feet seemed to mire in the snow. With every step, the distance between himself and the house seemed to grow farther, not closer.

As he ran, he continued to watch the scene with horror and growing anger. He shouted again to no avail. Just when he thought he was close enough to be heard, a sharp blade rose into the air over the woman on the ground. With all that was in him, he yelled, "No!" The blade descended even as the word left his lips.

Howls of laughter echoed in the night. A hand raised the mother's head above the men, who were jumping up and down in the ritual of the Malsi victory dance. Ivan drew to a stop. His breath escaped him. He dropped to his knees, and his stomach could no longer be contained. He had seen much death in his battles all over the world but there was something different here he could not explain to himself. *I have got to escape this insanity.*

He retched his guts out into the snow, staining it with the bile from his stomach. He caught his breath and retched again and again. His sides started to ache. When the waves of nausea subsided, he took clean snow and rinsed his mouth. He sat in the snow, trying to clear his mind. As he did, Hassan approached.

The team leader looked down on Ivan where he sat. "It is good the men did not see you in this condition. They would wonder if you had the stomach for a fight, or the nerve to lead them."

Ivan took some more snow into his mouth and spit out more of the foul taste that was in it. "There was no need for that slaughter."

Hassan said, "What do you care? Those are not humans."

Ivan looked up at him. "Which ones?"

Even in the dark, Ivan could tell Hassan had sharpened his gaze. "You start to worry me, General."

Ivan stood so he would be eye level with Hassan. "Worry you?"

Hassan had a threatening tone to his voice. "You do not sound very respectful of the Malsi way."

Ivan put an edge in his voice. "No, Team Leader, it is you who worries me. You and your men cannot even carry out a simple command. 'Bring me prisoners for interrogation.' A direct order and one that was very clear. Instead of that, we have your men doing as they please. If you cannot control your men, especially in such a simple operation as this one, how can I expect you to be able to control them in a real fight?"

Hassan's voice lost some of its harshness. "Do not worry, they are battle tested."

Ivan spit again. "The men who took the house need to be executed immediately. Being battle tested is no excuse for not following orders.

Also, I want a new cook assigned to me. The one I have now nearly poisoned me with the garbage he served for dinner. See to it."

Hassan took a step back. "As you wish."

Ivan stared at him hard. "Team Leader."

"Yes?"

"Be careful how you speak to me. I will not tolerate insolence."

Hassan gave him a salute. "I understand perfectly. You will have a new cook for the late meal. The men will be harshly punished when we rejoin the main force."

Hassan tromped off though the snow. Ivan watched him leave; his words still echoed in the back of Ivan's mind: "They would wonder if you had the stomach for a fight."

CHAPTER FORTY

THE BATTLE OF NEW LEAVENWORTH

M YST WAS AWAKENED BY the sound of a loud knock on a wooden door. She opened her eyes to a dense blackness. She caught her breath and tried to remember where she was. *The fort. There is going to be a battle.* She tossed the bed covers off herself, put her feet on the cold stone floor, and called out, "I will be ready in a moment. I know the place you want to go and will lead you there. Just one moment of privacy please."

She dressed quickly, draped her cloak over her shoulders, and opened the door. She greeted Shelly and the soldier she remembered as Carver. "I am ready; I will take you to the goods we brought to trade."

Shelly stepped back in surprise. "You know why we are here?"

Myst blinked in the harsh luminescence of the hallway. "Of course. The only thing anyone cares about us is what we have to trade. I know where our goods are, and Skye told me to take you to them. My only concern is that it is dark, and the journey is long. We may not return in time for our goods to be of value."

Myst thought Shelly's face looked harder than she remembered.

Shelly said, "Time is not the problem. We have means of getting to your cache with ease. As for darkness, we make our own light."

Myst suppressed her smile. "Then we must hurry through the dark."

In the Command Staff headquarters, Moore completed his briefing on the defenses and the staff stood to leave when a massive explosion shook the room, knocking some off their feet. Dust blew through the air, and those still standing steadied themselves on whatever was near.

Colonel Moore called to John, "Do the Malsi have many big guns?"

John shouted back, "On the way here, we scouted them and only saw one. It's a 120mm howitzer and if you don't have something to shoot back with, we are going to be in a world of hurt. What about the tanks we saw?"

Moore said quickly, "Decorations, they haven't run in years and the cannons are inoperable. We are reduced to a few guns, mortars, and a lot of bows and arrows but we mainly use those to hunt to save bullets. We don't have the tools to produce new guns or very accurate ammo. We expended most of our good stuff in the early years when everything went to hell."

Skye saw her father's eyes narrow. "Not good." Another explosion rocked the room. "We need to turn that thing off, fast."

Skye trailed Colonel Moore, her father, and Major White to an observation point that was dug into the side of the mountain above the fort. She sucked in a deep breath as dawn revealed the scene in the clear area in front of the first wall of the fort.

People streamed into the fort through the main gate in what looked like a loosely controlled panic. Soldiers armed with rifles and some with lances and clubs kept people in line on the road, urging them to hurry. The people pulled carts and wagons and carried those things dearest to them. The wall of the fort stood thirty feet high and consisted of layers of thick rocks. It had a slight bow to it and met the mountain cliffs one hundred yards on either side of the twenty-foot-wide gate.

John said to Moore, "I'd like to take my men and try to get to the cannon. We know these guys and how they deploy. I think we'd have the best chance of success."

Moore responded, "I'll send some of my men with you, we know the territory."

Skye looked to her father. "Of course I will go with you."

John raised an eyebrow. "Skye, I love you dearly. I do not think I could stand it if after all this time something happened to you. Besides, we will be quite occupied and will not be able to look after you."

Skye winced. It was as if he had slapped her in the face.

Behind she heard Moore let out a soft whistle. "Careful about your judgments, Colonel Erikson. I have no intention of getting into a family matter, but this woman can take care of herself. I have seen her in action."

Skye tried not to sound pleading. "Please, Father, I am a defender of the village. I have skills you don't know."

He responded, "That may be. Nonetheless you do not know the vicious nature of this enemy, and I will not expose you to it."

Skye's swallowed hard, and she looked away in despair. Soldiers prowled the ramparts built onto the thick walls. Most carried rifles but a few had only spears and bows. She wondered where Myst was. A rumbling blast from afar signaled another incoming round from the Malsi cannon. Skye flinched at the sound and the horrible screeching the projectile made as it hurtled through the air seeking its target.

This time the impact was near the inner court, where the refugees were seeking shelter. The huge explosion sent people and animals flying in all directions. Smoke billowed from the yard and those not hit screamed in terror loud enough for those high above in the observation platform to hear them clearly. The soldiers tried to keep order on the road and prevent complete chaos from enveloping the fort.

She heard her father say, "I think the spotter is on the ridge right over there, below the two cedar trees." She could hardly believe her ears; *Didn't he see what I just saw? Some of those people were killed …*

Major White answered, "I think you're right. We'll have to get a team out there. It will take a couple of hours though."

John sighed, "If we had a sniper rifle, we could get him from here. That might not stop the shelling but at least it would knock off their accuracy a little bit."

Skye looked to the place her father had described. Squinting into the glare the sun created on the fresh snow, she found she could see two men in dark robes sitting calmly below two towering trees. One had binoculars and was studying the fort. He said something and a moment later the second man waved signal flags to a point well out of her sight. A few seconds later, another shot from the lethal cannon was on its way.

This round exploded near the base of the wall and luckily missed the refugee trail. Colonel Moore stated flatly, "We can't take much more of this. We need to get the spotter and the artillery piece. We'll have to send two teams. Volunteers only."

Skye could not stifle her question. "How far do you think that is … from here to the one you call the spotter."

Major White said, "Just short of a thousand yards as the crow flies. We've ranged it before. Unfortunately, the terrain makes it more like two miles for a man to travel."

Skye turned to Moore. "You said that when my animals were brought in they had all my things. Are they near?"

Moore eyed her curiously. "Yes, why?"

"If someone can show me to them, I believe I can be of some assistance with this problem."

A few minutes later, she returned to the platform with her favorite rifle. On seeing it, her father whistled and said, "A Marine Corps M40A1 complete with a 10X scope. We only stashed a few of these. You know how to use it?"

Skye nodded and chambered a round.

Her father said, "It's not that I don't trust you but show me a shot away from the spotters. I don't want to spook them if you miss."

She tried not to let irritation into her voice. "I don't have many rounds, it is custom-made ammo."

He replied, "I know, I'm the one that stashed it, remember? Not to put too fine a point on it, if you need more than one shot per target, we will need another shooter. Consider it a windage round."

Skye pointed to a Humvee across the valley that she estimated was close to the same distance as the spotters, but out of the line of site from their location on the mountainside. "There, the guy on the right in the orange."

She put the rifle to her shoulder, got the sight picture she wanted taking into account the elevation change, held her breath, and squeezed the trigger. The weapon jumped in her hands and she raised her eye above the sight in time to see the orange-clad figure get blown off the back of the Humvee.

Almost at the same time, another report from the howitzer sounded and she watched as another projectile exploded near the gate, scattering people in panic. She looked at her father and said, "Not to put too fine a point on it, but are we going to let them do that all day?"

He shook his head. "Fire away."

Skye leveled her rifle at the spotter on the ridge. Through her telescopic sight, she saw the man laugh with his companion and take a bite of something. She steadied her weapon on the rock wall in front of her and let out half a breath and held it. The man raised his binoculars and looked right at her. She softly said, "Hello," and then squeezed the trigger and fired the rifle.

The recoil kicked the muzzle up and the butt into her shoulder. She steadied it again, peered through the scope, and saw her target laid flat out on the ground.

From behind her, Colonel Moore let out a breath. "Nice shot."

Skye shifted her aim to the shocked signalman, who stood looking around as if trying to see where the shot came from. An instant later, he lay dead beside his companion.

Her father placed his hand on her shoulder. "I'm sorry to see the skills you have needed to develop in these times. Those were shots not taken lightly or without considerable skill. Please forgive me for doubting your abilities."

Skye lowered her eyes. "You have been gone so long, there is no reason for you to know me."

Her father put his hand under her chin and raised her face so that their eyes met. His piercing blue eyes held a sorrow she had not seen before. "I will go with my men and we will defeat this enemy. When we return, I hope you and I can learn more about each other. Please give your mother my love. You must return with the vaccines before it is too late."

She blinked hard to keep tears of disappointment and anger back. "I am a warrior and belong in battle with you. Yet I also know how to follow orders. I will do as you command."

He put his arms around her, and she let her arms stay at her side, not able to muster the warmth of a hug.

Her father and the others left her standing alone on the observation platform. She turned back to the view of the valley as the sounds of their footsteps on the rock surface disappeared behind her. Then her stomach turned. At the edge of the clearing in front of the fort, a huge army emerged from the woods a mile away.

The first to appear was a long line of men in dark robes. With the binoculars, she could see they carried spears and swords. Interspersed with these weapons, she saw some rifles and automatic weapons. She estimated they had a higher ratio of guns than the defenders did. Beyond that, there seemed to be more of them in sheer numbers. Colonel Moore had said they had five hundred soldiers in the fort and another six hundred civilians. She estimated there were at least that many men advancing across the valley. She slung her M40A1 over her shoulder. *Not enough bullets to do any good against that many. Better rearm with something better suited to this battle.*

As she descended from the lookout platform, she saw the enemy advance into the clearing then form into a line that stretched across the two hundred yards of the valley.

When the last of the people on the road saw the Malsi army, there was a huge surge as the refugees abandoned all their carts and pressed into the gate. Once the last of them was in, the massive wooden doors swung shut, sealing the main entrance to the fort. Skye wondered if their fate had been sealed as well.

John walked with Colonel Moore through the labyrinth of tunnels underneath the fort. "If we take the cannon out, I'll shoot a green flare in the air. If you don't see it, expect more shelling."

Moore showed him into a large room with iron gun racks on either side. "Our armaments have not fared well over the years. We do still have some that will be useful to you. How is the enemy armed?"

John looked over the mostly empty racks. "Surprisingly poorly. They have a small quantity of guns, which they use sparingly. We think they have limited ammunition. They mostly rely on primitive weapons and numbers."

Moore unlocked one of the racks with a metal key. "That is a little good news. Perhaps we won't be overwhelmed by fire power."

"This Malsi force you face is cunning and bold. If you think you've won today, you must prepare for a greater battle in the future. At first their tactics will look clumsy and stupid. They will often send a wave of conscripts in human wave attacks to test defenses and set up the main force for the kill. I will take my men and take out that gun as soon as we can."

Moore shook his hand. "Thanks for your help. I look forward to seeing you again. I wager it won't be that long. A squad of my men will join you at the eastern exit. It is well hidden and will allow you to get out without being seen."

John glanced around the room to make sure they were alone and then spoke in a low tone. "If you survive this attack, and I don't return, take care of Skye. She can help you more than you know. We must not let these bastards get to Stehekin."

Moore raised an eyebrow. "I will look after her, though from what I've seen she may end up looking after us. I will see you again, my friend."

John extended his hand and they shook again. "You must like underdogs. I'll see you when I see you."

Skye watched as the Malsi army advanced unimpeded through the snow. She paced back and forth in the observation post as Lieutenant Eyer, who had just joined her, surveyed the situation with two of his men. The Malsis were four deep and started to chant in a way that sounded both hypnotic and terrifying at the same time. They pounded their weapons together, which added to the cacophony of sound that grew closer with each moment. *Where the hell is Myst?*

Skye wanted to do something—anything—but the fort's defenders had not been given the order to fire yet. Then an idea struck her. At the head of the advancing force, a man strode as if he was bullet proof. He carried a raised black and yellow flag and was clearly conveying commands to the rest of the troops. Skye took her AR16A and flipped the safety off. She set it on the rock wall in front of her and took aim at the standard bearer a hundred and fifty yards away.

Lieutenant Eyer tapped her shoulder. "What are you doing?"

She looked at him over her shoulder; his eyes were soft and his manner one of concern, not questioning. She answered, "Looks like there are a lot more of them than there are of us. I'm hoping if I kill the first one, then maybe the rest of them will get scared and run away."

The lieutenant smiled and nodded. "Me too. Fire at will."

Skye returned her attention to the sight on her rifle. She carefully took her aim and squeezed off a shot. The bullet flew true and the flag carrier slammed to the ground, his colors falling with him.

She held her breath as the Malsi army paused as one. A complete silence filled the air, and the whole world seemed to stop. The silence was pierced by the sound of the big gun firing again. The projectile shrieked through the air, and Lieutenant Eyer knocked Skye off her feet and covered her with his body. A massive explosion erupted on the mountain above them, and a cascade of rocks and boulders rained down around them.

When the dust settled enough for her to see, she was shocked at the flesh wounds on Eyre's body, wounds that would have been hers had he not thrown himself on her. They staggered to their feet to see the Malsi army running at full speed toward the fort, screaming in rage. Skye looked to the lieutenant to apologize. "Guess that didn't work."

He dabbed the blood from one of his wounds with a bit of fabric from his shirt. "Never works if you don't try. Suggest we get below to see how we can help."

Skye hurried into the infirmary, anxious to see Eagle, but she did not want to delay her return to the ramparts to join the fight. She was startled to see every bed full and many people sitting against the wall or laying on the floor. Moans of pain filled the room, and the doctors were all engaged with wounded patients. Many of the hurt were women and children; Skye's heart cried out when she saw a little girl tucked under a bloody sheet.

She made her way to Eagle's bed and was pleasantly surprised to see him looking much better than the day before. The ugly red streaks had left his face, and his eyes were bright and attentive. He smiled when he saw her. "Skye, how goes the battle?"

She took his hand in hers. "Not well. We are severely outnumbered, and the enemy has a cannon that is raising hell with us. My father has gone to take it out. Unfortunately, I think his chances are nil."

Eagle stammered, "Your father?"

Skye touched his lips with her finger to quiet him. "If we survive the day, there will be much for me to tell you. Know this, I have found it to be a privilege to travel with you and to be able to call you friend." She reached into her pack, took out her pistol, and pressed it into Eagle's hand. "This enemy we fight is crueler than I can tell you. Do not allow them to take you prisoner." She looked into his troubled eyes. "Understand?" He slowly nodded.

Skye stood, kissed him on the forehead, and then said, "I must join the battle." Holding back a tear, she quickly turned and walked away.

She pretended not to hear when Eagle's voice called behind her, "Skye, I love you."

I know.

Skye reached the fort's wall carrying her rifles and bow just as another explosion shook the courtyard. The force of the impact knocked her to her knees, and more screams of agony were carried in the air. She got to her feet and made her way to the battlement and found Lieutenant Eyer shooting arrows. The scene was massively confusing. The top of the fort wall was filled with men and women, all carrying some type of club or hoe or other handheld weapon.

At the front of the wall, soldiers fired rifles and arrows toward the Malsi army. The lead elements had reached the base of the wall and were now trying to employ ladders to scale the face of the fort. Gunshots punctuated the air. Skye looked at the field in front of the fort and her skin started to crawl. If anything, there were more Malsi troops than she had imagined existed. *This is impossible. Hurry, Myst!*

The Malsi army charged over their own dead, whose blood stained the snow. Acrid smoke filled the air, causing Skye's eyes to water. She called to the lieutenant, "Where do you want me?"

He pointed to a spot on the wall beside him. "Right there. I hope you have some bullets, 'cause most of us are out."

She took her place, raised her M16A1 rifle, and in short order fired her last ten bullets, dropping a Malsi with each one. With the weapon now useless, she dropped it on the ground and fired the final rounds she had for her sniper rifle. With no more bullets, she went to work with her bow.

She detected the army moving with deliberation to the north of the wall. She yelled to Eyer, "An army flows like a river, ever searching for the weakest point."

The lieutenant smiled between shots with his bow and said, "Sun Zu." He motioned down the wall. "The lowest point will be the gate. We must defend it at all costs."

The attacking army was relentless. Malsi troops started to reach the top of the wall, climbing the metal ladders they had carried across the battlefield. The first to reach the top were dispatched by the soldiers and citizens with clubs. Skye could see that the onslaught was going to continue into the afternoon. Then she saw a sight that made her blood run cold.

Three trucks with armored bulldozer blades on the front were making their way across the clearing. Colonel Moore appeared by her side. His face was streaked with blood, but Skye could not tell whose it was. His voice was cracked and dry when he said, "Your father was right, this is a clever enemy. They used their troops to draw our fire and now they bring up the trucks to batter the gate."

He made a signal to someone behind them and Skye heard a loud *WHOOSH* and the sound of a projectile fly overhead. A moment later, the lead truck burst into flames and spun out of control, running over several of the enemy troops.

Skye watched in fascination as the other two trucks kept coming. There was another *WHOOSH*, and this time there was an explosion behind the racing vehicles. Skye heard Moore say, "Damn."

A third shot from the fort's mortar hit the trailing truck dead on, turning it into a flaming death trap for the occupants. The one truck that remained was almost to the gate. A rain of arrows peppered it with no effect. Skye braced herself for the impact but was unprepared for what happened next.

When the truck hit the gate, it exploded with a deafening force and a wall of fire that blew the gates off their hinges. The impact knocked everybody on the walls off their feet, and many of those in the courtyard were blown into the air. The Malsi troops near the gate were knocked over, and all of the ladders shook off the wall and fell to the ground, taking their climbers with them.

Skye regained her feet and found the world was silent. Stunned fighters in and out of the fort gazed around with shocked faces. Looking to the field in front of the fort, Skye's muscles tightened as she saw two more trucks coming. The Malsi troops were getting to their feet, and her stomach turned as she saw them start to charge the now open gate.

She looked to the courtyard and saw troops of the fort rallying to the breech in the defenses. Civilians pressed behind them, waving their clubs in the air. She could see people shouting though she heard no sound. In front of her, Colonel Moore pointed into the fort with his mouth moving, shouting orders, and she realized she had no idea what he was saying.

She shook her head and rubbed her ears but it had no effect. From her vantage point, she could see the Malsi army converging on the gate in great numbers. Inside the courtyard, a brutal hand-to-hand contest was being waged between the leading edge of the Malsi force and the troops and citizens of the fort. Skye concluded that if the trucks that were approaching held explosives like the last one, and if they were to drive into the courtyard and detonate, the battle would be lost. *I will not concede this fight.*

She drew one of her last arrows from her quiver. It was one of only two flamers she had brought with her. She loaded the bow, ignited the tip, drew the string back, and let it fly. The arrow arched across the sky, trailing a thin white smoke. She held her breath as it tracked straight to the lead truck and blasted through the driver's side of the windshield. The truck immediately spun out of control, rolled on its side, and billowed into flames that set off a thunderous blast that shook the battlefield.

She drew her last flamer and was loading it into the bow when something stuck her in the shoulder and slammed her to the ground. Her head hit the rock surface of the wall, and her world exploded into a riot of sound and pain.

The screams of the battle below reached her, and she put her hand to her shoulder and pulled it back, covered with blood. *Damn. I've been shot.*

She faintly heard a familiar voice cry, "Skye!" It was Myst. In the same instant, she saw Lieutenant Shelly and another trooper race along the wall, carrying a machine gun and belts of ammunition. Moments later, the staccato sound of the gun was the most distinct sound of the battle. A distant explosion told her they had dispatched the last truck.

Myst came to her side. "Bet you thought we'd be too late."

Skye tried to smile. "You might be."

Myst took a cloth from her pocket and pressed it to Skye's shoulder. "Would have been back sooner but we stopped for a picnic."

Skye winced at the pressure. "Did you have a nice time?"

Myst pulled Skye to her feet. "Marvelous, simply marvelous. And you, have you been enjoying yourself?"

"Been to better parties."

Myst took Skye by the hand. "Let's get you to a doctor."

Skye looked over the battlefield as a green flare burst in the sky. Colonel Moore shouted to her, "Looks like your father took out the big gun!" The sight of the flare brought a huge cheer from the defenders. Skye had a sense of great relief, followed by an unfamiliar hollowness that crept into her heart.

Skye and Myst made their way down the wall to the sound of machine guns clearing the Malsi from the courtyard.

The infirmary was jammed, and the wounded spilled out into the hallway. When Doctor Choy saw Skye, he finished with the person he was working on and went directly to her. After a quick examination, he smiled and told her she only had a flesh wound, placed a bandage on it, and went to the next patient. She held her throbbing shoulder with her hand. *Only a flesh wound. Criminy, I'd sure hate to have a real wound.*

Skye and Myst started to make their way through the infirmary to Eagle. Without warning, the far wall of the room exploded, sending doctors and patients tumbling like rag dolls. Skye was partially shielded from the blast by the doorway, and she and Myst missed the brunt of the impact.

Dust and smoke filled the room. Skye peered at the wall and was horrified to see Malsi fighters coming through the hole that was there. She reached beneath her cloak and drew her KaBar. Beside her, Myst pulled out a short sword. Skye looked at the fighter nearest her, screamed her battle cry, and charged him. The surprised man backpedaled one step before she plunged her blade into his stomach.

Myst attacked the next Malsi, felling him with a cut across the chest. Skye whirled and found her next foe to be more prepared. This one blocked her thrust so she kicked him in the groin. As he curled over, her blade laid him down. Something hit her arm and the knife was knocked from her hand and clanged to the floor.

A Malsi with a club smiled at her and raised it above his head, ready to strike her. She drew her dagger from her vest and slashed his throat before he could swing. She turned to the next fighter and was surprised to hear a shot and see him collapse in front of her.

Eagle fired five more times and dropped two more Malsis. Smoke curled in the air and the defenders faced the breach in the wall but no more attackers came through.

CHAPTER FORTY-ONE

JUST THE START

AT DAWN, BARZAN STOOD on the roof of his command vehicle on a rise above the fort. He could see smoke still billowing from the inside and people emerging from the breached walls collecting wounded and dead from the battlefield. The taste of death stuck in his mouth; he took a flask of whisky from his pocket and took a long pull on it.

The vile liquid stung his throat but nonetheless he swished another swallow around his mouth, creating a burning sensation on his tongue and lips. Then he spit the whole of it out on the ground.

To his surprise, Ivan called up to him, "Careful, my commander, one should not waste such a rare thing."

Barzan gave him a thin smile. Ivan's uniform was black with soot, and blood stained his left arm. "Thought you were dead, as you should have been when the attack failed." He tossed the flask to his general.

"Good to see you too, my commander." Ivan took a long pull on the drink and swallowed deeply. "What are your orders?"

Barzan looked back to the battlefield. "Defeat tastes sour in my mouth. Reminds me of our first assault on London. I think our old friend has been here. This battle has been costly; our enemies have won this day. However, even now I have troops exploring a trail to the interior."

Ivan took another drink. "Da."

Barzan jumped off the truck and landed on both feet next to the general. "We beat him before. We will annihilate him next time. Come, we must revisit our plan."

From a mountain peak overlooking the fort, John and Les watched Barzan's command vehicle and escorts turn down the pass heading west. Les lifted his binoculars and zoomed in on the lead car. "Think he's had enough and is going to gather his kiddies and high tail it back to the Old World?"

John rubbed his hands together to promote some warmth against the morning chill. "Not a chance. What he wants is at the end of the lake."

"You could at least humor me for a bit. So what are we going to do? Go back to that nice warm fort with those nice people and get drunk till we can't stand up?"

John smiled. "Exactly." Then he started toward his lead vehicle. "After that we head home and rearm."

John saw his friend raise an eyebrow. "Home? I did not think we'd ever make it."

Les let out a sigh and turned to the few troops that were left with him.

"Let's point these things east and get the hell out of here."

CHAPTER FORTY-TWO

HOME AGAIN

COLONEL MOORE WALKED THROUGH the cool air to the readied horses with Myst, Skye, and her father. Skye watched Myst mount Sunchaser and then eased herself onto Midnight's back, her shoulder still aching. Colonel Moore looked up at her. "Are you sure you don't want an escort?"

Skye smiled at him. The morning sun was fresh, and a light new layer of snow hid the ugly scars of the battle that had raged a day ago. "It is a kind offer and I greatly appreciate it. However, we must travel fast, cross unfriendly territory, and move in stealth. The meds have to be delivered as soon as possible. One thing you can do is to please take care of my companion. I will return for him when I am able."

Her father looked at her and touched her leg with his hand. "I wish I was going instead of you but for the time being my place is here. I believe the Malsi are not done yet, and I want to try and find out what plans they have. Tell your mother and the others to be vigilant. We will return home as soon as we can."

Colonel Moore nodded. "I give you my word I will send your father and his troops to you as soon as possible. Thank you for all of your help. I fear we will need it in the future. It is nice to know we have an ally in you."

Skye answered, "We must all help each other. It is the way the world is supposed to work. You have my best wishes until we meet again."

She looked at her father. "I will do as you ask, and I will try to arrange for supplies to be sent here but I'm not sure how. Please hurry, we all miss you and the others."

Her father kissed his hand and tapped her knee with it and stepped away. "Be safe."

Skye nudged Midnight, and the horse broke into a trot with Myst and Sunchaser right behind.

Moore turned to Lieutenant Shelly. "I feel sorry for anyone who gets in their way."

Midnight turned off the mountain trail into the open east valley. A cold breeze hit Skye in the face and she took a deep breath, relishing the freshness. Still a fear gripped her heart. They had been away from the village too long. The meds needed to be delivered; she called to Myst, "Come, Myst, we must fly!"

Midnight and Sunchaser burst into a gallop and raced into the pass.

The End